HAPPILY EVER AFTER

A Baywick Novel

CHERYL HOLT

Cover Design: Dar Albert, Wicked Smart Designs, www.wickedsmartdesigns.com
Paperback and Digital format: Dayna Linton, Day Agency, www.dayagency.com

ISBN: 979-8-88525-160-0 (Paperback):
ISBN: 979-8-88525-164-8 (Digital Book)

Library of Congress Pending

First Edition: 2022

10 9 8 7 6 5 4 3 2 1

Printed in the USA

Praise for *New York Times* Bestselling Author
CHERYL HOLT

"Best storyteller of the year . . ."
Romantic Times Magazine

"Cheryl Holt is magnificent . . ."
Reader to Reader Reviews

"Cheryl Holt is on my 'favorite authors' list. I can't wait to see what she'll write next."
The Reading Café

"A master writer . . ."
Fresh Fiction

Here's what readers are saying . . .

"OMG! I just started reading this series yesterday. It was hard for me to close my Kindle and go to bed. So, so good!"
Artemis

"Cheryl Holt has packed in so much action that the reader is constantly spellbound. So many characters, so vividly portrayed! Rogues, unfaithfulness, loyalty, and delightful dialogue. You will love this book!"
Gladys

"It was fabulous! I laughed, I cried, I got angry, and I smiled. I read the whole book without stopping."
Robin

"Action, drama, and intrigue. I read it in one afternoon. I couldn't put it down!"
Gina

"You just can't wait to turn the page to see what happens next. Outstanding!"
Margaret

"This book is such an emotional roller-coaster. I cried and laughed and cheered. It was so good!"
Colleen

BOOKS BY CHERYL HOLT

LINKED HISTORICAL ROMANCE SERIES

BAYWICK
HAPPILY EVER AFTER
LOVE EVER AFTER

CADS
CAD'S WISH
CAD'S PICK
CAD'S CHOICE

LOST GIRLS
SOMEONE TO LOVE
SOMEONE TO CHERISH
SOMEONE TO WED

ALWAYS
ALWAYS
ALWAYS YOURS
ALWAYS MINE

JILTED BRIDES
JILTED BY A CAD
JILTED BY A SCOUNDREL
JILTED BY A ROGUE

FOREVER
FOREVER YOURS
FOREVER MINE
FOREVER AFTER
FOREVER

BABY CALEB DUET
ONLY YOU
ONLY MINE

LOST LORDS OF RADCLIFFE
HEART'S DELIGHT
HEART'S DESIRE
HEART'S DEMAND
SCOUNDREL
HEART'S DEBT

RELUCTANT BRIDES
WICKED
WANTON
WONDERFUL

LORD TRENT
LOVE'S PROMISE
LOVE'S PRICE
LOVE'S PERIL

SPINSTER'S CURE
PROMISE OF PLEASURE
TASTE OF TEMPTATION
DREAMS OF DESIRE

EROTIC HISTORICAL ROMANCES
LOVE LESSONS
TOTAL SURRENDER
ABSOLUTE PLEASURE
COMPLETE ABANDON
MORE THAN SEDUCTION
DEEPER THAN DESIRE
FURTHER THAN PASSION
TOO HOT TO HANDLE
TOO TEMPTING TO TOUCH
TOO WICKED TO WED
SECRET FANTASY
FORBIDDEN FANTASY
DOUBLE FANTASY

HISTORICAL ROMANCES
SWEET SURRENDER
NICHOLAS
 (REPUBLISHED AS MY SCOUNDREL)
MY ONLY LOVE
MY TRUE LOVE
THE WAY OF THE HEART

CONTEMPORARY ROMANCES
MOUNTAIN DREAMS
SEDUCE ME
KISS ME
LOVE ME

NOVELLAS
MEG'S SECRET ADMIRER
KNIGHT OF SEDUCTION
SEDUCING THE GROOM

OTHER NOVELS
A SUMMER WEDDING AT CROSS CREEK INN
MUD CREEK
THE WEDDING
SLEEPING WITH THE DEVIL

NONFICTION
LITTLE MIRACLES

HAPPILY EVER AFTER

A Baywick Novel

Chapter One

"I CAN SEE A small strip of blue. It's probably the ocean, don't you think? It's visible right out our window."

Excited over the tiny view, Emily Shaw smiled at her cousin, Peggy. Emily had never previously been to the sea, so every detail was novel and thrilling. But Peggy was over on the bed, having flopped down in a snit the instant the housemaid had dropped their bags and left the room.

Peggy pictured herself as being very grand and important, an arbiter of all that was posh and fashionable. Nothing was ever good enough for her, and she found fault in every direction. In contrast, Emily was content in every situation, and she tried to be optimistic and happy. She could never understand why a person would choose to be negative or miserable.

From the moment their coach had crested the hill, and the village of Baywick had been spread out below them—like a painting in a storybook—Peggy had been muttering derisively. She'd envisioned a bigger town, larger buildings, wider streets, but Emily hadn't harbored any expectations. She was simply glad to have a holiday, to have escaped the pressures of home.

She'd never wandered far from their rural property of Hexham, so every mile of their journey had been a delight. Every bend in the road had brought new and intriguing sights. Not for Peggy though. She wasn't impressed.

They would spend the summer in Baywick, loafing like wealthy ladies of leisure, even though they were no such thing. Emily was the poor relative, and Peggy was the spoiled daughter of what had once been a rich family. Before her father's finances had fallen off a fiscal cliff, Peggy had traveled extensively. She'd been to London and even Paris. On another lucky occasion, she'd visited the luxury resort of Brighton, which was just up the coast.

It was where the glamorous and notorious members of High Society reveled. In her estimation, no locale could possibly be as magnificent. Her immediate opinion had been that Baywick wasn't magnificent, wasn't what she'd anticipated, and she'd already convinced herself that they shouldn't have come.

A slight breeze wafted in the window, and Emily inhaled a scent that had to be salty ocean air. She'd never smelled a similar aroma, and though it was odd to admit, it made her feel as if she'd finally arrived where she'd always belonged.

"Let's take a walk," she said. "There's a promenade around the bay. We should explore the area."

"It's too hot."

"It's not hot. It's a lovely afternoon in June, and you're being ridiculous. Why are you so grumpy?"

"The town is such a disappointment. Clearly, we were tricked by the brochure we received. We were riveted by words like charming and quaint, but in reality, the text should have read dull and boring."

Emily blew out an exasperated breath. "We've been here for five minutes. How can you be so sure it's horrid?"

"All the chic people will be in Brighton." Which they couldn't afford; Emily had checked. "Why would any prominent gentlemen stay in this pathetic hovel? How will we meet any of them?"

Peggy had recently been jilted by her fiancé, Teddy, so she was hoping to find a candidate to replace him.

"I am not in Baywick to meet gentlemen," Emily said, "so I don't care if we cross paths with any of them or not."

"Of course you don't. You're a spinster, and you're resigned to remain one, while I would like to change my life for the better. If I don't wed—and fast—I truly don't know what will become of me."

Emily had the same worry: What would become of them? But she had a whole summer to pretend that no catastrophe was looming. She was twenty-five, and Peggy was twenty-three, and Emily's advanced age practically guaranteed that marriage would never be an option.

It wasn't an insult for Peggy to call her a spinster. It was simply a fact that she had no dowry or prospects, and she'd taught herself not to fret about it. After all, none of the men to whom she'd been most attached—mainly her father and uncle—had behaved in a manner to instill confidence that she should put her security in the hands of a male.

Her father, God rest his soul, had been swept into a fraud scheme that was supposed to have made him a quick fortune. He'd perished from a lung ailment, but he'd been killed by shame and humiliation too. Her mother had died when Emily was a baby, so he'd been her only parent.

She'd been sent to live with her uncle's family, but he'd gotten himself into debt with his extravagant habits, so he'd mortgaged everything to the hilt. When he'd passed away, they'd been stunned to discover how little was left. His wife, Florence, had inherited their estate of Hexham from him, but there was no money for repairs or wages for competent employees, so it was gradually falling apart.

Florence was ill with consumption, and it was a death sentence, so her health could fail at any moment. What would happen then? So far, she'd managed to keep their creditors at bay with pleas and sweet-talking, but Peggy didn't have her charm or grit.

Once Florence was gone, the creditors would swoop in and seize the property, and the notion was terrifying. As a child, Emily had staggered through that very scenario. After her father had been brought low, men had arrived with wagons and had carted away their belongings, and she still had nightmares about that day.

She'd been delivered to her uncle with a single satchel of clothes. Within a year, she'd outgrown every item, so even those few garments had been lost to her.

"Can't you muster a bit of excitement?" she asked Peggy. "It's our first afternoon. Will you constantly whine about Baywick? Or will you ceaselessly bemoan your severed engagement until I can't bear to listen another second?"

"Aren't I allowed to complain? I was badly used."

"If you insist on obsessing, how will we have any fun? I thought—for the summer anyway—we agreed to put our woes behind us. Isn't that the reason we traveled to Baywick?"

"I said I'd *try* to put them behind me. You've never been jilted, so you could never understand how distressed I am."

"I can't incessantly commiserate. For months, I've sat through unending accounts of your varying levels of anguish. I'm over it."

"What else would we discuss? In your entire life, have you ever been acquainted with a female who was jilted?"

"No, I haven't been. It's very rare."

"You ought to exhibit a tad more sympathy for my predicament. I'm so devastated that I may never recover."

Emily swallowed down a scoff. Peggy had never exactly been possessed of deep emotion. It wasn't her nature to weep or regret, and she'd only ever loved herself. She wasn't heartbroken over her feckless betrothed. No, she'd been hideously embarrassed by him. If she could glom onto another suitor, she'd forget Teddy in an instant.

Emily had never liked Teddy. He'd been pompous and pretentious, and the minute he'd stumbled on a prettier, richer girl, he'd reneged on the betrothal. His parents had helped him to cry off, and Florence had been too weary to fight with them.

Emily hadn't been shocked by Florence's reluctance to intervene in the debacle. Florence had been her uncle's second wife, so she was Peggy's stepmother and Emily's step-aunt. Peggy and Florence had never been close, and Peggy had never been interested in being mothered.

As his grounds for spurning Peggy, Teddy had claimed there were rumors that she was a tart, that she'd had an amour with a boy in the village and all the neighbors knew about it. Emily had heard the gossip too, but she suspected Teddy had spread it himself in order to justify his callous conduct.

She suspected too that he'd realized Peggy didn't bring much to the table as a bride. Her dowry was spent, and while she would inherit Hexham on Florence's death, it was a decrepit ruin. He would have received no funds from Peggy that would have enabled him to restore the beautiful old place, so he'd found a wealthier wife.

Emily wished him happy—she wished everyone happy—but she doubted he would be. He was too vain to ever be content, and in that, he'd matched Peggy perfectly. His fickle desertion of her cousin underscored Emily's sense that she was fortunate to have escaped the fetters of matrimony.

In her view, men were arrogant asses who repeatedly made bad decisions. What sane woman would deliberately shackle herself?

"I'm taking a walk," she said. "You can dawdle in here and feel sorry for yourself, but I intend to explore."

"You'll act like a tourist? That's so crass."

"Well, I *am* a tourist. Why can't I act like one?"

Peggy was in a foul mood, so it was futile to argue with her. Emily went to the door and opened it. Peggy rose up on an elbow and said, "When will you be back?"

"Probably in an hour or two. Why don't you try to nap? Maybe if you rest, you won't be quite so grouchy when I return."

"I'm not grouchy," she snapped.

Emily laughed. "No, definitely not."

She left, and though Peggy called to her again, she continued down the hall to the stairs and the lobby.

They were staying at *Mrs. Darlington's Holiday House for Young Ladies*. There had been an advertisement about it in the London newspaper, and she'd been enticed by the description. It catered to females who wanted to travel, but who had no relatives to escort them. It was a quiet, clean abode that offered chaperoned trips and excursions.

Guests were welcome to tarry for a few days or for a few months, and a familial atmosphere was encouraged, as if the residents were fond cousins.

Emily had never heard of a hotel that catered just to female guests, and normally, she wouldn't have paid any attention. But for some reason, the advertisement had lit a fire under her usually placid demeanor.

Baywick was a new town, designed by investors to rival Brighton. They hoped it would grow to be a popular spa. She'd been overwhelmed by the peculiar notion that she had to see it for herself. After voicing several sly hints about how charming it sounded, it was her Aunt Florence who'd finally suggested they go and enjoy themselves.

They couldn't really afford it, but Florence had been adamant.

Emily reached the lobby and was tying the strings on her bonnet when the proprietress, Mrs. Darlington, came out from the back. She had a basket over her arm, as if she was about to run errands. They'd chatted briefly when Emily and Peggy had initially checked in, but a maid had shown them up to their room.

Mrs. Darlington was a bit older than Emily, perhaps thirty or so, and she appeared gregarious and friendly. They were the same height and shape, with slender torsos and a vivacious energy in their strides when they moved. They both smiled constantly, seeming to have the same type of sunny personality.

They might have been sisters, but for Emily having blond hair and green eyes, and Mrs. Darlington having chestnut hair and blue eyes.

Emily was fascinated by her. It was rare to cross paths with a woman who owned her own business and handled her own affairs. She was *Mrs.* Darlington, so Emily figured there was a husband lurking behind the scenes. Or was she a widow?

"May I help you?" Mrs. Darlington asked.

"I was thinking I'd take a walk. My cousin is napping, but I'm eager to explore. Is it safe to be out and about by myself?"

"Baywick is very safe, but if there's ever a time when you're not comfortable, you can always request that a maid tag along. Any of them would be glad to accompany you."

"You don't mind if they're dragged away from their duties?"

"Their *duty* is to ensure you have a lovely visit." Mrs. Darlington gestured toward the door. "I'm going out too. Shall we go together? I can point out the important landmarks."

"I'd like that very much."

They departed, their pace leisurely. Mrs. Darlington was acquainted with everyone. Women nodded cordially, and men tipped their hats. It was a pleasant interval, with Emily feeling no need to fill the void with conversation.

The hotel wasn't directly on the water, but set at the edge of a quiet lane. It was a neat and tidy building, three stories high, painted white, with black shutters and trim. There were flowerboxes under the windows, and a discreet sign announcing its name.

From the outside, it looked like a large residence that might have once been owned by a banker or successful merchant. The front door opened onto the street, but there was a small garden at the rear, with benches and a fountain that bubbled under a grove of fruit trees. It was the perfect spot for a summer sojourn.

Suddenly, the street ended, and they were spit out at the sea. Baywick was nestled around a pretty bay, with a promenade that curved the length. There was an island off shore, and people were loafing on its beach, rowboats pulled up on the sand to carry them back when they were finished.

Farther out, a jetty had been constructed, and white waves crashed over the black rocks.

People were strolling or sitting on benches and gazing out at the sailboats gliding by, but there were bigger barks and schooners anchored beyond the jetty. It was mesmerizing and amazing, like a colorful painting of a British coastal town.

She was from a rural, landlocked farm, so the sight was enlivening in a manner she couldn't explain. Perhaps she was meant to live by the ocean and had simply never realized it.

"Oh, my," she said, as she sighed with delight. "It's so beautiful."

"I've always thought so." Mrs. Darlington gestured to the other end of the bay. "Those strange rocks poking up from the water are The Needles. You can take a hiking excursion on the cliffs of the headland above them if you're game to try. The view is spectacular."

"I would like that. While I'm on holiday, I want to experience everything."

Then Mrs. Darlington indicated the island. "That's Pirate's Cove. There are rowboats that are free to borrow, and if you can find a gentleman to man the oars, you can pop over for a picnic."

"Were there pirates here in the past? Is that why it's called Pirate's Cove?"

"I'm told there were pirates, but it might be a rumor the investors spread so the place would sound more exciting."

Emily chuckled. "How long have you been here? It's such a new town. I can't suppose it's been very long."

"I actually arrived before the architects snuck in and bought up the adjacent countryside. I purchased my building when there was nothing to see but beach grass."

"Do you mind being surrounded?" Emily asked.

"Not really. When I can offer guests more entertainment, it's better for business. Previously, many ladies found it very boring. There weren't many activities, but now, there are shops, teahouses, and dressmakers. There is a theater and a dance pavilion." She leaned nearer and murmured, "There's even a gambling club."

Emily blanched. "I'm shocked that the community leaders would allow it."

Mrs. Darlington shrugged. "One of the major investors is Mr. Archie Covington. He's quite a dandy, and he hopes to draw from the fast crowd in Brighton. If there was no gambling, the rich and glamor-ous wouldn't visit us."

There was a twinkle in Mrs. Darlington's eye that made Emily laugh. It reinforced her burgeoning sense that they had a similar opin-ion about how the kingdom operated. It seemed they had very much in common.

"Are there any rich and glamorous people present at the moment?" Emily asked. "My cousin, Peggy, is desperately praying there might be."

"I believe Mr. Covington is staying for the summer, and his toplofty friends often stop by. Do you know the Covington family?"

"No, I wouldn't run in the same circles."

"Well, his brother is James Covington. Lord Roxbury?"

It took Emily a minute to recognize the name. "Lord Roxbury—the explorer?"

"The very one."

"My goodness. Is he with his brother? That would be very exalted company indeed."

"Evidently, he's tiptoed in," Mrs. Darlington said, "but he's hid-ing. He hasn't been spotted, and after his recent ordeal, it's probably not surprising that he'd tuck himself away. If I'd been tossed into that sort of debacle, I'd hide too. I imagine the normal world is loud and hectic to him."

Emily had read about Roxbury in the newspaper. Who hadn't? He'd been away from England for so many years that it had been assumed he and his crew were deceased. But a few months earlier, he'd sailed into London, with only a smattering of his men having survived their tribulations.

Everyone was blathering over his failed expedition, but none of the survivors would discuss the details, so what had happened remained a mystery. The more stories circulated, the more repugnant they became: that the crew had run mad and killed each other, that they'd been starving and had eaten each other.

There was no end to the vicious accounts, and Emily felt sorry for him. She agreed with Mrs. Darlington. If she'd suffered a comparable calamity, she'd be hiding too.

"He's such a curious person," she said. "What would you predict? Will he burrow out of his hole so we can meet him?"

"It's a small town, and it's difficult to keep out of sight. I'm betting he'll stagger out of his cocoon before too much more time has passed."

"The chance that we might catch a glimpse of him will have my cousin entranced for days. Perhaps weeks."

They grinned, the perception of friendship growing by leaps and bounds, then Mrs. Darlington said, "I hate to sound rude, but I have to finish my errands. Would you like to come with me? You could visit some of the shops I frequent and learn more about the area."

"Will you be disappointed if I decline? This is my first trip to the seashore, and I'd like to walk on The Promenade."

"You should do that, rather than plod along with me, but I should mention that it's Friday, and there is a public dance at The Pavilion on Friday and Saturday nights."

"A dance! How delightful!"

"The music and buffet aren't worth it, and there are always more ladies than men, so you may wind up sitting much of the evening. Or maybe Archie Covington will drag some of his London chums over from Brighton. That would enliven the event."

"And Lord Roxbury might put in an appearance too."

"We've been waiting with bated breath for that glorious moment to arrive."

They smirked in unison, then Mrs. Darlington left, and Emily strolled down The Promenade. She felt completely at home and was already wishing she never had to leave. She continued until she was too tired to keep on, then she turned and headed for the hotel. Hopefully, Peggy would have taken a nap and would be in a better mood.

If she wasn't, Emily would tell her about Lord Roxbury and his brother being in Baywick, about Mr. Covington regularly bringing gentlemen over from Brighton. She'd tell her about the dance that would be held that evening.

If that news didn't perk her up, Emily didn't know what would.

Chapter Two

"I WISH MORE MEN were here."

Emily smiled at Peggy and said, "Maybe tomorrow night will be better."

They were huddled in a corner at the town's dance pavilion, and while Peggy's hopes had been raised about the affair, it was very much like the country festivals they had at home. Baywick hosted a dance every Friday and Saturday night, so the local citizenry never made much of a fuss about it.

It was easy to pick out the other tourists who were on holiday. They were attired in fancier clothes, had dragged out jewels and curled their hair. She and Peggy were looking quite smart, and she was happy to have had a reason to dress for a party.

Peggy had blond hair and blue eyes, and she was wearing a blue gown that enhanced her coloring. A maid at the hotel had styled her hair, and she could be fetching when she tried, but all the expensive garments in the world couldn't hide the frown lines that marred her face. She appeared as if she'd be a disagreeable person to know—and she generally was.

Recently, she'd grown very chubby too, and her flowing skirt couldn't conceal her rotund figure.

Emily's gown was green, and it enhanced the blond of her hair and the emerald of her eyes. The Shaws were a family of blonds, and usually, their eyes were blue. Only Emily's were different, and she'd inherited them from her beautiful, long-deceased mother.

Being the opposite of Peggy, she was slender and lithe, and she moved with a fluid grace. She didn't attempt to be elegant or supple; it was simply a natural trait. It was another attribute she'd inherited from her mother, and she liked to think—if her mother could see her decked out in her finery—she would be very proud.

As Mrs. Darlington had predicted, there were many more women than men in attendance. Archie Covington hadn't strutted in with a troupe of male friends, so she and Peggy had each danced exactly once. With Peggy's penchant for criticism on a short fuse, she'd soon be demanding they return to the hotel.

"Shall we eat?" Peggy asked. "There's not much else to do."

There was a buffet in a separate room, but Mrs. Darlington had served supper before they'd departed, so Emily wasn't hungry.

"You go on," Emily told her. "I need to step outside for some fresh air."

"If you abandon me, how will I entertain myself?"

"Come with me." Peggy shook her head, and Emily said, "Or stand here and flaunt yourself as if you're extremely exotic, and perhaps another gentleman will escort you out onto the floor."

"I believe I'll try that. It's a dance, so I should be dancing, and while we're in Baywick, would you do me a favor?"

"That depends on what it is."

"I want you to call me Margaret."

Margaret was Peggy's given name, with Peggy being her nickname, and Emily smirked. "I'm not calling you Margaret. No one has ever called you that. You've been Peggy to me for twenty-three years, and I'm not changing how I address you."

"*Peggy* is ordinary and common. If I'm introduced to a handsome swain, I'll make a bad first impression."

"I doubt we'll be meeting any handsome swains. At least not tonight."

"We have the whole summer though."

"True, and if the man of your dreams blusters up and sweeps you off your feet, and you can persuade him to call you Margaret, I will celebrate forever. In the meantime, you'll always be Peggy to me."

Huge doors opened out onto a wide verandah, and Emily hurried toward them so Peggy couldn't waylay her further. There were stairs that led to The Promenade, and she went down and began to stroll. It was a balmy evening, and she hadn't stopped to fetch her cloak. It was too warm, and she didn't need it.

She was eager to get away from the crowds, and she continued on until the noise from The Pavilion had faded away. Then she found a bench and sat down, smiling with pleasure over how perfect the interval was.

Her mind was furiously working as she pondered whether she might remain in Baywick after Peggy left at the end of August. How could it be accomplished? She would spend the next two months contemplating the issue. Wouldn't it be lovely if she could rearrange her life?

She rose from the bench and climbed down a set of stairs onto the beach. It was much darker below The Promenade, and she located a large boulder and leaned her hips against it. Off in the distance, a thunderstorm was brewing. It was too far away to hear the thunder, but the lightning was dramatic.

After a bit, it occurred to her that she could smell a cheroot burning. She glanced around and was disconcerted to see that there was a man leaned on an adjacent boulder. He was only a few feet away, but he'd been so quiet that she hadn't noticed him.

He was bundled for very cold weather, draped in a heavy coat and wool hat, as if he was freezing. She was in her party gown, with not even a shawl to cover her arms. The temperature was that mild.

Her initial fear was that he was a vagrant or criminal, but he didn't exhibit any threatening gestures. He realized she was peeking at him, and he said, "Have I startled you?"

"Yes, but I'm pretending you haven't."

"I was trying to be invisible, but I wasn't successful."

"Are you having a private moment? Shall I leave you to your musings?"

"No, you needn't leave on my account," he said. "How about you? Are you having a private moment? It looks to me as if you are. Shall I tiptoe away?"

"I'm simply enjoying the beach and the storm on the horizon, so you're not interrupting."

"You're very brave to have snuck down here."

"Or very stupid."

He chuckled, and his voice was cultured, his posh London accent very clear, but it sounded rusty, as if he didn't laugh very often. He tossed his cheroot into the water, and there was a *hiss* as the tip flared out. The silence grew oppressive, and she was struggling to devise a way to politely depart, but there didn't appear to be one.

"Are you on holiday?" he asked. "Or are you a resident?"

"I'm definitely on holiday. I just arrived this afternoon."

"What is your opinion of the place so far?"

"It's delightful." He snorted in a derogatory manner, and she said, "You don't agree? You don't think it's delightful?"

"I haven't expended much energy considering whether I like it or not."

"You're still debating? What would it take for you to decide it's wonderful?"

"When I figure that out, I'll let you know."

She snickered with amusement, deeming him to be very odd. "How about you? What brought you to Baywick?"

Her question had him scowling, as if the answer was a complex puzzle. Ultimately, he said, "I have no idea."

Which made no sense. "Are you a resident then? Are you here on business? Are you an architect? Are you a builder?"

"I guess I'm visiting, but not really."

"Is that a riddle I'm supposed to solve? Are you being deliberately mysterious? Or are you merely wishing I wasn't so nosy?"

His scowl deepened. "Am I being obnoxious?"

"Not yet, but you might cross the line very soon."

He winced at that. "What possessed you to choose Baywick though? You could have picked any town, and Brighton is just up the road. Why Baywick?"

"The London newspaper ran the most engaging advertisement. From Mrs. Darlington?" He shook his head, indicating he wasn't familiar with her, and Emily said, "She owns a hotel for female travelers. It seemed very unique, so my cousin and I were anxious to try it for ourselves."

"And is it unique? Are you charmed?"

"Yes, absolutely."

"A hotel for females?" he said. "I've never heard of such a thing."

"Neither had I. It's why I was so intrigued, and I'd never seen the ocean, so I was tantalized by the possibilities that were presented."

She studied his winter clothes, and she had a recurrent character flaw that she butted in when she shouldn't. She couldn't stop herself from mentioning the obvious. "You're bundled up as if it's January. Are you cold? How could you be? It's such a pleasant evening. I hope you're not ill."

"I'm not ill. I just have trouble feeling warm. It's as if the blood in my veins has turned to ice." He paused, then scratched his ear. "Was that a strange comment? I swear, it's been so long since I've chatted with a woman that I can't remember how to converse like a normal person."

"What a bizarre remark. Why haven't you been chatting with any women? Where have you been? In prison?"

"Close enough."

She blanched. Was he a criminal after all? He had the accent of a toplofty gentleman, but that didn't mean he was one.

He'd noticed her reaction and waved away her concern. "Don't mind me. I'm being ridiculous."

"I wouldn't describe you as ridiculous. I'd say *peculiar* fits you much better."

"Yes, I'm very peculiar," he confessed. "I didn't used to be, but I've slipped off the road of what's ordinary, and I can't get myself back onto the correct route."

"Sir, that is another remark that is completely bewildering. If you keep talking, I'll wind up worrying that you're a tad deranged."

She offered it in a teasing way, but he muttered, "Sometimes, I wonder if I'm not exactly that. Perhaps I should lock myself in an asylum."

She swallowed down a gasp, having prodded at issues she shouldn't have addressed. She was desperate to wipe away any awkwardness, so she grinned at him and said, "What is your name? May I be incredibly forward and ask you what it is?"

"It's Roxbury."

"Roxbury . . ..as in James Covington, Earl of Roxbury?"

"The very one."

Lord Roxbury was the explorer whose feats had been so widely reported. He'd sailed off to the Arctic North to draw maps and search for the Northwest Passage, and he'd been gone for such an extended period that the Covington family had started to believe he was deceased. His younger brother, Archie, would have been installed as earl, but without warning, Roxbury had surprised the whole world and had returned from the dead.

He and his men hadn't told anyone what had happened to delay them. Or if they had, she hadn't heard any details.

Mrs. Darlington had claimed he was in Baywick, but he hadn't been sighted, so Emily had been pitched into a marvelous adventure. When she informed Peggy and the other guests at the hotel about it, they would be green with envy.

"My, my, but aren't I wallowing in high company?" she said. "There were rumors that you were in residence, but that you were hiding. Instead, I find you lurking—quite alone—in the dark and wrapped up as if it's about to snow. Can you defend such unusual behavior to me?"

She shifted on her boulder so she was facing him. If she bumped into him again in the light of day, she wanted to be sure she'd recognize him. He shifted too, and they were near enough that their feet were almost touching.

The sole sound was the swish of the surf onto the beach. She was isolated with him, and it was generating a sense of intimacy that was entirely misplaced, but she might be able to pry out any secret.

"Since you know who I am," he said, "I expect you realize that I've been away for years."

"Yes, exploring in the Arctic North. Is that why you constantly feel as if you're freezing?"

"I will thoroughly humiliate myself and admit, yes, it feels as if I'm freezing—even though I'm not. I assume the affectation will pass the longer I'm in England, but for now, I'm indulging it."

"There's nothing wrong with putting on a coat," she insisted, as if they were conspirators in his baffling conduct.

"It's the middle of June, so you are not the only person who's speculated over my mental state."

"You should ignore what other people think." She voiced it very firmly, as if she was a born troublemaker herself, but no one in the kingdom followed the rules more closely than Miss Emily Shaw. "Apparently, you've suffered in the past, but with you being home, you should participate in any activity that brings you comfort."

"I will keep telling myself you're right."

Their conversation dwindled, and they stared at each other. He was assessing her features as if committing them to memory.

She was assessing him too. He was a big man who would tower over her if he'd been standing on his feet, but with him leaned on the boulder and wearing heavy clothes, she couldn't be certain. She was curious about the color of his hair, but it was concealed by his cap. She was curious too about his eyes, and she predicted they'd be blue.

It was very strange, but they might have been acquainted for ages, and she was riveted by the most potent perception that he was carrying many burdens and was dying to shuck them off onto her shoulders.

"Was your ordeal very bad?" she quietly asked, the question popping out before she could tamp it down.

"Yes, it was very bad," he replied.

"There has been such terrible gossip about it, and it must be exhausting to endure so much strident attention. How are you dealing with it? In light of your current condition, it appears you're having problems adjusting."

It was a hideously inappropriate comment, and she couldn't believe she'd uttered it. He evaluated her for an eternity, formulating a response. Clearly, he was on the verge of confiding in her. He was stretched very tight, like a string on an archer's bow that was about to break.

Then he folded in on himself and discreetly tucked his anguish away.

"My brother helped to build Baywick," he said, deftly changing the subject.

She was relieved that he hadn't given her a dressing-down for being impertinent. "Yes, I was told that he'd been involved."

"He did it while I was out of England."

"You should be proud of his endeavors. It's a lovely town."

He tsked derisively. "You've extolled its virtues, but then, you also admitted that you've only been here for a single day, so you might not be the best judge."

"Wasn't it developed for visitors exactly like me?"

"When I found out how much he'd spent on the design, I was upset. He begged me to come and review the investment for myself."

"Is that why you can't decide if you're a tourist or a resident?" she asked.

"Yes. I'm tasked with discovering how splendid it is, but I'm too grouchy to keep an open mind."

"You're like my cousin, Peggy, who accompanied me to Baywick for the summer. She's grouchy too, so she's not enjoying herself. Perhaps

I should introduce you, and you can compare notes about how there's nothing to like."

He laughed. "I'm *trying* to like it."

"You should try harder. Have you seen any of the attractions? There are hikes and boat trips, teahouses and quaint restaurants. Theater troupes travel from London and Paris. There is a concert hall too, with some of Europe's premier musicians contracted to perform."

"You sound like a paid endorser. If you continue gushing so enthusiastically, you'll soon have me convinced that it's very grand."

Her cheeks heated with embarrassment. "I must seem horribly provincial to you. Are you making fun of me?"

"No. I'm delighted to have stumbled on you. You've furnished me with an entirely new perspective—one that wasn't delivered by my anxious brother."

"Mrs. Darlington mentioned that numerous prominent families have constructed homes in the neighboring hills. Are you one of them?"

"Yes, we can claim the very ostentatious seaside manor of Wave Crest."

His tone was very sarcastic, and she clucked her tongue like a fussy nanny. "It means you're wealthy enough to own it, yet you're complaining. You should be a little more grateful that you're able to afford such an extravagance."

"You are absolutely right. May I please learn your name, so I will know who is scolding me and warning me to behave?"

"It's Miss Shaw. Miss Emily Shaw, and I wasn't scolding you. I was explaining that, to me anyway, Baywick is a very dear spot, and with some effort on your part, you'll begin to recognize that it is."

He grinned. "I stand corrected."

"I like it so much that, if I could figure out how to stay forever, I would."

"Maybe you'll devise a method to accomplish it."

"I doubt it, but I have a vivid imagination, so I will pretend it could happen."

"Why couldn't it happen?" He stared intently, as if he was truly curious.

"I'm a spinster with no money. How could I pick up and flit off to a different location?"

"You're a spinster? How old are you? Eighty?"

"I'm twenty-five. How old are you?"

"Thirty, going on a hundred, but you don't look a day over ten."

"I guess that was a compliment, so thank you."

"It's difficult to be a female, isn't it?" he said. "I'm a man, so I can pack a bag and journey where I like. I can change my life and change my fate. You're a woman, so you're held down by rules that keep you stuck where you are."

She'd never viewed herself as being *stuck* before, but she definitely was. She was bound to Aunt Florence and Hexham, with no funds or connections to give her a safe harbor after her aunt and Hexham were lost. Wasn't that an accurate description of being stuck?

Now that he'd pointed it out, she'd obsess and chafe over her lot. She'd pine for a better ending, but she never dreamed big dreams. That was the road to deep discontentment, and she never liked to mope or lament. Negative thoughts never led to a good conclusion.

She'd been chatting so avidly with him that she hadn't been focused on her surroundings. Suddenly, the tide encroached very close, close enough to wet their shoes.

She hadn't noticed a wave approaching, but he had. He jumped out of range, and he grabbed her by the waist and yanked her away too. He was very strong, and he lifted her with ease. The quick move had her tumbling sideways, and she crashed into him. His body was hard as a rock, and he was fit and trim, providing evidence of physical endeavor.

It was very odd, but for just a moment, Time seemed to stop ticking. The sea breeze ceased blowing. The surf didn't lap on the shore. The universe was marking the encounter, making sure they marked it too.

But she didn't live in a world where strange men grabbed women they didn't know, and they both realized it immediately. He dropped his hands as if she'd grown so hot that he'd burned them. She might have admonished him for being too forward, but he chortled merrily, which she was convinced he didn't do very often.

"The water almost swamped us, Miss Shaw," he said, "and you're dressed in such pretty clothes. I hope we haven't ruined your slippers. Did they survive?"

She glanced down, and her feet were dry. "It was a near disaster, but I believe they're fine, so I'm lucky. If they'd been soaked, I could never have invented an alibi that would have satisfied my cousin."

"We should probably return to The Promenade while we can still escape. The tide will be coming in for an hour or two, so the water will continue to rise."

He gestured to the stairs, and they had to wait for another wave to sweep in and back before they could hurry over and climb up. They were positioned directly under a lamp, so she was able to get her first clear look at him.

He was the most handsome man she'd ever seen, with black hair and very blue eyes. His hair was worn longer than was proper and tied with a strip of leather, as if he couldn't be bothered to cut it. His eyes were twinkling, as if he'd engaged in mischief with her.

"Are you walking far?" he asked. "Shall I escort you to your destination?"

"That's not necessary. I'm attending the Friday night dance, so it's not much of a distance." He gaped at her as if he had no idea what she was talking about, and she added, "There's a pavilion? And a public dance every Friday and Saturday night?"

"Oh, I'm glad you apprised me. I should spend more time with you, so you can instruct me on details my brother insists I've been too lazy to discover. He swears I'll like the place sooner or later."

"I swear you will too. Do you dance, Lord Roxbury?"

"I haven't in years."

"Then you should start again. I will brazenly invite you to the event tomorrow. If you stroll in the door, all the ladies will expire from delight."

He smirked. "I think a party like that might be a bit beyond me."

"We'll likely cross paths over the summer, so I will constantly nag until you relent and join us. I can be very adamant."

"I might actually relish your badgering."

He was studying her as if he was searching for a clue he couldn't find. The interval became awkward, and she needed to head to The Pavilion, but her rendezvous with him had been too thrilling. She couldn't bear to have it end.

"Why don't you get going?" he eventually said. "I'll keep watch to guarantee you arrive safe and sound."

She snorted with feigned aggravation. "How can you have any effect on my security? You didn't even know there was a dance pavilion. If you don't know where it is, how can you be certain I've reached it?"

"I'm learning many things from you, Miss Shaw. I'll note the building you enter, and from this point on, I will be possessed of new information about the town."

"Goodnight, my lord. It was a pleasure to sneak away with you, and in the future, if you see me out and about, stop and say hello."

"I will."

She'd been dismissed, so there was no reason to linger, and she supposed he'd assume she was drooling over him like a besotted ninny. She physically pulled herself away and marched off. After a few strides, she peeked back and said, "When I tell my cousin, Peggy, that I met you, she'll die of envy."

"I can't imagine why."

"Haven't you heard? You're the invisible mystery-man of Baywick, and for several minutes, I had you all to myself. I can categorically state that you are real and not an apparition."

She whipped away and kept on. She could feel him behind her, his focus hot as a dagger. She was anxious to steal a final glimpse of him, but she forced herself to stare straight ahead. As she made it to The Pavilion, she skipped up the steps to the verandah, and she went to the rail and leaned on the balustrade.

She eagerly peered at the spot where she'd left him, positive he'd be lurking and gazing fondly, but he'd already faded into the shadows. The rat! She'd thought he'd be avidly observing her, that he wouldn't have been able to tear himself away.

Was she surprised by his lack of interest? No. When had any man ever behaved as she was hoping or expecting?

She scoffed at her foolishness, then rushed inside to locate Peggy who, no doubt, would be bored silly and demanding they return to the hotel. For once, Emily would be glad to agree.

She'd just reveled in a private interlude with James Covington. After that amazing adventure, nothing else seemed the least bit exciting.

Chapter Three

JAMES COVINGTON STOOD ON the beach, staring out at the ocean. He was hiking at the local landmark called The Needles. It was named for several stone pillars that jutted up out of the water, as if they were a giant's fingers.

He would grudgingly admit that the area was spectacularly beautiful. There was a high cliff behind him, and The Needles poked up to the sky in front of him. Off to his right, Baywick was nestled around the curved bay. He was quite a distance away, but he could see people strolling on The Promenade, enjoying themselves in the warm June sunshine.

The temperature was balmy, and for once, he wasn't shivering. He'd left his heavy coat at home and was hiking in his shirtsleeves, the sun warming him.

He walked over to a promontory of rocks and scrambled up to the top. The greater height provided a stunning view of the coast that wound toward Brighton. The air was fresh, the vista spectacular, and he told himself to smile and feel lucky.

He was back in England. He was alive. He'd survived when so many others hadn't. He had to remember to count his blessings on a regular basis. He had to quit letting himself be consumed by guilt.

Far out on the horizon, a large schooner was passing by, its sails full of the wind, so it clipped across the water. Earlier in his life, the sight would have had him hungry to be on it, anxious to traipse off to an unexplored spot on the globe. Not anymore.

After his failed trip to the wilds of the Arctic North, sailing ships didn't appeal to him in the slightest. In fact, he suspected he would never travel again, just so he'd never have to board a vessel. It would vividly remind him of how easily tragedy could strike, how difficult it was to manage in dangerous circumstances, how despicably men could behave when faced with adversity.

His plan was to never place himself in a desperate situation ever again. He wanted nothing to change and nothing to vex him, and his low attitude certainly made him wonder how he'd stagger through the summer. His brother, Archie, had begged him to tarry at Baywick, at their new manor house of Wave Crest, but every detail of the elegant, costly residence fueled his fury.

He'd been lost for so long that people had started to believe he was dead. Archie, who was actually his half-brother, had been the loudest voice in claiming it. He'd been spurred on by his mother, Bernice, who'd demanded that Archie be declared earl.

As a result, bankers and others—who should have been more cautious—had allowed Archie to get his hands on too much of James's money. Archie had invested in numerous schemes, but he had no aptitude for business, and he was very stubborn. He wouldn't take advice from those who were smarter than he was, and he thought he was always right.

A few of his endeavors had been successful, but most hadn't been. He'd been spending like a drunken fiend, feeling entitled to finally revel like an aristocrat and having no sense of economy or budgeting. Their deceased father had set up a trust fund for him as his inheritance from the estate, and their oldest brother, Edward, had been the trustee. But Edward had died while James was away, then James had vanished, and there had been no one who could have forced Archie to live within his means.

His mother, Bernice, should have controlled him, but she was just as greedy and covetous as Archie. To top it off, Archie had turned twenty-five, so the balance of the trust fund had been given to him in a lump sum.

If James had been present in England, he might have found a method to stop the disbursement, but he hadn't been, so the pile of money had been dumped on his irresponsible younger sibling. James hadn't pushed Archie for an answer as to how much of it remained, but if he'd already squandered the entire amount, James wouldn't be surprised.

The conclusion would be that Archie would need James's financial support throughout his life. Archie was a gambler and wastrel who'd repeatedly proved that James couldn't accumulate the assets necessary to pay for his extravagant habits.

James was rich, but conservative with his fortune. He envisioned decades of fighting with Archie over money, and the whole notion was exhausting.

One of Archie's biggest expenditures had been his Baywick venture. The architect had convinced a collection of men to fork over loans so he could build the town. Archie insisted Baywick would eventually rival Brighton in popularity, but James couldn't imagine that occurring. Not with the Prince Regent having decreed Brighton his favorite spot in the kingdom. With that opinion widely disseminated, who would ever meander over to Baywick?

If the quaint town never achieved a dedicated following, what would happen to James's investment? Whenever he asked himself that question, he recollected how he'd like to wring Archie's neck.

He was still lurking up on the rock promontory, when a woman came into view from around the base of the headland. She was alone, although there were others farther back, so it looked as if a hike was in progress.

He was about to let her walk on by, but as she neared, he realized it was Miss Shaw who'd chatted with him the previous night. She'd been funny and kind, and she'd stumbled on him when he'd been at his very worst, dressed in a winter coat and skulking in the shadows like a deranged lunatic.

At the time, he'd only observed her in the moonlight, then under a lamp, and he'd thought she was very fetching. He was delighted to report that, on closer inspection, he'd been correct: She was gorgeous, with lush blond hair the color of golden wheat, and striking green eyes that twinkled merrily as if she was always happy.

For some silly reason, he yearned to linger in her company and hope some of her cheery disposition might rub off on him.

She was short and slender, wearing a pink gown that enhanced her complexion and made her even more beautiful. She'd tugged off her bonnet and was carrying it by the ribbons, but she wasn't paying attention. If she wasn't careful, she'd be dragging it in the sand.

On seeing her, he suffered the sweetest wave of excitement, as if he'd been waiting for her to arrive. She had a peculiar effect on him, one he didn't understand. Even though they were strangers, he'd felt so much better when he was with her.

"Ahoy, there!" he called down. "Isn't it my partner in mischief, Miss Shaw?"

She glanced up at him. His feet were braced, his hands on his hips, so he was posed like a statue. He was grinning like a fool; he couldn't help it.

"Lord Roxbury?" she asked. "Is that you? Why are you out and about in the middle of the afternoon? I could have sworn you were a nocturnal creature who only slithered out of his secret burrow in the dark of night."

"I'm trying to be more spontaneous. You ordered me to learn more about this town I suddenly own. You seemed so certain that my mind could be changed, so I'm working to alter my negative assessment."

"Have you discovered any sights that tickle your fancy? Might I expect that you have and you're growing less critical?"

"I'm not critical," he said. "My tastes are very discriminating."

"No, you're critical and persnickety, but then, you're an earl, so I suppose you're born to be fussy. Isn't it a rule or something?"

"I believe it is."

For an instant, they didn't move. He stared down at her, a thousand conflicting thoughts racing through his head. He was anxious to dawdle with her because his mood would improve, but it was risky for them to socialize. A gentleman of his station never flirted with a young lady of hers, and she would misconstrue his behavior.

Although he pictured himself as a very manly man, he was incredibly lonely. He missed the crew members who'd survived with him. They'd bonded during their ordeal, then they'd parted in London, having vowed to never discuss any of what had transpired. On his end though, he was dying to talk about all of it.

He'd only had Archie and Archie's mother, Bernice, to welcome him back, and while they acted as if they were glad he'd returned safe and sound, they really hadn't been. His resurrection from the dead meant that Archie wasn't earl, and James was quite sure they'd just as soon have had him disappear forever.

He had to regroup so he could begin to thrive in his old life, but he was tormented by memories of his tragedy, was awash with insomnia and bad dreams, and he was so muddled in his thinking that he had no business being cordial with Miss Shaw. He would enjoy it too much, and she would misinterpret his interest.

Then again, over the past few years, he'd made so many mistakes. If he made one more with Miss Shaw, he'd simply add it to his list of unforgivable errors.

He clambered down, leaping to the ground like an agile acrobat.

"Why are you wandering by yourself again?" he asked. "I've now crossed paths with you twice, and you didn't have a maid trailing after you either time."

"I'm not a posh Londoner," she said. "I'm used to planning my own schedule. I can definitely stroll down a beach by myself."

"Aren't you worried you might encounter a villain with evil intent?"

"The only one I've encountered so far has been you."

"Ha! You already know me so well."

She smiled a pert smile that charmed him, then she pointed behind her. "I'm here with several guests from my hotel."

"You're merely pretending to be free and independent?"

"Yes, but I'm probably just very old-fashioned."

They ambled away, so she was gradually separated from her companions, and it seemed completely natural that they'd saunter off together. He was perched much too close to her, the hem of her skirt swishing over his leg with each stride. She exuded a scent that called to him on an almost feral level. He was positive no other man could have detected it. It was an aroma designed to tantalize him and no other.

Their silence was comfortable, but after a bit, she asked, "Will you allow me to boast?"

"Of course. Boast away."

"I told the other ladies at the hotel that I met you. They were green with envy, so I am a celebrity among them."

"If your acquaintance with me can render you a celebrity, then it's obvious the bar is set very low."

"It's the sole occasion anyone has been jealous of me, so I must wallow in their adoration before they realize it is entirely misplaced."

She laughed, her gaze impish and delightful, and his heart flip-flopped in his chest. He was so entranced by her that he could barely stop himself from linking their fingers as if he was her adolescent beau.

What was wrong with him? He suspected his fascination with her was being fueled by his isolation, by his feeling that the Earth had tipped off its axis and he'd lost his equilibrium. The pace of his life was too hectic, and he couldn't run fast enough to keep up.

"Did you enjoy the rest of your evening?" he asked. "How was the dance?"

"We went home. After my secret rendezvous with you, how could a paltry ballroom compare? Plus, my cousin, Peggy, was complaining, so we left."

"You're giving me too much credit for enlivening your night."

"Yes, I am. I'm deliberately fawning over you and stroking your ego. Am I having any effect?"

He chuckled. She was sassy and impertinent, and she wasn't impressed by him, but then, with his condition quite reduced, he wasn't very impressive.

"Yes, you're being very effective at stroking my ego," he said, "and I love to be fawned over."

"Is it fun to be an earl? Do you like it?"

"I haven't been one all that long, so I'm still figuring out how to view it."

"Why is your title new? Has your father recently passed away? If so, I offer my condolences. I don't know much about you or your family, so it's possible I will utter stupid comments and make a total fool of myself."

"Are you in the habit of being foolish?"

"Not in my conduct, but I frequently babble ridiculous remarks."

He chuckled again. "My father perished when I was a boy, so my older brother, Edward, was earl. He died when I was in the Arctic North."

"You had no idea?"

"No."

'You've suffered a string of tragedies, haven't you?"

"Yes, I have, and it's all been too much for me to handle."

The words burst out of him. He was a very typical British male who kept a stiff upper lip and tried to never whine or feel sorry for himself. But he'd returned to find his dear Edward deceased—on top of everything else that had occurred. And Archie in charge and reveling like a king.

"You've been home for how long?" she asked. "Three months? Four?"

"Three."

He must have looked very glum, and she grinned to cheer him.

"So you've been an earl for three months," she said, "and I will brazenly state that you're very good at it. You've grabbed the reins with no difficulty. You know exactly how to be arrogant and vain."

"Arrogant *and* vain? I thought I was being friendly and accommodating."

"No, you're very noble, very grand. Your magnificence practically oozes out of you."

He snickered. "Just for you, I shall tamp it down."

"Don't behave normally on my account. It's amusing to watch you strut and preen."

They had reached a spot where a stream flowed out of the rocks and into the ocean so they couldn't continue down the beach. He wouldn't mind getting his boots wet, but he didn't suppose she'd like to ruin her shoes. He'd explored the area before he'd bumped into her, and over the eons of time, the surf had carved caves into the base of the cliff.

He pointed to one of them and said, "May I show you a cave? The roof sparkles, as if it's constructed of diamonds. I found it a bit ago. Are you game to look at it?"

"I am absolutely game to look, and I'm glad to hear you've been exploring. You're acting more like an ordinary person today."

He rested a palm on the small of her back, relishing the excuse to touch her, and he guided her over to the cliff and motioned inside.

She glanced up at him. "I've never been in a cave. Is it dark in there? Should we have a lamp?"

"No. Light shines in from the entrance. You can see just fine."

He sensed her trepidation, and he stepped in front of her to lead the way. She hesitated, so he clasped her hand, as he'd been yearning to do. He drew her through the narrow opening, then it widened into a large grotto. There was a pool in the middle that reflected and illuminated the ceiling.

"Oh, my," she said, gasping with pleasure. "Isn't that splendid?"

"I thought so. I'm thrilled I stumbled on you so I could share it with someone."

"Have you any idea what sort of rocks they are? Or why they're sparkling?"

"No, I have no aptitude for geology or scientific explanation."

"Let's pretend they're really diamonds," she said. "We'll sneak back at midnight and fill our purses. We'll be rich forever."

"I like the sound of that."

They stared up at the ceiling, and they were still holding hands. She hadn't pulled away, and he definitely hadn't. He liked standing close to her so he could perceive the odd aura she emitted. Was she aware of the effect she had on him? He was sure not. She was genuinely unique and lacking in any guile.

They walked over to the pool of water and peered down into it. It was pitch black.

"How deep would you imagine it is?" she asked.

"I wouldn't hazard a guess, but if I didn't know how to swim, I wouldn't jump in and hope I'd be able to climb out."

"Perhaps it descends to the other side of the world. If we leapt in and floated down, we might surface in China."

They chuckled quietly, and she leaned nearer. The edge was slippery with moss. She lost her footing, and she was far enough away that she wouldn't have fallen in, but he grabbed for her anyway, not wanting her to trip and hurt herself.

Suddenly, his arms were wrapped around her, and she was snuggled to his chest, their bodies pressed together all the way down. She was a slender woman, but very shapely, and he could feel her pert breasts, her flat tummy, her curvaceous thighs.

He'd always been a randy rogue, and he was swamped by a wave of lust, which was humorous and embarrassing. It underscored how isolated he was, how disconcerted in his thinking and moods. He couldn't allow himself to be attracted to a fetching commoner who was kind and pretty, but despite his mental chastisement, he didn't release her.

He was being pelted by the eeriest sense that Fate had tossed her into his path for a reason, and until he discovered what that reason was, he would never be shed of her.

As if from a great height, as if he was watching some other idiot behave like a lunatic, he dipped down and kissed her. He couldn't help it. For a brief instant, his lips brushed hers, and she stood very still and permitted him to proceed, but she was wiser than he was. She eased away to put plenty of space between them.

"We shouldn't be kissing," she said, her tone scolding.

"Yes, but you're a female, and I never listen to females."

"It's highly likely that you're too much man for me."

"I'm too much *man* for every woman."

"I'm certain that's true." She pointed to the entrance. "Will you escort me to my companions? They'll be wondering where I am."

"I don't want to take you to them."

"Do you always get your way?"

"Yes. Always."

She smiled a smile as old as Eve's, then she asked the strangest question. "Are you lonely, Lord Roxbury? You seem to be."

He scoffed. "If I was, I'd never admit it."

She started out, and like a puppet on a string, he went with her. They ducked outside, and after being in the dark cave, the sun was very bright. They blinked and blinked to stabilize their vision.

"Would you like to meet the other ladies from my hotel?" she asked.

"No offense, but I'd rather be boiled in hot oil."

She laughed. "They'd drool over you. I promise, so you'd like it very much."

"Maybe another time."

"What will you do instead? Will you lurk on this deserted beach by yourself?"

"Probably not. I've had all the adventure I can abide for one afternoon. I'll head home."

"What's the name of your manor? Wave Crest? Where is it located?"

"We're on the other side of this headland. There's a valley that fronts the shore. My brother picked it as the best spot for a house."

"And what is your opinion? Is it the best spot?"

"It's all right," he blandly stated. In reality, the place was spectacular, a haven any man would love to claim as his own. In that, Archie had been very shrewd for a change.

"I will ponder you hiding there," she said.

"It's very ostentatious. Archie built it, and he never does anything halfway, so you needn't worry that I'm trapped in dire surroundings."

"Will you come to the community dance tonight?" she asked. "I'm betting you won't."

"I won't come, but I swear I'll *think* about coming."

"Ooh, you are such a nuisance."

"I've heard that about myself. May I call on you at your hotel?"

He hadn't realized he would pose the request, and it was a ridiculous suggestion, but at the notion of parting from her, he was terribly woeful and anxious to see her again very soon.

She studied him curiously. "Why would you call on me?"

"I have no idea."

He must have looked particularly bewildered, because she mockingly retorted, "You were supposed to flatter me and insist you will die a little each day until you can be with me again."

"That would sound awfully close to poetry, and I'm not very romantic."

"Neither am I, and there's no purpose I can deduce that would justify your stopping by. But I hope I will bump into you when I'm traipsing about. It's been marvelous to chat with you again."

He dipped down and stole another kiss. It was quick and fleeting, and it was accomplished before she had a chance to deflect it.

She shook a finger at him. "You could be dangerous to my equilibrium, so we definitely won't wander off in the future. I shouldn't risk it."

"Are you afraid you might misbehave?"

"Yes! You're a man who could coax a woman into any sort of immoral conduct."

"Would you include yourself in that group? Might I ever be lucky enough to corrupt you?"

She smirked. "We will never put ourselves in a position where we have to learn the answer to that question. Goodbye."

She marched off, and he watched her depart, figuring he must appear as mournful as a spurned suitor.

"I miss you already," he declared like a besotted fool, and the words were so unusual for him that he wondered if he wasn't getting ill.

She glanced over her shoulder. "I might miss you already too, but I won't fan the flames of your massive ego and confess it."

They shared a conspiratorial grin, then she vanished around a pile of rocks and was gone.

He dawdled, listening to the waves crashing, to the birds cawing in the sky. Once his pulse had slowed to a decent rhythm, he muttered, "What the hell is wrong with me?"

There was no one to respond to the query. He was alone, and he liked to be. It was why he'd fled London—so he could have some peace and quiet. But since he'd met Miss Shaw, he didn't want to be by himself. He would have liked to loaf with her the whole afternoon.

His yearning was potent and bizarre. If he'd believed in supernatural powers, he'd almost worry that she might have bewitched him. He didn't dare run into her again or he might land himself in all kinds of trouble, so he turned and went in the other direction, heading to the empty parlors at Wave Crest.

Archie had accused him of coming home quite mad, and perhaps his brother was correct for a change. Perhaps he'd completely tipped off his rocker. If he was contemplating an affectionate friendship with Miss Emily Shaw, there was likely no other explanation for what was happening.

Chapter Four

ARCHIE COVINGTON WALKED OVER to the fireplace and pitched a stack of letters into the flames. He watched until they were reduced to ash, as if by burning them, the senders would cease to harass him.

It had been a pile of grim news: demand for payment from merchants, tailors and others, late notices from creditors, even a few legal documents to apprise him that he was being sued in the courts.

He was in a very deep fiscal hole, and he had no idea how to climb out of it, but he blamed James for his predicament. If James had simply stayed dead, there would be no brutes hounding Archie.

He'd never been adept at budgeting, and it was so expensive to carry on in an elevated fashion in London. How was a fellow to survive in such bloodthirsty waters? If a man wasn't able to spend, and spend freely, he was naught but chum in the water.

James had vanished for five years, and Archie had been incredibly patient in waiting to learn his fate. Their oldest brother, Edward, had refused to discuss the possibility that James might have perished. He'd also refused to make plans as to what they'd do if James never returned.

After Edward had passed away—from a virulent influenza—Archie had taken swift steps to protect the title. He'd begun the necessary proceedings to have James declared deceased, even though family members were typically required to delay seven years.

Archie had used Edward's sudden demise as a valid argument that they'd suffered *two* deaths, so he needed to move forward more rapidly than was usually permitted. He'd started reveling extravagantly, shored up by the prospect of receiving James's money. Yet most of his purchases had been financed by promissory notes.

Then James had strolled in the door, bold as brass, as if he hadn't been gone a single day. His appearance, like Christ resurrected, was too infuriating to abide. Archie liked James very much, and he would never engage in ill-wishing, but if James had died on that frozen tundra, Archie's current situation wouldn't be quite so horrid.

He was in the front parlor at Wave Crest, and supper was about to be announced. It would be just himself and James, with no guests. He'd invited several London acquaintances to come for the week, and they'd sworn they would, but none of them had arrived. The bastards!

They were over in Brighton, and their fickle decision to remain there was a permanent thorn in Archie's side.

He'd once caroused there with them, but to his great consternation, he'd been banished from the glamorous town. It was a shameful verdict that he'd never confessed to anyone. No, he merely pretended he'd grown weary of the tedious spot and was eager for different surroundings.

There had been a minor incident with a young lady who was a distant cousin to the royal family. After their tryst was over, the little liar had claimed she hadn't been amenable to Archie's passionate advance. During the episode, she'd vehemently protested, but everyone knew girls didn't really mean it when they objected, so he hadn't heeded her complaints.

She'd fought like a wildcat, and her efforts to escape had left him overly excited, so unfortunately, he might have roughed her up a bit. It was all her fault, but the end result of the debacle had been a skirmish with her brothers, as well as a private word of condemnation from the Prince Regent himself.

Archie had immediately become a pariah, and he'd had to pack his bags and depart—with a stern command levied to never show his face there again.

He was still fuming over his unfair treatment, and it was the primary motive for his investing so heavily in Baywick. It was just down the road from Brighton, and he was determined that it be better and more fun than Brighton, so he could lure away the rich and notorious characters who loved to gambol there.

He wasn't having much luck though. With Baywick being located so close to Brighton, his friends would promise to visit him, but at the last second, they would head to Brighton instead. It was a maddening conundrum he couldn't fix.

He was terribly afraid the venture had been a huge waste, and with James constantly nagging, Archie couldn't convince him that it had been a viable scheme. James was thirty to Archie's twenty-five, and even though James was five years older, he might have been fifty years older.

He lorded himself over Archie in ways that were exhausting. He was smarter and more discerning than Archie. He was arrogantly confident, certain he was a god among peasants, and he repeatedly made Archie feel immature and stupid.

With it being just the two of them for supper, the meal would be uncomfortable. Since James had come home, he'd been behaving very strangely. His temper was short, his attention span even shorter, and Archie avoided him as much as he could. James was incensed by how Archie had seized control after Edward's death, and whenever they chatted, their conversations devolved to bickering.

Edward had never given up hope that James might still be alive, but Archie had yearned to be earl with a hunger that was indescribable. In light of his actions to expedite the transfer of the title, it was difficult to insist he'd been praying for James's safe return.

James entered the parlor, and a footman poured him a whiskey. He took the glass, then plopped down on a sofa nearest the fire. For some reason, he was always cold, as if the frigid North had altered his anatomy. He was wearing a thick wool sweater, the collar pulled up around his ears.

"Gad, James," Archie said, trying for levity, "it's a balmy summer evening. Must you dress as if it's January?"

"Don't fret about my clothes, Archie. I'm positive there are bigger issues to torment you."

Archie wondered if James's odd donning of winter attire might be grounds to have him committed to a mental asylum. He was exhibiting such peculiar habits. Might any of them indicate he was now a lunatic?

The minute the disloyal thought flitted by, Archie shook it away. He had to stop obsessing over how he could step past James and become earl. Edward's demise and James's disappearance had set that conclusion in motion, but it had all crashed down quickly enough.

He ignored James's sarcastic tone and asked, "How was your day? Were you able to take in any of the sights?"

"I hiked over the headland and explored The Needles."

"What was your opinion of it?"

"It was interesting."

James's expression was very bland, as if the spectacular geology wasn't remarkable. Then again, James had sailed across the globe and seen things that few humans had ever observed, so he wasn't easily impressed.

Archie sighed with exasperation. "Will you be a grouch all through supper? Anymore, you're such awful company. I wish I could improve your mood."

"My mood is fine, and you're trying too hard to persuade me to like Baywick. As I've explained over and over, it's charming."

"You don't act as if you think it's charming." Archie sounded as if he was whining. "Even your optimistic comments are tinged with mockery."

He was standing by the hearth, while James was seated, his intense gaze digging deep. Archie might have been back at boarding school and about to be paddled for an infraction. He would have begun to pace, but figured he'd have seemed guilty of a hideous transgression, so he went over to a chair and sat too.

He hadn't done anything wrong by investing in Baywick—well, other than his spending funds that weren't his own—but James liked to peer down his nose at lesser mortals so they trembled under his scrutiny. Archie was no exception.

For his entire life, he'd lived under James's shadow. James was tall, dark, and handsome, possessed of their father's stunning looks and imperious manner. His hair was black as a raven's, his blue eyes sharp as a blade. They could cut right through you and leave you flayed.

In contrast, Archie completely resembled his mother, Bernice, as if his father had provided no seed for his creation. He had blond hair and blue eyes, but his hair was already thinning on the top, and he was having to invent clever ways to conceal what was occurring.

He was much shorter than James's height of six feet, and where James was broad and brawny, strong and fit, Archie was small and chubby, slight and uninspiring.

James was wiser, wealthier, and more important than Archie, and he was lauded and respected by all. With his return from the Arctic

North, he was considered even more grand. Archie had never equaled his brothers in wit or charisma, and it was widely recognized that he was the runt of their father's litter.

He toiled valiantly to obtain the acclaim he deserved as the son of an earl, but despite how he struggled, he rarely received it.

There was one area where he excelled over James. He was the better dresser, but even though he employed the most expensive tailors, their designs couldn't obscure the paunch developing around his belly.

"Could we not argue about Baywick for a change?" James said. "You'll give me indigestion."

"I just want you to like the place, to understand the vision we had when I joined with the other investors. Is that too much to ask?"

"I understand your reasoning. The problem I'm having is that it's easy to throw money at a project when it's not your own."

"Mother and I thought you were dead!" Archie should have let the subject rest, but he felt so ill-used.

At his shrill protest, James's focus grew piercing. "You oughtn't to remind me that you held my memorial service, and could the topic of my supposed death be another one you don't raise right before we go in to eat?"

"You can't keep blaming me for the actions I took after Edward died. You were missing for five years. How long should we have waited? Forever?"

James didn't answer the question. "Where is your mother anyway? You mentioned she'd be arriving soon, but might I hope she's decided to stay in London?"

"She's coming next week."

"I will be on pins and needles until then."

James's derision was exhausting. He and Bernice had never gotten on. She had been their father's third wife, having wed him when she was young and silly, and it had been a horrid mismatch. She'd never been very maternal either, so her attempts to mother her husband's boys had been unsuccessful. She'd only ever cared about Archie and how her marriage could lift him up.

"You're determined to complain and criticize about every little detail," Archie said, "so why travel here with me?"

"I told you that I had to see what you'd done with so much of my money. And I was anxious to flee the gossip that's swirling in the city. You know that. This was a good spot to hide."

"Why is that?" Archie scathingly inquired. "Is it because there's no one visiting Baywick who actually matters? Is it because there's no one of importance to stumble on you and report your whereabouts to the newspapers? Are you telling me this is a failed enterprise?"

Archie's tone was very strident, but he couldn't help being furious. James simply prodded at all his insecurities.

"I didn't say I think it's a failure." James enunciated each of his words, as if speaking to a dunce. "The town seems very busy to me."

"But none of the best people have flocked to us."

James shrugged. "Who can predict if they ever will? It's so close to Brighton. I'm not sure it's sufficiently different to set it apart. Why would it be worth the bother of coming here instead of there? Have you ever pondered that dilemma?"

It was the worst assessment James could have offered, and if Archie had been a weepy person, he'd have cried like a baby.

"Despite your low opinion," Archie bitterly asked, "will you tarry for the summer? Even though you hate it? You promised you would."

"I don't hate it."

"You don't sound as if you love it."

"It's growing on me."

It was an olive branch of sorts, tossed out to smooth over their rancor before they went in to dine, and it was furnished just in time too. The butler summoned them to their meal, and they stood and headed to the adjacent room.

As they approached the table and were being seated, James casually said, "There was a large stack of mail delivered this morning. It was all addressed to you, and I could swear a few of the envelopes might have been legal notices. You're not in financial trouble, are you?"

Archie's bowels seized up. He absolutely could not permit James to discover his dire fiscal condition. On his twenty-fifth birthday, the balance of the trust fund he'd inherited from their father had been disbursed to him, and he'd already spent it.

He couldn't figure out how he'd frittered away such a huge amount, but he had to maintain his status as an earl's brother, as a man of Quality, as a gentleman of style and discernment. He couldn't go about, looking like a pauper. What would his acquaintances think?

"No, no," he said, forcing a smile. "What a preposterous notion. Of course I'm not in financial trouble. In fact, I'm swimming in wealth. Let's eat, shall we?"

James stared him down, as if he'd call him out on the lie, but apparently, he'd castigated Archie quite enough for one evening. He gestured to the butler, and the man stepped forward and poured their wine.

"Come in! Come in!"

Bernice Covington grinned at Archie's fiancée, Temperance Moore. She was twenty-one and a very plain, dull female. Bernice thought it was ridiculous that a fortune had been showered on her. Then again, she was a great heiress, and a massive dowry made any woman more attractive.

Bernice herself was wed at eighteen, so she was only forty-five. She was still beautiful, her blue eyes shrewd and cunning, but her blond hair had thinned and faded to silver, hinting at her age in a manner she didn't like.

She was plump now too, and it was exasperating. Most people viewed an excess of weight as a sign of prosperity, but she'd relished the days when she'd been slender and lithe, and men like her prominent husband had perked up when she'd strolled by.

In contrast, Temperance was no beauty and never would be. Her features were pleasant enough, but she was short to the point of being tiny. Her hair was brown, her eyes too, which Bernice didn't like. The prettiest girls were always blond, but beggars couldn't be choosers. It was difficult to find an heiress, and Archie deserved a rich bride.

Temperance had initially been engaged to Bernice's stepson, Edward, when he'd been earl. His untimely death had had Temperance wondering if she shouldn't cry off, but Bernice had slyly convinced her to betroth herself to Archie instead.

After all, she'd agreed to bind herself to Edward so she could become Countess of Roxbury. With Edward out of the way, and James having been considered deceased, Archie should have been raised up. Temperance had simply substituted one fiancé for another, but now, James was back, Archie wasn't the earl, and there were vicious rumors circulating that Temperance was about to jilt Archie.

The prospect of her walking away with some other gleeful beau was too much for Bernice to abide.

She was heading to Baywick for the remainder of the summer, and she was terribly afraid—should she depart the city—the blasted ninny might renege when Bernice wasn't around to stop her. Bernice had to keep her close so she realized she would never be allowed to slither off Bernice's hook. There would be no breach of promise.

They were in the front parlor of her London house—well, it was James's house, but why quibble?—and she'd carefully staged the room to remind Temperance of how grand and prestigious the Covington family was. They were old aristocracy, with centuries behind the title, and Temperance was from a lowly clan of upstarts that was involved in the sugar trade in the Caribbean.

She'd be lucky to join them, was lucky to have been picked by Bernice as a suitable candidate for her only son.

Refreshments were served, but the conversation was stilted and uncomfortable. Eventually, Bernice said, "I've received a letter from Archie."

"How nice." Temperance's tone was disinterested, as if she could barely recall who Archie was. "Is he enjoying his holiday?"

"Oh, he's not on holiday. He's very busy, meeting with investors, attending meetings. He's been the centerpiece of the whole enterprise at Baywick; if they hadn't had his guidance and expertise, they'd never have dug a single shovel of dirt."

Bernice was a realist, and she'd be the first to privately confess that Archie was lazy and incompetent. He'd had very little to do with Baywick being built, but that admission was between herself and God.

"I've heard it's a quaint town," Temperance said.

"It's really charming."

"I'm glad it turned out so well."

Temperance was glaring at Bernice as if Bernice was a nuisance, and the girl's pompous attitude was incredibly annoying. It was a common problem with heiresses. They assumed their money made them special. It aggravated women like Bernice who *were* special in their own right and didn't need to prove it.

"I've had a clever idea," Bernice said, "and I thought I'd share it with you. I'm traveling to Baywick next week, and I was wondering if you'd like to accompany me."

"To Baywick?" Temperance stared down her pert nose as if Bernice had just proposed a trip to Hell.

"We've opened our cottage, and Archie constantly has acquaintances popping over from Brighton. There's a dance pavilion and a theater. It's become quite sophisticated."

"Is the Earl there too?" Temperance asked.

"Yes, James is there."

"Is he staying for the summer?"

"That's the plan. The gossip in London has been horrendous, and newspaper reporters were hounding him. Archie suggested he escape to the country."

"Does he like it there? What is his opinion of Baywick?"

"He's fallen in love with it." Bernice gushed the reply, then realized she was probably spreading it on too thick. "What do you think? Would your father let you tag along? You could tarry for the month of July. It would be nice for you and Archie to socialize before you tie the knot."

"Would you be there to chaperone me?"

"Yes, certainly. Shall I write to your father? Shall I ask him if you can go?"

"You swear Lord Roxbury is there?"

Bernice didn't like how she kept inquiring about James. When James and Archie were together, there was no comparison between them. James was tall, handsome, and imposing. People were in awe of him. Men respected him. Women dreamed of bedding him.

Archie had few attributes to recommend him over James. He was good looking enough, but he was chubby and balding. He was very friendly in a manner that brooding, unhappy James could never be, but frivolous females preferred the dark, sulky type. What if Temperance shifted her focus to James?

For a moment, Bernice hesitated, debating whether she dared take Temperance to Wave Crest.

As quickly as the dilemma arose, she just as quickly discarded it. There was no reason to worry about Temperance's motives. She was engaged to Archie, and despite what she might wish, James would never be interested in her.

Even if he'd been fully recovered from his ordeal, he was very rich, so her fortune wasn't an enticement. Plus, if he'd been contemplating matrimony—which he wasn't—he could choose a candidate from the most beautiful women in the world. He didn't have to settle for a plain, brown-haired girl who was ordinary in every way but for her dowry.

It was Archie and Bernice who needed her money. Bernice's husband, Archie's father, hadn't liked her very much, and she'd been a third wife. Upon his death, she'd received a cash gift as her inheritance, but she'd already spent it. Archie had squandered his trust fund disbursement too, and with James being back, Archie couldn't dip his fingers into the estate accounts.

They *needed* Temperance's money, and if the annoying child thought she would visit Wave Crest merely to flirt with James, he would immediately cut her down to size. And of course, Bernice would ensure no romance blossomed. Temperance wasn't exactly a temptress, and she had no qualities that would induce James to notice her.

"Yes, James is at Wave Crest," Bernice said, "but we'll rarely see him. We'll be too busy with Archie, as he squires us to all the best places."

"I'm positive it will be divine." Temperance didn't look as if she meant it in the least.

PEGGY STOOD NEXT TO the buffet table, sipping a glass of wine. The Saturday night dance was in progress in the adjoining room, and so far, it had been a very tedious affair. Nothing had happened to render it any different or more amusing than the Friday night debacle.

There were many more ladies than gentlemen in attendance, so she'd had just one opportunity to take a turn on the floor. The same musicians were playing the same uninspired tunes. The wine and hors d'oeuvres were the same options that had been served the prior evening.

It was only her second day in Baywick, and this would be the story of the entire summer. The coastal sojourn would never be fun or worthwhile, so why had she let Emily convince her to make the trip?

Her stepmother, Florence, had egged them on too, insisting they should go and enjoy themselves. Peggy had been hoping Baywick would provide a few months of excitement, but clearly, she'd miscalculated. She ought to persuade Emily to leave early, but her cousin could be very stubborn, so she doubted Emily would agree.

Out in the main room, a stir of animation suddenly swept through the subdued group. Voices were louder, conversations more vivacious. It sounded as if new guests had arrived. Praise be!

She put her glass down on a nearby table, then went over and peeked in to see what was occurring. A half-dozen London dandies had strutted in. They were in high spirits, stylishly dressed, and liking how the country rubes were agog over them.

Emily hadn't accompanied her that evening. She'd worn herself out, hiking on the sea cliffs and had pleaded fatigue, so Peggy had glommed onto some other women from the hotel.

One of them was standing close by, and Peggy walked over and whispered, "What is it? Who's come?"

"It's Mr. Archie Covington," her companion whispered back. "He's Lord Roxbury's brother and a chief investor in the town."

Peggy bit down a gasp of surprise. Emily had told her Roxbury and his brother were in residence, but she hadn't wanted to believe it.

"Which one is Mr. Covington?" she asked.

"The short blond. I don't know the men with him, but he's very popular with a certain fast crowd. He often has chums who pop over from Brighton."

"Could they be cordial with the Prince Regent?"

The other woman shrugged. "Probably, but who can guess for sure? In any event, they're rich bachelors, so this night just got a whole lot more intriguing."

Peggy moved to where she'd be more visible. The musicians were starting another set, and the men were asking ladies to dance. Lines were forming.

She studied Mr. Covington. He was pudgy around the middle, and he wasn't exactly handsome, but he wasn't bad either. From the cut of his clothes, it was obvious he was very wealthy, and that always made a fellow better looking.

He was affable and extroverted, and the people with him were laughing and clapping him on the back. As she watched, he drew a flask from his coat and took a swig. He passed it to his friends, and they had a swig too. They were snickering, preening over how they'd commandeered the room. They viewed themselves as being very toplofty and relished the notion that their exalted presence would save the party.

Peggy viewed herself as being very exalted and important too. She had a keen eye for fashion, and she recognized Quality when it was right in front of her. There was no question that she should be included in their tight circle.

They grabbed various women by the hand and dragged them onto the floor. Upon having their attention bestowed, it was like winning the lottery. Each chosen girl beamed with pride, as if they'd been sin-gled out for their unique beauty and special character.

Mr. Covington gazed about, searching for a partner, and being much more discerning than the others had been. She could practically sense his determined impression that he was elevated above everyone else.

Peggy felt the same way. None of the other females could compete with her.

Pick me! Pick me! Pick me!

She was mentally shouting the words at him. And . . ?

Like magic, his hot focus fell on her. He sauntered over and asked, "May I have this dance?"

Peggy gave a vain toss of her blond hair and said, "I would be honored."

Chapter Five

"I LOVE IT HERE."

"I'm glad."

Emily smiled at Mrs. Darlington. They were in the front parlor of her house that she'd turned into a hotel. It was early in the afternoon, and it was quiet. Peggy had been out late, and she hadn't yet dragged herself out of bed. Emily was loafing, and Mrs. Darlington had just come in from running errands. She'd handed off her basket to a servant, then had sat down to chat.

"This is only my third day," Emily said, "and I'm already wishing I never had to depart."

"That sentiment is often voiced to me, but my guests always wind up going home in the end."

"I don't have much to go home to. We live with my widowed Aunt Florence. She's ill with consumption."

"I'm sorry to hear that. It's such a terrible disease."

"Her husband perished several years ago, and we were shocked to discover that he'd been a spendthrift. For the moment, we've held onto our property of Hexham, but after Florence passes away, I can't predict what will happen."

"Once the worst occurs, would you consider moving to Baywick to work for me?"

Emily lurched up in her seat as if she'd been poked with a pin. "What a lovely idea! Thank you for suggesting it. I would consider that."

"One of my employees is getting married and leaving town with her husband, so I'll need to replace her. The wages would be pathetic, but you'd have room and board."

"If I could stay here forever, I would think I'd died and gone to Heaven. Are you really serious about this?"

"Yes, I'm serious. From the instant we met, I sensed that we were destined to be friends."

Emily beamed with delight. "I appreciate your sharing that. I felt the same way, but if I'd admitted it, I was afraid you'd deem me mad."

"I make quick decisions about people. I either like them or I don't."

"I'm the exact opposite. I'm slow to form an opinion, so perhaps we'd be a good team. You could be swift and abrupt, and I would be measured and methodical. I'd temper your more outrageous impulses."

Mrs. Darlington laughed. "It sounds as if we would be partners in crime, so you should probably call me Mary."

"I will, and you must call me Emily."

Mary leaned nearer and murmured, "And I'm not a widow."

Emily frowned. "Why claim to be one then?"

"It helps me in business. Female guests are more likely to book a reservation if they believe it to be the case." Mary smirked. "Apparently, a widow automatically possesses an abundance of wisdom and maturity that a single woman lacks."

"Do your employees know?"

"Yes, and they keep my secret. Don't tell anyone. I wouldn't want the truth to circulate."

"My lips are sealed, and I shall enjoy having learned this private tidbit about you. It feels as if we're conspirators."

A servant brought them a tray with tea and cakes, and they served themselves, chatting about everything and nothing. Then Mary said, "Your cousin and the other ladies returned late last night. Evidently, there was some excitement at the dance. Archie Covington showed up with some of his London friends."

"Mr. Covington is Lord Roxbury's brother?"

"Yes. He's quite a dandy, and he's very set on himself. I find him to be incredibly pompous, and I can't abide his brand of male arrogance."

Emily chuckled. "Remember that I met Lord Roxbury? I found him to be very dashing. Is Mr. Covington dashing? Does it run in the family?"

"I haven't ever laid eyes on the Earl, so I can't compare them. Mr. Covington is short and chubby and, by my very fussy feminine standard, a tad ordinary."

"They're not the least bit alike then. Lord Roxbury is dynamic and remarkable. I bumped into him again yesterday when I was hiking at The Needles."

"The two of you are practically bosom buddies."

"I think he's lonely," Emily said.

"Or maybe he's playing on your sympathies so you'll pity him and be kinder to him than you ought to be."

"No, he's genuinely glum. His recent ordeal has left him bereft."

"That could be, but if you stumble on him in the future, be careful. I don't trust any nobleman. They view women as chattel, and his brother has a hideous reputation."

Emily raised a brow. "What type of reputation? Normally, I wouldn't gossip, but I'm fascinated by Roxbury."

"You shouldn't be fascinated by him, and if it starts to seem as if you are, I'll yank you to your senses."

"What are some of the stories about his brother?"

"There are just rumors, not stories. I've never had a bad tale confirmed with direct knowledge. Mr. Covington revels with a very fast crowd. If I had a sister, I wouldn't allow her to socialize with him."

"I'll have to ask Peggy about him. Mr. Covington is precisely the sort of fellow who would tantalize her. I hope they didn't cross paths."

"I'm sure they did. And I'll have a word with the other ladies who were at the dance. If his friends are lingering in town, they shouldn't schedule any outings with them."

"If Mr. Covington is wicked," Emily asked, "do you suppose Roxbury is too?"

"I have no idea about the Earl. He's only just arrived, so there hasn't been a chance for gossip to spread."

"He didn't appear debauched to me. If I had to describe him, I'd say he's sad and adrift. He's peculiar too, as if he's forgotten how to be happy."

"You are too understanding, aren't you? Please don't be sucked in by his low mood. I can't tell you how many females in history have been convinced they could save a man who didn't deserve to be saved."

"I swear to never suffer an ounce of compassion for him."

They snickered in unison, and the conversation might have wandered away from the Covington brothers, but there was a knock on the front door to interrupt them. No servants were nearby, so Mary rose to answer it herself.

When Emily heard the person's voice—and his question—she could have fainted from shock.

"I am James Covington. Lord Roxbury? I'd like to speak with Miss Emily Shaw. She informed me that she's your guest. Might she be available?"

Mary peeked over at Emily, her eyes wide with amazement, as if she was seeking permission to let him in. Emily shrugged, figuring they couldn't shut the door in an earl's face.

"Yes, she's here," Mary replied. "Come in, won't you?"

He strutted in as if he owned the house, and Mary curtsied as he went by, but he barely noticed her. He assessed the foyer and the parlor, critically absorbing every detail, as if he was about to purchase the building.

He saw Emily over on the sofa, and he said, "Hello, Miss Shaw. I've arranged a picnic. Will you join me?"

The query was abrupt and completely bizarre. She was reeling from the fact that he'd chased her down, and she stammered, "A picnic . . . .? Well . . ."

Were they sufficiently acquainted for them to traipse off together?

No, and Mary's warnings about noblemen were still reverberating. Then again, Emily was twenty-five and a spinster. She was level-headed and pragmatic. If she wanted to walk out with a handsome gentleman, she certainly could. She had no chaperone to forbid it. Mary might not be too keen on the prospect though, and Emily liked her so much. She couldn't bear to upset her.

Manners first. "Lord Roxbury," she said to him, "may I present my friend and the owner of this hotel? Mrs. Mary Darlington."

"Hello, Mrs. Darlington." He didn't bother to glance at her.

"You know how to make a bold entrance," Emily told him, then she looked over at Mary. "What is your opinion, Mary? Shall I oblige the Earl or not?"

Clearly, Mary couldn't deduce how to refuse him either, and she scowled, supplying no hint of what Emily should choose.

Emily grinned up at Roxbury and asked, "What are you planning, my lord? Before I consent, I ought to have some notion of what you're envisioning."

"I thought I'd row us over to the Pirate's Cove."

"A boat ride *and* a picnic? How could I decline such a fabulous invitation?" She said to Mary, "Will you mind if I accept?"

Mary regrouped from her momentary astonishment. "I'm not your nanny. It's not up to me."

Emily couldn't guess if Mary was being sincere or not. It could simply be that, with the Earl in the room, she was afraid to be frank.

"Will I be safe in your company, Lord Roxbury?" Emily asked him. "I've heard some disturbing stories about your brother. Are you possessed of the same dissolute tendencies? Or can I trust you to behave?"

He didn't respond to the slur about his own character, but he was perplexed over his brother's reputation. "There are stories circulating about my brother?"

"Apparently so," Emily said. "Should I fear for my virtue?"

He snorted at that. "It's just a picnic, Miss Shaw. Your virtue will survive."

She persuaded herself that he was correct: It was just a picnic. What could happen? And she wasn't exactly a flirt. She could spend an afternoon with him, then return in fine shape. She was sure of it.

"I would love to visit the Pirate's Cove," she said.

"Shall we go now?" He offered her his arm.

"Yes, it can be now." She smiled at Mary. "I'll see you in a few hours."

Mary told the Earl, "Please bring her home in a good condition, Lord Roxbury. I run a reputable business, and I can't have reports spreading that I've condoned mischief."

He frowned at her. "I'm the dullest creature ever born. In my entire life, I don't believe I've ever engaged in mischief."

Emily and Mary both sputtered with amusement, deeming the comment hilarious, and Mary said, "Sir, you are a nobleman. I'm positive you're trained at birth to engage in mischief."

"I'll try to rein in my vile inclinations—just for the two of you."

"I would appreciate it."

Mary opened the door, and Emily and the Earl departed. As Emily went by, Mary yanked her shawl and bonnet off a hook and handed them to Emily.

"Take these," she said. "Wear the bonnet and cover your skin as much as you can. The sun will be very hot on the water. I would hate to have you burn."

"Thank you," Emily replied. "With Lord Roxbury being so pompously hasty, I'd forgotten I might need them."

"I'll bring you back in one piece," he said, "and I promise you won't be sunburned."

"I shall hold you to it."

He was weary of the delay, and he practically dragged her out to the street. She rolled her eyes at Mary, viewing the whole interlude as unusual, then Roxbury lifted her into his carriage, and they rumbled away. She allowed herself a quick instant to wonder if she hadn't gone mad, or if *he* hadn't gone mad, then she remembered she couldn't recollect when she'd last frivolously socialized with an intriguing bachelor.

She would thoroughly enjoy herself, would chat and become better acquainted, and she wouldn't worry a single minute.

"Do you think I'm mad?"

"I was just pondering that very question," Miss Shaw said to James, "and my answer is *yes*. You're absolutely mad."

James nodded vigorously. He couldn't explain why he'd been so desperate to be with her. When the idea for a picnic had occurred to him, it had rattled loose a thread of exhilaration that was still tugging at him in absurd ways.

Before he could talk himself out of it, he'd ordered his chef to pack a basket, and he'd headed into the village.

They were at the end of The Promenade where there was a public dock. The town provided free rowboats and skiffs, so people could traverse the bay, and he'd sent a servant to reserve one and have it prepared. He steadied her as she climbed into it.

As he'd journeyed back to England from the Arctic North, he'd vowed to never go out onto the water again, but he supposed he could endure a short trip over to the Pirate's Cove.

He climbed in after Miss Shaw, and the attendant handed him the picnic basket. He stowed it under a bench, then he clutched the oars and pulled hard. The small craft leapt away, rapidly conveying them toward their destination.

"I assume you know something about boats," she said, grinning.

"Yes, you scamp. I grew up on the ocean. I'm sure I can row us a few hundred yards."

"Are you from a nautical family? Were your ancestors in the navy?"

"My uncles were. Not my father. He was earl, so he wasn't permitted to pursue activities that might have been hazardous."

"Were you in the navy yourself?"

"No, but my boarding school was a military academy. We had classes where we learned navigation and how to tend the sails on various kinds of ships."

"I'm so envious. When I went to school, we simply studied home administration. And, of course, we were regularly drilled on social deportment. No one ever considered that we might like to learn to sail too."

"Have I previously mentioned that I'm glad I was born a man?"

"How did you become an explorer?" she asked.

"A friend of mine organized an excursion down the Nile in Egypt."

Her jaw dropped. "You've been to Egypt? Ooh, I'm so jealous."

"He needed an investor, so I chipped in, and it bought me a spot on his crew. After that expedition, I was hooked on adventure."

"Are you still hooked? From the reports in the newspapers, I suspect some of the excitement has faded."

He pulled a little harder on the oars, using them as an excuse not to respond.

If he'd been in London, he might have presumed she was prying for information she could share with others or perhaps even sell to a reporter. Everyone was eager to have the wild rumors verified, but he and his men had agreed they wouldn't discuss what had happened.

He was dying to expound though, and a flood of words raced to the tip of his tongue. He was afraid, should he offer even the blandest comment, he'd babble many secrets that were none of her business.

They were already across the bay, the island swiftly approaching, so he could focus on that and ignore her remark.

There was another dock, and several boats tied to it, so others were visiting. They wouldn't have the place all to themselves, which was probably a blessing. If they'd been truly alone, who could guess how he might have behaved? Anymore, he was that dangerously unpredictable.

He secured them to a piling, then he clambered out and extended a hand to her. As she stood up, the boat rocked, and she swayed so far to the side that they were lucky she didn't pitch overboard. He grabbed her, practically plucking her up onto the dock.

She wasn't frightened by her near-mishap, and once she'd regained her balance, she laughed merrily.

"For a moment there," she said, "I thought I was a goner."

"Can you swim, Miss Shaw? I should have asked before I dragged you away from dry land."

"I'm not much of a swimmer, but the water is very clear, and I can see the bottom. If I'd tumbled in, I could have waded to shore, but I might have ruined my dress."

She was gazing up at him, looking fetching and jolly, and her sunny mood was infectious. He wanted it to wash over him, to imbue him with some of her cheery disposition. How did she manage it? How was she always so happy?

Their conversation dwindled, and he was staring like a fool, like a besotted boy, and he was delighted to have snuck off with her. He was eager to kiss her, but he'd done it the prior day in the cave under the cliffs, and she'd scolded him and left. So he didn't dare attempt another embrace.

He intended to spend as many hours with her as he could seize for himself, so he couldn't scare or annoy her where she might demand he take her back to her hotel. It dawned on him—now that he'd absconded with her—maybe he'd never take her back.

She was the one to ease away. She spun and marched down the dock to the beach. She peered both ways, then at him. "Have you been here before? Do you have a favorite spot?"

"No. This is my first visit."

"Let's walk until we stumble on the perfect location, preferably in the shade."

The sun was shining down, and for just an instant, she seemed to be bathed in golden light, as if there was a halo surrounding her. It made her green eyes sparkle, her blond hair glow. He picked up the basket and came over to her. Not pausing to debate, he broke his self-imposed rule and kissed her. He shouldn't have, but he did it anyway.

She didn't chastise him, but she said, "Is this to be a romantic picnic?"

"Yes, if I can convince you that a bit of romance might be worth it."

"I doubt you'll succeed. I'm a tough customer, so I won't blithely fall for your charms."

"You think I have charms?"

"Yes, but that's the only time I'll admit it."

He chuckled and linked their fingers, as if they were sweethearts strolling home from church. They kept on around a bend, to an arbor under a leafy hedge. It faced the bay and the town, and they could see people over on The Promenade.

"What is your opinion?" he asked. "Does this meet your high expectations?"

"It's exactly what I was hoping to find."

He had no idea what his chef had packed in the basket, but he opened it to discover a blanket neatly folded on the top. He drew it out with a flourish. "*Voila!* You won't have to sit on the sand. We'll be able to dine like a civilized couple."

They spread it out, then she ordered him to relax, while she puttered about in a wifely fashion. He couldn't remember when he'd last had a young lady fuss over him. Perhaps he never had and that was why he couldn't recall.

It was very comfortable, very domestic, as if they'd been wed for a dozen years and had often loafed on a deserted beach.

She emptied the basket, and it contained an extravagant meal, with a sliced meat pie, breads, cheeses, and even a small cake. Three bottles of wine had been included, and as she pulled them out, she snickered gaily.

"Was your chef aware it was to be just the two of us?" she asked. "Is he supposing we're drunkards? Or is he supposing *you* are a drunkard? Should I be worried you'll drink yourself into oblivion? I pray you won't, for I need you sufficiently sober to row me back across the bay when we're finished."

"When I claimed to be dull and boring, I wasn't joking. I have no bad habits, so I've never once over-imbibed."

She snorted. "Liar. You're a nobleman, so your life is likely an entire book of bad habits."

"That would be my brother, Archie. I'm actually quite a tedious fellow."

"I don't believe it for a second."

He poured them both a glass of wine, and when they would have clinked the rims together, she stopped him.

"We should have a toast," she said. "What shall it be?"

He pondered, then said, "How about this: to you."

"No, that's terribly dreary. How about: to *us*? To our becoming friends? It seems so improbable to me that we'd be cordial, but here we are."

"Yes, to us and our new acquaintance. Why do you imagine we met?"

"I'm telling myself it's one of the mysteries of the universe," she said.

"There's no explanation?"

"No, none at all."

She sipped her wine, as she snooped in bowls and dished up two plates. They ate in a companionable silence, with neither of them feeling the need to fill the void with conversation.

After a bit, she said, "I wish I could stay in Baywick forever, and Mrs. Darlington who owns the hotel? She invited me to work for her."

His pulse raced at the prospect. "Would you like to do that?"

"I told her I'd chew on it. Matters at home are difficult. My cousin, Peggy, and I live with my aunt. She's in failing health, and I can't predict what will transpire after she passes away."

"You don't have any other family?"

She smirked. "Not any worth mentioning."

"This might be a good option for you then."

The news had stirred a peculiar surge of excitement in him. If she moved to Baywick, he'd see her frequently. She'd be in residence and available for socializing. It was madness to reflect on that scenario, but then, he'd been hearing repeatedly that his ordeal had left him deranged. If he behaved like a lunatic over her, who would be surprised?

"Mrs. Darlington's suggestion has given me plenty to contemplate," she said. "What about you and your plans? Will you tarry in Baywick for the whole summer?"

"Would you like me to tarry?"

She clucked her tongue with annoyance. "Don't be a tease. There is no reason for you to arrange your schedule according to what I might prefer."

"Well, I hadn't intended to dawdle for more than a week or two, but whenever I anticipate a return to London, I nearly break out in hives. I can't make myself go."

She frowned. "Is it because of the rumors?"

"Yes, and I ran to the coast to avoid them. It's been embarrassing to be so daunted by a few stories."

She reached out and patted his hand, and the gesture was sweet and endearing. "Don't pay attention to idiots. They know nothing about you."

"It's not that I care about their opinions. They're urging me to talk about what occurred, but my men and I agreed we wouldn't. I would never renege on my vow to them."

"Good for you." She studied him, her gaze probing and sympathetic. "What happened there? May I inquire? Was it awful?"

"It was horrid and grueling, and the details are more distressing than I would ever reveal to you."

"I won't pry then," she said, "but if you should ever like to unburden yourself, please feel free. I'm very discreet, and your secrets would always be safe with me."

It was the most precious comment she could have offered, and another wave of painful remarks begged to spill out. He wanted to confide how men had died of cold and starvation, how they'd fought and killed each other over trifles, how some of them had mutinied and carried on like animals.

He'd learned the hard way that human beings had an enormous capacity for violence, for betrayal and disloyalty. He'd witnessed and survived the worst conduct men could exhibit. He wouldn't discuss any of it.

He was getting lost in her pretty green eyes, and he yanked away and pointed to the water.

"Have you ever waded barefoot in the surf, Miss Shaw?"

"No, I never have."

"Would you like to? Or are you afraid you might faint if you saw my toes?"

"Would you faint if you saw mine?" she countered. "You wouldn't deem me to be loose, would you?"

"I would never think that about you."

She grinned. "You'd have to swear you'd never tell a single soul."

"I'd never tell; I swear."

"Then, yes, I should love to try it."

His grin matched hers, then he leaned on his elbows and extended his foot. "You'll have to remove my boots. They fit tightly, and I doubt I can shuck them off on my own."

She didn't hesitate, but leapt up to oblige him. She pulled off one, then the other, and tossed them away. He busied himself, tugging off his stockings and rolling up his trousers, while she scooted behind him. He could hear her kicking off her slippers, lifting her skirt, untying her garters and tugging off her own stockings.

She came around to stand in front of him, and she'd knotted the hem of her skirt to hold it up to her knees, so he had a shocking view of her bare calves. But he wasn't complaining!

She grabbed his hand, then they dashed across the sand, eagerly waiting for the tide to sweep over their feet. The water was freezing, but she hadn't realized it would be, and she squealed with merriment.

They played for an eternity, and it was the first time in ages that he'd frolicked as if he was young and carefree. For a few minutes anyway, he could ignore his woe and just enjoy himself. Through it all, she was charming and happy, like a child being given new toys.

Eventually, they grew tired. They returned to the blanket, replaced their shoes and stockings, and relaxed. She cut into the cake, and they shared a slice, with him feeding her bites off his fork. It wasn't that intimate—they were merely eating a piece of cake—but then again, it was outrageously intimate. The simple act was very thrilling.

"You didn't wear a heavy coat today," she said, "or a woolen cap. Is your perpetual chill waning?"

"I'm struggling to keep from behaving so strangely. It's exasperating to have others whispering that I'm mad."

"Perhaps I'm helping you to feel better. You've been curious as to why we met. Perhaps that's why." She smiled at him and said, "If all that's required to improve your condition is a picnic on the beach, then maybe I'll drag you over here every afternoon."

"Would you spend every afternoon with me if I asked you?"

"No, but we can pretend I would."

"Why wouldn't you?" He sounded petulant and spoiled.

"I have no business socializing with you."

"You like me more than you should."

"You might be correct, and just as *I* have no business socializing with you, *you* have no business socializing with me. It can't become a habit because I would begin to count on it too much."

"I would count on it too," he admitted, "but wouldn't it be spectacular to have a summer romance? When a person is on holiday, a flirtation is practically expected."

"I'd miss you too much when it was over. I'm tender-hearted, and I have to watch myself with you so I don't jump in over my head. I shall take you in small doses, but never swallow the entire bottle."

"You talk as if I'm a false tonic."

"Are you?"

"Probably," he said, and she laughed.

He stole a quick kiss, the only one he'd dared since they'd stepped out of the boat. She sighed, but didn't scold him, so apparently, he was making progress.

He laid down and stretched out on the blanket, as she puttered around, picking up their mess and repacking the basket. She refilled their wine, then gazed out at the bay as if she'd never seen a more perfect sight.

To his great surprise, he dozed off next to her. He'd come home with many problems, the most vexing being his insomnia. On the rare occasions when he was able to fall asleep, he woke in fits and starts, so he never completely rested.

For once, he slumbered hard and deeply, but soon, he was pitched into the middle of a dream that regularly plagued him. In it, he's trudging through a blizzard in a tattered coat and boots. The frigid air is more piercing than can be described, the snowflakes hitting him in the face, like biting hailstones.

He's wandering blindly, and he's separated from his men! His panic is growing, and he's shouting for them, but there's never any answer! The wind sucks his words away! Then . . . ?

He leapt to consciousness, with his pulse pounding and his senses rattled. He glanced about quite wildly, then he remembered he was safely back in England, and he slumped down.

Miss Shaw was seated beside him, and she was obviously distraught, which was mortifying. He prayed he hadn't cried out, that he hadn't mumbled comments that might have disturbed her.

"I'm sorry," she said, "but we need to get going."

She pointed to the sky, and it had clouded over as if it might rain. She'd covered him with her shawl, and he pushed it away and sat up.

"I had a nightmare," he said.

"Was it scary? It seemed to be."

He scowled. "Was I babbling incoherently? I hope not."

"You moaned and were very troubled, and I yearned to shake you out of it, but I couldn't decide if I should or not."

She squeezed his hand, and he linked their fingers. He gaped about, anxious to focus, to feel less discombobulated.

"I constantly have a bad dream," he said. "It's always the same. I'm lost in a snowstorm, and I can't find my men."

Her expression became pitying, and it simply underscored the fact that he shouldn't mention his peculiarities. What sane person could understand them?

"The terror and potency will fade as time passes," she said. "I'm sure of it."

"I will tell myself you're correct."

He shivered violently, but then, the sunny afternoon was over. She noticed his discomfort and draped her shawl over his shoulders.

"Wear it—just for a minute," she said. "Warm yourself."

His cheeks heated with chagrin. "You must think I'm deranged."

"No, you're merely a tad tormented, but I like being with you as you work yourself through it. I'm your friend, and you can show the *real* James Covington to me."

"The *real* James Covington is a lunatic."

"I rather like him anyway."

He drew her to him, their foreheads pressed together, their breath mingling. They stayed like that for a long interval, then he kissed her as he was always desperate to do. Once they were back in Baywick, he wouldn't be able to display any signs of fondness, so he lingered, enjoying himself.

She joined in the embrace with a tremendous amount of affection, and her eager response was a balm for his weary soul. They might have dawdled forever, but from far off, thunder rumbled, reminding them that the weather was changing fast.

They jumped up, and she grabbed the blanket, while he grabbed the basket. Holding hands, they raced to the dock, not caring if any of the island's other visitors observed them, but they needn't have worried. The boats that had been there when they'd arrived were all gone, the other sightseers having had the sense to depart much earlier.

"I better return you to Mrs. Darlington before you're soaked," he said. "If you come home wet and bedraggled, I'll never hear the end of it."

"The sky wouldn't dare rain on me. I'm too happy."

He helped her into the boat, then climbed in after her. He cast off and swiftly rowed them to shore. His carriage was parked at the dock, his poor driver having had to wait for him. James managed to load them into the vehicle just as the first raindrops splatted on the ground.

They proceeded to the hotel at a brisk pace, the horses and driver in no mood to spend an extra second out in a torrent. Their fleet speed meant they reached their destination in the blink of an eye. A maid was watching for Miss Shaw, providing evidence that their prolonged delay hadn't passed unremarked.

"Thank you for a perfect picnic," she said.

"Thank you for accompanying me. I had the best day ever."

"So did I."

They stared like halfwits, and it was so hard to keep from kissing her goodbye, but he couldn't. The driver had opened the door, and the maid could peer in to where they were snuggled on the seat.

Miss Shaw slid away as he murmured, "I'll see you again shortly. I'll figure out a reason

for it to occur."

"I'll be looking forward to it," she murmured in reply, then she scooted out.

The maid rushed over with an umbrella so she could duck under it. The rain had begun to pound down, preventing more of a farewell. She gave him a quick smile, then she and the maid hurried inside.

His driver didn't ask for instructions. He latched the door, clambered onto the box, and set the horses trotting out of town and toward Wave Crest.

James snuck a final glance at the hotel, wishing Miss Shaw had been peeking out a window, but if she was there, he couldn't locate her. He leaned against the squab and took stock of his condition, and he was astonished to realize he felt content and rested.

But he was missing her already, and he was mentally searching for excuses as to how he could arrange a social engagement for them. It would have to be very soon. He simply couldn't imagine letting too much time go by.

Chapter Six

PEGGY STOMPED DOWN THE street toward the hotel. The rain that had poured down the previous day had moved on, and it was sunny and warm, the sky clear and very blue.

She'd expected the town's shops to be worth investigating, that they'd carry unique items worth purchasing. But no. The objects on display had been no different from what she would have been able to buy in rural, dreary Hexham. She hadn't even found any ribbons that were pretty, and she supposed she ought to be celebrating. The meager fare meant she hadn't had to waste any money.

She was trying not to be irked, but her mood was foul. She blamed her irritation on Emily who'd spent the prior afternoon with Lord Roxbury. The entire afternoon!

It wasn't fair. Peggy had met Roxbury's brother at The Pavilion, then he'd rejoined his friends. There had been so many women salivating over him, and she'd just been one face in the crowd. Yet Emily and Roxbury were practically bosom buddies.

"Miss Shaw! Is that you?"

The man's voice, calling to her from down the block, had her whipping around to see who had summoned her. She was new to the area, so the chances of her being recognized were slim to none.

To her great shock, Archie Covington was leaning out a carriage window and waving to her as if they were old chums. She'd assumed she hadn't made a lasting impression, but he recollected her name! He was gesturing for her to walk over!

She hustled down to his vehicle and flashed her merriest grin. "Mr. Covington! This is a delightful surprise, and I must state that I am flattered you remember me."

"How could I have forgotten? Ever since we danced, I was hoping we'd cross paths again."

The comment left her absolutely breathless. "I was hoping for it too."

"Why are you out and about?" he asked. "Are you running errands or are you strolling for no reason?"

"I was running errands, but I didn't find the ribbons I needed, so I'm headed to my hotel. Mrs. Darlington's? It's *The Holiday House for Young Ladies*. My cousin and I are staying there for the summer."

"I know it and Mrs. Darlington very well." He puffed himself up. "You must have heard that I'm a major investor in the town. I'm privy to every little detail about the place. How are you enjoying yourself? Have you been charmed?"

"Oh, yes," she lied, understanding that she dared not be negative. "It's a divine spot."

The adoring remark was precisely what he'd anticipated. He nodded as if he'd been administering a test and she'd passed it.

"May I give you a ride?" he asked. "I realize it's a short distance, but it's so warm. I would hate to have you overheated."

Her stepmother, Florence, had never imparted much useful information about men or how a female should act around them. Nevertheless, Peggy grasped that it would be the height of folly to climb into his carriage. Yet when would she ever have another opportunity like this in the future? In her small, tedious existence, how often did an earl's brother roll up and offer to convey her home?

She'd be mad to refuse, and besides, she wasn't exactly a virtuous maiden. It was a huge portion of why she and Emily were hiding in Baywick: so the rumors would die down at Hexham.

Over the years, a neighbor boy had frequently lured her into the barn and had touched her in ways she shouldn't have allowed, so she'd learned what occurred when a couple snuck off. She'd relished those encounters and had gleefully participated.

Then she'd been betrothed to Teddy, and he'd been quite romantically determined too, so she'd let him attempt several naughty deeds.

In the end though, he'd jilted her for a much richer girl, and he'd embraced the rumors about the neighbor boy as his excuse to cry off. Never mind that he'd behaved just as egregiously. In the very same barn!

She was jaded enough to accept that it was how the world worked. A male could skate through any transgression, but a female had to guard herself every minute. If she made the tiniest error, she was doomed forever.

Mr. Covington was a gentleman, from a prominent family, so she didn't imagine he would be as amorous as Teddy or her neighbor, but who could be sure?

As she debated the issue, he sensed her hesitation and said, "If you'd rather not, that's fine."

"No, no, I'd love to have a ride."

The prospect of his leaving without her was terrifying. She glanced around, but no one in Baywick knew who she was, so she yanked open the door and scrambled in.

She tumbled onto the seat across from him, as he drew the curtains closed. Very rapidly, they were sequestered in the darkened vehicle. If she'd been a naïve ninny, she might have been disturbed by his actions, but she wasn't.

He was a famous Londoner who had fancy friends and who liked to revel with a wicked abandon. That meant he was the type of beau Peggy had been waiting for her whole life. Could she snag him for her very own?

"Do you have to be back anytime soon?" he inquired.

"Some of the other guests were planning a walk on The Promenade, but if I fail to join them, I doubt anyone will miss me."

"Marvelous. If you're in no hurry, we could drive for a bit."

"I'm definitely in no hurry."

He retrieved a liquor flask from his coat and downed a hefty swig.

"Are you a drinker, Miss Shaw?" he said, and he waved it at her.

"Not usually." Not ever! Her stepmother, Florence, felt only trollops imbibed of hard spirits, so they weren't permitted at home.

She grabbed the flask and downed a hefty swig too, managing to swallow without coughing or having her eyes tear up. She took a second, and a third, merely to impress him.

"This will appear awfully forward," he said, "but would you call me Archie when we're alone like this?"

"I would like that. It will seem very cozy."

"And what is your Christian name? What should I call you?"

She thought of dreary, boring Peggy Shaw, and she didn't want to be Peggy. She straightened her shoulders and rested a bold hand on his knee. "It's Margaret, Archie. You simply must call me Margaret from this point on."

"Margaret, it is," he murmured. "I think we're going to be very good friends."

"LET'S THROW A SUPPER party."

James gaped at Archie as if he'd suggested they strip off their clothes and run naked through the streets.

They were in the receiving parlor at Wave Crest, with James seated on a sofa and Archie standing in front of him. He was deliberately blocking James's view of the beach out the window, so he'd have to pay attention and not daydream.

It was the middle of the afternoon, the minutes ticking by at a snail's pace. James was feeling like a trapped lion that needed to burst out of its cage. He kept pondering Emily Shaw, how she was just over the headland in Baywick. He could have saddled a horse and quickly been at Mrs. Darlington's hotel.

The pull she exerted was so powerful that he ought to tie his ankle to a chair so he didn't rush into town and behave like an idiot.

"Why would we have a party?" James asked Archie, sounding horrified.

"Because we're cordial fellows? Because we have an image to maintain among the local citizenry? Because we have to set the style in this burgeoning metropolis?"

"The very idea exhausts me."

"James! When I badgered you into coming to Baywick, you promised you'd try to be sociable, yet all you do is hide and nitpick."

Archie's tone was scolding, as if James had always been a great trial, which was hilarious. Their father had sired three sons, and if any of them had been a trial, it certainly hadn't been James.

Male laughter wafted by from out on the verandah, reminding James that they had company he hadn't sought. It was a dozen of Archie's rowdy cohorts who were on their way to Brighton. They'd popped in to see Archie before continuing on to the other, more popular spot. His brother was anxious to keep them in Baywick as long as he could.

Wave Crest was a magnificent retreat, so it was precisely the haven James had required when he'd traveled to the coast, but he was suddenly chafing at the solitude it provided. He blamed his foul mood on Miss Shaw. Prior to stumbling on her, he'd been content to wander the empty rooms like a ghost in a museum.

Now though, he was chomping at the bit for something interesting to happen. If they had a party, he'd be busy with arranging the details, so perhaps he'd stop obsessing over her.

"What were you envisioning?" he asked, and apparently, he was about to relent. "I haven't the faintest notion of who we would invite."

"I know who should be included, and my chums are here, so we have to round out the guest list with some females. We can dig them up at that women's hotel. That Mrs. Darlington's? It's jam-packed with a group that would die to fraternize with us."

James's pulse raced. A gala would furnish him with the perfect excuse to see Miss Shaw again without his appearing too besotted. "Have you been introduced to any of the people who are staying there? Would you be comfortable inviting them?"

"I met some of them the other night, and they were rather dazzled by me, so yes, I would be comfortable with it."

"We'd serve supper, but would we have dancing too? How much of a crowd are you contemplating?"

"It should be quite large," Archie said, "so we should have dancing. We'll have to drum up some musicians."

"This is getting more complex and expensive by the minute."

"It's the reason we have servants, James, so they can *serve* us. The butler and housekeeper will do most of the work. You simply have to stroll in at the designated hour and look pleasantly agreeable—even if you're not."

"Your mother hasn't arrived, so we don't have a hostess." They were bachelors and couldn't host young ladies without one. "Is there anyone who would be suitable? How about Mrs. Darlington? She's competent and cordial. She might be amenable."

Archie scoffed with derision. "Gad, no. We have to maintain some level of polish. Otherwise, the locals will start to assume we're not very grand. I'm happy to lower myself so we have plenty of guests, but we're not having an innkeeper up-jump into a position where she doesn't belong."

At Archie's obvious snobbery, James rolled his eyes. "You'll probably have to put her on the guest list though. She has her reputation to consider, so she'll likely want to come as a chaperone."

"That would be fine, but she can't be in charge. What are you thinking by suggesting it?"

"It must have been a bout of temporary insanity." James was being incredibly sarcastic, but Archie didn't notice.

"We should ask the Rutherford sisters to act as co-hostesses." James drew a blank, the name meaning nothing to him, and Archie said, "They're spinsters? They're major investors with you. You should meet them."

"I suppose I can bite the bullet."

Archie tsked with exasperation. "Wipe that frown off your face. It's a party. Not a funeral."

James leaned nearer and spoke softly, so the men out on the verandah wouldn't hear him. He was already having second thoughts. "The house will be overrun by strangers. What if they gape and pester me with insulting questions?"

Archie smirked. "You give yourself too much credit for being interesting. I'm positive no one will pay any attention to you."

"If a single person mentions my expedition, I will proceed to my bedchamber, pack a bag, and immediately head back to London."

"You will not. You'd never be that rude."

"I might be," James claimed.

In a prior period, before he'd been battered by life, he'd been a very social fellow, but that intriguing individual had been lost in the Arctic North. Other than the fact that he'd have a chance to be with Miss Shaw again, the entire endeavor left him cold. Literally. He had to fight off a shiver.

"You can be such a child," Archie told him. "Since you returned from your journey, you've grown quite unlikable."

"I was always unlikeable. Are you just realizing that I am?"

"You're worse than you used to be."

"I can't argue the point."

"And *I* won't argue about the party. We're having it, and that's that. All right?"

James reminded himself that it would bring Miss Shaw to Wave Crest. He liked the idea of her strolling through the parlors and leaving her essence behind. Perhaps, after she departed, the place wouldn't seem so empty.

"Yes, Archie, let's have your party. I'll quit complaining."

With Archie receiving permission, he practically skipped out of the room. On witnessing his elation, James felt a little better about being generous. They quarreled too often, and he scolded Archie too vehemently. Usually, Archie deserved to be scolded, but their constant bickering was ruining their sibling bond. If a mere party could deliver such joy to Archie, why not oblige him?

"THE PARTY IS ON."

Archie made the announcement, then blustered onto the verandah where his London chums were seated at the patio tables and whining about being bored. He was terribly afraid they would cut short their visit and travel on to Brighton, and he would implement any scheme to keep them in Baywick.

"Will it be a meal only?" his friend, Tiger, asked. "Or will it be a meal and dancing?"

"Supper and dancing."

His friend, Gordo, murmured so James wouldn't hear, "How did you convince your brother? He's so ferocious. I can't believe he agreed."

"He's not that bad," Archie said. "After you become acquainted with him, you'll understand what I mean."

At the comment, the group snickered, as if they'd been quietly gossiping about James, and Archie suffered a flare of resentment. James was insanely brave, tough as nails, and loyal to a fault. Wherever he went, he was famous and celebrated, and his failed expedition was a minor setback on his road to magnificence.

What had this motley crew ever accomplished? How dare they condescend!

But as quickly as his fit of pique arose, it sizzled out.

His friends were the wildest dandies of the demimonde. They drank and gambled, caroused and flirted, and their wicked antics were legendary. They were third and fourth sons of wealthy men, some of them noble, some not, and they had too much time on their hands.

They were eager to engage in mischief—the more debauched, the more they relished it.

They'd bonded as boys at boarding school, and they had nicknames like Tiger, Gordo, and Feisty. The monikers described their personalities, and they all had one except Archie, so it seemed as if he didn't truly belong in their tight circle. He struggled to overcome the impression, behaving more despicably than any of them just so they'd be glad to associate with him.

"Will there be young ladies to entertain us?" Gordo asked. "Are there any young ladies in this godforsaken place?"

"Of course there are," Archie said. "What kind of gathering would it be without them?"

"How many will be invited and how pretty will they be?"

"Who cares how pretty," Tiger said. "I want to know how loose."

They guffawed and banged their glasses on the tables.

Archie told them, "It will be the ones we met at the public dance. They're staying at that women's hotel."

"You expect us to go slumming, Archie?" Feisty said. "With common ninnies? I'm shocked—shocked!—I tell you!"

Feisty was being facetious, and the remark produced whistles and lewd boasts about the sorts of things they'd ultimately attempt with the women.

They liked to prey on unsuspecting maidens. They sought out females who were determined to alter their dreary lives. Archie and his friends altered them, but not in the way the girls were hoping.

It was a game they played: tricking innocent misses into furnishing what they should only relinquish to their future husbands. There were rules, steep bets, and money changing hands. Prizes were even occasionally awarded—when a seduction was particularly outrageous.

They were twenty-five that year, so they probably should have grown up and abandoned such a juvenile pursuit, but the competition was so fun. Why call a halt? And girls were so bloody gullible. They were introduced to an earl's brother or a baron's cousin, and they instantly began to hear wedding bells. They never realized they were being moved like pieces on a chess board.

"I've already picked Margaret Shaw," Archie said.

"You can't pick this early," Tiger protested. "We have to have an equal chance to assess the contestants."

"Sorry," Archie said, "but I jumped the gun. I've lured her away for a carriage ride, so she's falling in love with me."

"How is that fair?" Gordo complained.

Archie thought they might gang up and insist Margaret be tossed onto the pile for everyone's consideration, but she would be so easy to manipulate. He was ten steps ahead of them, and they hadn't even started.

Tiger waved away the problem. "Oh, let him have her. He's partial to insipid blonds, and he'll swiftly wear her down. He'll have delicious stories to tell when he's finished with her."

Tiger's comment swayed them, and the matter was settled. Archie would flirt with—and try his best to ruin—Margaret Shaw. He'd do it without a ripple in his conscience, and it would never occur to her that she was being deceived. He was more driven than the others to get what he wanted. They were lazy and entitled, and if a female fought too vehemently, they backed down.

Not Archie. He found the chase to be thrilling, the culmination exquisite. He never took *no* for an answer, which was why he'd been banned from Brighton. One would think the humiliating predicament would have taught him a lesson, but it hadn't.

Margaret Shaw was exactly the type who tickled Archie's fancy the most: naïve, anxious, trusting, and eager to please. She was ripe for the plucking, and he would brazenly seize whatever he could coerce her into providing.

⸻ 4 ⸻

"Who is it from?"

Emily and Mary were in the front parlor of the hotel, loafing on the sofas and once again enjoying a pot of tea and some cakes. While they'd been chatting, a messenger had arrived with an envelope for Emily. When she'd flicked the seal and had seen the decorative words that had been penned, she could have fainted from shock.

Lord Roxbury had scribbled a personal note at the bottom: *Don't you dare refuse.*

She glanced at Mary and said, "You won't believe it, but Lord Roxbury has invited us to a supper party. With dancing afterward."

"At Wave Crest?"

"Yes, and we're to bring all your current guests. He'd simply like to be apprised as to how many it will be, so his staff can have enough chairs at the dining table."

Mary raised a brow. "You told me your picnic with him was very innocent. Was there more to it than you've shared with me? No offense, but I came to Baywick before it was ever a town, and I have never been included in any event hosted by the Covington family."

"I swear it was just a picnic," Emily said. "We ate, talked, and walked on the beach, so I have no idea how I've garnered his favor."

Mary was clearly dubious, and Emily's cheeks heated, supplying stark evidence that she had to be lying. But she wasn't lying. Not really.

The only part she hadn't mentioned were the delightful kisses he'd bestowed, but that was a private secret she'd never reveal.

"I've been acquainted with a few noblemen," Mary said, "and when they deign to socialize with women like you and me, they always have an ulterior motive."

Emily shrugged. "That's generally true, but the Earl is lonely, and doesn't his brother have friends visiting? They probably need some females to join in the dancing."

"I'll work hard to convince myself that your assessment is correct."

Mary was frowning and troubled, and Emily asked, "What's wrong?"

"I'm leery of aristocrats, and I have my business to consider. I'm not a chaperone or nanny, but I would hate to have an incident arise that wound up reflecting badly on me."

"You shouldn't worry so much. It says there will be hostesses. Alice and Charlotte Rutherford?"

"Ah, that eases some of my concern. They're spinster sisters, from a very grand family, and they'll ensure the festivities are done up properly. If they're in charge, it won't be a bachelor's bacchanal."

"Is that what was vexing you? Having spent time with Lord Roxbury, I can categorically state that he is very stoic and level-headed. I can't suppose he has any tendencies that would distress you. Or if he does have them, he'd be too polite to exhibit them."

"He might not be inclined to misbehave, but his brother and his brother's friends aren't quite so sensible. Mr. Covington has a horrid reputation, remember?"

At the notion that they might not attend, Emily felt terribly disappointed. "Should we decline then?"

Mary grinned mischievously. "Are you mad? I've wanted to snoop through the parlors at Wave Crest since they pounded the first nail. Of course we'll accept."

"I'm so relieved to hear it. I expect it will be lovely."

"We'll go, and we'll be so gorgeously attired that they'll wish they were commoners so they could court us."

Emily laughed. "I'll keep repeating to myself that it's our goal."

Peggy tromped down the stairs with her bonnet tied and a shawl draped over her shoulders. She must have decided she was too bored to continue hiding in their room.

"Guess what's happened?" Emily said to her.

"What? And if it's something stupid, don't tell me. I'll be so annoyed."

Emily shook the invitation at her. "Lord Roxbury has requested our presence at his beach home of Wave Crest for supper and dancing. He's asked all of Mrs. Darlington's guests to come, so it includes you and me."

Peggy's jaw dropped so far that Emily was amazed it didn't hit the floor. "Are you joking?"

"No. It's to be held Wednesday evening."

"Let me see that."

Peggy marched over and grabbed the invitation. She read it over and over, then she smirked. "Be still my heart!"

"I thought it might excite you."

"We're going, right?" Peggy asked. "You won't devise some silly reason as to why we can't?"

"Oh, we're going," Emily said, "and I'm certain it will be the best night of our lives."

Chapter Seven

EMILY WALKED THROUGH THE garden behind Lord Roxbury's beautiful beachside home of Wave Crest. The paths were lit with lanterns, so it was easy to see her way. The sun had set, and the stars were twinkling.

Supper had been marvelous, the food delicious, the wine flowing freely, and the conversation lively. Mr. Covington's London friends were jolly and raucous, and they'd teased and laughed with a humorous abandon. She suspected they were scoundrels, possessed of awful reputations, but they were handsome devils from wealthy families, so the ladies had been delighted to socialize with them.

They'd gush about it the entire summer, all of them yearning for more invitations when Mr. Covington had rich visitors.

As to Emily, she was simply hoping Lord Roxbury would invite her back for a smaller gathering. With so many people in attendance, her view of the residence had been confined to a few downstairs parlors, and she'd love to have a tour of the whole house.

She reached the water's edge, and there was a bench perfectly situated to loaf and gaze out at the ocean. She slid onto it. She was far enough from the party that the noise had faded, so the only sound was the swish of the waves on the shore.

Out on the horizon, a lamp glowed on a passing ship, and she wondered who was on board and where they were headed. The sight stirred an unusual burst of wanderlust, which was amusing. She'd never envisioned herself as a traveler, and she supposed she was merely eager for a better future to occur.

It dawned on her that she was very lonely, and the realization was a surprise. She was twenty-five and nothing amazing had ever happened to her. She was beginning to imagine that nothing ever would.

She smelled smoke from a cheroot, and she peered about, positive it would be Lord Roxbury hiding in the shadows. She'd come to Wave Crest, secretly expecting they'd be together every second, as if they were ardently devoted, but that had been wishful thinking.

They had no connection to one another, and in front of his other guests, he couldn't have singled her out. He was very charismatic though, so there had always been a crowd around him. They'd peppered him with questions about his adventures, but they'd tactfully avoided any mention of his recent debacle. Had his brother warned them to steer clear of the topic?

Once they'd gone into supper, they'd been seated at opposite ends of the table, so they hadn't been able to chat. After the meal, as they'd retired to various parlors for cards and dancing, he'd disappeared. She'd been in no position to ask after his whereabouts, and she'd been horribly depressed that he'd vanished.

She didn't particularly like his brother or his brother's rowdy friends. They were near to her same age, but they seemed very immature to her. She wasn't keen to drool over them, and she'd simply wanted to snuggle down on a sofa with Roxbury.

He likely assumed he'd cleverly concealed his presence, and she said, "Why have I stumbled on you in the dark again, Lord Roxbury? It's enough to make me worry over how your mind works."

"If you ever discovered how it works, you'd run away in a terrified hurry."

"I'm certain that's true."

"How is the party? Is it limping along without me?"

"Yes, it's quite merry, and I am sorry to report that no one has missed you."

He snorted, then he tossed his cheroot into the grass and imperiously commanded, "Come with me."

"To where?"

"To the gazebo."

"You have a gazebo?"

"Yes, and we'll have more privacy there. My brother invited too many people, and they're all strolling in this blasted garden. If we tarry here, we'll never have a moment to ourselves. We'll constantly be interrupted."

"You're awfully sure I'd like to be alone with you."

He tsked with mock offense. "It doesn't matter what *you* want. It's what I want that counts. I'm an earl, remember? There's no use arguing."

She chuckled and facetiously said, "You definitely know how to woo a girl. Is this your normal method of seduction? You issue orders and point out that you must be obeyed?"

"Yes. Am I succeeding?"

"I believe you are."

She stood and clasped hold of his hand, and he snickered pompously.

They started off, but shortly, another couple approached. He pulled her into some bushes, and they dawdled, barely breathing, as the pair sauntered on by. Then he dragged her off in the other direction, and they might have been naughty schoolchildren, playing a prank.

The gazebo loomed before them. It was painted white, and the moon was up, so it looked silver and appeared to shimmer. They reached the three steps that would lead them into it, and she hesitated.

"If I climb inside," she said, "will you behave yourself?"

"Let's hope not."

He didn't pause so she could debate or second-guess. He simply dashed up and hauled her in too. She could have yanked away, but the pathetic fact was that she was delighted by him and would never have declined.

The small building was round, with benches on the edge, and they were covered with plush cushions. He picked a spot where they'd have a clear view of the garden. If anyone came toward them, they'd see them immediately. He sat down and tugged her down with him.

She'd presumed she'd seat herself next to him, but he had other ideas. He nestled her onto his lap, her breasts crushed to his chest, her bottom pressed to his hard thigh.

With no words exchanged, he dipped in and kissed her, and she wrapped her arms around him and kissed him back with a great deal of enthusiasm. It was very passionate, with an almost desperate feel to it, and she tried to recall if she'd ever observed a man and woman as amorously involved as they suddenly were. She didn't think so.

His lips had captured hers as if he would drink her in, and his hands roamed over her torso, as if he was imprinting her shape and size into his palms. She shouldn't have allowed him to be so forward, but she'd been swept into the deluge, and she was too inundated by sensation to control herself. The raucous interlude made her recognize why young ladies were so carefully chaperoned.

Older, wiser women understood, as she had not, that amour was additive and perilous. He was sending jolts of pleasure through her anatomy, and she was softening, was leaning into him, yearning to receive more of what he was supplying.

It was when he began plucking at the combs holding her hair in place that she balked. The lengthy locks were pinned up in a pretty chignon, and if they fell down, she'd never be able to repair them.

"Lord Roxbury," she murmured as she drew away.

He frowned, bewildered as to why they'd stopped. "What? What is it?"

"You can't take down my hair."

"Oh, oh, of course I can't," he agreed.

He left her hair alone, but he didn't desist with his dedicated advance. He kissed her again, becoming even more passionate, even more obsessed. The interval grew wilder, as if she was on a raft and careening down a river. She was floating free and couldn't swim safely to shore. She could only grab for purchase and pray she was still in one piece once they were finished.

They dallied forever, Time seeming to halt, so they might have been snuggled together for a minute or an hour or a year. She'd lost track. Finally, the intensity waned, their lips parting. His eyes were twinkling so, for a change, he looked relaxed and lighthearted.

"I've been wanting to do that ever since you walked in the door," he said. "It's why I tiptoed out. I caught myself either ignoring you or gaping at you like a lunatic."

"Was that your ploy? You were gaping at me and ignoring me in equal measure?"

"Yes. I couldn't figure out how to act around you. I was eager to sit with you on the sofa and chat about your day—with no strangers to interrupt."

"I'm glad that's what was happening. When you barely spoke to me, I thought perhaps we weren't as cordial as I had imagined."

He smirked, gazing at her mouth. "We've settled the matter of whether we're cordial or not."

"Before I arrived, I had constructed this fantasy in my head about how the evening would go. It hadn't occurred to me that the other guests would prevent us from carrying on in our usual way, so I'm thrilled that we crept off." She inhaled a sharp breath. "Did that sound terribly brazen?"

"Yes, but I've never deemed a bit of brazenness to be a bad trait in a female. In my company, you may be as bold as you like. I don't mind."

She sighed with happiness. "How long have we been out here?"

"Too long, I'm sure."

"We should get back. Or, at least, I should get back. Mrs. Darlington and my cousin, Peggy, will have missed me."

He wrinkled up his nose. "I don't care about them. Let them speculate as to where you are. And isn't your cousin's name Margaret? I could have sworn that's how she was introduced."

"She's putting on airs to impress you. Her Christian name is Margaret, but she's always been Peggy to me. She's socializing with an earl, so she's trying to appear more grand than she really is."

He chuckled at that. "The two of you are so different. Is your relationship with her genial or rocky?"

"She can be a difficult person to like. She believes she's better than everyone else, and she's very spoiled, but I've learned how to handle her."

"She's exactly like my brother, Archie. Who spoiled her? Her mother? Her father?"

"No one spoiled her. She turned out horrid all on her own."

His chuckle became a laugh. "How about you? You're very sweet, so obviously, you were never spoiled."

"I'm delighted to hear you say so. With Peggy as my kin, I have to be extra agreeable to compensate for her failings."

"Who were your parents?" he asked. "Who was your father?"

"My mother died when I was a baby, and my father was a gentleman. He fell on hard times and passed away much before he should have. I went to live with my uncle and his wife, Florence. Florence is Peggy's stepmother."

"Do you like her?"

"She's wonderful, and we're very close. She's ill though, and it worries me."

"Why aren't you at home nursing her? You're the sort who would."

"It was *her* idea for us to visit Baywick. I had seen an advertisement for Mrs. Darlington's hotel in the newspaper, and I showed it to her. I must have seemed particularly glum because she insisted we make the trip."

"I'm lucky she encouraged you. If she hadn't, you wouldn't be in Baywick, and my meeting you is the best thing that's happened to me in ages."

"Flatterer," she scolded. "You should be cautious in tossing out your compliments. I receive so few of them that it will stir my vanity and I'll start to assume I'm much too posh to associate with you."

"Heaven forbid." He smiled a delicious, riveting smile.

"Could I ask you a question?" she said. "Actually, it's a bit of a favor."

"You can ask me. I can't guarantee I'll grant it, but you can ask."

"Wave Crest is so beautiful. It's what I would have designed for myself if I'd had the means to build a cottage on the beach. Could I call on you some afternoon and have you give me a tour of the entire house?"

"I would love that. Yes, absolutely, I'll have you back when the rooms aren't overrun by my brother's rowdy companions. You can snoop through every inch."

"Thank you. Now then, I have to return to the party."

"I've already shared my opinion about it. I'm having much more fun out here."

"I'm friendly with Mrs. Darlington. If she suspected I was misbehaving, I'd be so embarrassed. I'd never be able to explain what we're doing."

"What are we doing?" he asked. "Can you clarify it for me?"

"No. I've never so much as had a beau, so romance is a mystery I've never unraveled. You're a rich, sophisticated earl, and I'm simply a spinster from a small village in rural England. I can't guess why we're loafing like this."

"Can't it just be because we like each other?"

"I suppose, but I've liked many men in my life, and I've never snuck off to a dark gazebo with any of them."

"I am ecstatic to be the first then."

He was staring at her with enormous affection. Was he growing fond? Could it be?

The notion was dear and terrifying. She was lonely, and he had a keen ability to prod at her worst impulses. She was anxious to make him happy, to furnish whatever he requested, merely so she'd have more chances to cavort with him, but that was deranged thinking. She was quite sure he would ultimately seek boons from her that a female only considered tendering after she was a wife.

She wasn't a fool. A nobleman never wed a girl like her. She wasn't Cinderella, and he wasn't Prince Charming. There was no future for them, but he'd swept into her world like a blazing comet, lighting it up in splendid ways, and nothing would ever be the same.

Their brief acquaintance had her chafing at her meager existence, yearning for more, craving in a manner that was pointless and would leave her discontented in the end. Yet even as she recognized the perils, she wouldn't change a single facet of her conduct toward him.

She couldn't decide if she was being especially stupid with regard to him or if she was naively gullible. It was likely a little of both, but despite what was driving her, she couldn't tarry.

"I'm going now," she said, and she slid off his lap. "I enjoyed supper very much."

He waved away the remark. "It was my brother's idea. If it had been left up to me, I'd have dined by myself and moped until bedtime."

"I hope you were serious that I can have a tour of the house."

"I'm planning on it. I will send you a message when I have it arranged. I'll have a carriage fetch you."

"I'll look forward to it."

She had to depart for the manor, but she couldn't pull herself away. It seemed wrong to abandon him.

"Are you feeling all right these days?" she asked, prying where she shouldn't.

"I'm mostly all right," he said, and out of the blue, he inquired, "Would you call me James?"

"No. That wouldn't be even remotely appropriate, but you're welcome to call me Emily if you'd like."

"I will."

They smiled fondly, and there were many comments swirling, as if there were other, more important issues that ought to be mentioned, but they didn't dare address them.

"Will you come back to the party?" she asked. "Will I see you before I head to the hotel? We're having our carriage prepared for midnight."

"You probably won't see me again, but I'll be in touch."

She was on the verge of spitting out affectionate words that she couldn't utter in his presence. She just liked him so much, which was idiotic and hazardous. Instead, she simply said, "Goodnight."

She whipped away and dashed off, and she didn't glance over to discover if he was watching her go. She continued on to the verandah, and she climbed the stairs and rushed inside. It was crowded and loud, the abundance of wine and liquor making everyone overly jolly.

She struggled to calm her racing pulse, to smooth her animated expression. Once she was more in control, she wandered through the rooms, ending up in the large hall where people were dancing. Peggy was standing along the wall, sipping a glass of wine, and Emily went over to her.

"Where have you been?" her cousin asked.

"Walking in the garden," Emily lied. "It's too hot in here."

Peggy studied her, and Emily tried not to fidget. She wanted to peek down to ensure her clothes were straight and her hair in place, but Peggy's focus was too curious.

"You look funny," Peggy said. "Did someone upset you?"

"No, and how is it that I look?"

"As if you have a secret. What is it?"

"I don't have a secret," Emily insisted. "How could I have? Nothing exciting ever happens to me."

"Nothing ever happens to me either, but maybe, this is the summer when our luck will finally change."

"I doubt it will," Emily said, "but I will keep hope alive."

PEGGY ENTERED THE DARK parlor and closed the door, tamping down the noise from the festivities that were in progress in another part of the manor. There was no fire burning, but it was a warm night, so it wasn't necessary.

She ambled over to the window and stared out at the garden. The paths were lit with lamps, and couples were strolling. Farther out, the ocean brushed the shore, but she couldn't hear it.

Behind her, the door opened and shut, and she whispered a prayer that her dreams were about to come true. Then she spun around.

Archie Covington hurried over to her. Without hesitating, he pulled her into his arms, and he kissed her furiously. He was a very good kisser, and she was no novice herself, but she was torn over how much skill she should exhibit. She couldn't bear to have him think she was loose, but she also couldn't have him thinking she was boring or provincial. He was very sophisticated, and he would lose interest.

"I wasn't certain you'd be here," he whispered as he drew away.

"I wasn't certain myself." She was whispering too.

"I'm so happy that we've had a chance to sneak away like this. All evening, I was anxious to get you off by yourself."

He'd slipped her a note at the card table, and when she'd read it and saw he'd requested an assignation, she'd nearly fainted.

From the moment she'd arrived at Wave Crest, he'd mostly ignored her. Initially, she'd pouted, then she'd recognized that he had a house full of company, and he couldn't shower her with any extra attention. By arranging their rendezvous, he'd fixed what was wrong, and she was gleeful as a child on Christmas morning.

Her life was about to be completely altered. She was at the beginning of a process that would ultimately make her Mrs. Archie Covington. She would never tell anyone though. If she mentioned it, especially to Emily, she'd be laughed out of the room. But she'd always been destined for greater things.

She hadn't been eager to travel to Baywick, but she'd met Mr. Covington almost immediately. She viewed it as a sign, as if she'd cast a love potion to bind him, and she was sufficiently vain to believe that she would quickly have him wrapped around her little finger.

"I hate that we have so many guests," he said. "It means I couldn't be alone with you."

"We're alone now, so it worked out."

"Yes, but we're being furtive and dodgy."

Peggy went out on a limb. "We could be more cordial in front of everyone. I wouldn't mind."

"Oh, my dear, I wouldn't dare. I look at you, and I'm quite over-come by affection. My infatuation would be noticed, and others would realize how very smitten I am. I wouldn't be able to conceal it."

Peggy's heart literally skipped a beat. "I might be a tad smitten too. Doesn't it seem as if we've always known each other? I feel so close to you."

"That's my perception exactly!"

They were fated to wind up together. It was so clear to her, and she was trying to figure out how to lead him to the proper destination.

"I have to return to the party," he said. "I'm the host, and if I'm gone too long, I'll be missed. You might be missed too. We shouldn't stir gossip."

"I can't stand that our encounter was so brief."

"I agree, and we have to attempt it again. Often and soon. How can we manage it? Are you chaperoned at all? Is there someone watching your every move?"

"No. My cousin is staying at the hotel with me, but she's not my nanny. I'm free to organize my own schedule."

"There are public dances on Friday and Saturday nights."

"I'll plan on being there."

"We could leave The Pavilion, when we're not being observed, and hide from prying eyes."

"I'd like that very much."

"Could you ever steal away on other occasions?"

"Maybe." Peggy was aware she shouldn't consent, but with him gazing at her so fondly, she simply couldn't refuse. "What sorts of meetings were you imagining?"

"I'd like to take you to our gambling club. Women are allowed, and it provides a more risqué type of entertainment that I relish. Would you like to be my guest? You're so much fun."

"If I suggested it, my cousin would perish from shock."

"You wouldn't have to tell her, would you? It could be our secret." He studied her intently. "All of my chums bring their lady friends, but I never have anyone to accompany me. Won't you be the first?"

She was practically salivating with an unsated hunger. He was opening a door to the life she'd always wanted to live, to the life she'd always expected to have. How could she not grab for it?

"I've never been to a gambling club," she said, even as warnings were clanging in her head.

"You would like it there so much. There's an elevated level of members that you won't find in the rest of the town. Only the best people are admitted, and we can behave however we like. We wouldn't have to pretend we're stodgy and straightlaced."

She snorted. "Perhaps I am stodgy and straightlaced."

"No, you're not," he fervidly said, thrilling her to her very core. "You're the precise kind of girl who could make me happy forever."

His words were so riveting that she was surprised she didn't collapse in a stunned heap.

She felt as if he was administering an exam, testing her to see if she deserved to walk about on his arm. She was anxious to prove that she belonged with him, and she might have been perched on a very high cliff and about to jump over. Where would she be when she landed?

Well, she knew where: She would be Archie Covington's bride. As they socialized, he'd grow to like her more and more, until he realized he couldn't live without her. She wouldn't consider any other conclusion.

"I can revel whenever and wherever you like," she boasted.

"Marvelous. I will send you a note when I have an evening arranged." He kissed her desperately, his passion fierce. Then he physically yanked himself away. "I have to go, but promise me we'll be together soon. Don't let me down. Swear you won't!"

"I will never let you down," she vehemently replied.

He went over and peeked into the hall, then he vanished.

She stood in the quiet room, her heart pounding, her joy swirling to such an astounding height that she could barely breathe. She struggled to calm down, and once she was certain her expression was smooth and her nerves steady, she returned to the party too.

Her face showed no emotion, but she was smiling on the inside, celebrating this bizarre opportunity. Who could have guessed that Baywick would render such a spectacular chance?

Any sensible, moralistic female would have declined to oblige him, would have declined to sneak off, but the pathetic fact was that she was no better than she had to be. She would use her debauched habits and tastes to lure him in so he'd fall in love with her.

In the end, wedding bells would chime, and she'd have his ring on her finger. She was absolutely convinced of it.

Chapter Eight

"You're turning me into a sloth."

Mary Darlington spoke the comment to Emily, and they laughed.

"I couldn't let you remain inside," Emily said. "The day is too lovely. You deserve to have a break."

"Yes, but my boss is an ogre. If I grow too lazy, she'll never stop scolding me."

They were headed to The Promenade to watch the sailboats glide across the water. The sun was out, the temperature balmy, the winds light. Emily was carrying a parasol, but they hadn't needed shawls. It was that pleasant.

Emily had suggested the walk, and Mary had amazed herself by agreeing. She had a competent staff, so the world wouldn't end if she pampered herself for an hour, but normally, she wouldn't have traipsed off with a guest.

It wasn't appropriate, and it destroyed the boundaries that ought to exist between them, but she liked Emily and had from the start. Emily wanted to move to Baywick in the future, and Mary had offered her a job, even though she didn't expect her to ever show up and accept it. It was simply too difficult for a female to completely rearrange her life.

Mary's proposal had put them on a novel footing. They weren't guest and proprietor any longer. They were something different: new friends certainly, and perhaps employer and employee later on. For the moment, they could stroll around the bay as if they'd been acquainted forever.

"Did you enjoy yourself at Lord Roxbury's supper?" Mary asked.

"Yes, very much," Emily said. "How about you?"

"It was a tad too boisterous for me. I didn't particularly care for his brother's friends. They were a little frivolous for my tastes."

"Just a *little* frivolous?"

"Maybe a lot frivolous."

Emily snickered with amusement. "You are horrid."

"The sons of the aristocracy are widely viewed as a national nuisance. I've never been able to abide any of them."

"Have you known many of them?" Emily asked.

"I've known enough, and Mr. Covington and his chums are examples of the worst of the species."

"What did you think of Roxbury?"

"I didn't really talk to him. He wasn't eager to socialize."

"He's not happy or gregarious, but he's definitely not annoying like his brother. I doubt he liked the party. He would have hated to host so many people. The whole reason he's in Baywick is to cherish the solitude."

"And we wrecked it by barging in," Mary said.

"I hope we can wrangle another invitation to Wave Crest someday. It's such a magnificent house. I'd like to have a tour when it's not brimming with a pack of loud, obnoxious scoundrels."

"It is magnificent," Mary concurred. "If I'd ever had the money to design my own beach cottage, I'd have copied it exactly."

Emily smiled. "That's my opinion."

They were almost to The Promenade and were about to cross the street onto it, when a fancy yellow gig flew by. It was traveling at such a high rate of speed that they had to jump back as it passed. They were in a busy area, so the driver was going much too fast.

A few onlookers shook their fists and shouted at him, but the driver was oblivious to their reprimands and continued on as if the pedestrians were invisible.

"Wasn't that Lord Roxbury and his brother?" Emily said.

"I didn't see. Who was holding the reins? It wasn't the Earl, was it? He seems too calm to flit about in such a slapdash manner. It had to be Mr. Covington. If he's behaving like a maniac, I won't be surprised."

"Yes, it was Mr. Covington."

"It's such a conspicuous carriage, and I haven't noticed it in town before. I'm betting he just purchased it, and he's showing off."

The gig careened around the harbor, as if the public thoroughfare was a private raceway belonging to the Covington brothers. It was typical that they'd act as if they owned the road, as if they could barrel over some peasants without consequence. Her dislike of wealthy dandies soared to a new height.

She was about to remark on her burgeoning disdain when she glanced over at Emily who was gaping after Roxbury with a yearning that was pitiful to witness. She was visually beseeching him, as if she could drag him back merely by wishing hard enough.

Her potent focus was depressing, and Mary supposed she should have been more serious about chaperoning Emily. Yet she wasn't a governess, so it wasn't any of her business if Emily engaged in a summer romance with the attractive nobleman. But Emily was her friend, and Mary had her hotel's reputation to protect. She should never have allowed Emily to go on that picnic.

She should have put her foot down, but she hadn't known how. It was always the problem with the aristocracy. A common person had no idea how to refuse any of them.

Emily was frozen in her spot, and Mary urged her onward, pretending she hadn't noted how woefully Emily was staring. It was exhausting to have her pining after the ridiculous man, but he was an acclaimed national hero. If Emily had become ensnared in his web, who could blame her? From Mary's own humiliating past, she grasped how easy it was to fall into an amorous trap.

They ambled in silence for a bit, the stroll suddenly uncomfortable, as if Emily was chewing on a thousand words she didn't dare speak aloud. They neared an empty bench, and Mary pointed to it.

"Shall we sit?"

At the sound of Mary's voice, Emily was startled, as if she'd been so lost in her misery that she'd forgotten Mary was by her side.

"Yes, let's sit," she agreed.

They plopped down and peered out at the pleasure boats sailing by. Mary fumed and wondered if she should commiserate, pry, scold, or simply butt out. She was in no position to offer advice or rebuke, but if Emily was being drawn into a dicey relationship with Roxbury, didn't Mary have a duty to caution her?

If she remained silent, and disaster struck later on, she'd never forgive herself.

"Could I ask you a question?" Mary said. "I'm not being nosy. Well, I *am* being nosy, but I hope you won't be angry."

Emily frowned. "I could never be angry with you. What did you want to know? You can ask me anything."

"Would you like to tell me about Lord Roxbury? Can you explain what's happening between you and him?"

"Nothing's happening." Emily's tone was very firm, but she couldn't hold Mary's gaze.

Mary sighed. "I'll just blurt it out, all right? When he passed by, you appeared so wretched. Obviously, there's more occurring than you've confessed. Has he misbehaved with you?"

"No, no, it's not that," Emily hastily said, but her cheeks heated with chagrin. "It's just that I like him so much. He and I have a powerful connection we can't fight."

"Has he told you he feels a connection? He's openly admitted it?"

"Yes, but I've sensed it too." Emily shrugged. "He's very lonely, as am I. I guess it's bonded us in a manner we shouldn't have permitted."

"You comprehend, don't you, that he would never develop a genuine affection? He might flirt and flatter, and it would seem very sincere, but it would be an illusion. He would never have honorable intentions."

"Yes, I understand that."

"Are you being candid with me and yourself? Do you truly recognize that it's impossible with him? He's such a famous fellow, and he's so accursedly handsome. Have you convinced yourself you could snag him? Is that it? If so, I have to warn you to be careful."

"He's kissed me," Emily mumbled. "On several delightful occasions."

"Oh, my."

"At our picnic and at the supper party. I ran into him when I was in the garden after the meal had ended. He was taking the night air, and we chatted in the gazebo."

Mary bit down a gasp. "He asked you to sneak off?"

"No, I bumped into him purely by accident."

Mary's skepticism rose to the fore. She doubted that was how it had actually unfolded. She was sure Emily's version of it was what she believed, but who could predict how Roxbury had viewed it? He might have been stalking her, watching her leave the house, then pretending he'd stumbled on her.

"You shouldn't be alone with him," Mary said.

"I realize that."

Mary's cheeks heated too. "I'm not your mother, your sister, or your chaperone. I'm barely your friend, really, but I'm very worried about this."

"You needn't be. Since the party, I haven't seen him. He promised he would bring me back to Wave Crest, so I could tour the manor, but I haven't heard from him. I've had to accept that he didn't mean it."

"If he invited you for a tour, would you go?"

"Yes—if you came with me."

"I couldn't. Nor should you. Not after he's been seducing you."

"He hasn't been seducing me." Emily clucked her tongue at Mary's assessment. "I wish you wouldn't describe it like that. You're making my bond with him sound sordid and wrong, as if he'd been tricking me."

"I'm so afraid he might have been."

"We've shared a few kisses, but I was a willing participant. I'm not a frivolous girl, and I'm an excellent judge of character. His conduct hasn't been coercive. Whatever transpired, I *wanted* it to transpire."

Mary was very jaded, and she wouldn't credit Roxbury with innocent motives. He had traveled the globe, had observed sights that no humans had ever witnessed. He was rich and sophisticated, and he'd probably engaged in a thousand affairs. He would absolutely have learned how to tempt a poverty-stricken woman like Emily, and he'd guarantee his interest appeared plausible and romantic.

"Could I tell you a secret about me?" Mary said.

"If you think you should."

"I only ask that you never repeat it. No one in Baywick is aware of my full history, and I'd like to keep it that way."

"Should you confide in me then? Maybe you shouldn't reveal it."

"It could furnish an important lesson for you." Mary inhaled a deep breath and slowly let it out, feeling as if she was struggling under water with a heavy weight on her back. She spat out the comment before she could lose her nerve. "I had my own amour with an aristo-crat's son. He encouraged my fondness to lure me into it."

"My goodness."

"I fell in love and assumed he'd marry me, and I was so desperately attached. He swore we'd be together forever, that he could persuade his parents to allow us to wed."

"You're not a widow, so he must not have followed through."

"No. I was young and gullible, and he was adept at cajoling me. My father was a university professor and my mother a vicar's daughter. I was fetching, smart, and educated. I told myself I could fit into his world, that I would eventually be welcomed there."

"What did your parents think? Did you confess it to them? Or was it all clandestine and furtive?"

"My parents were deceased by then, so I was on my own and easy prey to a scoundrel like him. He set me up in a little apartment, and we carried on as if we were man and wife, but it crashed down fast enough."

"What happened to end it?" Emily asked.

"Despite the fantasy I had concocted, his father would never have consented to a marriage. In fact, my dearest darling was betrothed to his cousin and had been for years."

"That rat!"

"Yes, that's a perfect description of him. Rather than his discuss-ing our marriage with his father, he disclosed our liaison and begged his father to rid him of an unwanted problem—that being me. His father's clerk visited to inform me I would never see him again. I was forced to sign some papers about never contacting him, and I was supplied with some funds to vanish. It's how I bought my hotel. I used his blood money to build a new life for myself."

She didn't add the worst part, the part she would never divulge to anyone. She'd been increasing with his child, and once she'd apprised him about the baby, he'd left and had never returned. It's why his toplofty father had intervened in the debacle, why he'd paid her to be silent and disappear.

She'd given birth at an unwed mother's home outside York, but the child had died immediately after. The entire experience had been more grueling and distressing than she could clarify or explain. She'd been all alone, with no parents to advise her, no relatives to offer assistance, no haven where she could have recovered from her many losses.

Somehow, she'd found the fortitude to stagger forward and reinvent herself. She'd slunk off to another area of the country, where she was a stranger and her scandal concealed. She'd started a business that provided her with a steady income, but one where she wouldn't have many dealings with men.

Her hotel catered to female travelers, and she'd surrounded herself with female employees. She only had female friends, and when she ran errands, she tried to interact with shopkeepers' wives, so she didn't have to speak to their husbands. She worked valiantly to separate herself.

Men could be too powerful, too vicious, too callous, and she would never lower her guard ever again.

"Mary, I'm so terribly sorry," Emily said, and she clasped Mary's hand and squeezed her fingers. "Please tell me your heart is not still broken."

"I picked myself up and moved on."

Tears flooded her eyes, but she was too proud to let them fall. She never talked about those dark days. Her reticence was partly due to shame and the need to hide her sordid past, but it was also because there was such a well of grief and rage bubbling just beneath the surface. She was always afraid, if she unleashed it, she might incinerate the whole world with her fury.

"It was ages ago," she said, "and I never discuss it, but I decided you should hear about it. I hope it will serve as a warning. I'm intimately familiar with men like Roxbury. I'm aware of what it's like to meet a fellow like him, to have him cast his attention in your direction. We're women, and we make foolish choices."

"May I put your mind at ease? I recognize the perils you've pointed out. I have no future with Roxbury, and any fondness he's exhibited is a chimera I can't trust."

"He probably fancies you. His regard is probably genuine, but it doesn't mean anything."

"I figured that out on my own." Emily chuckled, but glumly. "He hasn't contacted me since the supper party, and I suspect he won't contact me. I was such an irrelevant acquaintance that I've been forgotten."

Mary doubted that very much. He'd ignore Emily until he was bored and anxious to fill an empty afternoon or evening. Then he'd ingratiate himself again, but she said, "I will persuade myself to believe that's true."

"Why would he and I socialize? It's not as if we wander in the same circles, and he doesn't plan to remain in Baywick for long. He's likely already packed his bags to return to London."

Mary would cross her fingers that he was leaving. She didn't admit it though. She simply nodded. "We'll conclude this conversation then, and I will pray I haven't upset you by being too blunt."

"Gad, no," Emily said, "and it's humorous to have you scolding me. My entire life, I've been so dutiful that I've never been chastised about my conduct. I like it that you care enough to admonish me."

"I promise to nag at you whenever you need it."

"I'm certain this will be the one and only occasion it will ever be necessary."

"I'm certain of it too."

Mary wasn't serious. It would depend on whether Roxbury left or not. Emily might swear to avoid him; she might convince herself that she would, but if he waggled a finger at her, she would come running and give him whatever he sought.

In that, every female was exactly the same. A man like Roxbury was simply too hard to resist.

"WHAT ARE YOU DOING?"

"I'm looking in the mirror to see if my hair is standing on end."

"Very funny."

James glowered at his brother and said, "Who's being funny? I feel as if my life flashed before my eyes a dozen times."

"We wouldn't have tipped over. The vehicle is perfectly balanced, and I am an expert at handling the reins."

"That's debatable, and thank you for not plowing over any pedestrians."

Archie had bought a bright yellow gig that was sporty and very fast, and he'd been eager as a puppy to show it to James. James had stupidly agreed to accompany him on a ride, but it had been a huge mistake. Archie was a menace on the road. He intimidated other drivers and relished the chance to scare them into pulling over. They were lucky they hadn't had an accident.

They were back at Wave Crest, the house quiet. Archie's obnoxious companions had finally headed on to Brighton, but to James's surprise, Archie hadn't gone with them. James had tried to get an explanation as to why, and Archie had claimed he liked Baywick much better.

The remark was obviously a lie, but James hadn't pestered him as to why he was being furtive. He was simply glad his cohorts had departed.

They were in the front parlor, having a whiskey. Archie was on the sofa, and James had been over by the mirror and pretending to study his shocked face. He went over and sat on a chair, just as the butler brought in the afternoon mail.

Archie received several ominous envelopes, but he didn't open any of them. He slid them behind him, so James wouldn't catch of glimpse of who had written.

"What have you there?" James asked. "Is it a pile of overdue notices from your many creditors?"

"Don't be ridiculous. Why would I be late in my payments to anyone?"

"Why indeed?"

"Although if you could spot me a few pounds, I wouldn't complain."

"No."

Archie scowled. "No, what? If I'm a tad short at the moment, how is that my fault?"

"You're an adult, Archie. You're responsible for your spending habits."

"While you were away, I had access to the estate accounts, but they've been yanked away. I'm having a slight—very slight!—problem because of the abrupt change. It wouldn't kill you to help me."

"If you're so lacking in funds, how did you purchase your gig?"

"On credit, of course. How would you suppose? It's how a gentleman acquires the necessities."

"You're not about to be the earl. You realize, don't you, that the man who sold it to you will retrieve it once you fail to pay? You don't have the title of Roxbury to throw around as protection against bad fiscal behavior."

Archie glared at him, as he struggled to devise an excuse that would move James to be generous. His brother had always been a conniver and manipulator. James was used to his prevarication and plotting, and he was familiar with Archie's sly looks. He flashed them in his attempts to seem innocent and trustworthy, when he was neither.

"I should get a share of your profits from Baywick," Archie suddenly declared. "I was so involved with the planning and financing. It would only be fair."

"As far as I can discern, there haven't been any profits. I was never very good at mathematics, but I believe your portion of nothing is zero."

"There will be profits," Archie insisted. "I'm sure of it."

"I hope you're right. I would hate to have to recoup my losses by raiding your trust fund. How is the balance anyway?"

Archie blanched, then quickly recovered his aplomb. "The balance is fine."

James scoffed. "Do you think I live in a bubble? Do you think I have no bankers to consult with me? Do you think I never hear gossip about you?"

"Who would gossip?" Archie blithely retorted. "I never engage in any dubious conduct, so there can be no stories to circulate."

"Don't beg me for money," James said. "Yours is squandered, and you have to develop a strategy as to how you'll support yourself from this point on."

"My strategy is clear: If I ever land myself in a jam, you'll bail me out. We're brothers, and you'd never permit me to suffer."

"Keep telling yourself that's true."

They were quiet for a bit, Archie fuming, while James glanced through his own letters. There was one from his shipmate, Captain Pettigrew, who'd survived their expedition. Whatever Pettigrew had to impart, James couldn't bear to read it.

The last news James had received as he'd fled London was that the expedition investors were scheduling an inquest to find out what had happened, why so many of the crew had perished. James didn't intend to ever talk about any of it. He'd cut out his tongue before he would.

Archie broke the fraught silence. "Remember those cousins who came to our party? The two Misses Shaw?"

James stared at his mail, not keen to have Archie note any piqued interest. "Yes, I recall them. Why?"

"What is your opinion of them?"

"I thought Emily Shaw was sweet and pleasant. I thought her cousin, Peggy Shaw, is exactly like you. She's foolish, spoiled, and immature, so she could be your female twin."

"I am none of those things, and her Christian name is Margaret."

"Yes, but Miss Emily told me her cousin was putting on airs for us. She's Peggy to everyone who knows her."

"What if we invited them to supper again? Just them with no other guests."

"No, never."

"Why not? What could it hurt?"

Archie's tone was very crafty, so James frowned at him and said, "What are you up to? Are you pursuing mischief with Peggy Shaw? If you are, I demand you desist immediately. We're not in London where sins can be committed with impunity. We're in rural Baywick, and this town is too small to conceal an indiscretion."

"When have I ever behaved stupidly?" Archie asked.

"How about always?"

"It would be fun to socialize with them. Margaret—or is it Peggy?—is so impressed with us, and she gushed about Wave Crest being very grand."

"So what? Will you rub it in her face? You act as if we're kings and we should show off for our vassals. What is wrong with you?"

"I like having silly girls fall in love with me."

"Leave her alone or I'll send you back to London. Then I'll track her down and tell her that Wave Crest is mine and you're a penniless idiot."

Archie smirked with annoyance. "She'd never believe you. She thinks I'm amazing."

"The poor child. Apparently, she has no common sense whatsoever."

Archie smirked again and finally opened one of his letters. He grimaced. "Mother has been delayed. She's arriving next week instead of this weekend."

"Oh, goody," James snidely said.

"If we want to have any genuine amusement, we should engage in it before she's here. For instance, if we had the Shaw cousins to—"

"We're not having them! Stop badgering me!"

James was being much too stern, but he couldn't abide the notion of having Emily at Wave Crest. During her prior visit, he'd promised her a tour of the manor, but on further reflection, he'd recognized that it would be madness to proceed.

He was bewildered, grieving, and half out of his mind with wretched musings, and she was beautiful and kind. He'd been using her to fill his dreary hours, but that was deranged and cruel. He had no business fraternizing with her. Any attention he focused on her would be misconstrued, and he did it simply so *he* could feel better, but she had to be wondering if a relationship wasn't forming.

He would never let it form, and he had to tamp down his obsession. There was only one way to deal with his burgeoning affection: He had to stay away from her.

She'd been the sole bright spot in his sojourn at Baywick, and he thought, rather than send Archie to London, he should pack his own bags. He was that anxious to ignore her, but it was so difficult.

"Fine!" Archie snapped, yanking him out of his miserable reverie. "We won't invite them. It was just a request. You don't have to bite my head off."

"Sometimes I do. You never listen to me, and I hate it when you nag."

"I wasn't nagging, and perhaps you should lie down and rest. It's obvious you're out of sorts, and a nap might improve your mood."

"Thank you for that wise advice. You've always been so concerned for my welfare."

James pushed himself to his feet and stomped out.

He was weary of his brother, weary of loafing in the country, weary of the slow days and his endless rumination that never led to a good place.

He marched to his bedchamber to grab a coat, and he had an old spyglass in his dresser. He grabbed that too, then he snuck out a rear door and hiked over to the headland and up to the top. From the summit, he could see down into Baywick, could see the harbor and the bay, the lanes carefully plotted out, the homes and shops that looked like miniature dollhouses.

People were strolling on The Promenade, and he stared down at them until he found who he was searching for: Emily, seated on a bench with Mrs. Darlington. She was pretty as a picture, attired in a green gown that would enhance the color of her eyes, a fetching bonnet covering her gorgeous blond hair.

He liked watching her so much, and his enjoyment was terrifying. He needed to escape Baywick before he behaved recklessly with her, but he supposed he wouldn't go. Not yet anyway.

For an eternity, he spied on her, and eventually, she and Mrs. Darlington stood and started back to Mrs. Darlington's hotel. Once they crossed the street and moved between the buildings, he lost sight of them. Then he turned away and climbed down the hill to Wave Crest.

The afternoon stretched in front of him like the road to Hades. There would be tea, then evening brandy with Archie, then supper for just the two of them. All of it seemed impossibly grueling, and he straightened his shoulders and went inside, ready to endure the worst.

Chapter Nine

EMILY STAGGERED UP THE trail to the top of the headland above Baywick. She wasn't normally a hiker, but another guest at the hotel had made the climb, and she'd encouraged Emily to try it. The summit provided spectacular views of the town and the bay, as well as a huge swath of the ocean.

If she peered down the other side of the hill, Wave Crest would be nestled in the valley below, and she deliberately refused to glance over. What would be the point?

She'd met Roxbury shortly after arriving in Baywick, and she'd foolishly allowed him to overwhelm the initial portion of her visit. But after she'd attended the supper at his home, she hadn't heard from him again.

She'd been moping and pining away to an insane degree and Mary, who was shrewd and wise, had forced her to recall that her flirtation with Roxbury had been very wrong, and obviously, he'd already grown weary of her. Or perhaps he'd realized, as she had, that it had been completely inappropriate.

That was the excuse Emily was using to clarify his disappearance from her life.

It was very windy on the promontory, and a stiff gust wafted up and over the cliff. She braced herself and grabbed for her bonnet, even though it was tied under her chin. Her shawl was hanging loose, and it was carried into the grass where it tumbled away.

She laughed with exasperation and chased after it, snatching it up before it could be sucked away and lost. As she draped it across her shoulders, she peeked over and Lord Roxbury was standing there. He hadn't seen her though. He was holding a spyglass and studying a ship that was barely visible out on the horizon.

Having shed his coat, he was in his shirtsleeves, the cuffs rolled to reveal his bronzed forearms. He hadn't shaved, so his cheeks were darkened with stubble, and he appeared enticing and dangerous, like a pirate or highwayman bent on mischief.

He was attired in tan trousers, knee-high black boots, and a flowing white shirt. The breeze flattened the fabric to his chest, so every inch of his muscled frame was delineated. The sight tickled her innards in a feminine way that was so exciting it embarrassed her.

He wore his hair longer than the current fashion, and the strands were mussed and blowing behind him, adding to the perception that he was a swashbuckler. She thought he should be gripping a sword rather than a spyglass.

She nearly called a hello, but Mary's warning was still ringing in her ears. There was no reason to be cordial, and clearly, he wasn't keen to pursue a friendship. On her end, if she chatted with him, the fleeting interaction would simply stir more discontentment.

She'd just ordered herself to scoot away, unobserved and unremarked, but he must have sensed her presence. He lowered his spyglass and turned toward her. For a moment, he had the strangest look on his face. He was assessing her as if she might be an apparition. Then he smiled and opened his arms to her, inviting her to run over and leap into them. She did exactly that.

He pulled her to him and kissed her fiercely. His lips captured hers, as if he'd drink her in, and he was touching her in places he had no business touching. Their loins were crushed together in a naughty manner, and it set off waves of desire that were too potent to understand or describe.

As always occurred when she was with him, the defenses necessary to keep him at bay rapidly crumbled, and she was anxious to furnish whatever he requested. She yearned to be by his side forever, to never be parted, and wasn't that the most absurd notion ever? Hadn't she just spent a lengthy interval convincing herself that she was better off without him?

"What are you doing up here?" he asked as their burst of passion eased.

"I'm hiking. What are you doing?"

"I'm loafing and lonely."

"I was going to sneak away."

"You silly girl!" His tone was dear and scolding. "Why would you have?"

"It seems futile, I suppose. After your supper party, you never contacted me again, and I figured you'd realized you should stay away from me."

"I had realized that," he said. "I've been very pragmatic. I thoroughly reflected on my burgeoning fondness, and guess what I've decided?"

"What?"

"I've been miserable without you, and I hate pretending we're not close."

"What should we do about it?" she inquired.

"I haven't the vaguest idea. What would you like to do?"

She could never truthfully answer that question—because a frank response might scare him to death. She wanted to marry him and live happily ever after. She wanted to remain with him until she drew her last breath. She wanted him to belong to her, to never consider belonging to any other female.

She was certain though that he was curious about more mundane issues, such as how should they socialize over the summer? Or how could they fraternize without it being awkward when he returned to London? Or how could he prevent her from misinterpreting his stunning attention?

She would be hearing wedding bells, and he would be wondering how he could dally with her without getting himself into too much trouble.

"Come with me," he said.

"To where?"

"Let's walk down my side of the hill, and I'll have my driver convey you to the hotel."

"I should head down to Baywick instead. You needn't put yourself out on my account."

"Of course you could trek down on your own, but I'm not about to let you. Now that I've stumbled on you, I can't allow you to flit off. You have to enliven the rest of my afternoon. I'm afraid I have to insist."

He linked their fingers and started down the trail to Wave Crest, and she followed after him without argument. All the while, she was kicking herself for being so foolish. How would she explain her visit to Mary?

She should have displayed more fortitude, but where he was concerned, she simply couldn't behave as she ought. What if he left for London shortly? What if this was the final time she ever saw him? If she declined this opportunity, and he departed, she'd always regret it.

They reached the bottom and went toward his house. He shifted away, so there was a bit of space between them. Anyone who observed them wouldn't notice that they'd been holding hands. He appeared chagrinned by the move, and he smirked at her.

"We're about to be swarmed by my servants," he said, "and perhaps even my brother, so I have to hide the fact that I'm completely besotted. I will have to carry on as if we're strangers."

"Can you manage it?"

"It could go either way, and I shall make no guarantees."

"Are you besotted?" she asked. "Is that what's happening? For I still can't describe it."

"What else could it be? Are you a sorceress who's bewitched me?"

"I have no magical powers," she told him. "If I've charmed you, I can't clarify how I accomplished it."

"I'm acting so oddly. Please don't think I kiss every woman I encounter up on the promontory."

She chuckled. "I would never think that."

"You are the only female who's ever driven me to stagger around like a lunatic."

"Was that a compliment? I couldn't tell."

"It's an admission that I'm wild for you."

"Well, then, aren't I lucky?"

"WOULD YOU STAY FOR supper?"

"No, I just can't."

James smiled at Emily, then snorted with disgust over how ridiculous he was being. They'd spent two hours strolling through the manor, and she'd snooped at a leisurely pace, oohing and aahing over every facet of the lovely residence.

He'd even showed her the master suite, watching her like an indulgent uncle as she'd wandered in the ostentatious rooms. Since meeting her, he'd become a foul, lusty character who constantly obsessed over prurient topics. Her presence in his bedchamber had him wondering if he'd ever be able to coax her into it for more debauched reasons.

They were on the rear verandah, seated at a small table and enjoying a glass of wine. They were staring across the garden to the ocean. It had been specifically designed so the paths and flowerbeds enhanced the view of the water.

"I'm jealous," she said. "This is all yours, and I shall greedily declare that I wish it was mine."

"Could you picture yourself living here?" He voiced the query in a light and teasing way.

"Absolutely. I'd have to grow very grand though, so I matched the magnificence. Then I would waltz into the village of Baywick, proclaiming that I was Mistress of Wave Crest. Everyone would be incredibly impressed."

"From the beginning, I thought it was a gorgeous spot," he said to her, "but you've made me like it even more."

"Thank you for giving me a tour."

"It was my pleasure."

They were sitting very close, their sides touching, their feet tangled together. He slid even nearer and stole a quick kiss. He shouldn't have, but he simply couldn't resist, and she shook a scolding finger at him.

"We're not kissing on your verandah," she said.

"No one saw us."

"You don't know who might have been spying."

"I'm not sorry."

He eased away, and they studied each other, as if committing features to memory.

"You look different," she said. "You must be feeling better."

"Yes, I'm definitely better. You have a soothing effect on me."

"Good. I like hearing that."

"Would you do me a favor?" he asked.

"Maybe. It depends on what it is."

He had the letter from his expedition mate, Captain Pettigrew, in his coat. He hadn't opened it yet. If it contained bad news, he couldn't bear to be apprised.

He pulled it out and handed it to her. "Would you read this for me?"

She frowned. "That's a peculiar request. Why can't you read it yourself?"

"It might be disturbing, and if it is, I don't care to be distressed by it." He pointed to it. "Just share the pertinent parts. If there's terrible information included, you can skim over it. I'll deal with it later."

She assessed him, her pretty green eyes digging deep. She wasn't evaluating him as if he was mad. No, she oozed sympathy over his bewildered condition, and she appeared to want to figure out how to aid him. Well, if he had a solution to his myriad of problems, he wouldn't be wallowing in a pathetic morass of despondency and gloom.

She scrutinized the letter and asked, "Who is Mr. Pettigrew?"

"He was captain of our crew on the trip home. Our original captain perished, and Pettigrew had to assume command."

"Is he a friend?"

"Yes, I guess we're friends, as much as anyone from the voyage could be." He shrugged. "We were survivors, rather than intimates, and it's created an odd connection for all of us."

"How many men came back? I don't recall the number."

"Only twenty." Twenty out of eighty. "I'm consumed by guilt over the losses we incurred. I rail at the heavens to tell me why so many others died, but I didn't. Why was I chosen? I never receive an answer."

"I realize how profoundly it vexes you." She rested a palm on his cheek and said, "It will be all right, James. Whatever Pettigrew has written, we'll get you through it."

He laughed. "You finally called me James."

"Don't get used to it." She blushed, then flicked the seal and scanned the words Pettigrew had penned, showing him it was three full pages. "It's quite mundane," she said. "He thinks you're in London, so this must have been forwarded from town."

"Yes, it was."

"He misses you, and he's feeling adrift and suffering from enormous melancholy. He's worried about you and wonders how you're faring, if you're experiencing any of the same symptoms. He'd like to visit you."

James scoffed at that. What kind of visit could they possibly have? What would they discuss? It was James's specific intent to never speak about the tragedy. Not ever. If Pettigrew was eager to vent and mourn, James couldn't help him.

She scowled. "There is one tidbit you should probably know. It has naught to do with your expedition. He made it home safe and sound, only to discover he'd been widowed. It's thrown him off-balance."

James winced. "That's too bad. He had a miniature of his wife in a locket, and he often gazed at it and thought of her. Memories of her kept him going. He must be devastated."

"Why don't you invite him to Wave Crest? If he's as anguished as you are, a sojourn here would be beneficial."

"Does he mention the inquest or the newspapers?"

"No. It's merely a note to inquire after your situation and to notify you of his."

"Oh . . . good." He took the letter from her and shoved it into his coat.

"Is there to be an inquest?" she asked. "Why is it necessary?"

"The investors lost a ton of money, and they're determined to learn why."

"Will you have to testify?"

"Not if I can avoid it." He grimaced, as if there was suddenly a foul odor in the air. "We agreed we'd never talk about it."

"Might it be advantageous to confer with Pettigrew? Perhaps you'd feel better."

"I'll ponder it." He wasn't serious.

"Will you reply to him? Or I could write for you. I hate to imagine him waiting for a response, but never receiving one."

"At the moment, I can't decide. The very idea has my pulse racing."

She reached for his hand and gave it a tight squeeze. "Are you afraid to speak to him? Is that it?"

"I'm not afraid. I just won't chaw over the details. They stick in my throat as if I'm choking on them."

"I understand, and I will renew my offer to listen to your stories. I'd never tell a soul."

"I'm sure you wouldn't, but it would be too difficult."

The ominous narrative was simple, but terrifying. They'd been sailing in the Far North, when they'd hit an unseen object hidden under the water. It had ripped open the hull, and they'd had to abandon ship. They'd been mapping a huge bay, and they'd rowed to shore with as many supplies as they could quickly toss into their longboats.

They'd been all alone, in the tundra, and stranded for over two years. They'd survived due to the assistance of several native tribes that hunted in the area. Without their gracious support, none of them would have made it.

British explorers were the smartest, savviest humans in the world. They were the rulers of the globe, but dire circumstances had altered their crew into feral animals. They'd endured lying, cheating, hoarding, treachery, and double-dealing. There had been five probable murders. A few men had gone mad and wandered off into the wilderness, never to return. Some had starved. Some had frozen to death. Others had been felled by accident or illness.

At the end, there had been a mutiny, where their captain had been ruled insane and relieved of duty. He'd committed suicide, which was a shocking debacle James would never reveal. It would mean publicly divulging the man's mental breakdown, and James would never permit his widow or children to discover the truth about his shameful demise.

Who would talk about any of that? Who would confess it? Who would dare to describe it? More importantly, who would believe such a harrowing, implausible tale?

After two grueling winters, James and the remaining men had given up hope of rescue. Their stamina had vanished, and they couldn't have lived much longer. They'd voted to walk out and head south, and the Good Lord had been watching over them.

A British whaler had stumbled on them and whisked them to safety, and it was a conclusion he still couldn't fathom. The ocean was so large, the Earth so big. What were the odds of being found on a little speck of snow?

Recollection rattled him, and ice washed through his veins. He shivered violently, and she noticed and asked, "What's wrong? Are you cold? You can't be."

He waved away her concern. "I'm not cold. I'm just ridiculous."

"Yes, you are," she said, "but I like you anyway."

He sighed with pleasure and sidled a bit nearer, wishing he could meld himself into her so there would be no space between them.

The sun shone down on her beautiful hair, and her eyes twinkled with her affection for him. She looked fetching, lovely, and kind. She possessed all the traits a husband sought in a wife, but that was a dangerous realization. He was already too obsessed with her, and he couldn't be grabbing at reasons to like her even more.

"What should I do with you?" he asked, not really needing an answer, but intrigued as to what her reply would be.

"Why must you *do* anything? We're friendly, and I'm delighted to know that we are. We should leave it at that."

"I've tried to avoid you, and I had convinced myself it was for the best, but as this splendid afternoon has proved, that's a ludicrous plan. I want to see you every day. I can't bear to suppose we'll only meet by accident."

"We can't meet every day, and you're not serious. It would indicate that we'd formed an attachment."

"Haven't we?"

"Yes, but it's an impossible one. It can't take us anywhere we might like to be."

"Are we too British?" he asked.

"Yes, absolutely."

"Why can't we shuck off the rules that restrict a flirtation between us? We should enjoy ourselves for the summer, then we'll separate with fond memories once autumn arrives."

"I would grow entirely too smitten," she said, "and I'm not like you. I don't have a man's callous sensibilities. I'd become wildly devoted."

"Would that be such a bad thing? Your life sounds so dreary to me. What if you went home happier than you've ever been?"

"That's not likely." She exhaled a heavy breath. "I will humiliate myself by admitting that I would start to hear wedding bells. I'm sure I seem horribly provincial, but I would completely misconstrue your attention. I wouldn't be able to help myself."

She was correct, and at her mentioning wedding bells, he should have been alarmed, but the notion tantalized him.

He didn't picture himself as being in a condition to marry, and he'd been an earl for such a short period. He hadn't had an opportunity to ponder the females who were available out on the Marriage Market. A man in his situation was encouraged to pick a young debutante, one with a massive dowry and perfect bloodlines, but he couldn't imagine choosing a girl like that.

Not when he was so distressed. He needed someone like Emily who was older and more mature, who was patient and compassionate. She could weather his quirks without quailing.

Because of his ordeal, he suspected he'd always be strange, that his view of the world would be slightly tilted. He doubted he'd ever revert to the person he'd been before he'd left on his failed excursion. Emily Shaw would be the ideal candidate to be his bride—if he'd been contemplating matrimony, which he wasn't.

He clasped her hand and kissed the center of it, then he laid it on his lap, their fingers linked, as if he'd hold onto her and never let her go.

"Will we base our socializing on coincidence?" he said. "Will I only see you if I happen to bump into you?"

"I guess that's how it has to be."

"What if I don't agree with that scenario? I would like a different arrangement, and I should get my way. I'm an earl, remember?"

She chuckled. "Yes, I definitely remember, but you won't get your *way* with me. Not about this. I'm keeping us from racing to folly, and I would appreciate it if you would chip in and do your part."

He pulled her to him, and he rested his forehead on hers. They stayed in that position for quite awhile, then she drew away and said, "I should return to the hotel. I had intended a brief hike, but I've been away for an eternity. I'm certain I've been missed."

"If you depart, how will I fill the tedious hours without you?"

"You can sit out here and stare at the ocean. To me, that's a little slice of Heaven."

"I'm not sufficiently grateful for all I have, and it won't be any fun if you're not here to scold me about it."

"I could jot down a list of your blessings. You could read it over and over after I'm gone. It's as close as I can come to tarrying."

He would have engaged in a lengthy bout of begging, but he'd delayed her as long as he dared. There was a footman nearby in case James required tending. He sent him to the stables to have the carriage harnessed.

"You don't have to give me a ride into town," she said. "I can walk; it's no bother."

"I'm trying to be gracious, so you have to allow me to practice my manners."

She gazed out at the garden, taking in the paths and flowerbeds, as if she was positive she'd never visit again. But he was already scheming as to when and how he could invite her.

The vehicle was prepared much too quickly, and they went out to the front foyer. As with the garden, she studied the rooms they passed, absorbing every detail, as if she'd never be back. In the driveway, he lifted her in, and when he would have climbed in behind her, she stopped him.

"You can't join me," she said. "I don't want my cousin or Mary Darlington to know you brought me home. It's bad enough that I'll arrive in your carriage. I can't have you seated beside me."

He could have argued with her, but he recognized she was correct. Baywick was a small place, and he shouldn't be observed galivanting with her.

"You win," he said. "You may travel to your hotel without me, but only on this occasion. From this point on, I insist that you let me have my way. If you don't, my poor ego will never survive."

"I'll try to be more amenable in the future, but you shouldn't count on it."

"Could I plead with you to hike the promontory every day?" he asked. "If I thought you would, I'd meet you by *accident* every afternoon."

"I can't predict when I'll see you, but I suspect it will be soon. Fate keeps toying with us."

"I've noticed that."

He kissed her goodbye, then stepped away and shut the door. She leaned out the window and extended her hand. He drew her fingers to his lips and kissed them too. They were growing incredibly maudlin, their fondness too overt, so he motioned to the driver. The man called to the horses, and she was whisked away. James dawdled until she vanished from sight.

He spun to go inside, and when he did, Archie was across the lawn and glaring derisively. James's cheeks reddened with chagrin, for he couldn't deny he'd been caught in a terrible entanglement.

"Wasn't that Emily Shaw?" Archie asked.

"Yes, it was." James was anxious for it to sound very innocent. "I ran into her up on the headland. We were having a glass of wine."

Archie scoffed, not buying the story. "You're such a hypocrite. You warned me away from her cousin, Margaret, so imagine my surprise to find you carrying out your own seduction."

"I haven't seduced Miss Shaw, and I don't plan to either. Don't be ridiculous."

"In my view, you haven't seduced her *yet*. Are you intending a debauched summer, with her as the central entertainment?"

"Don't be crude, and I won't listen to any slurs about her character. We're cordial; that's it."

"She's in love with you! It was so obvious. Is she supposing you'll marry her? Have you promised you will? Is that what's occurring? If you're deceiving her, I will declare myself quite astonished."

"I repeat, Archie: We're cordial acquaintances."

"For pity's sake, you were kissing her!" Archie snorted mockingly. "I've never liked it when you lectured me, and as I age, I like it even less. You told me to leave Margaret alone, but in light of your shenanigans, all bets are off."

"My edict still stands. I won't have you flirting with her. Nothing good can come from it. Besides, you're betrothed to Temperance Moore. You ought to remember that fact."

"Ha! You have the gall to admonish me over my romantic foibles? Emily Shaw is about to be ruined by your grand self, so I'll ignore Margaret when you vow the same about her cousin."

Archie whipped away and stomped off.

James could have chased after his brother, could have asserted his motives toward Emily were honorable, but that would be a lie. Archie wasn't the sharpest nail in the toolbox, but he'd accurately judged James's reprehensible conduct. James should forget about her. He should pack his bags and flee to London before he dug a hole from which he couldn't escape.

But he didn't want to do that, and he wouldn't do it. He walked out to the rear verandah, to have another glass of wine and plot how he could bump into Emily again as soon as possible.

Chapter Ten

"What do you think?"

"It's fabulous."

Peggy smiled at Archie, then glanced around Baywick's merry, frenzied gambling club. A trio of musicians played in the corner, delivering one cheery tune after another. The fast tempos added an uninhibited quality to the festivities, elevating pulses and putting people on edge, so they behaved more negligently than they ought.

The chandeliers were lit, the gaming tables packed. It was the common room, for common gamblers, where they could bet small amounts. There were other, more private rooms in the back, where richer gentlemen could consort without having to rub elbows with the ordinary citizens in the front of the house.

Archie hadn't escorted her to them, and she wasn't sure why. She'd hinted that she'd liked to see them, but he'd furnished a vague reply as to why she couldn't. She yearned to join the more exalted group with a hunger that was almost palpable.

She'd gone to the public dance at The Pavilion with a young lady from the hotel. Emily had stayed home, having been exhausted after a day of hiking. Peggy's companion was just as rash as Peggy, and they'd tarried long enough that others would remember they'd been there, then they'd flitted out and had walked to the gambling club.

Archie had been waiting for her, and from the moment she'd clasped his arm and had sauntered inside, she'd been overwhelmed by the powerful perception that she'd finally arrived exactly where she was meant to be.

He'd given them each a pouch of coins, so they'd been able to wager. He'd explained the games to them, some simple, some complex, and they'd jumped in with incredible relish.

They'd quickly lost the money he'd supplied, but the bright colors and hectic atmosphere were intoxicating. She'd never felt anything like it, and she'd like to have her own heavy purse so she could have continued all evening.

"Let's sneak away from your friend," Archie whispered.

"She came with me, and I shouldn't leave her alone."

"She's fine; she won't miss us."

Peggy was torn over obliging him, but his pull was too strong. He linked their fingers and drew her away, hurrying them down a dark hall. They slipped into a deserted parlor, and he spun the key in the lock.

The space was designed for an assignation, as if the club offered pleasures it didn't advertise. There was a fire in the grate and plush pillows on the floor in front of it. A lavish fainting couch was pushed into one corner and a narrow bed in the other.

Her stomach roiled with trepidation, and she had a fleeting mental debate over how she'd respond if he led her to the bed. He didn't though. Instead, he guided her to the fainting couch. He stretched out and tugged her down so she was atop him.

For a second, she hesitated. A mix of alarm and elation were pummeling her in equal measure, and her wicked tendencies won the battle. She snuggled down, and with no conversation being necessary, he began kissing her. His hands were on her hips, their loins pressed tight. Down in his trousers, his phallus was hard as stone, and at the realization of how fervidly he desired her, she was awash with ecstasy.

"I'm so wild for you, Margaret," he said. "Are you wild for me?"

"How could I not be?"

"I wish we could constantly be together. How could we manage it?"

"You could fetch me from the hotel, and we could stroll on The Promenade. Wouldn't that be lovely?" He glared as if it was a stupid suggestion, so she rushed to say, "Or perhaps you could host another supper party. Maybe a smaller one where we could socialize more intimately. I'd like that."

"Alas, my brother is opposed to a party. He's still recovering from his ordeal, and he doesn't like having guests."

"My cousin mentioned that you have a new gig. She saw you driving it. What if you stopped by and invited me for a ride?"

"Mrs. Darlington is such a fusspot, and she wouldn't like it." He smiled in a devilish way. "I have the worst reputation. She wouldn't be too keen to have me courting you."

At his use of the word *courting,* she could have swooned. Was that how he viewed their blossoming relationship?

"I like men with bad reputations," she brazenly said.

"Yes, but I would hate to get you into trouble with her. If she was upset, she might evict you. You'd have to find other lodging during this busy period, and if you couldn't, you'd have to head home. I plan to enjoy the entire summer with you, and I couldn't bear to have you depart early."

"I never would. Nor will I let Mrs. Darlington control my conduct or choices. I'm simply renting a room from her. She's not my nanny."

"That's a very brave position, but you shouldn't cross her."

Peggy's pulse raced with dread. "Are you telling me it's impossible for us?"

He frowned as if she was being silly. "No, absolutely not. We will sneak away as often as we can. We merely have to be very careful with Mrs. Darlington."

"I have to be careful with my cousin too. Emily would never like to learn that I've been stepping out with you. She's such a stickler for the proprieties; I'd never hear the end of it."

He scoffed. "Your cousin is a stickler? My dear, you've completely misconstrued what sort of person she is."

"Meaning what? I've been acquainted with her my whole life. She's very prim and proper."

"I suppose she likes everyone to think so, but she's been secretly meeting with my brother."

"Their meetings haven't been secret," Peggy said. "He's called on her at the hotel, and we came to your party."

"She's been with him on other occasions, when no one is aware."

Peggy's jaw dropped. "Emily has been?"

"Yes, I caught her at Wave Crest yesterday."

"She told me about it, but she claimed she'd bumped into Lord Roxbury when she was hiking. She described it as being very innocent."

He scoffed again, more derisively. "I have no idea what they were really doing—they were alone for hours—but when he was helping her into his carriage, he kissed her quite desperately. I witnessed it with my own two eyes."

"Emily was kissing Lord Roxbury?"

"Yes, and they appeared ardently attached. It's shocking, isn't it? Clearly, you're as stunned as I am."

"I doubt *stunned* captures my level of astonishment. She's always been so moralistic and persnickety. When she notices my failings, she's quick to rub my nose in it."

"Perhaps, with her misbehaving herself, she'll cease being so sanctimonious. She especially shouldn't scold you about our flirtation."

"Too right, Archie."

He gazed at her with such deep yearning, as if he found her to be the most exotic female in the kingdom. His fondness was so blatant, so welcome. Where would it take them?

Well, she knew what she intended. Eventually, she'd have Archie Covington as her husband. He couldn't stare at her so stridently and not be falling in love.

He started kissing her again, and the embrace grew even more passionate. His tongue was in her mouth, his palms roaming over her breasts and arms, her back and bottom. He was flexing against her, igniting sparks of desire throughout her body.

She wasn't confused about what he sought, but she wouldn't give it to him. Not yet anyway. She was happy to engage in several naughty acts, but she would never cross any lines, not unless they were married. He probably thought he was leading her on, but she was leading him on too, and she'd get her way in the end. She was convinced of it.

They were distracted by giggling out in the hall, and a man and woman were whispering drunkenly. One of them jiggled the knob, and luckily, Archie had locked the door, so the amorous couple couldn't barge in.

Archie touched a finger to her lips, urging silence, as the man said, "It seems this room is occupied."

They giggled even harder and moved on. Once it was quiet again, he eased her off him, and they sat up.

"We should return to the gaming tables," he said.

"Yes, I should locate my friend too. I must find out what time it is. We've been in here forever, and I have to be back at the hotel by midnight. Mrs. Darlington has a curfew, so I can't be late. It's a firm rule, and if a young lady breaks it, she has to check out and go home. She's very strict about it."

"It sounds as if you're Cinderella."

"If I am, aren't you Prince Charming?"

"I believe I am." He motioned to the door. "We shouldn't walk out together. How about if you leave first? I'll follow in a bit."

"I can't bear to part from you."

"You'll see me again very soon."

"Swear it," she said, being much too vehement. "Swear I'll see you."

"I swear. I'll arrange an outing, and I'll send you a note."

"Don't make me wait too long."

She stood and went over to peek into the hall, then she paused to flash a wicked grin at him. It promised all sorts of depraved conduct, then she hurried away, positive she'd caught him like a fish on a hook.

"I NEED TO MENTION a problem to you," Mary said to Emily. "Could we talk in private?"

"Yes, certainly."

Mary guided her into a sunny apartment that had to be her personal lodging. It had big windows, colorful curtains, and comfortable furniture. Emily suspected a woman could be very content in such a cozy, beautiful place.

She figured they were about to discuss the possibility of her working at the hotel in the future, so she was totally unprepared when Mary said, "This is so embarrassing. Please don't be angry."

"I won't be angry, but what is it? Just spit it out and don't be embarrassed. I hate to suppose you would be."

"It's about your cousin, Peggy."

Emily blanched. "What's she done?"

"It's not what she's done, precisely. I'm simply fretting over an incident one of my maids witnessed. I decided a word of caution might be appropriate. Could you speak to her for me?"

"Yes, of course, and you're scaring me. What's wrong?"

"She and another guest attended the dance last night. You didn't tag along."

"No. I was tired from my hike, so I stayed home."

"I'm not blaming you."

"This is sounding worse by the second."

Mary tsked with exasperation. "I'm not handling this very well. Let me try again. You're aware of my midnight curfew?" Emily nodded, and Mary continued. "They arrived just as my maid was about to lock the doors. Her companion came in first, and as my maid waited for your cousin to come in too, she observed her climbing out of Archie Covington's carriage."

"Oh, no."

"He kissed her goodbye. Right out on the street in front of the hotel. His reputation isn't a secret, and my maid thought I should be apprised."

Emily was nearly too shocked to comment. "Peggy was kissing Mr. Covington?"

"Yes. I'm not informing you because I'm upset. It's not that. She's entitled to have friends while she's here on holiday, and I'm not her chaperone. I'm merely concerned about her fraternizing with Mr. Covington, but I'm not in a position to have that conversation with her."

"Well, I am, and I'm glad you told me about it. Peggy is prone to bad choices, and Mr. Covington could easily lead her astray."

"That's what I'm afraid of."

"I'll deal with this immediately. I'll explain the situation, and I'll be very firm with her. She'll listen to me."

"Thank you."

"You won't have to worry about her behavior ever again," Emily said, "and I'll see you later. Perhaps we can have tea."

"I'd like that."

Emily dashed out and tromped up the stairs to their room. As she'd left a few hours earlier, Peggy had still been in bed. She was relieved to find her cousin up and dressed. She was sitting on a chair by the window and staring out at nothing.

"Where have you been?" she asked as Emily bustled in.

"I was strolling, enjoying the sights."

"I'm starving, and I've missed breakfast, so I have to locate a restaurant that's serving food in the middle of the afternoon. There must be one in this godforsaken town. Would you like to join me?"

"Yes, we can go, but first, I have to discuss a difficult topic with you. Don't bite my head off."

"When have I ever bitten your head off?"

Emily snorted. "How about every occasion where I've raised a subject you don't want to address?"

"Are you about to scold me? For what transgression? I just got up. What crime could I have committed in my sleep?"

Emily walked over and sat in the chair next to her. "Mrs. Darlington has advised me that you rode home from the dance with Archie Covington."

Peggy clucked her tongue with offense. "Isn't she a busybody? Why would she assume my having an escort would be any of her business?"

"It's not that she's chastising you. It's that Mr. Covington has a low reputation, and she asked me to be sure you knew about it."

"He's a London dandy and an earl's brother. He carouses in the city with a very fast crowd. If he's maligned by these provincial rubes, I'm not surprised. They could never understand the sort of amusement that appeals to a man like him."

Peggy's tone was very snide, very caustic, indicating the conversation would be exhausting, but Emily pushed on. "Did you kiss him out on the street?"

"What if I did? Don't you dare admonish me over it."

"How have you become sufficiently acquainted with him that you would carry on in such a familiar way?"

Peggy shrugged. "I met him shortly after we arrived in Baywick, so we'd been introduced. Then he gave me a ride in his carriage the other day when I'd been out shopping. Since then, we've been very cordial."

"You were alone with him, in his carriage?"

"Yes, and don't lecture me about it. He's very fond of me, and I've captured his fancy."

"Peggy!" Emily fumed. "You shouldn't trot about with a strange man."

"He's not a stranger to me, and you oughtn't to complain about this. If you try, this quarrel will wander down a road you won't like to travel."

"What's that supposed to mean?" Emily asked.

"It means you shouldn't reprimand me for kissing Archie Covington. Not when you've engaged in the very same activity with Lord Roxbury."

Emily sucked in a sharp breath. "Who told you that?"

"Archie. Who would you imagine? He saw the two of you, so don't pretend it didn't happen."

There were a hundred issues Emily needed to debate, but she chose, "You're on a first-name basis with Mr. Covington?"

"Yes, so I won't listen to you berating me. You've been embarrassing yourself with the Earl, so you've lost the moral high ground."

Emily's cheeks heated. Peggy was correct that she'd lost any standing to protest her cousin's conduct, but still, a warning had to be delivered.

"I won't criticize you for what transpired last night. I simply have to point out that he's not the most reliable fellow. If he's flirting with you, it's entirely possible he has ulterior motives."

"What about you and Roxbury?" was Peggy's response. "Apparently, the notion has never occurred to you that he might have ulterior motives as well. Don't tell me you've been hearing wedding bells."

"I won't tell you that. The Earl and I enjoy an unusual affection."

Peggy smirked with derision. "As his brother and I do, and I must mention that your relationship with the Earl is much more shocking than mine with Mr. Covington."

Emily couldn't justify her antics with James. Instead, she said, "You could land yourself in a jam with him. There are stories about him and how he seduces girls like you with wicked intent. It would be awful if you were his next victim. You shouldn't stir any gossip."

"I'll keep that in mind," Peggy sneeringly retorted, "but if anyone is about to be the subject of lurid gossip, it will be you. Are you presuming Archie is the only person who saw you with the Earl? I'm certain some of his servants would have too. They'll chatter with their co-workers, and this is a small town. Word will spread quickly, so maybe you should worry about yourself before you start worrying about me."

"Roxbury and I are just friends."

"Archie and I are *just* friends too, but I'm thinking that he and I will end up as much more than friends."

Emily scowled, struggling to unravel what Peggy was claiming. "You believe he'll marry you?"

"Why couldn't he? He's already falling in love, so we'll soon learn who winds up with a ring on her finger. I'm positive it won't be you, receiving one from Roxbury."

Emily sighed with dismay. "Mr. Covington will never marry you, Peggy. How can I convince you?"

"You can't. Time will tell if I'm right or wrong, so I would appreciate it if you would butt out. Don't nag about my amour, and I won't nag about yours." She stood and marched out, pausing to grab her shawl and bonnet on the hook by the door.

"Where are you going?" Emily asked, gnashing her teeth over how they'd bickered.

"I have to find something to eat. I had expected you to join me, but you needn't bother. If I had to stare at your glum face through the whole meal, it would give me indigestion."

She stomped out, and as her footsteps faded, Emily turned to gaze out the window.

"That went well," she glibly said to the empty room.

She contemplated the two months they'd spend in Baywick. How much mischief would Peggy foment? How much drama might unfold?

Emily's affiliation with James was difficult, but she had a good head on her shoulders. She knew better than to count on him. What about Peggy and Mr. Covington?

They were a pair of spoiled brats, who felt the world owed them a favor, and Peggy had always assumed she deserved a bigger life than the one that had been provided. With the two of them having no limits to their voracious appetites, what catastrophes might arise?

The answer to that question was too terrifying to ponder, so she'd put on blinders and hope for the best. If they behaved recklessly and their frolics crashed down, she would ask James to help her clean up the mess. Each day she remained in Baywick with Peggy would be a gamble, and she would stagger forward and pretend no disaster was lurking.

What other option was there? Would they pack their bags and slither home to Hexham?

No! She wouldn't leave James a second early, so she wouldn't allow Peggy to render that conclusion.

Suddenly, her anxiety flared to such a height that she couldn't catch her breath. She grabbed her own shawl and bonnet and hurried off to stroll on The Promenade again. A brisk walk in the sea air would cure what ailed her. Wouldn't it?

If nothing else, she could sit on a bench and think of James on the other side of the hill. She would wonder where he was and what he was doing. Thoughts of him would calm her down. She was sure of it.

Chapter Eleven

EMILY SAT IN THE theater, surrounded by a packed audience. A famous European opera singer was on the stage, in the middle of an aria. The intermission was about to arrive, and it would be a relief. Emily wasn't exactly an opera fan, and the lyrics were in German, so it was hard to follow.

Still though, she was enjoying herself. The building was a stunning place, and it reinforced her opinion that Baywick had been planned by geniuses. The ambiance was so pretty that she might have been in Paris.

The aria concluded, and the curtain came down. People began leaving their seats, rushing to the lobby for a glass of wine. Others climbed to visit important citizens up in the boxes, while others stepped out for a breath of fresh air.

Peggy wasn't with her. She'd attended the public dance instead, which was just as well. Since their quarrel over Mr. Covington, their relationship had been incredibly strained, but Emily had convinced herself not to worry.

Peggy realized, should she misbehave and be caught, their summer would abruptly end. They'd have to jump onto the first mail coach bound for Hexham, and that dire possibility would encourage her to be careful. At least Emily was telling herself it was having a positive effect.

She wasn't Peggy's nanny, and if Peggy got a wild idea in her head, it was difficult to corral her into better conduct.

Emily was with three other ladies from the hotel, and they'd been swallowed up by the crowd. She trudged along behind them to the lobby, but it was filled to bursting, and she couldn't find her companions. She would have liked to have a glass of wine, but she was too short to shove to the front of the line and ask for one, so she went outside.

The theater had a patio that looked out at the ocean. It was jammed full too, and she wedged herself into a corner where she promptly found herself face to face with James. Dressed as he was in formal clothes, there was nothing about him that was similar to the bewildered man she'd met her first night in Baywick. He was elegance personified, a dashing scoundrel who put every other gentleman to shame.

His black suit was expensive and perfectly tailored, his cravat blindingly white and sewn from the finest Belgian lace. He'd smoothed down his hair with a pomade that made it glisten under the lamps. He appeared rich and delicious, the sort of handsome, charming rogue that mothers warned their daughters about.

They froze and gaped with astonishment, then he smiled and said, "I can't believe I've run into you again. Fate will not let me stay away from you."

"Why are you here?" she asked him. "A theatrical concert is a very normal way to spend an evening. Aren't you shunning *normal* events?"

"My brother had tickets, but at the last minute, he cried off on me."

"You poor boy. You're all alone?"

"Yes. How about you?"

"I'm with some hotel guests, but I got separated from them."

They were standing an acceptable distance apart, as if they were strangers. Yet she was desperate to hold his hand or maybe wrap her arms around his waist. It was simply so difficult to pretend they weren't intimately acquainted.

"How are you liking the performance?" he asked.

"It seems to be very good, but I'm not a connoisseur, so I'm not the best judge. How about you?"

"May I tell you a secret?"

"Yes, absolutely."

He leaned in and whispered, "I hate opera."

She chuckled. "I don't hate it, but I don't love it either."

"If I didn't suffer through the second act, I wouldn't necessary grieve over it."

She grinned. "Are you suggesting we sneak away?"

"Yes, shall we? Will anyone miss you?"

"Probably not. If I don't return to my seat, my companions will assume I grew bored and went back to the hotel."

"Instead, you could stroll down The Promenade with me."

"Why, Lord Roxbury, I thought you'd never ask."

He led her out of the crowd and down the stairs. He was a striking man, and everyone studied him as he sauntered by. They frowned and murmured, obviously recognizing him to be *somebody* and trying to figure out who. She might have heard a woman exclaim, *Isn't that Roxbury? I could swear it is,* but she wasn't positive.

He was in a hurry to whisk her away. His long legs ate up the boardwalk at such a fast pace that she was practically stumbling after him.

"I'm nearly running," she said, pulling him to a halt. "I can't keep up with you."

"I'm sorry. I'm so anxious to have you all to myself that I wasn't thinking."

He slowed down, and they ambled on. They passed empty benches, and she'd expected they might sit on one of them, but they didn't. They continued on and wound up at the public dock where rowboats could be borrowed during the day. He pointed at them and said, "Shall we take a ride?"

"It's the middle of the night. Is it safe?"

"It's safe when you're with me." There was a lantern hanging on an adjacent pole, and he grabbed it and gestured to a boat. "Let's do it. It'll be fun."

She never wanted to view herself as a stick-in-the-mud, so she nodded. "Don't you dare tip us over and don't you dare get lost."

"We'll just row over to the Pirate's Cove. The lamp will provide plenty of light. We'll be fine."

"You're mad. You know that, right?"

"Have I ever once—since I met you—denied being deranged?"

"No. Not once."

"Then I won't start denying it now, but I can promise we'll make it to the opposite dock with no problem."

He helped her in, then climbed in after her. He tossed away their rope tether, then he gripped the oars and quickly maneuvered them over to the island.

No one else had been ridiculous enough to head there in the dark, so they were very much alone. He tied them off, then lifted her out. They didn't walk out onto the sand, but plopped down on the end of the dock, their feet dangling, the lantern behind them and furnishing a warm glow.

They peered over at the town of Baywick. The Promenade was illuminated with lamps, many houses and businesses illuminated too. It might have been an enchanted fairyland, and she sighed with delight.

"Isn't this pretty?" she said.

"I'm glad I stole you away. It was worth it."

"I should have brought a bottle of wine. The occasion seems to call for it."

"I should have thought of it too, but this was an impulsive act."

"Are you in the habit of absconding with young ladies with no warning or preparation?"

"No, you're the very first one."

"I shall tell myself to believe you."

He scowled. "Why wouldn't you believe me?"

"You're an aristocrat, so women throw themselves at your feet. I picture you as having engaged in dozens of affairs. You've probably even kept mistresses. Isn't that behavior common among the men of your class?"

"My older brother, Edward, was that debauched, but I never was. From the time I finished school, I was traveling on expeditions. I never had the chance to be wicked."

"You're home now, and you're not going anywhere, are you?"

He fought off a shudder. "Definitely not. It's my determined goal to never board a sailing ship ever again." He pointed at their small boat. "For the remainder of my life, that's the only type of vessel that could tempt me."

"You have leisure hours to fill, so you can become debauched."

"I can't envision it. I'm very stodgy and boring, so I wouldn't have the vaguest notion of how to be wild and out of control."

He dipped in and kissed her, and she joined in with an equal amount of enthusiasm. Then she nestled herself to his chest, his arm over her shoulders to hold her close.

"Did you ever write to Captain Pettigrew?" she asked. "I've been worrying about him."

"I haven't managed it yet."

"My offer to pen a letter for you still stands. You could advise me of what to impart, and I'd put it down on paper for you."

He gazed at her with a tender expression that had her heart racing. He looked absolutely besotted, and she was in no better condition. Mary had begged her to be wary of him, and Peggy had accused her of forgetting her moral inclinations. They were both correct, and if she'd possessed an ounce of sense, she'd have demanded he row her to shore, but she didn't insist they leave.

When she was with him, it felt so right, so perfect, as if the universe meant for them to be together. Their fondness was too powerful, and the restrictions that should have prevented a relationship had vanished.

He nibbled on her neck, and she laughed and pushed him away.

"Stop that," she scolded. "I like it too much."

"I'm trying to turn you into a wanton."

"I will work very hard to ensure it doesn't happen."

"If I agreed to let you write to Pettigrew for me, would it lure you to Wave Crest for another visit?"

"I'd visit Wave Crest whenever you invited me, but I'd bring someone with me. I won't dawdle there with you alone."

"My brother saw me kissing you the last time you were there."

She tsked with aggravation. "He mentioned it to my cousin, and I got an earful about it. Were you aware they're friendly?"

"Yes, and they shouldn't be. I ordered him to stay away from her. He'd enjoy leading her on, and she'd misconstrue his intentions." The import of his words registered, and he blanched. "Oh, gad, that sounded awfully pompous. Am I as despicable as my brother?"

At his obvious discomfort, she chuckled. "As you've shrewdly deduced, I am in the exact same quagmire with you. I've already been warned—quite vehemently, I might add—that you are a cad who is toying with me."

"Who has warned you that I'm a cad?"

"Mrs. Darlington and my cousin. I swore you weren't, that you have the purest of motives, but they didn't believe me."

"What do *you* think I'm doing?"

"I think we share a strident affection. I can't fathom what's causing it or why it's occurring. When I'm away from you, I tell myself it's for the best, but then, we cross paths, and I'm so ecstatic that I can't persuade myself to ignore you."

"I view our connection the same way. We seem to have met for a reason, so perhaps we'll always feel tightly bound."

"Yes, that's how I feel: tightly bound to you. It's as if I've known you forever."

"What will become of us?"

She had some very firm ideas on what she'd like to have transpire. She'd like to marry him and live happily ever after, but that was a fantasy. She didn't dare discuss her true wishes, so she tossed the ball in his court, being curious as to what he'd say.

"What is your opinion about it?" she asked.

"I hadn't assumed I'd tarry in Baywick the whole summer, but I will change my plans for you."

The decision thrilled her. "I'll be here until the first of September."

"We should socialize as often as we can."

"And then what? Afterward, when I was home, I'd be broken-hearted. I have no prior experiences that would furnish me with the foundation I need to flirt for months, then forget about you. Could you carry on like that? Could you flirt all summer, then blithely return to London?"

"I can't imagine it, but I can't imagine avoiding you either. It's been how I've told myself to handle you so far, but with our being out on this dock by ourselves, it's clear my scheme has failed."

"Can a man and a woman of our disparate stations ever simply be friends? With how we instantly fall into passionate kisses, we're something more than friends. Is there a term to describe us?"

He shook his head. "No."

"It appears we're at an impasse. We can't avoid one another, yet we oughtn't to fraternize. What shall we do?"

"I won't worry about it. That's how I've staggered forward since I arrived back in England. I could be on a raft and floating down a river. I'm allowing the current to take me in any direction it pleases. It's how I've been dealing with you."

"What if we saw each other once a week? We could schedule various activities. What if you had a regular supper party and I was a guest? Or what if you hosted an evening musicale or theatrical reading? I could come to those sorts of events. It would provide the excuse we need to be together, and we wouldn't grow so frantically desperate when we encounter each other by accident."

"If I arranged a weekly musicale, would I be able to sneak off and kiss you in dark corners? For I have to confess that I want to misbehave with you. I have no interest in loafing in a stuffy parlor and having to pretend you're a stranger."

She snickered with amusement. "So Mrs. Darlington was right? You have nefarious designs on my person?"

"Apparently, I possess many nefarious designs with regard to you, and I am stunned to be suffering from them. I'm usually such a tedious fellow, and you've altered me so I'm greedy and covetous."

"You're not tedious, Roxbury. And no, if I attended a musicale at Wave Crest, we couldn't sneak off to any corners."

"Are you claiming it's impossible between us?"

"I guess it is."

He snorted at that. "Fate isn't listening. You constantly pop up when I least expect it."

They were quiet for a bit, gazing over at the town, at the twinkling lights, at the couples strolling on The Promenade. It was a perfect moment, and she was tabulating the details so she'd remember them later on.

"Are you feeling better these days?" she asked him. "I haven't seen you in a wool coat in ages."

"I'm much better. You're having a palliative effect on my condition."

"I'm glad to hear it."

"My mind is calming down, and I'm managing my ruminations." Then he added the most disturbing remark. "I might have to go to London in a few weeks."

"Before the summer is over? Why would you leave early? What's happening in London?"

"The inquest is definitely being held, so I'll be subpoenaed to testify. I don't suppose I should ignore an official summons."

"No, you shouldn't, but won't it be terribly difficult for you to talk about your ordeal?"

"Yes, so would you come with me? I won't be as distraught if you're there too."

She gaped at him. They were locked away in Baywick and enjoying a type of shipboard romance, the kind travelers pursued when they were far from home. Their isolation and lack of structure were skewing the boundaries of what was allowed, so it seemed they could consort in ways that weren't permitted or condoned.

Did he realize the significance of what he'd suggested? She couldn't traipse off to London with him. First and foremost, he was a bachelor, so she couldn't stay with him, and she didn't have the funds to reside at a hotel or coaching inn.

She couldn't sit in the front row at the inquest and provide moral support. She couldn't meet with him in the evenings after the hearings were over to commiserate and sympathize. There was no place for her in that scenario.

"Oh, James," she said, "I would love to, but it would be shockingly improper."

He shrugged. "I was lost for several years, in the worst circumstances, and I believed, over and over again, that I'd die there, alone and forsaken."

She winced and snuggled herself closer. "Don't tell me that. It distresses me so much."

"When I left England on my final expedition, I was very stuffy, very British. I always followed the rules and obeyed the strictures that constrained me, but I was changed by tragedy. Rules and strictures are ridiculous to me now. If I need you in London, why shouldn't you join me there?"

"You know why. You're adrift, and you're unmoored from the world you used to inhabit. But *I* still live in that world, and you'll eventually return to it. You'll recover and cease to feel so disconnected. In the meantime, I can't carry on so brazenly. I can't journey to London and flit about on the fringe of your life. I wouldn't have any idea how to accomplish it."

He smiled. "Is that a *no*?"

"That's a definite *no*."

He shrugged again. "It was worth asking. What if you'd agreed?"

"Will you have to depart early? I have such limited opportunities to be with you, and I like to think of you being just over the hill. I can't bear to imagine you not being there, even if it's only for a few days."

"I'll make sure my presence at the inquest isn't required before September. I will tarry in Baywick as long as you are here too."

She sighed with gladness. He was so charming, so dear. How would she survive after she staggered to Hexham at the end of the summer? She truly could not fathom it.

"Let's plan our next encounter," he said. "We shouldn't leave it to chance."

"How about if you host another supper party?"

"I will do that. I will arrange it and send you an invitation."

"I'll have to bring Mary Darlington, so don't envision a cozy meal for two."

"Will you walk in the garden with me after we eat? If I'm going to go to all the trouble of having guests, I should receive a reward. The reward I choose is to kiss you in my gazebo."

"We'll see if you can tempt me." She eased away from him and gestured to the boat. "I have to get to the hotel. I can't guess what time it is, but I have to be there by midnight. Mrs. Darlington has a strict curfew."

"If you're late, will you turn into a pumpkin?"

"No, but she'd probably evict me. The curfew is her method of guarding her reputation. She feels compelled to protect us from wandering off with strange men."

"And there's no one stranger than me."

He kissed her again, and he kept on for quite awhile. Ultimately, she mustered some fortitude; she stood and skittered away.

"You are a menace, James," she told him. "You entice me too thoroughly."

"I'm wearing you down. Shortly, you'll relent and give me whatever I request. Have I mentioned that I always get my way?"

"Yes, and have I mentioned that my cousin and Mrs. Darlington have warned me about you? Your comment sounded like an admission of bad motives."

He was gazing at her with such affection that she could barely stand to observe it. What was she supposed to do with that look? How was she to deflect it? Why would she want to deflect it?

"I would never hurt you," he murmured.

"You wouldn't *deliberately* hurt me, but I have to be careful." She extended her hand and said, "Come. I've loafed too long, and I have to hurry."

"I'd rather sit here with you all night and watch the sun rise."

"I'll like that too, but I'm trying to exhibit my common sense."

"Common sense if highly overrated."

She pulled him to his feet, then he helped her into the boat and rowed them back to the public dock. They tied off, then started down The Promenade. They strolled slowly, their fingers linked, their heads pressed close as if they were madly in love.

Was that what was occurring? She was beginning to think, on her end anyway, that it might be happening. She'd never been in love, and she had no idea of what the signs could be, but her heart was aching, as if it had doubled in size. She felt as if she'd die a little each minute until she could be with him again. Wasn't that love?

They reached the last corner, and he drew her into an alley and kissed her goodbye. It was sweet and poignant, and tears stung her eyes. How was she to weather the storm of emotion he stirred? How bereft would she be when they parted in September?

The best path would be to pack her bags and flee to Hexham without apprising him, but she wouldn't. She would stay in Baywick and let the chips fall where they would.

"We should get you home," he said. "I can't have Mrs. Darlington lock you out. She's very fierce, and I wouldn't like to be scolded by her for corrupting you."

"Plan your supper party."

"It will be very soon. I promise."

They stared, a thousand remarks swirling that could never be voiced aloud. Then he nodded toward the hotel.

"You have to depart first," he said. "If it's my decision, we'll dawdle here forever."

"Thank you for the boat ride."

"Thank you for accompanying me. I'm ensnaring you in my web."

"I'm enjoying it."

They sighed together, then she whipped away and rushed to the door. As she arrived, she glanced over, and he was directly under a lamp. He looked decadent and dissolute. He might have been the worst London dandy who'd been gamboling around the city.

In case anyone was nearby, she didn't acknowledge him, but dashed inside. The front parlor was empty, so she was able to climb to her room without encountering Mary, Peggy, or any of the other guests, and it was a relief. She was so happy that she couldn't have uttered a single intelligible word.

PEGGY OPENED THE DOOR at the back of the hotel and tiptoed in. Dawn was breaking on the eastern horizon.

The prior evening, when she'd snuck off to meet Archie, she'd stolen a key from an unsuspecting housemaid. It had been insurance lest she came in late. She'd been determined to revel with Archie and his friends and positive she'd miss the curfew. It would have been humiliating to have left them early, and she refused to seem provincial in their very sophisticated eyes.

She'd spent the whole night at the Gentleman's Paradise Club, which was the fancy name for Baywick's gambling den. Archie had brought her into the private, members-only area, where the rich and notorious were allowed to wager without having to rub elbows with the commoners out in the front.

With him inviting her into them, with his including her, she viewed it as further evidence of his growing infatuation. It had been the greatest experience of her life.

He'd delivered her to the hotel in his carriage, and they'd shared many passionate kisses on the way. Her hair was down, her gown askew, and she'd tugged off her slippers, so her tread wouldn't be heard on the floorboards.

She was suffering from a giddy elation that was making her feel invincible, but there were dangers lurking. The main one was Emily noticing her furtive entrance. They had separate beds though, and her cousin slept like a log, so the chance of discovery was very small.

She crept up the rear stairs to her door, and as she reached for the knob, she almost shook a fist in triumph over how easy it had been to return undetected, but suddenly, a scullery maid appeared down the hall.

They both froze, assessing each other and taking stock of what they were witnessing. Peggy frowned and raised a finger to her lips, warning the girl to silence, and she coupled it with a fierce glower, visually indicating there would be consequences if she stirred trouble.

Mrs. Darlington's servants were emboldened to report on the guests, and Peggy deemed it to be outrageous behavior. They ought to know their place, and they didn't warrant any elevated authority.

The ninny nodded her understanding, then she vanished like smoke, as if Peggy had terrified her. Good! Let her be afraid. It would keep her quiet.

Peggy slid into her room. Emily was slumbering deeply, the curtains pulled, so it was very dark. Furtively, she stripped to her chemise and drawers, then she went to her bed and slithered under the blankets. She held her breath, peeking over at Emily, but Emily hadn't moved.

Peggy grinned and forced herself to relax. She'd arrived safely, with no one the wiser except for the stupid scullery maid. The blasted child wouldn't dare tattle, and if she tried, Peggy would call her a liar. It would be Peggy's word—that of a paying customer—against the lowliest servant.

She drifted off, thinking of Archie and the fun she'd had at the gambling club, thinking of his boisterous friends and how they'd welcomed her in their tight circle of merriment. She dozed off, dreaming of rings and weddings and being absolutely certain that everything would work out perfectly.

Chapter Twelve

"Would you sit?"

Mary Darlington was behind the desk in her office, and she gestured for Emily to take the chair across. This was a formal meeting, the sort Mary hated to hold, and she didn't want Emily to suppose they were about to have a friendly chat.

Her expression was very grim, but she couldn't force herself to seem happy. She liked Emily very much, but her business came first. The world was a hard place for a female, and Mary didn't dare engage in any conduct that might tarnish her reputation.

Women didn't generally travel on their own, and they didn't feel comfortable residing in a hotel. She tried to run an exemplary establishment, where there would never be a reason to complain about the service Mary offered. Her every action revolved around that issue. Her rules had to be followed to the letter. She never made exceptions and, when an infraction was committed, she never showed any mercy.

"You look terribly glum," Emily said. "What's wrong?"

"We have to have another awkward discussion," she said, "and it's exhausting me. It's about your cousin again."

"Oh, no," Emily murmured. "What's she done now? After you and I talked the other afternoon, I was very blunt with her. I was certain she'd listened to me."

"Well, she didn't listen, and you needn't talk to her again. I'm afraid we're far beyond that point."

Emily frowned with dismay. "What are you saying?"

"She stayed out all night. I informed the two of you about the curfew when you initially arrived, and you insisted you understood it. I explained that there would be ramifications if you ignored it."

"She was in her bed this morning when I awakened."

"She snuck in as the sun was peeking over the horizon."

"Are you sure?" Emily asked.

Mary's scullery maid was lurking in the corner, and Mary motioned for her to step forward. "Tell Miss Shaw what you observed."

"I was lighting the fires, Miss Shaw," the girl said. "Your cousin crept up the rear stairs. Her hair was down and her clothes disturbed. She'd removed her slippers so she could tiptoe in without anyone hearing her."

Mary added, "I can't figure out how she got inside. I checked the locks myself before I retired, but she managed it somehow."

Her words fell like an anvil, crashing between her and Emily like a hammer bashing at their relationship. The maid glanced at Mary, appearing nervous and wary, and Mary shooed her out.

She and Emily were silent until her strides faded, then Emily said, "I'm so sorry—and so embarrassed. What should I do?"

"*You* need do nothing. You can tarry for the rest of the summer as you planned, but your cousin will have to leave. Immediately. She can find other lodging in Baywick—that's up to her—but she can't remain here."

Emily's shoulders slumped. "May I plead her case? May I beseech you to change your mind?"

"You can't change it."

Mary had evicted a few guests over the years. There were ladies who reveled in the freedom of being away from home, who forgot the boundaries of what was allowed. Previously, it hadn't been that difficult to proceed, but because of her fondness for Emily, this occasion was extremely painful.

No matter how the incident resolved, Emily would blame herself. It wasn't fair that Mary was placing the burden on Emily, but it couldn't be helped. Mary should have dragged Peggy Shaw down—after all, she was the guilty party—and had this thorny conversation with her, but it was easier to let Emily handle it.

Emily would notify her cousin of the consequences. Mary would simply hide like a coward and wait to be apprised that Peggy Shaw had left.

Tears flooded Emily's eyes, and Mary winced and said, "Don't cry. It will devastate me. I hate what's happening, and I wish there was a different route we could travel."

"These are tears of shame, and I can't tamp them down."

"You shouldn't be ashamed. This isn't your fault."

"Where was she?" Emily asked. "Have you any idea? I thought she was at the dance. I went to the theater myself, and she wasn't here when I returned. I didn't worry about it, and obviously, I should have."

"I don't care where she was, but it's clear she has an independent streak that's problematic."

"I could threaten her, so she realizes she's perched on a very sharp ledge. It might rein in her wilder proclivities. Could you permit me to try?"

"No, because I don't believe she can rein them in, and I won't twiddle my thumbs until she involves herself in trouble that would impact me."

"What if *I* guaranteed her behavior?" Emily was practically begging.

"You shouldn't vouch for her; it's a losing proposition." Emily was crestfallen, and Mary said, "I hope you can understand my position. I can't risk having my good name attached to her mischief."

"If she leaves," Emily said, "I'll have to leave with her."

"I recognize that, although—as I mentioned—you don't have to go. Or you can visit us later on. You'll always be welcome, but unfortunately, your cousin will not be."

Emily stared down at her lap. An excruciating interval wound out, and finally, she said, "I like Baywick so much. I should have known it wouldn't last."

"It's not the end of the world. You can return on your own."

"I can't imagine how I would. After I'm home, I'll never escape. It's why this sojourn meant so much to me." She pulled herself together and asked, "When would you like us to depart?"

"Now." Emily winced, and Mary said, "I can't have her on the premises another night. I apologize, and I shall pray you forgive me."

Emily waved away Mary's remark. "There's naught to forgive. This is your property, and we agreed to abide by your rules. To my great regret, Peggy has never felt that rules should apply to her."

"That's a dangerous attitude for a woman to have. Once prior, I convinced myself that I could carry on with a reckless abandon, and I was brought low quickly enough."

Emily peered around, as if confused about where she was. "I'm too bewildered to make a cogent decision. Can you advise me?"

"I've contacted the coaching inn, and they have one room available. It will give you time to figure out a plan. If you're determined to remain, you'll have to search for other lodging, but it's the height of summer, and the town is full. I can't guess if you'll succeed."

HAPPILY·EVER·AFTER 177

"I wasn't ready for my holiday to be over," Emily muttered quite miserably.

"You needn't be hasty. I can have a maid walk over and reserve the room for you. You can go there and debate your next move."

"You're being so nice to me, but I haven't earned any courtesy."

Mary leaned nearer, her gaze intent. "Don't blame yourself."

"I should have minded Peggy better, but that's been the story of my life with her. I attempt to boss her, but I can't."

"She's a hazardous character. Watch yourself with her. If you elect to tarry in Baywick, you must remember that you're visitors. Her antics will reflect badly on you."

"I'm afraid of that, so we should just head home."

"You can take the mail coach any morning or afternoon. It passes through twice a day."

Mary didn't comment further, for she suspected, despite how Emily might chastise or endeavor to fetter her cousin, it wouldn't help. Peggy Shaw seemed like the type who would bluster forward and break things, but a female couldn't conduct herself so brazenly.

A male could, but not a female. It was an unwritten law that governed the world.

She waited, studying her friend and simply eager for the terrible meeting to be over. Eventually, Emily stood and said, "Thank you for permitting me to stay with you. It was much too brief, but I loved every minute."

"Come back on your own," Mary said. "You'll be welcome."

"Or I might get lucky and rent other accommodations. We could still see each other occasionally."

Mary doubted that would happen, but she said, "If you locate something, send me a note. Or if you depart for Hexham, let me know that too. And write to me after you've arrived. We should correspond."

"I would like that very much."

Emily staggered out, then Mary motioned to a maid who'd been hovering in the hall.

"The Shaw cousins are checking out," Mary told her. "Have someone run to the coaching inn for me. Tell them we'll reserve their final room."

"I'll deal with it immediately."

"Give the two ladies a half hour to chat about their situation, then knock on their door and apprise them that you're there to pack their bags. I want them gone without delay."

The staff was aware of what had transpired, that the eviction was imminent so, at Mary's command, the woman didn't so much as raise a brow. She merely nodded and said, "I'll handle all of it for you. Don't fret."

She hurried out, and Mary exhaled a weary sigh. She struggled to never be hardhearted or cruel, but often, cruelty was required. She'd like Emily to return in the future, but for the moment, Mary had to assume she'd never see her again.

"Stop nagging. Please!"

Peggy glared at Emily, and for once, Emily glared back, which was surprising. Normally, Emily was the most placid person in the kingdom. For her to exhibit any upset was bizarre, and Peggy accepted it as an indication of how egregiously she'd mucked up their summer.

"Are you even sorry?" Emily asked.

"Yes, yes, I've admitted it a thousand times already."

"I like Mary Darlington, and we're friends. Have you any idea of how humiliating it was to sit across from her and hear that she was kicking us out? I am sick with regret."

Peggy didn't like Mrs. Darlington and thought her hotel was overrated and common, but she wouldn't mention it. Emily's standards were much lower than Peggy's. She'd never traveled before, so she was content in any base condition.

"I hate that she treated you so poorly," Peggy said, "and she shouldn't have dragged you into it. If she was angry with me, she should have spoken to me directly. It was ridiculous for her to have involved you."

"Where were you anyway? Don't tell me you were with Mr. Covington. If he was the cause of this mess, I will wring your neck."

"I wasn't with Mr. Covington," Peggy lied. "I was out with another guest."

"Doing what until dawn?"

"We went to the Gentleman's Paradise Club."

"Isn't that the gambling hall?" Emily asked.

"Yes, but females are allowed in it too. I've never been to a gambling den, and I couldn't resist." Peggy smirked when she probably shouldn't have. "It was very exciting, and I didn't realize how the hours were racing by."

"You were wagering? We don't have money to waste on such folly. What's wrong with you?"

"There were tables where we could play for tiny stakes. I recognize that matters are dire at Hexham, but surely we won't be beggared if I spend a few pennies to amuse myself."

They were at the coaching inn, having rented the very last room. When they'd first been escorted to it, Peggy had informed the proprietor that they didn't want it, but he'd snottily replied that it was this room or no room. It was small and dank, located on the main floor, next to the kitchen. Cooking odors wafted by, many of them not very appetizing, and she wouldn't be in any rush to eat their food. She refused to dawdle in such a wretched place, so Emily had to get busy and find a better option.

Her revelation that she'd been wagering was too much for Emily. Her cousin lurched over to the sole chair and plopped down. She was bent over, her elbows on her knees, and she was so miserable that Peggy actually suffered an unusual wave of embarrassment. On occasion, she could be oblivious and selfish—she couldn't deny it—and she'd pushed Emily to her limit.

"I'm sorry," she said again, and she meant it. She wasn't sorry that she'd caroused all night, but she was sorry that she'd been caught, sorry Emily was so distressed, sorry Mrs. Darlington had scolded her. "I didn't think I'd committed a horrible crime, and I can't believe it's blown up into such a huge morass."

"You were aware of Mrs. Darlington's rules, Peggy. Why must you always behave like this? Why can't you just act as is expected of you?"

"I was having fun." Peggy was nearly boasting, as if that explanation could wipe away any sin.

"Was it worth it to stir all this trouble?"

Peggy thought it categorically had been, but she didn't suppose she should admit it. Instead, she said, "I apologize that the ramifications have impacted you, but what now? What should we do?"

"We should head home—tomorrow on the mail coach."

Peggy's entire body was gripped with alarm. She couldn't leave Baywick, couldn't leave Archie. "No, absolutely not. Florence sent us to enjoy the summer, and we're staying."

"How will we? The town is packed with visitors, and even if we could stumble on an available spot, it wouldn't be appropriate. Mrs. Darlington specifically catered to young ladies. If we move into a more general type of hotel, who can predict what kind of seedy environment we'd encounter?"

"Don't worry so much. We'll be fine."

"I'm not certain we will be, so you have to prepare yourself. I'm not convinced we should tarry. Not when you've disgraced yourself like this. I'm shocked by your antics, and I'm writing to Florence to ask her advice. I'm positive she'll order us to depart immediately."

Peggy scowled. "Why would you bother Florence? She's sick, and we shouldn't disturb her. We're adults. We had to relinquish our lodging, but there have to be other choices that would suit us."

"I don't know, Peggy." Emily appeared exhausted and mortified. "I'm too ashamed to ever bump into Mary Darlington again. Can't we go home? Won't you agree?"

The more Emily whined, the more obstinate Peggy became. She wouldn't allow a witch like Mrs. Darlington to chase them away. She wouldn't allow a tattling servant to ruin their summer. She had to be near Archie, and until he took the necessary steps to make their amour official, she couldn't vanish.

"How about this?" she said. "Let's at least search before we give up. Florence was so excited about our trip, and she'd be disappointed if we returned early."

It was easy to manipulate Emily by mentioning Florence, and it always worked. "I suppose we can try, but only for a day or two. If we don't succeed right away, we're leaving and that's that."

"Would you quit looking so glum? I'm always lucky, and you're the optimist in our dynamic duo. Can't you pretend we'll manage it? Just for me?"

Emily tamped down a furious retort, then said, "You have to swear your nonsense is ended. You have to promise you'll behave better in the future. I can't deal with you when you act like this."

"I swear I will be the most boring person you've ever met." Emily snorted with disgust, then pushed herself to her feet and trudged to the door. Peggy asked, "Where are you going?"

"I'll speak with the proprietor about where to start any search for a room, and I shall pray Mrs. Darlington didn't tell him she kicked us out."

"Would she have?"

"She probably wouldn't have gossiped, but her servants might have. If so, then every other establishment will be closed to us."

Emily left, and Peggy sat, letting the air settle. There was a desk in the corner, with a writing tray on it. She went over and penned a note to Archie, informing him of what had happened. He would be greatly humored by her breaking curfew, by her being caught.

She folded the letter and stuck it in the bodice of her dress, then she snuck out to the barn to locate a stableboy who could deliver it to Wave Crest.

Archie was so fond of her. When he learned of her troubles, she had no doubt he'd gallop to their rescue, like a knight on a white charger. She couldn't guess what miracle he might provide, but he'd built the bloody town. Surely he could fix their paltry lodging problem.

She imagined him blustering in, imagined Emily's stunned face when they were saved by him. It would be the perfect conclusion.

JAMES WAS RELAXED IN his carriage and riding through Baywick. He'd been chafing at Wave Crest, and he'd begun to feel trapped, so he'd had his driver harness the vehicle so he could tour the surrounding countryside.

The road meandered down the coast, and there were rolling hills that opened up to cliffs and ocean vistas. Several times, he'd had the man stop, and he'd climbed out to soak in the views. Eventually, he'd have to slither back to London. He had his rural estate of Roxbury too, as well as numerous other properties he'd inherited with the title.

He needed to put in an appearance at all of them, but for the moment, he was so content in Baywick. Perhaps it should be his permanent residence.

As he'd been sightseeing, the weather had turned, a storm blowing in, so his leisurely excursion had been cut short. It was raining, fat drops plopping on the roof, so his driver had to be miserable, but James wasn't in any rush.

He'd thought Emily might be out walking, and he'd bump into her. He'd told her he'd arrange another supper party, and he was ready to send out the invitations. The news would have furnished him with an excuse to pull over and chat, but he hadn't stumbled on her. To escape the deluge, pedestrians had hurried to their destinations, so the streets were empty.

He'd considered popping into the hotel to surprise her, but that was an insane idea, so he'd continued on past without making a fool of himself.

He was approaching the edge of the town, the coaching inn up ahead, when he noticed a woman entering the main yard. She was unprepared for the torrent, with no cloak or umbrella, and she staggered along blindly. Her condition was incredibly bedraggled, and she was morosely hunched over, as if she'd lost her last friend.

He studied her, then blanched with dismay. Was it Emily? Out in the rain? What was she thinking?

He pounded on the roof, and his driver yanked the horses to a halt. He jumped out and raced after her.

"Emily!" he called, his summons drowned out by a crack of thunder, so he tried again. "Emily! Is that you?"

She froze and straightened, then peered over at him. "James? What are you doing here?"

"I was passing by, and I saw you. You silly girl! Why are you out and about?"

He marched over and clasped hold of her hands. They were cold as ice, and she was completely drenched. How long had she been outside? Was she mad?

"You're in a desperate state," he said. "What's wrong? Why are you so far from the hotel? Why are you out in this tempest?"

"Oh, James, I'm having the worst time, but I'm too dejected to discuss it. I simply have to get inside, so I can dry off and warm myself."

He frowned. "You're staying at the coaching inn? When did that happen?"

"It doesn't matter when. I can't talk about it. Please forgive me, but I'm too uncomfortable for words. I'll explain later."

He wasn't about to let her flee. He tightened his grip and led her toward his carriage, and he lifted her in and sat her down. He couldn't bear how she was shivering, and there was a drawer under the seat, where he kept a cache of supplies.

He opened it and retrieved a woolen blanket that he draped over her shoulders. There was a flask too, that was filled with whiskey, and he pressed it to her lips.

"Take a drink," he said. She shook her head, but he was insistent. "Just a few swallows. It will start your blood flowing. Do it for me?"

She was malleable as a baby and offered no further protest. She downed several gulps as he'd demanded.

As they'd stood out on the road, he'd assumed her cheeks were wet from the rain, but it was clear she'd been crying. He couldn't stand to suppose she was distraught, and his heart lurched in his chest.

"Why aren't you at Mrs. Darlington's?" he said. "You have to tell me."

"I'm too embarrassed to confess it."

"It's obvious you've suffered a small catastrophe. Apprise me of what's occurred, and allow me to fix it for you."

"You have no obligation to fix it, and it would be presumptuous of me to bother you."

"I've been loafing all afternoon because I'm so bored, so I would be delighted to expend a bit of energy on your behalf. In fact, you'd be doing me a favor if you charged me with a task."

"We were evicted by Mrs. Darlington." She spoke the comment so quietly that, initially, he wasn't sure he'd heard her correctly.

"I don't believe it!" he said. "How could you have upset her?"

"It wasn't me; it was Peggy. She was out carousing until dawn, which is against the rules, and we were kicked out."

"You had to move with no notice or warning?"

"Yes, and tonight is our last night," she said. "I've been trying to find other lodging, but I've had no luck. We're going home in the morning."

The pronouncement was like a punch in the gut. She couldn't go! If she wasn't in Baywick with him, what was the point of anything?

"You can't leave," he said.

"I've exhausted every lead, so we have no choice but to depart."

"You should have contacted me."

She gaped at him as if he was deranged. "Why would I have?"

"I could have helped you."

"If I'm having difficulties, it's none of your affair."

"We're friends though, aren't we? Of course I should be permitted to assist you. You should have come to me immediately."

"And begged you to do what?"

She looked totally bewildered, and he couldn't decide how to proceed, so he kissed her. He dipped in and brushed his lips to hers.

"Why are you crying?" he asked.

"I've been walking all day, meeting with landlords who were rude and dismissive. Then I was trapped out in the rain. I feel as if the universe has cursed me."

"I'm here now, so there's no reason to lament. We'll devise a solution. You're being overly dramatic, and this is not as bad as it seems. Not from my perspective anyway."

"I'm so sad!" she said, his remark unleashing a flood of despair, "and I'm so angry at my cousin. I'm mortified that Mary Darlington was caught in the middle of it. Peggy is so inconsiderate, but I'm the one who's impacted by her awful behavior. She couldn't care less. I've searched everywhere for other accommodations, but she's barely left our room. She treats me as if I'm her servant, and she blames me for failing to rent something. We have to go home, but I don't want to go home! It means I'll never see you again!"

Her voiced grievances brought on a wave of misery, and she began to weep, so he snuggled her to his chest.

He'd never previously comforted a distraught woman, and he was stunned to discover that he liked it very much. Her anguish niggled at his masculine instincts, so he yearned to protect her from harm. She was a damsel in distress, and he should rescue her.

He held her until there were no tears remaining. She was limp as a ragdoll, her limbs rubbery, as if her bones had melted.

While she'd vented her woe, his mind had been busily working, struggling to deduce the best way to aid her. The answer, when it occurred to him, was so obvious that he was shocked it had taken so long to figure it out.

"You have to excuse me, James," she eventually said, "but I need to change my clothes and start packing."

"You're not leaving," he told her.

"Weren't you listening? I have no other option."

"There's one option you haven't pondered, and it will be perfect."

"What are you talking about?" she asked. "I've investigated the whole town, and there's no place available. I'm sure of it."

"It's a spot you haven't thought of, and I guarantee there is plenty of space for you and your cousin."

She scowled. "Where is it?"

"Wave Crest. You're coming there with me, and I won't hear any argument to the contrary."

She was horrified. "I can't stay with you at Wave Crest."

"Yes, you can. Who is there to tell you that you can't? I'm delighted by the idea, and my opinion is the only one that counts."

Chapter Thirteen

"Surprise!"

At hearing the female voice, Archie whipped around, being stunned to find Margaret Shaw peeking out of a Wave Crest bedroom.

"Margaret?" he asked, his shock evident. "Am I hallucinating?"

She frantically motioned for him to walk over to her, and she grabbed his wrist and pulled him inside.

"Did you get my letter?" she asked. He must have looked confused by the question, because she hurried to say, "About our being evicted by Mrs. Darlington?"

"Oh, yes, I got it. I was astonished to learn she'd treat you that way. Particularly when you're a special friend of mine. I've been working my fingers to the bone, trying to locate other lodging for you."

He'd always been a convincing liar, and she flashed a worshipful smile. "The minute I realized we were in trouble, I just had to contact you."

"What happened with Mrs. Darlington? You mentioned something about coming in late."

"Yes, she has a curfew, remember? I broke it the night we were gambling. I didn't return to the hotel until dawn."

"You scamp! You're so naughty. I distinctly recall warning you to be careful."

"A housemaid saw me, and the little witch tattled."

Archie tsked with exasperation. "I hate servants who feel free to interfere with their betters."

"Don't I know it. If I was still residing there, I'd wring her scrawny neck. But guess what?"

"What?" He was so bewildered to have her on the premises that he couldn't form a coherent sentence.

"I'm staying here! With you!"

"How did that happen?"

"Your brother swooped in and rescued us. He ran into my cousin, Emily, and when she shared our tale of woe, he tossed us in his carriage and brought us home."

"Are you joking? I simply can't fathom James being so accommodating. How could she move him to be so generous?"

"I think he fancies her."

"You're right, of course. I'd forgotten about his odd infatuation."

He'd seen James kissing the blasted woman out in the driveway, but it seemed too peculiar to be believed. After surviving his ordeal in the Arctic North, he was half mad, so it was completely typical that he'd glom onto a fetching commoner.

"He's agreed to help us," Margaret said, "because he's so fond of her. Isn't that hilarious?"

She raised an impish brow, being incredibly humored by Archie's deranged brother, and Archie wondered about Emily Shaw. Obviously, the amour would end badly for her. There was no benefit for her to participate, but as Margaret was proving, a highborn gentleman could coax a lowborn female into some very stupid behavior.

"I'm amazed by the entire situation," he said.

"I'm amazed too, but I'm even more delighted. We can be together constantly. With our being locked away in the same house, it won't seem strange if we socialize."

"Our flirtation will definitely be easier to accomplish."

"That's my exact opinion."

"And I won't implement any curfews," he said. "If we decide to revel until dawn, who is there to tell us we can't?"

Even as he uttered the comments, his mind was busy, assessing the dangers, the advantages, and the problems her presence might create.

His mother would arrive the following week, and she was planning to tarry for the remainder of the summer. She never interfered with Archie's schemes, and if he was caught in mischief, she always took his side, so she was irrelevant to any conduct he might instigate with Margaret. If Archie seduced her, his mother wouldn't care.

What about Margaret herself? From how gleefully she was preening, it was clear his nefarious strategy toward her was succeeding apace. When she gazed at him, she'd be hearing wedding bells, so she'd want to make him happy.

He was gleefully picturing her in her nightclothes and being tucked away down the hall. He would be able to sneak in for naughty visits, so he'd have many more chances to coerce her into tawdry acts she should never attempt.

In the few encounters they'd managed so far, he'd worked to push her down the carnal road, but she always called a halt just as matters grew interesting. He supposed she was holding out until she had a ring on her finger, but he'd dealt with many girls like her, and he had numerous tricks up his sleeve that would bring him what he craved.

He was still playing his lewd game with his friends, still trying to be the first one to fornicate with an unsuspecting young lady before the summer was through. Margaret Shaw was the perfect candidate, and she'd wound up right where he needed her to be.

They'd been huddled by the door, murmuring quietly, but footsteps sounded out in the hall. They froze, listening as a maid walked by.

Archie couldn't be discovered in her bedchamber. James had warned him to leave her alone, so Archie didn't dare defy him. Not overtly anyway. When a maiden's virtue hung in the balance, it was worth a bit of risk to continue the pursuit. The prospect of dire consequences was thrilling, and the chase was very fun.

"I should go," he whispered, once it was silent again. "We can't be so reckless, not when you've only just strolled in."

She flashed a saucy grin. "Perhaps you can tiptoe in later. After everyone is asleep?"

Had any man in history ever received a more blatant invitation? She was practically begging to be ruined. Why not oblige her?

"I will eagerly ponder your exhilarating suggestion, Miss Shaw."

He winked, then hurried away. He didn't glance back to see if she was watching him depart. He doubted she was. No, she'd be dreamily staring out the window and aquiver with ecstasy over the opportunities that James had produced by delivering her to Wave Crest.

Girls could be so silly.

He bristled with disgust, then rushed off to find James and inquire as to how long he expected the Shaw cousins to tarry. How much time would Archie have to carry out his plan to the bitter end?

"It's like we're living in a fairytale."

Emily glared at Peggy and said, "Don't get used to it."

"Why shouldn't I? Wave Crest is so beautiful, and Lord Roxbury is delighted to have us as his company."

"No, he's not. We've imposed horribly, and he's being unusually kind."

"Aristocrats are never kind to people like us. Not unless they have an ulterior motive. What could his be?" Peggy pretended to speculate, then she said, "Might it be that you've charmed him, and he's determined to be closer to you?"

"It's nothing like that. He simply stumbled on me when I was in a hideous condition, and he felt sorry for me."

"I've been told that his Arctic expedition turned him to stone, but maybe he still has a heart beating in his chest."

"Peggy!" Emily snapped. "We're not denigrating him under his own roof. Speak politely about him or don't speak about him at all."

Emily frowned over at the door to ensure it was tightly shut. They were ensconced in the pretty bedchamber James's housekeeper had opened for her, and they were about to head down to supper.

Several of Mr. Covington's friends were visiting again, so it would be a table of boisterous, obnoxious dandies. Their conversations were laced with comments and innuendo that bordered on the risqué, but never quite crossed into inappropriate territory.

Emily assumed she and Peggy would be the sole females in attendance. Hopefully, their presence would prevent the dialog from growing too ribald.

She tamped down a scoff of annoyance. She'd like to wish them all to perdition, but she wasn't in a position to complain about any issue. She especially couldn't protest the type of guests James welcomed.

He'd rescued her from disaster, and when he'd been so sympathetic, she could only smile and be grateful for what had been offered. She didn't dare have an opinion about much of anything.

If Archie Covington chose to fraternize with a group of rogues, it wasn't any of her business, and the situation wasn't exactly improper. It wasn't as if she was locked away with a pair of bachelors. She and Peggy were together. Maids had been appointed to tend them, and James's stepmother would join them shortly.

If Emily and Peggy were still in residence when she arrived, there would be an older woman to lend them an air of respectability. Emily had to stop fretting so much.

Peggy was dressed and ready to descend to the front parlor, but Emily had been fussing with her hair, anxious for it to be perfectly styled. She went over to the bed to select the fan she'd take with her. She'd brought three of them from Hexham, and none of them seemed right. She was so nervous!

With James fetching her into his home, their liaison had been pushed to a new level that was very dangerous. She felt as if she was auditioning for an actress's role, but she hadn't learned her lines.

"How long will Lord Roxbury let us stay?" Peggy asked.

"I can't guess how he views it, but I intend that our sojourn will be very brief."

"Don't be ridiculous. We should presume on his generosity for the whole summer."

"You can just get that bizarre notion out of your head. We won't dawdle one second longer than we have to."

Peggy shrugged. "We'll see what happens."

"I need you to swear that you'll behave yourself. I can't have you engaging in mischief that might reflect badly on him."

"You're worried about me?" Peggy snickered disdainfully. "He fancies you. If anyone requires a lecture on moral conduct, isn't it you?"

Emily was unwilling to have a discussion about her relationship with James. She couldn't explain it, and she certainly couldn't justify it.

"I will continue to look for a room in Baywick," she said.

Peggy groaned. "Don't do it, Em! Why waste the energy when we can remain here instead?"

"I refuse to be a burden."

"Roxbury won't mind if you tarry. In fact, I'll bet he's devising ways to keep you from ever leaving."

"In the deluded world where you wander, I'm sure that's true, but you have completely misconstrued what's occurring. I was in a desperate situation, and he assisted me. It's temporary! I will search for lodging in town, and I'll give it two weeks. If I have no luck, we'll return to Hexham. That's what we should have done anyway. I shouldn't have listened to Lord Roxbury."

"I'm relieved you did though, and I will work valiantly to frustrate your efforts to rent a dreary room. I won't allow you to act like a fool."

They were on the verge of a quarrel, and she couldn't bear to bicker, not when they were about to go down and mingle with Archie Covington's friends.

"Promise me I won't be embarrassed by any of your antics," she pleaded. "If I ever have to sit through a meeting with Roxbury, like the one I sat through with Mrs. Darlington, I'll throw myself off a cliff."

Peggy chuckled maliciously. "Well, there are plenty of cliffs nearby, so you'll be able to locate one easily enough."

"Peggy! Don't joke about this."

"Will you cease your agonizing? I will be so meek and modest that people will start to wonder if I'm a saint."

"Don't be smart. Be good. Be sensible for a change."

"You're such a fusspot."

"I notice you haven't promised," Emily said, sounding like a scold.

Peggy rolled her eyes. "I *promise* Emily, and we'll become Roxbury's favorite guests. He'll beg us to stay forever, so do your part to charm him, won't you? Let's have him chomping at the bit to keep you here. Then he will keep *me* here too."

Peggy swept out, and Emily grumbled with exasperation, then followed her to the stairs.

"Lord Roxbury! There you are."

Peggy smiled at the elusive nobleman. She'd hunted everywhere and had finally stumbled on him on the rear verandah as he was about to walk down and stroll in the dark garden.

During the evening's socializing, he'd been mostly invisible, so there hadn't been a single second where she could have chatted with him, and they definitely needed to converse. The blasted man was totally infatuated with Emily, and his fondness was so blatant that it was almost painful to witness.

Peggy should have been jealous that Emily had gotten so fortunate, but she wasn't. Roxbury was too old, too grouchy, and too peculiar, so Emily could have him. But could Emily be persuaded to *want* him?

Her cousin could be so silly. How often did a young lady of limited means even cross paths with an earl? To have him besotted was incredibly strange, and Emily ought to be more excited about the opportunities it presented. She ought to be scheming as to how she could improve her future, but she wasn't a conniver, and her mind didn't work in devious ways.

"Hello, Miss Shaw." The Earl nodded politely, but it was clear he was eager to escape. "How are you liking Wave Crest?"

"It's absolutely divine. I'm comfortably settled in my bedchamber, and your staff has been more than kind. I'm very grateful to you."

He waved away her words. "I hated to have you experiencing difficulties, and I was glad to pitch in and help."

"Your property is so beautiful." She exhaled a weary sigh. "I'll miss it very much when we depart."

"There's no hurry. I informed your cousin that you're welcome to tarry for as long as you like."

"That's a sweet sentiment, but Emily is already gearing up to search for lodging in town again." He scowled at the news, and she leaned in and murmured, "She insists we're imposing on you. Are we imposing? I hope you can assure me we're not. I couldn't bear to suppose we're a burden."

"You're not a burden, and what's this about Miss Emily searching for lodging?"

Peggy snorted with annoyance. "I probably shouldn't have mentioned it."

"No, no, tell me what she's up to."

"She's determined not to be a bother, and she's convinced herself that she can find a suitable arrangement. I complained that she won't, but she won't listen to me. If she doesn't rent a room for us by next week, we'll head home."

He froze, and she perceived a thousand remarks flying to the tip of his tongue, but he couldn't voice any of them. He was pursuing such an inappropriate amour with Emily that he couldn't refer to it aloud. He really ought to be ashamed of himself.

Emily was gullible and trusting, and she never harbored negative opinions about others. He could lure her into any dicey scandal, and Emily wouldn't recognize the dangers until it was too late. Yet it was the habit of aristocratic men that they believed they had the right to reach out and seize whatever they craved.

If Roxbury desired Emily, he would likely obtain what he sought in the end, so where would that leave her cousin? Nowhere good, but Peggy couldn't worry about Emily. Archie was at Wave Crest, so Peggy had to remain on the premises too. She couldn't be thwarted in her goal of winning him merely because Emily shouldn't be in close proximity to Roxbury.

"Don't concern yourself with lodging or any other issue," he ultimately said. "This house is huge, and we have plenty of space. There's no reason for you to return to Baywick."

"I've explained that to Emily, but she can be very stubborn. She's fretting about *you* and how you view our arrival."

"I'm fine with it." He seemed irked with Emily, which was what Peggy had been trying to accomplish. "If I hadn't wanted you here," he said, "I wouldn't have invited you."

"I'm delighted to hear it, and I thank you again for being so kind."

"I'll talk to your cousin," he firmly stated. "I'll point out how ridiculous she's being."

"I shall pray you have better luck than I did."

"She'll heed me," he said like a threat, and he motioned toward the manor. "Some of the men are starting a card game. They were looking for a fourth player."

She knew when she'd been dismissed, and she grinned. "I'm a great and relentless card player, so I will pull up a chair and beat them soundly. I love putting arrogant oafs in their places."

He chuckled, then continued down into the garden. It was a small party, with no couples in attendance, so the lamps weren't lit to encourage strolling. The moon was up though, so he could easily see his way.

She watched him until he was swallowed up by the shadows, then she smirked with amusement. Men were such simple creatures, and she understood them so well. She ought to write an instruction book so other women would have a clearer idea of how to handle them.

By morning, Roxbury would have persuaded Emily that they would reside with him for the rest of the summer. Peggy had no doubt about it.

Hopefully, Emily would keep him busy and happy. Peggy needed him distracted, so he wouldn't notice her as she carried out her own scheme against his brother. In another week or so, she'd have her life organized precisely how it was meant to be.

Chapter Fourteen

EMILY STIFLED A YAWN and entered her bedchamber. It had been a hectic day, and her nerves were frayed. She'd like to fall into bed and sleep for a week.

Mr. Covington's supper party was raging in the lower parlors. He and his friends would probably still be gamboling when she came down to breakfast.

As she'd headed up the stairs, she'd dragged Peggy up with her. There weren't any other female guests on the premises, so it wouldn't have been proper for her to have tarried with a group of such raucous, boisterous men.

They'd quarreled over whether Peggy would oblige her or not, but in the end, Emily had won the argument. Peggy had accompanied her, which was a relief, but a frustration too. Why was every little incident with her cousin such a battle?

Suddenly, a man said, "I didn't think you'd ever call it a night."

She jumped and whipped around to find James slouched on a chair in the corner.

"What are you doing?" she demanded. "You can't assume this is all right. Are you mad?"

"Yes, we've established, over and over, that I'm quite mad. Besides, it's your fault that I snuck in."

"How could it be my fault?"

"I waited for you out in the garden, but you never arrived."

"I took a stroll five different times myself, but I never bumped into you."

"We didn't cross paths, so if I want to be alone with you, I guess I have to do it in here."

"You're not staying."

She went and peeked into the hall. It was empty, and she motioned for him to depart, but he simply motioned to her instead, urging her to walk over to him.

She tsked with exasperation and shut the door. "Aren't you listening? You can't stay!"

"It's my house," he said like a bully, "and I can enter any room I choose."

"Yes, you can, but not while *I* am in one of them and getting ready for bed. What if your brother found out? What if a servant saw us? I'd never survive the shame."

"You are my special friend. Who would dare to criticize you?"

His view of the dilemma was absolutely typical. If they were caught, no disgrace would attach to him. It would completely crush her though.

She was still over by the door, hovered like a frightened rabbit. It was annoying to be so anxious, but she couldn't quell her unease. Deep inside, she was positively gleeful over his appearance, and she was worried about what she might ultimately allow.

He grew tired of her disobeying his grand self, so he stood and marched over to her. She watched him approach, and it was very strange, but she felt as if her destiny was unfolding, as if her whole life had been leading her directly to this moment.

Without her understanding his intent, he scooped her up and proceeded to the bed. He tossed her onto it and tumbled down after her. She wound up flat on her back, with him stretched out atop her. It had happened so fast that there wasn't a single second where she could have protested.

Before she could complain, he dipped down and kissed her. It was quite a desperate embrace too, and he gave her no opportunity to wonder if she should participate or not. She simply leapt in and kissed him back with an equal amount of enthusiasm.

They continued forever, and at the beginning, it was incredibly passionate and even a bit frantic and rough. Gradually though, it became more tender and affectionate. He broke off to nibble her cheek, her neck and nape, sending goosebumps down her arms. All the while, he was whispering endearments about how glad he was that she was with him, how delighted he was that they could be together.

His words were hazardous to her moral compass, for they pulled at a thread of feminine longing. She wanted to be the woman he cherished, and she couldn't tamp down the torrent of yearning he stirred.

Eventually, he shifted off her and onto his side. She rolled too so they were nose to nose. They grinned like naughty schoolchildren.

"Are you feeling better?" he asked.

"Much better, but that doesn't mean you can loaf in here. One of us has to use some common sense, and obviously, it won't be you. If we are to muddle through this quagmire you've created by inviting me to Wave Crest, we have to establish some ground rules as to how we'll interact."

"Why would we have to have any rules? This is my castle and I'm king of it. That's all you need to know."

"You can't just barge in and tantalize me like this," she said.

"Ha! I already did, so your comment is ludicrous."

"You're aware of what I'm telling you, James. You demanded I move to Wave Crest, and I'm very grateful for it, but am I safe with you or not?"

He scowled. "What an absurd question. Why wouldn't you be safe?"

"I am a spinster who is far from home, so I'm very vulnerable. I can't permit you to exacerbate my low condition."

He smirked. "Your cousin told me a secret about you."

"Oh, no. What was it? I'm almost afraid to inquire."

"She claims you're planning to resume your search for lodging in Baywick."

She considered denying the charge, then decided there was no reason to be furtive. "Yes, I intend to search."

"I'm not about to let you, so you can shove that ridiculous notion right out of your pretty little head."

"Well, we can't remain with you. By your tiptoeing into my room—the first night I'm in residence too!—it's patently clear that we oughtn't to wallow in such close proximity. It's too dangerous."

"I've always liked some danger in my circumstances. Life is more interesting that way."

"I don't like it at all. I refuse to provide you with unlimited chances to ruin what's left of my good reputation. I'm lucky I'm a stranger in Baywick. If people were acquainted with me and realized why I fled the coaching inn, I'd be destroyed by gossip."

"I never worry about gossip."

"Of course you don't. You're a rich gentleman from a prominent family, but I'm just an ordinary female from a small village in the country. You can act however you like, but I don't dare."

He shrugged. "Bernice will arrive in a few days, so any difficulties about your being on the premises will be corrected."

"Bernice is your stepmother?"

"Yes, and Archie's mother."

"Do you swear she's coming?"

"Would I lie about it?"

"Maybe, and I'm terrified that rumors will filter into Baywick."

"Why would you care? As you mentioned, you're not from here. If there are idiots who are determined to titter and snicker, let them."

"I care about Mary Darlington and what she might hear. She and I are friends, and if she discovered that I'd flitted off with you, I'd be so embarrassed."

He scoffed with irritation. "You fret over the silliest issues."

"I have to fret. I don't have the luxury of an important name that would allow me to misbehave. Even if no one in the area knows who I am, I wouldn't like to have lurid tales circulating."

He laughed. "I promise we will stir no lurid tales."

"Don't joke about it, and you must promise me you won't sneak in again."

"I can't promise that because I wouldn't be sincere, but we should agree to this: We'll both tarry at Wave Crest until the beginning of September. Wasn't that your original schedule? To dawdle for the summer? We should agree we'll do that."

"I will—if I can find a place for Peggy and me."

"Hello, Emily! Hello!" He tapped a playful finger on her ear as if it was plugged. "You've found it! You will stay with me, and we're not arguing about it."

He was smiling at her so affectionately. She'd never had a man stare at her as he was staring, and she was starting to yearn and crave in a manner that was insane. She wanted to consent to whatever he requested, wanted to give him whatever he sought. She was eager to make him happy and damn the consequences.

Her desire to please him was alarming. She was swiftly ignoring every rule she'd ever learned about moral conduct. There was the added problem too that he was a nobleman, and there were always horror stories about aristocrats. They thought they were better than everyone else, so they were selfish and greedy.

By dallying with him, she was risking very much, while he was risking nothing. If he trifled with her, he would be carrying on exactly as was expected. But if *she* dabbled with him, and her errors were ever exposed, she'd be ruined.

He could never flirt with pure motives. They could never bond as equals, could never enjoy a beautiful and satisfying amour. It was impossible. Yet recognizing all of that, understanding all of that, she opened her mouth, and the words that emerged were, "I guess I can remain with you until September."

He snickered with amusement. "That wasn't so hard, was it?"

"It was pretty hard."

She was frowning, and he put his thumb on her forehead and rubbed away the worry lines that were forming.

"I wish you weren't so nervous about this," he said. "You seem so miserable."

"I'm not miserable. I'm delighted to be here, but I'm scaring myself because, when I'm with you, I constantly make bad choices. I'm afraid of where it will take me."

"It will all work out. We'll be fine."

He shifted onto his back, and he pulled her to him, so she was draped over his chest. She lay very still and absorbed every detail, committing them to memory so she'd never forget.

"Could I ask you a question?" she said after a comfortable silence.

"You can ask, but I can't guarantee I'll answer. Or I might answer, but I won't tell you the truth."

She pinched the skin at his waist, and he chuckled.

"Be serious," she said.

"I am being serious. You're a female and I'm a male. When the Good Lord created the world, he set me above you. If I need to spew a falsehood—for your own benefit—then I will."

She snorted with mock offense. "You're being incredibly arrogant, and I hate an arrogant man."

"You don't hate me."

"You're correct; I don't." She sighed, anxious to push on. "After we go our separate ways, what do you envision happening?"

"I haven't reflected on it overly much, but I imagine we'll have a wonderful summer, filled with interesting activities, then we'll . . . we'll . . ."

He cut off, and she could sense he was scowling. She rose up on an elbow, so she could observe his expression. He looked terribly vexed.

"You must realize why I've inquired," she said. "We will be fond all summer, then we'll part as if we're strangers. How will we manage that precisely? Will we ever see each other again?"

"Probably not."

"Would we correspond?"

"I doubt it," he said. "I'm a very lazy letter writer."

"Would you miss me?"

He flashed a delicious smile. "Every second."

"So we'll flirt, kiss, and grow more firmly attached, then you'll send me home with a broken heart?"

"That sounds awfully dreary. I hope it won't end like that."

She'd never been especially close with any male, so she couldn't decide if he was particularly obtuse or if obliviousness was common in the species. Could he really toss her away? Was he that coldblooded?

"You refuse to admit it," she said, "but it's shocking that you snuck into my room. If I had a father or brother to speak for me, we'd be marching to a quick wedding." She leaned in so they were nose to nose. "Are you concerned about how you're behaving toward me?"

"No one knows that I'm with you, and no one will ever know."

"You can't be sure of that."

"I'm sure enough," he said, like the haughty aristocrat he was.

"I'll climb out on a limb and suggest—if we were caught together—you'd never marry me. Is that where I am with you?" He winced with dismay, and she hurried to say, "You can spit it out. I'm not a green girl with stars in my eyes. I'm merely trying to figure out where I stand with you."

His gaze was warm and dear, but he didn't jump to offer a marriage proposal. No, he crushed her with candor. "I'm sorry, but I would never wed you, and I'm embarrassed that you've raised the possibility, for my replies will make me appear to be the worst scoundrel."

"I asked you to tell me the truth, so I can't complain when you do."

"It's nothing personal," he ludicrously told her, "but in light of the mental tribulations that I developed during my recent ordeal, I'm in no condition to pick a bride."

She thought his reticence was completely connected to her low status. She was certain, if a rich princess with a fat dowry strolled by, he'd race to the altar, but she wouldn't argue the point. Instead, she said, "What's your purpose with me then? Are you expecting to ruin me? Is that it?"

"I would never dishonor you, but would you rather I ignored you? Would you rather I sent you and your cousin home?"

"No, but I'm simply conflicted over our motives. It's morally wrong for us to dally without matrimony being the conclusion at the end."

"I grasp that fact, so will you start to view me as unethical and horrid? I never assumed I was a cad, but maybe I am."

"You may be a cad, but I'm just as complicit. I want to spend every minute by your side until I depart in September, so what does that indicate about my character? Is there a word for a female cad?"

"I don't believe there is, and I can only state that we are a very pathetic pair."

He snuggled her down again, and they were silent, pondering.

She was stunned that she'd posed her query about marriage. She shouldn't have, but she was digging herself into a very deep hole with him. Whenever she began to suppose they might have a future, she had to remember his expression when he'd responded.

He'd appeared genuinely regretful, but she'd noticed a bit of scorn there too, as if he pictured himself as being much too grand for her. No doubt he felt she'd been foolish to pester him, that she'd greatly overstepped the bounds between them.

She smiled, eager to smooth over the awkward exchange. "I will be very greedy and confess that I'd like you to be mine forever. I wish we could lock ourselves in at Wave Crest and never leave."

"I'd like that too. Let's pretend it could happen just that way."

She nestled even closer, ordering herself to be content with what she'd managed to snag for herself. She would have him for her very own for the remainder of the summer, and it was a small miracle for which she would always be grateful.

The room was quiet, the candle casting comforting shadows on the walls, and she was exhausted from the long day. She dozed off without realizing she would, and when she opened her eyes, it was full morning.

Without glancing over to check, she knew he'd left, and she wondered if he'd drifted off for awhile too. The prospect of his sleeping by her side underscored how reckless they were being. When had he tiptoed out? What if a maid had come in at dawn to light the fire? What if he'd been caught with her?

They were lucky that no scandal had arisen, but many nights would pass before she fled in September. Who could predict what mischief she would ultimately allow?

She should have been aghast at her wretched conduct, should have been ashamed of herself. At the very least, she should have been alarmed over her negligence. But she was glad she'd dared, glad she'd had him all to herself for a few hours, and she couldn't wait to be with him again—no matter what it cost.

My, my, but wasn't she in trouble?

Chapter Fifteen

PEGGY STOOD ON THE edge of the ballroom. She'd come to the public dance at The Pavilion with Archie and his friends. When they'd suggested she tag along, she'd been too excited to refuse, but the event wasn't unfolding as she'd expected, and her temper was sparking.

Their arrival had certainly enlivened the proceedings, but Peggy had danced with each of them exactly once, then she'd been left to loaf with the other wallflowers.

Her sojourn at Wave Crest wasn't as rewarding as she'd assumed it would be. She'd figured her constant presence in the manor would garner her extensive opportunities to ensnare Archie, but so far, she hadn't had any luck.

Each night after Emily and the Earl went to bed, she snuck down to revel in the downstairs parlors. Emily naïvely believed Peggy went to bed too, but after Emily vanished, Peggy rushed down to cavort with the raucous group.

She gambled and chatted with them in a charming way, proving she could fit into Archie's social world, but it hadn't moved them down the road toward matrimony. Archie had caught her a few times when she was alone and had dragged her into deserted parlors to deliver some stirring kisses, but he'd always draw away before matters could get very interesting.

He claimed he desired her desperately, but he never engaged in acts that would have led them to the altar. It was very frustrating, and she couldn't deduce how to climb out of the depressing rut where she was trapped.

He was out on the floor with another girl, and Peggy was fuming. She viewed him as *hers,* and she didn't like to share. The tune ended, and new lines formed. He asked yet another girl to step out with him. The stupid cow was grinning like a fool, simpering and cooing as if Archie walked on water, and Peggy couldn't bear it.

She slipped out to the verandah to stare at the ocean. The sight should have provided solace to raise her mood, but it didn't.

Why couldn't her plans ever work out? Why couldn't she ever latch onto the things she craved most in life? Was it too much to hope that Archie Covington would fall in love with her? Why shouldn't he?

She was pretty and vivacious. She and Archie enjoyed the same hobbies and entertainments. His friends thought she was cheery and fun. She'd be the perfect wife for him, but he treated her as if she was no one special.

She was so miserable, and she simply wanted to return to Wave Crest and lick her wounds in private. She'd ridden to town in Archie's carriage, and his driver was parked outside. She decided to seek him out and inquire as to whether he could run her home, then come back for Archie.

She had to try. If she didn't escape The Pavilion, and the merriment occurring, she might go mad.

She crept through the building to the front, then hurried down the street to where their driver was sitting on a rock wall and smoking a cheroot. He was polite and obliging, and without argument, he agreed to take her.

It as a short trip over to Wave Crest, and the house was quiet, a single lamp burning in the foyer. A lone footman was waiting up for Archie. She headed straight to her room, and he sent a maid up to tend her. She changed out of her clothes and had her hair brushed and braided for the night. She dismissed the maid, then gazed out the window.

The stars were out, and she made a dozen wishes: that Archie would propose, that it would happen soon, that they would live happily ever after.

Behind her, the door opened. She glanced over, expecting the maid had forgotten something, but to her stunned surprise, it was Archie. She could have fainted from shock.

"Why aren't you still at the dance?" she asked.

"You left without a word. I had to check that you were all right."

He closed the door and marched over to her. He kissed her sweetly, his expression warm and endearing. He'd been so tantalized by the other young ladies at The Pavilion that she was amazed he'd realized she'd departed. But he had realized it! Her morose attitude fled in an instant.

"I was so jealous," she said. "I thought we'd spend the whole evening together, but you barely noticed me."

"Don't be silly. I couldn't have showered you with any extra attention, but I watched you constantly. Couldn't you sense it?"

"No. You were focused on everyone but me."

"How could I look at another? You're meant to be mine."

He started kissing her again, and she jumped into the embrace. He'd been fierce with her previously, as if he couldn't get enough of her, and this occasion was no exception. His tongue was in her mouth, his hands in her hair. He yanked the ribbon from her braid, so he could riffle his fingers in the lengthy strands.

She was attired in just a summery nightgown. It was an older garment, white, with flowers embroidered on the bodice. It had been washed too often, so it was faded and worn. The thin fabric made it seem as if she was naked, and as he stroked his palms over her body, his hot touch scalded her.

The encounter escalated rapidly. He was easing them toward the bed, and he tumbled them onto it. Where in the past, he'd mostly been a gentleman, he was suddenly overcome by uncontrollable lust.

He wasn't particularly large in size, but with his weight crushing her, she felt trapped. He was fumbling with the buttons on his trousers, so she knew what was about to transpire.

"Archie!" she murmured, trying to squirm away. "Please! Let's stop."

"I can't stop. I love you, Margaret! Don't you love me too?"

At having him declare himself, she was nearly apoplectic with joy. "Yes, I love you too! I've been so eager to tell you, but I was worried you wouldn't like to hear it."

"We should keep on then, shouldn't we? It will seal our affection so we can never be parted. Allow me to remove your nightgown, and we'll continue on to paradise."

"I can't. We have to be married first. It's a sin if we're not."

The mention of *marriage* was like throwing cold water onto the mattress. He frowned and said, "You can't want me for a husband. I could never be worthy of you."

"I adore you, and I think you're wonderful. Of course you'd be worthy."

"You believe that? Truly?"

"Yes! I'd be so lucky to have you."

He drew away and sat on the edge of the bed, his elbows on his thighs, his head hanging down, as if he was incredibly dejected.

"Wouldn't you like us to wed?" she asked. "Wouldn't it be marvelous?"

"I would have to obtain my brother's permission." He snorted with derision. "Then I'd have to talk to my mother and persuade her, but she's so accursedly fussy, and she's never even met you. It might take years to bring them around. I'm afraid you'd grow tired of waiting for me to convince them."

"Would they really be opposed? Are you certain? Roxbury seems to like me."

Archie scoffed. "James is mentally deranged. His reasoning was scrambled during his ordeal, and he's lost his ability to behave rationally. Who can guess how he might respond? What if I asked and he refused? What would we do?"

The notion that Roxbury might reject their request was too awful to abide, and she said, "It would kill me if he declined to give us his blessing."

"It would kill me too, darling." He remained slouched over his lap, furiously pondering. Finally, he peeked at her and said, "There's another way we could accomplish it. What if we wed in secret? We could proceed without informing anyone, then, once the time was right, we'd proclaim our union. The deed would be done, so my brother's complaints would be pointless."

"That sounds terribly dodgy. What preacher would help us?"

"I'm sure this will astonish you, but my friend, Gordo, has a small church income from his father. He's officially a curate, though he never brags of his position. He's authorized to perform weddings, and if we sought his assistance, he'd marry us. He likes you, and he'd bite his tongue until we were ready to apprise the whole world."

"I wouldn't like it to be a secret," she said. "Would it have to be? Are you positive?"

"You have to remember about my brother and mother. I don't trust what their reaction might be, and if James wouldn't consent, we'd be thwarted forever."

Peggy felt as if she was standing on a very high cliff and about to jump over. A *secret* wedding would be tawdry and wrong. Marry—without telling anyone? Marry—without garnering Roxbury's blessing? Marry—without her being introduced to his mother?

Alarm bells were ringing in her mind, but they were ringing so softly she could barely hear them. Archie was offering her the exact spot in life that she'd always assumed she was destined to occupy, and he understood his mother and brother. He understood how to deal with them. Wasn't it better to forge ahead, then beg for forgiveness later on?

She was so excited, but confused over what was best. She desperately needed advice from an older, wiser female, but there was no one who could play that part. She yearned to flit down the hall, to awaken Emily and seek her opinion, but she had no doubt her prim, stuffy cousin would be aghast.

She'd order Peggy to be patient, and she'd demand Peggy take the usual route: discussions with Florence, contracts drafted, a year-long engagement, announcements in the newspapers. If Peggy insisted she couldn't tolerate any delay, that she was anxious to be Archie's bride immediately, Emily would likely rush to the Earl and tattle. She would ruin Peggy's chance.

What were the benefits of Archie's scheme? What were the detriments? On the spur of the moment, she was too overwhelmed to deliberate over them. She only knew that Archie was prepared to defy his brother so he could have her as his wife. He was that determined.

As to herself, she sensed—in a powerful way—that if she failed to reach out and seize this opportunity, it would vanish, and the wedding would never occur. He was eager to give her everything she'd ever wanted, practically on a silver platter. How could she deny him? How could she deny herself?

"What is your answer, darling?" he asked, his eyes searching hers. "Will you marry me right away? Will you make me the happiest man in the kingdom?"

"Yes, Archie, I will," she said. "When shall we do it?"

ARCHIE SMIRKED AT HIS friend, Gordo, and accepted the purse of coins Gordo delivered as his prize.

"You win the game every bloody time," Gordo protested. "I can't figure out how you manage it. Tiger and I are much more charming than you, but you always finish first."

"You don't possess my ruthless attitude. I refuse to be defeated, and women are such gullible creatures. It's simple to trick them."

"Miss Shaw is madly in love with you," Gordo pointed out. "It might be difficult to skate away from this one. She's staying in your brother's house. Are you sure you've thought this through? She's such an unpleasant girl. Very plain and ordinary too. I'd hate to have you wind up in a morass with her."

"I am a master at seduction," Archie said, "just as I am a masterful escape artist. There is no female alive who could attach a fetter to my ankle. Not unless I was inclined to have it placed there."

"You better hope that's true."

They were at Wave Crest, after having snuck into a rural church down the road. There was no caretaker or regular vicar, with both of them stopping by once a month to perform Sunday services. The building was nearly always deserted, so they'd conveniently commandeered it for his *wedding* to Margaret Shaw.

He still couldn't believe how effortlessly he'd persuaded her. He'd told her they'd need to keep it a secret, and she'd agreed without argument. He'd told her they might have to be silent for ages about their nuptials, and she'd vigorously nodded. Gad, he'd told her Gordo was a curate! And she hadn't questioned the preposterous falsehood!

Her naiveté boggled the mind. It really, really did.

There had been four men in attendance with Archie and Gordo. They were Archie's friends who were all as morally debauched as he was. They'd traveled on to Brighton, and Gordo would leave shortly too.

If someone ever tried to assert that there had been a ceremony—Margaret, for instance—they would categorically swear that they hadn't been in Baywick on the date alleged and she was a deranged liar.

"Will you join us in Brighton after you've deflowered your bride?" Gordo asked, his tone snide. "Everyone will want to chaw over the details."

It was the most amusing portion of their ruse: when they guffawed over the details. Archie couldn't show his face there though, but he didn't dare admit it.

"Actually, I'll probably tarry with her for a few days," he said. "I'll enjoy myself, then I'll meet up with you in London. By then, I'll have an excess of stories to share."

"You're a dog, Covington. Have fun, and don't do anything I wouldn't do."

"Ha! I shall do everything you'd do and quite a bit more besides."

"What will become of your Special License?" Gordo asked. "Will you frame it?"

"No, but I will burn it immediately."

A Special License was a document that could be obtained from a bishop in order to marry in a hurry. Otherwise, a month's delay was required before a couple could tie the knot. His friend, Tiger, had forged a copy, and the fake license had lent an air of credibility to the proceedings. Margaret had eagerly signed her name at the bottom.

Archie escorted Gordo out to the driveway, watching as he climbed on his horse and rode away. For a brief moment, he suffered an attack of conscience. He was a horrible person. He couldn't deny it, but Margaret was so needy and trusting. Her yearning to be noticed, to be accepted, practically oozed out of her, and her pathetic traits helped him to rationalize his conduct.

When she learned how she'd been tricked, she would be devastated, but she was very stupid. She'd behaved like an idiot and had landed herself in a terrible jam. How was that Archie's fault? He wasn't her nanny, and he had no obligation to save her from herself.

He crept into the house, being careful not to awaken anyone, then he tiptoed up the stairs. As they'd arrived back from the church, he'd sent her up to her room to get ready for bed. His phallus was hard and aching just from envisioning how entertaining the rest of the evening would be.

He'd deflower her, then he'd fornicate with her over and over. He'd keep on until he'd had his fill and was growing bored with the charade. Then . . . ? He'd return to London and resume his normal routines.

He reached her door, and he didn't bother to knock. After all, he was supposedly her husband. She was sitting on a chair by the window, attired in her nightgown. It was the one she'd worn previously, with the flowers embroidered on the bodice. The garment made her look young and fresh, like a dairymaid ripe for the plucking. Her hair was brushed and curling over her shoulders, and he realized she wasn't the homeliest girl he'd ever ruined.

She appeared timid and scared, as a virgin should be, but excitement shone in her eyes too. She couldn't wait to finally belong to him, and he would put on a good show. He spun the key in the lock, then came over to her, and he checked the clock on the mantle, having to track the time so he wasn't caught in her room.

It was nearly midnight, and the scullery maids rose around five in the morning to light the fires. It meant he had five hours to amuse himself.

He pulled her to her feet and kissed her soundly. "My darling bride," he said, whispering, "let me see how pretty you are without your clothes."

He grabbed the straps on her nightgown, quickly tugging down the fabric to bare her breasts, and she panicked and clasped his wrists.

"Must you remove it so soon?" she asked, whispering too. "Can't we chat and cuddle a bit first?"

"No, Margaret, I've been lusting after you from the minute we met, so I'm afraid I must have you naked as fast as I can accomplish it. It's a wife's duty to take off her clothes—if that's what her husband requests. I'm sure you want to please me, don't you?"

She gnawed on her cheek. "Yes, I want to please you."

"Then don't argue over what I'd like to have happen. You should never quarrel with me. We recited the vows, and you promised to obey."

"Yes, I promised, and I wasn't quarreling. I'm just nervous. I didn't think I would be, but I am."

"It's perfectly natural to be nervous, but you can't prevent me from doing whatever tickles my fancy. Now then, let's rid you of this matronly nightgown, and we'll get started."

Chapter Sixteen

"EMILY! IS THAT YOU?"

Emily spun to see Mary Darlington approaching. She smiled and hurried toward her. She hadn't crossed paths with Mary since she'd left the hotel. She'd wanted to send a note to inform her that she was still in the area, but she'd been too embarrassed to admit she was residing with James.

She couldn't clarify her current situation in a way that wouldn't sound salacious and dangerous, and Mary would never understand.

She and Peggy had walked to Baywick together. Emily had needed to escape Wave Crest for a bit, but their trek had been incredibly awkward. Peggy was in a strange mood, being unusually giggly with delight, as if she was on the verge of blurting out a great secret. In the end, she hadn't revealed what it was, and Emily hadn't pressed.

Whatever was plaguing her cousin, Emily couldn't deal with it. She was too absorbed with her own dilemma regarding James. Did she have a moral compass? Apparently not.

Peggy was shopping, and Emily had been strolling on The Promenade and waiting for her to finish. Then they'd hike back to Wave Crest. Emily was using the interval to contemplate her choices and her future.

She was falling in love with James, which was the very worst conclusion. He was an earl from a rich, prominent family, while she was plain, ordinary Emily Shaw from Hexham. It was bizarre that he'd grown fond of her, and she should have run away from his burgeoning affection, but she couldn't convince herself to flee.

He had many issues vexing him, but his mental state was quickly improving. Very soon, he wouldn't be so lonely and disturbed, so her calming influence wouldn't be required. Where would she be then? Shouldn't she save herself before she got in too deep?

The problem for her though was that she couldn't bear to part from him, and evidently, she didn't mind if she got in too deep.

She desperately yearned to discuss the predicament with someone who would listen and commiserate, and she'd like for it to be Mary. In light of her prior experience with a nobleman, she could provide valuable advice. Then again, because of her calamity, she was also the very last person in whom Emily should confide. Mary would be horrified over Emily's conduct.

"I'm amazed that you're still in Baywick," Mary said. "I was positive you'd departed. I've been watching the mail every day, hoping for a letter that would apprise me you had an uneventful trip home."

"We didn't leave. We tried to, but we wound up finding a place."

"I feel awful about what happened," Mary said, "and I'd like to wring your cousin's neck for forcing my hand. Have you forgiven me?"

"I was never angry with you, so there's nothing to forgive. It was Peggy's fault, and it's been the story of my life with her that she lands herself in jams, but the consequences pummel me."

"Where are you staying?" Mary asked. "You must tell me what sort of room you found, and if it's terrible, lie to me and claim it's beautiful. If I learn I've cast you into a hovel, I'll be so mortified."

"We're definitely not in a hovel." Emily debated, deciding she should just spit it out. "I'll confess what occurred, but you must promise you won't faint. And please don't scold me."

Mary scowled. "Is that a riddle I'm supposed to solve?"

"Let's sit down, and I'll explain what I mean."

They were next to The Promenade, and she took Mary's arm and led her to an empty bench. As they seated themselves, Mary's scowl intensified, and she said, "Are you about to share bad news?"

"You'll probably deem it to be bad, and very idiotic too, but I can't deduce how I view it."

"Isn't that clear as mud?"

"We nearly went home," Emily said. "There was no lodging to rent, and I was ready to pack my bags, then I bumped into Lord Roxbury."

"Oh, no. Why am I certain this tale won't end well?"

Emily's cheeks heated. "I'd been caught in the rain, and I was trudging to the coaching inn when he passed by in his carriage. I was wet and miserable, and he stopped to offer his assistance."

"He conveyed you to Wave Crest? Your cousin too?"

"Yes. Have I shocked you?"

Mary studied her, then shrugged. "I'm not shocked. Roxbury is a charming, famous man, and it's a huge house. He has space for two guests, but have you fully considered the ramifications?"

"Believe me, I've thought of little else since I arrived, but it's not as risqué as it sounds. Mr. Covington's mother is coming. She should be here tomorrow, so we won't be there alone."

"Well . . . good." Mary paused, then added, "Isn't it good?"

"I guess it is. I haven't been able to persuade myself that I should have accepted his hospitality."

"Has he misbehaved with you?"

"No, no, it's not that!" Emily's declaration was much too vehement. "He's been a perfect gentleman every second."

Mary looked dubious, as if she realized Emily's comment couldn't possibly be true, but she was much too polite to admit it.

"How long will you tarry there?" Mary asked.

"Until the beginning of September. That was my original plan. Am I being extremely rash?"

"I'm not the best judge of what's rash about this. Where noblemen are concerned, I'm too jaded, but I'm very worried about you. I'll never trust Roxbury to have pure motives."

"His stepmother is joining us, so her presence will wipe away any hint of impropriety."

Mary patted her hand. "Are you trying to convince me or yourself?"

Emily sighed with regret. "I've been dreading my having to have this conversation with you. I was positive it would be difficult, and I was correct. I can't justify my conduct."

"Roxbury is a handsome rogue, so be careful. Remember yourself. If he starts to seem overly fond, and if he spews flattery, don't listen. It's how you can be trapped."

Emily yearned to blurt out that he'd been spewing too much flattery, to the point where she might act recklessly, but she had no idea how to confess it.

"I like to think I'm level-headed," she said, "and that he's not playing me false."

"You *are* level-headed, but it's hard to be lucid when a man like Roxbury is affectionate. I'm living proof of how stupid a female can be."

"You weren't stupid, Mary," Emily loyally told her. "You were young and vulnerable, and a practiced scoundrel took advantage of your naiveté."

"In hindsight, I recognize that to be the case, but I reveled in every minute of his seduction. It was only when it crashed down on me later on that I recollected how I should have been more cautious. No offense, Emily, but why would Roxbury fall in love with you? He could wed a great heiress or maybe even a princess, so why would he choose you instead? You have to ask yourself that question constantly or you'll be in so much trouble."

Emily knew Mary's words were very wise. Why would Roxbury fall in love with her?

She was sure he *didn't* love her, not yet anyway, but she was desperately hoping he'd grow to love her in the future. In a very silly, very feminine manner, she longed for them to march to the altar, but that was a deranged dream.

"Roxbury and I are friends," she firmly stated, "and I'm delighted that he invited me to spend the summer. You're aware of how much I enjoy Baywick. He's given me the chance to remain, and I'm grateful for it."

"It's the chance I yanked away by being so fierce with you. I wish I'd been less strict. I miss having you at the hotel."

"You've discovered I'm here," Emily said, "so we can socialize. Lord Roxbury claims his stepmother will host many parties, so there will be soirees and entertainments at Wave Crest. I'll have you placed on the regular guest list."

"And we can attend the theater and other events."

They smiled, feeling as if they'd reached a sort of peace accord, even though they hadn't been quarreling. They chatted a bit more, then Mary had to return to work. Emily walked her part of the way, and was saying goodbye, when a fancy coach lumbered past them. It took up so much of the narrow lane that they had to squeeze themselves against a wall to let it roll on by.

It was pulled by six white horses in an ornate, expensive harness. The animals had colorful ribbons braided into their manes and tails. Liveried footmen hung from the corners of the vehicle, and there was an ornate crest on the door.

"Who could that be?" Emily asked. "Are we about to be overrun by royalty?"

"No, it's not royalty, although she pretends she is." Emily frowned, not understanding, and Mary said, "That is Archie Covington's mother, Bernice Covington. She's the Dowager Countess of Roxbury, and she gads about like a queen."

"Lord Roxbury seems very reserved to me, so they must be very different people. I wonder if they're cordial."

"I'm betting not. Did you notice she had a companion with her? It's probably Archie's fiancée, Temperance Moore."

"He's engaged?" Emily said. "I didn't realize it. Neither brother has mentioned it."

"Archie blusters about as if he's a bachelor, so I'm not surprised." Mary leaned nearer and murmured, "Archie has no money of his own, and Miss Moore is an heiress. Originally, she was betrothed to Roxbury's older brother, Edward, but he died, and Archie's mother convinced her to betroth herself to Archie instead."

Emily was murmuring too. "I never met Edward Covington, but I figure Archie is quite a step down from him."

"When the switch of fiancé was made, it was assumed James was dead and Archie would become earl."

"But James Covington is back, so Archie Covington is ... what?"

Mary wasn't usually a snide person, but she snickered with disdain. "He's a poverty-stricken younger brother, with bad habits, lewd friends, and terrible vices."

Emily winced. "Why am I suddenly thinking I won't have a quiet summer sojourn after all? Do any of them get along?" A thorny problem presented itself. "What about Lord Roxbury? If Miss Moore wants to be a countess, might she set her sights on him? She's already moved from one sibling to another. What's to stop her from moving yet again?"

As Emily posed the question, her heart dropped to her shoes. She was flirting so shamelessly with James, and this was precisely the kind of dilemma that could arise in the middle of her insanity. She was wallowing in fantasies, picturing them married, but he would wed according to his station. If he didn't, he'd wind up miserable forever, and—like magic—an heiress had arrived out of the blue.

"I have no idea if Miss Moore might be scheming," Mary said, "but I predict you're about to have some very awkward moments at the supper table."

Emily rubbed her temples. "I feel a headache coming on."

"Your idyll at Wave Crest just grew a lot more interesting."

"Or a lot more exhausting."

They gaped until the coach vanished. Bernice Covington and Miss Moore would be in residence when Emily and Peggy returned from their lengthy stroll into town. Were the two women aware that James had female guests? If they weren't aware, what would their opinion be when they found out?

Mary had loafed too long and had to go, and she startled Emily by hugging her tight. Emily lived in a world where people rarely expressed their fondness physically. She hugged Mary back just as tightly.

"Take care of yourself," Mary said as she drew away.

"I will."

"I'm so glad I bumped into you, and I'm relieved to have you in Baywick, even if it means you're staying with Roxbury."

"I'm glad I bumped into you too. I was so afraid you'd be angry with me."

"It was the other way around. I thought *you* would be angry with me." Mary added, "Don't be a stranger."

Then she kept on. Emily watched her depart, then she went to The Promenade and sat on a bench to wait for Peggy.

Her mind was awhirl as she pondered James even more fervidly. She had plenty of issues to contemplate, and now, she had an heiress to stir into the mix. What if Miss Moore fancied James? What if he reciprocated her regard? What if he was excited by the prospect of her money flowing into his bank account? Where would it leave Emily?

Ooh, she was so foolish! And yes, so very gullible!

When Peggy finally strutted up, Emily was in quite a state, but she didn't dare reveal any of her tortured musings. The afternoon was waning, and they had to return home and dress for supper. She'd expected they would have one more quiet evening before James's stepmother sauntered in, but the woman was on the premises, so everything was about to change.

Peggy was holding a parcel, and Emily said, "What have you bought?"

"Just some ribbons. They're no better than what I could have purchased in Hexham, but I bought them anyway."

Emily chuckled. "Were there coins burning a hole in your reticule?"

"I'm tired of constantly looking the same. If a ribbon can enliven my features, it's a small price to pay. Let's go; I'm eager to get back."

Emily stood, and they started toward the road that led out of town and over the headland. Emily was beginning to recognize some of the locals, and she was thrilled when they smiled and nodded their own recognition.

"I saw Mrs. Darlington," Emily said, even though the woman was a sore subject.

"What did the rude harridan want?" Peggy's tone was very snide.

"She's my friend, so don't insult her."

Peggy snickered crudely. "Actually, it's her fault we wound up staying with Roxbury, so I should probably send her a thank-you gift."

"When she and I were chatting, an ornate carriage drove by, and Mrs. Darlington told me it was Mr. Covington's mother. She's come a day early, so she'll be at the house when we arrive."

"I can't decide if that's good news or bad. I guess it will depend if she's a witch or an angel."

"Even if we don't like her," Emily said, "we should try to make her like us. We shouldn't upset her. She might request that Lord Roxbury have us pack our bags."

"Don't worry about her." Peggy was exhibiting a confidence Emily didn't feel. "We won't be packing our bags. We're totally ensconced in the family, and there's no one who can complain about our being at Wave Crest."

Emily deemed it a peculiar remark, and she said, "Well, we should be pleasant and accommodating. There can't be any bickering."

"We have no reason to fight with her. Why would there be bickering?"

"She's brought a companion with her, and I'm not sure how the young lady will affect the mood of the involved parties."

Peggy scowled. "A young lady? Who is it?"

"Mr. Covington's fiancée. Apparently, he's engaged, but neither brother bothered to mention the situation to us."

Peggy stumbled and nearly fell, and Emily leapt to steady her.

"Are you all right?" Emily asked.

"Yes, yes, there must have been a loose rock in the dirt."

Emily stared at her cousin and frowned. "My goodness, Peggy, you're white as a ghost. Have you injured yourself?"

"No, I tripped!" Peggy was much too insistent. "What's this about Mr. Covington having a fiancée? He couldn't possibly have one. Why would Mrs. Darlington tell you that?"

Emily shrugged. "Because it's the truth? Her name is Temperance Moore, and she's a great heiress. She was initially engaged to their older brother, Edward. Were you aware they had an older brother?"

"I seem to remember them talking about him."

"When he died, Mr. Covington's mother convinced Miss Moore to switch her betrothal to Archie. He had hopes of becoming earl, so Miss Moore agreed to the match, but with Lord Roxbury returned from the dead, who can predict what Miss Moore is thinking? It might cause some fireworks, so we should be prepared."

Peggy was looking paler by the moment, and Emily was afraid her cousin might faint, but they were quite a distance from Wave Crest. She couldn't collapse. How would they get back?

"This Temperance Moore . . ." Peggy's teeth were clenched so tightly that she could barely speak. "Mrs. Darlington claims she's engaged to Archie? I mean to Mr. Covington? You're positive that's what she told you? You're not mistaken?"

"No, I wasn't mistaken. He's been betrothed to her for ages, but I didn't hear when the wedding is to be. Why?"

Peggy scoffed. "Mrs. Darlington is incredibly confused. She must have mixed him up with some other man."

"No, she knew all about it. Evidently, Miss Moore's path to being the Roxbury countess has been in place for years."

Peggy staggered, and Emily grabbed her again.

"Honestly, Peggy, what's wrong? Are you ill? Shall I flag down a passing vehicle and ask for a ride? People here are so kind. I'm certain someone would assist us."

Peggy straightened and glared at the headland, as if she could peer through it to the manor on the other side. She had the strangest grimace on her face, as if she was bewildered or perhaps terrified.

Then she pulled herself together and said, "We don't need to flag down anyone. I'm fine. We should hurry to Wave Crest though. I have a few matters to handle immediately."

"Can we please arrive quietly? And we must ingratiate ourselves to Mr. Covington's mother. She can't mind our being there or she might pressure Lord Roxbury to kick us out. I'm not ready to slither off to Hexham just yet."

"I repeat: We will never be kicked out, and if Mr. Covington's mother assumes she can manage it, she'll be in for a huge surprise."

It was a perplexing comment, and Emily didn't have time to inquire about it. Peggy took off, and she was practically running. For a minute or two, Emily tried to keep up, but she couldn't. She slowed to a crawl and followed along at a leisurely pace, while Peggy raced on and disappeared over a hill in the road.

There was too much drama occurring at Wave Crest. Emily's folly with James was stirring most of it, and Bernice Covington and Miss Moore would add to the stress and tension. She was in no rush to reach the property one second sooner than necessary.

Chapter Seventeen

"Guests, James? Really? You might have warned me."

"Why would I be required to apprise you when I have company?"

James glared at Bernice, and his temper was automatically on a slow boil. It was his perpetual state when he was with her.

They were in the front parlor, seated on sofas, and having a late afternoon glass of wine. It was just the two of them, which he never liked, and he was anxious to escape and change his clothes for supper. Bernice had arrived a day early, and she'd brought Temperance Moore with her, so he was already wishing he'd put his foot down and had refused her permission to visit.

He didn't know Temperance and couldn't imagine why Bernice thought he should host her. Was she staying all summer? Was Bernice? He couldn't abide Bernice, and he was too surly to be cordial to Temperance who was a stranger to him.

In his view, any girl who would willingly shackle herself to Archie was slightly deranged. He also didn't like how she'd been engaged to Edward, but had switched to Archie the minute Edward died. Obviously, she yearned to purchase a title at any cost, and there was a greedy aspect to her actions that he didn't like.

Bernice should have asked him if Temperance could come, and he was already struggling to figure out how he could convince them to depart immediately.

Bernice was his stepmother, but he'd never liked or respected her. She was his father's third wife, a flighty, vain shrew who'd joined the family when James was a boy. Her disagreeable qualities had driven their father away from home, so he'd mostly gamboled in London, while James and Edward had been stuck in the country with her.

She had few maternal instincts, and those she possessed had been lavished on Archie. She'd rarely behaved in a way that had benefited him or Edward, and she'd repeatedly been a drain on their energy, patience, and assets. She constantly chafed over Archie being a third son and how he wasn't receiving his share of whatever boon was being distributed. Whether it was acclaim, wealth, or status, she never felt he was given his due.

Then, when James had been stranded in the Arctic North, she'd leapt to have him declared deceased, to have Archie installed in his place. She and Archie had burned through their own inheritances, then had tried to persuade bankers and others to relinquish riches to which they hadn't been entitled.

She was an extravagant spendthrift who flaunted her position as countess like a queen, and James was lucky he'd staggered to England when he had. He'd seized control of his fortune and properties before she could beggar him.

"I walk in the door," she protested, "and instantly discover that you have a pair of single females residing with you. You and Archie are bachelors, and Temperance is with me. What am I to make of your risqué arrangement with the Shaw cousins?"

"I don't care what you make of it. Emily Shaw is a friend, and she was in dire straits. I helped her by offering her shelter when she couldn't find lodging in Baywick. I won't hear any objections about it."

"Am I your mother or not?"

He smirked with derision. "No, Bernice, you're not my mother, so don't feign an interest in my habits or acquaintances. And don't you dare lecture me."

He'd just jabbed at one of her petty grievances. She pretended to be the greatest mother in history, but she wasn't, and in light of the mischief she'd implemented when he was away in the Arctic North, they couldn't confer without bickering.

On her end though, she realized she had to tread cautiously around him. She had no money remaining, and she lived as a charity case in his various homes. He provided her with a meager allowance, but he didn't have to provide it, and he could cut it off whenever he chose.

She smiled a placating smile and said, "I was merely inquiring as to your intentions with regard to them. I didn't mean to upset you. You simply shouldn't have welcomed them without me in the house. You're being a tad reckless, aren't you? What would people say if word spread in Baywick? In such a small area, their reputations would be tarnished forever."

"Well, you're here now, and you will be our hostess, so those issues are irrelevant. They're not staying with two bachelors. They're staying with you. Don't nag."

"I never nag," she ludicrously insisted, "but what about Temperance? If her father learned they were present, he'd be aghast. She can't be expected to socialize with them."

James rolled his eyes. "They're not peasants in the field. They're not scullery maids. They're charming young ladies from a good family, so don't antagonize me over them. You won't like how I react."

Bernice sniffed with affront. "You can be such a bully, James. It's an odious trait, and I wish you'd tamp it down."

"Is there any other feature of my personality that you'd like to criticize? Otherwise, I shall go to my room and dress for supper."

"I don't know why I try to talk to you."

"Neither do I, and you don't have to tarry at Wave Crest. If you're not happy, you can return to London."

It was a cudgel he wielded with her. He was head of the family, and he held the purse strings. He struggled to respect the fact that she'd been his father's wife, but she fatigued him beyond his limit. He should have ignored his loathing, should have been a bigger man, but their mutual aversion was too potent and too ingrained.

She reined in her sarcastic attitude. "Of course I won't leave. I've so recently arrived that I doubt my bags have been unpacked. What would I tell Temperance? What would she think? Despite how I painted it, she'd recognize that you'd kicked us out."

"Yes, that's my main worry: What would Temperance think?"

"She will be your sister-in-law," Bernice said. "You have to make an effort with her. Don't be a brat about it."

"When is the wedding to be? I haven't heard that there's a firm date."

"I'm hoping for next spring."

"Is she hoping for that? Will she follow through now that Archie won't be earl?"

A hint of rage showed in Bernice's expression, but she quickly masked it. "Yes, she'll follow through. Why wouldn't she?"

"Wasn't she shopping for a title? With Archie losing out on the chance to inherit, he's not the fiancé she assumed she was buying. What if she cries off?"

A muscle twitched in Bernice's jaw, indicating she'd been fretting over the predicament. She'd never admit it though. In her view, Archie was a perfect catch for any girl.

"Why don't you scurry off and change your clothes?" she said, her tone furious. "It's obvious you're in no mood to have a civil discussion, but I would appreciate it if you'd at least attempt to be cordial. If you can't or won't, what sort of summer will we have?"

"As I previously mentioned, you can return to London. I'm not stopping you."

He marched out and had nearly escaped when she called, "I'm told there's to be an inquest about your failed expedition."

He halted and glanced over his shoulder. "Yes, that's the rumor."

"Have you been subpoenaed?"

"No, but I guess I will be."

"You will disregard any summons," she staunchly stated. "You will *not* give any testimony. I really can't have it."

"*You* can't? Why would you suppose I'd heed your opinion about it?"

"It's our name that will be dragged through the mud. It's my and Archie's names. My God, James, they're tittering that you became cannibals! That men ate each other to survive! Will you spew that type of shocking detail and send the entire country into a collective swoon?"

He scoffed. "No one ate anyone. Men starved though. And they froze to death. Is that information enough to satisfy your sick curiosity?"

"I forbid you to speak about any of it."

"It's not up to you, Bernice, and whatever I choose to do, you won't be consulted."

"I am Dowager Countess, and I am ordering that you will not shame us."

"I'll keep that in mind."

He whipped away and continued on to the stairs and the safety of his bedchamber. Perhaps he wouldn't come back down to dine. The experience might delay his mental recovery by decades.

"ARE YOU SURPRISED TO SEE ME?"

"Yes, I'm very surprised."

Temperance flashed a frosty smile at Archie. She didn't know him at all, and she'd never spent much time with him. When they were together, she always found herself a tad startled to realize that she might wind up married to him.

His older brother, Edward, had been tall, handsome, and charming. He'd exuded a magnetism commoners expected from the aristocracy, but rarely observed in them. With his dark hair, blue eyes, and broad physique, he'd looked exactly like James. They could have been twins, their stellar bloodlines clearly evident.

In contrast, Archie was short and chubby, was blond and pale, was smirking and fawning. He wasn't ugly, but he'd never be described as anything but ordinary.

She didn't like to suppose she was fickle. She had her father's pragmatism, and she never liked to imagine she'd judge a fellow on his facial features and masculine vigor, but apparently, she harbored the tastes of the silliest debutante.

There was an air about Archie, one of ingratiation and obsequiousness, that grated, as if he was never certain of his place in the world. He worked too hard to be liked, and he suffered from a constant need to prove he was important and interesting.

"Are you glad I came?" she asked.

"Yes, of course I'm glad."

"Sorry, but I had to inquire. Ever since I arrived, you've seemed anxious."

"I was just busy today. That's all."

"This visit was your mother's idea. She insisted it would give us a chance to become better acquainted."

"She's correct," he said, practically gushing. "There are a thousand ways we can entertain ourselves."

She doubted that very much. "Such as?"

"Baywick is a lovely town, and you're aware that I was a major investor. I will escort you to all the sights so you can see how successful I've been."

She'd heard the stories of how little he'd had to do with the construction or implementation. Her father kept tabs on him, so he was followed and investigated, and the news they unearthed was never good.

Archie had eagerly pursued a legal case to have James declared deceased, then he'd borrowed lavishly against his future elevation. Now, with his brother home, Archie's scheme had failed, and the estate's bank accounts were lost to him.

The remaining issue involved his inheritance from his father. It was entirely possible that he'd squandered every penny, but they hadn't been able to find out for sure. Her father was shrewd with his money. It's why he'd grown very rich, and while they were dangling a fortune at Archie Covington, they wouldn't deliver it if he'd simply fritter it away on gambling and vice.

She and her father relentlessly debated whether she should cry off or not. Was it worth it to marry into the Covington family? After all, James could die, especially if he continued his adventuring, and Archie might still be earl. But what if James lived to be a hundred? What if she wed Archie and never received the benefit she'd been hoping to purchase, that being *entrée* into the British aristocracy?

She'd finally cornered him out on the rear verandah. It was the first minute she'd had to be alone with him. He hadn't been present when they'd arrived, and he'd come in late, strutting into the dining room after they'd begun eating. He'd been disconcerted to have her seated at the table, and he hadn't fully recovered his aplomb.

Supper was over, and it had been very awkward. Lord Roxbury and Bernice had traded barbs through the whole meal, with Bernice repeatedly raising topics that aggravated him. Her hostile conduct, exhibited in front of several people, reinforced Temperance's belief that Bernice would be a horrid mother-in-law.

The two Misses Shaw had been an odd addition to the guest list. Initially, she'd worried they might be doxies, but upon meeting them, that suspicion had been wiped away. Yet Roxbury and Archie were bachelors, so their having a pair of females on the premises wasn't appropriate by any standard.

Obviously though, she was to have no opinion about the situation. Or she could have an opinion, but she had to keep it to herself. No one was allowed to question the behavior of the great and grand Lord Roxbury, due to his mental condition being incredibly fragile.

Emily Shaw had been agreeable and cordial, chatting breezily about sights in the area, but her cousin, Margaret Shaw, had been surly and unlikable. She'd glared at Temperance with extreme malice, and Temperance couldn't guess how she'd stirred such animosity.

She wouldn't waste any energy unraveling the root cause. Temperance wasn't highborn, but her father's wealth set her far above a nobody like Margaret Shaw.

"May I show you the gardens?" Archie asked. "I had them designed for beauty and pleasure, and you'll be very impressed."

"It's dark out so there wouldn't be much to see."

"How long will you stay with us? Mother is intending to tarry for the rest of the summer. Will you tarry too?"

"How long would you like me to stay?" she asked. "You haven't exactly seemed thrilled to have me stroll in."

From the moment he'd realized she was sitting at the supper table, he'd been jumpy as a cat on a hot roof. He was very nervous and constantly glancing over his shoulder, as if he was afraid of being attacked from behind.

He didn't have a chance to reply. Suddenly, from over in the doorway, a woman said, "Mr. Covington, may I speak with you? I'm trying to figure out a curious problem, and you're the only person who might know the answer."

They peered over at Margaret Shaw. Archie couldn't completely conceal a ripple of disgust, as if he harbored a powerful dislike for her, but he could be a suave fellow when polish was required, and he quickly masked any contempt.

"I'm busy, Miss Shaw," he told her, "but I'll be in soon. I'll find you."

The churlish girl hovered, as if she'd scold Archie for some reason, but in the end, she spun away and stomped off in a huff. Archie watched her depart, and he had such a peculiar expression on his face that Temperance wondered if they'd been flirting. Miss Shaw was precisely the type who would grow smitten and Archie precisely the type who would have encouraged her.

He was a terrible libertine, and her father had warned her, if she proceeded to the altar, she'd have to develop a very thick skin. He would have regular affairs, but she didn't like him very much, and would wed him for the opportunity to be a countess, so would it matter if he chased trollops? Would she care? She couldn't decide.

Archie leaned nearer and murmured, "She's such a nuisance. My brother invited her and her cousin to reside with us, but it's made her overly proud. She thinks she owns the place."

"Will they be staying long?" she inquired. "Might I request that their sojourn with us be very brief?"

"I'll talk to James about them. I'll attempt to persuade him to send them away, but he's fond of Emily Shaw. I'm not sure if he'll listen to me."

"Should I talk to him?" she asked. "He didn't notice how insolent Margaret Shaw was being to me. Perhaps I could point it out."

"No, no! You shouldn't confer with him on any important subject. His mental state is precarious, what with his recovering from his ordeal and all. His fuse is very short, so he has a bad temper. If you utter one wrong word, he lashes out."

"You're worried he'd lash out at me? I haven't witnessed any boorish behavior."

"You haven't been here a sufficient period to have been confronted by it."

"Why don't you go in and locate Miss Shaw?" Temperance waved toward the door. "She's quite eager to converse with you."

Archie scoffed with derision. "I don't have to drop everything and rush after her merely because she's demanded it."

"Might she be sweet on you?" Archie couldn't hide a wince, and she said, "A tart like that would misconstrue any attention you paid to her."

"You're correct; she would."

"Maybe you should tamp down any fires that might be flaring."

"A wise idea." He squeezed her hand. "We'll chat in the morning, if not before. I'll show you the gardens, then we can take a tour of the village."

"I can't wait."

He left, then she went down into the garden on her own. She was entirely capable of assessing the spot by herself. She didn't need a man to escort her anywhere, and besides, she'd seen Roxbury heading down a dark path. It would be the perfect moment to accost him.

❧

"HELLO, LORD ROXBURY. FANCY meeting you here."

James bristled. He'd been sneaking to the gazebo, hoping Emily would join him there, but who did he immediately run into but Temperance Moore?

He had no desire to socialize with her, and he wondered if she'd been following him. The prospect raised his hackles.

"Hello, Miss Moore," he said. "It's a lovely evening. Are you enjoying the garden?"

"It's very nice. I'm a city girl and not much of a one for nature, but it's clear the design is remarkable."

He was anxious to continue on, but she stared him down, practically insisting he invite her to accompany him for a stroll. He couldn't avoid it, even as he desperately prayed Emily wouldn't observe them. What would she think?

He bit down a smirk. Apparently, he was immersed in such a deep amour with Emily that he couldn't bear to make her jealous.

"Would you like to walk with me?" he asked.

She nodded and clasped his arm, and they sauntered off. He should have had mercy on her and selected an inane topic of conversation, but he wasn't about to exert himself. He suspected *she* had a topic she was dying to address, and he was happy to let her take the lead.

"May I ask you a question?" she said after a lengthy and very awkward silence.

"You can ask, but I can't guarantee I'll answer."

It was the reply he gave to everyone these days. People were constantly delving into subjects that were none of their business, and usually, they were simply keen to confirm lurid gossip. He never obliged any of them.

"I've been pondering my betrothal to Archie," she stunned him by admitting.

He was shocked by her brash comment. They were barely acquainted. Why would she seek his opinion? Why would she expect him to provide it?

He figured there were a hundred issues with Archie that would have her hesitating and wary, and he asked, "What has you pondering?"

"If I was your sister, would you advise me to proceed with the wedding or to cry off?"

It was such an appalling query that he flinched. "I don't believe I should confer with you about this situation."

She scowled up at him. "It seems I've startled you by being too blunt. It's a failing of the Moore family; we're much too direct."

"I can see that, and I will be very direct too. Are you contemplating a severance? Is that what's happening?"

"Whenever I'm around Archie, I'm riveted by how different we are. I'm convinced we wouldn't suit."

"That's quite a stirring declaration, and I'm more certain than ever that we shouldn't be discussing this."

"Who else should I discuss it with? His mother thinks he's marvelous, but I'm positive you have a more realistic view."

"You should probably speak to your father about it," he said.

"I have spoken to him. Frequently. We've thoroughly investigated Archie, so he's not a mystery to us."

"Then I shall simply mention that my half-brother has numerous faults, and a woman should carefully reflect on them before marching to the altar."

"My father and I have been debating the dilemma. I engaged myself to Archie because I assumed I would be a countess. I felt the detriments were worth the benefits of my obtaining a title."

"Yes, a title has value beyond imagining." He was being very facetious, but she didn't appear to notice.

"I'd still like to be a countess," she brazenly announced, "and I decided I should inform you that I'd like to deliver my fortune to a man who can furnish that ending."

It was a pompous and dreadful assertion that hinted at double-dealing and betrayal. She was eager for them to conspire against Archie, and while James wasn't the most devoted sibling, he liked to suppose he possessed a bit of loyalty.

He'd never sabotage Archie's marital chance, and if Miss Moore was having second thoughts, it was outrageous for her to have raised them with him. She was wagering that James had no moral compass and would jump at the opportunity. It underscored the general perception that women shouldn't have money.

Any windfall left them overly impressed with their own importance, as evidenced by the fact that she saw no problem with financially ruining Archie.

What kind of person was she? What kind of man did she picture James to be? If he was as treacherous as she presumed, why would she want him as a husband?

He'd always had a bad temper, but his ordeal in the Arctic North had lit a permanent spark to it. The littlest incident could set him off, and he struggled relentlessly to remain calm. Regrettably for her, she'd pushed him to the edge of his tolerance for nonsense, and she'd just vividly reminded him of why he loathed being surrounded by his family.

Aside from a few distant cousins, Archie and Bernice were his sole relatives. Archie was bound to marry Miss Moore, so it was highly likely she'd become a member of the small group he recognized as kin. The notion nauseated him.

"I will state this once and only once," he said, his tone aggrieved, his anger barely controlled, "so please pay close attention. Archie is my brother, and Bernice has been my mother since I was a boy. They are counting on the match to go forward, and I would never take any action that would prevent it."

She noted his fury and was anxious to clarify her position. "I was merely being candid. You could have my dowry, instead of your brother, and you'd be a better steward. If I've distressed you by suggesting the possibility, I most humbly apologize."

"Your apology is not accepted. If further nuptial negotiations are required, I have no idea why *you* would initiate them with me. The contract is between Bernice and your father, and you should butt out."

"It's a lot of money," she blithely said.

"I don't care."

He'd given her a dose of the sort of frank conversation she claimed to relish, but she didn't like to be on the receiving end of it. She winced, then straightened. "You don't have to be so curt with me. I'm trying to have a rational and very private discussion with you, and you've misconstrued my intent."

"I haven't misconstrued. You were tossing out bait to discover if I could be hooked by a deceitful scheme where we would do our best to destroy my brother."

"I have no scheme," she huffed. "I've simply revealed my reasoning."

"No, you were expecting I'd be inclined to betray him. Well, I'm not inclined, Miss Moore, and therefore, you are not welcome to stay in my home for any portion of the summer. Not a day. Not a minute."

She frowned. "Are you kicking me out? You can't be."

"You will need to invent an emergency in London that will necessitate your fast departure, and you will leave as soon as your transportation to the city can be arranged."

She was made of stern stuff and didn't recoil from his hostile manner. "I hate that I've enraged you. I didn't mean to."

"No, you meant to corrupt me and injure my only sibling, and I am heartily disgusted by your antics. Goodnight."

He whipped away and stomped off, and he headed to the manor and the shelter of his bedchamber. His mood and disposition were never elevated, and she'd forced him to recollect that he shouldn't be socializing. He'd traveled to the seashore to recuperate in the peace and quiet. He couldn't abide this type of strife, and he refused to be drawn into the debacle of Archie's marriage.

Whether Archie shackled himself to Miss Moore or not, it was entirely up to Bernice and Miss Moore's father. James wouldn't involve himself.

Let the rest of them bicker and spat. Let them fight over the huge pile of money Miss Moore was waving in their faces. He would have no part of it, and he speculated as to how quickly Miss Moore would pack her bags.

How rapidly would he be shed of her? If she didn't flee swiftly enough to suit him, he might actually enjoy throwing her out bodily.

He reached the house and snuck up the back stairs to his room, where he shut and locked the door. For an eternity, he stared out the window, but it was too dark to see much of anything, so the view provided no solace. He paced, drank some whiskey, paced some more.

He thought about his life, his past, and his future. He thought about his tragic expedition, about his comrades, most dead, some not. He thought about how the calamity had reshaped him, how it had left him battered, drained, and very, very angry.

He was so bloody unhappy, and he wondered when his mental and emotional difficulties would begin to fade. What if they never faded? What if he always remained just as disordered and bewildered as he was that very moment?

What did he want for himself? What should he choose? Where would he like to be in five years? In ten? How could he continue on as he was, being mired in guilt and horrific reminiscence? How could he live with himself?

He stormed out and went to find Emily. She would know what he should do, and she wouldn't hesitate to tell him.

Chapter Eighteen

EMILY WAS SEATED AT her dressing table and ready for bed when her bedchamber door opened. She glanced over to find James sneaking in. Even though she knew it was very wrong, she'd been hoping he'd visit.

Her hair was down and brushed out, and she was wearing a summery nightgown, a robe over the top, so she was covered from chin to toes. She wasn't exactly flaunting any bodily parts, but still, it was an outrageous situation.

The entire evening had been difficult. Supper had been awful, with the conversation during the meal stilted and draining. Bernice Covington was the most unpleasant person she'd met in ages, and Miss Moore was a snot and a snob.

Peggy had been sullen and bristling over some sort of issue, and Archie Covington had strolled in late, without explanation or apology. Emily had worked valiantly to be cordial and chatty, but it had been a losing proposition. The whole thing had been wretched.

Briefly, she'd considered walking to the gazebo, figuring James would eventually follow her there, but she'd given up on that idea. She might have bumped into other family members whom she'd been determined to avoid. She'd had all of their nonsense she could stand, so she'd claimed exhaustion and had headed to bed early.

Now, here was James, arriving right on schedule to improve her mood.

She spun on the stool to face him, and she grinned. "I'm not impressed by your ability to host a supper party. That was the most miserable one I've ever endured."

"I agree, and I shouldn't have put you through such an exasperating ordeal."

"Are your family gatherings always this maddening?"

"Usually, they're much worse."

"Will you be offended if I state that I don't like your stepmother? Or your brother's betrothed?"

"No, you won't offend me. I have no great affection for either of them."

"I've never been fond of your brother. How do you retain your sanity when you're surrounded by such dreadful relatives?"

"I've mostly traveled out of the country. It was a means to escape them."

She snorted with amusement. "Smart man."

He'd been lurking over by the door, and he pushed himself away and came over to her. He dipped down and kissed her soundly, then he drew away and went over to the bed. He plopped down on the pillow, an arm braced behind his neck.

"I have been fending off criticism and complaints all day," he said.

"How have you weathered them?"

"Not well."

"And you don't like to be pestered or berated."

"No." He shifted onto his side so he could look at her. "Bernice had the audacity to scold me for inviting you to stay at Wave Crest."

"I imagine you told her it's your house and she should mind her own business."

"Yes, I used those precise words. I was away for years, so she'd started to assume everything belonged to her and Archie. They haven't been eager to relinquish any of it back to me."

She hated to see people fighting. "I'm sorry that they're so rude to you."

"Not as sorry as I am." He smirked with disgust. "She also ordered me to ignore any subpoena I receive to testify at the inquest. She doesn't want our name in the newspapers."

"It's not up to her," Emily loyally insisted. "I can't believe she'd dare to command you."

"She's scared I'll admit that my men and I became cannibals. It's the gossip in London, and apparently, she has such a low opinion of me that she suspects it might be true. We froze and starved, but we didn't eat anyone."

"Would you like me to march down the hall and punch her in the nose? Is she always this horrid to you? Or was she showing off for my benefit? She's the type who pretends to be very grand."

"She's always been horrid. She was my father's third wife, and I've never liked her. We've never gotten along."

"That's too bad."

He waved a hand, as if their failed relationship was irrelevant. "Guess what else happened to vex me."

"From your angry expression, I'm almost afraid to inquire."

"I was accosted by Miss Moore! She actually informed me that she'd still like to be a countess, and she would be willing to set Archie aside and marry me instead." He frowned ferociously. "What kind of woman would suggest such a scheme? What kind of character must she possess deep down?"

"What did you tell her?" Emily asked, nerves rattling her.

"I told her to invent an emergency and head home immediately."

"You didn't!"

"I did, and I am so enraged. I'm not the best brother, but can you picture me behaving so despicably? I'm totally stunned. The worst part was her absolute certainty that I'd be delighted to betray Archie. For money! It boggles the mind."

"So what now?"

"Hopefully, she'll slink off as I've demanded."

"What if she doesn't? She's awfully impressed with herself. What if she refuses to obey you?"

"I'll toss her out bodily."

Emily laughed. "You would not."

"I might. I'm that furious."

"What if she ultimately weds your brother? You'll constantly recollect your conversation with her. How could she suppose you'd harbor any respect for her after this?"

"I'm betting it's immaterial. I'm positive she's about to cry off."

"You'll be lucky if she does. She was so haughty to me at supper. What would it be like to have such a snooty, hostile person as a sister-in-law?"

"You dealt with her like a gracious queen."

"I'm flattered that you think so," she said.

"I'm more amazed by you every day."

"You're being terribly complimentary. You must want something."

"You are very perceptive."

Suddenly, he didn't appear quite so troubled or overwhelmed. He sat up and motioned for her to come over to him.

"Explain what you're planning first," she said. "I don't like the look in your eye, and since you're loafing on my bed, I'm sure I've deduced what it is."

"You'll never have deduced it. My brain works in such convoluted ways that I am a complete enigma. You'll never figure it out."

"How about if I remain right where I am? It might be the safer route. I act like a dunce around you, and if I stay over here, perhaps I'll exhibit a bit more fortitude."

"I don't want you exhibiting fortitude. I want you happy and amenable."

"That's what is worrying me."

He slid to his feet and grabbed two chairs. He placed them so they were facing each other, then he pointed to one. "Sit. I have an important topic to discuss, and I'm not about to raise it when you're so far away."

"Are you about to blurt out a bad idea? Should I be wary?"

"I never have bad ideas. This is a wonderful decision, and it just might be the answer to many of my prayers."

She hesitated, debating. He was sly and confident, and that combination of traits might prove deadly to her reputation. Yet in the end, she went over as he'd requested. Where he was concerned, she couldn't stand her ground.

She seated herself, and he eased down too. He clasped her hands and linked their fingers. He was smiling with such affection that she was alarmed. He might spew any wild remark that probably shouldn't be uttered aloud.

"I have a possible solution for us," he said. "You won't like it, and you'll automatically devise a thousand reasons why it's deranged, but you have to listen to me and ponder my suggestion. Don't scoff and tell me I'm mad."

"You *are* mad. Haven't we previously agreed that you are? But I shall try to keep from stating the obvious."

"Thank you. I appreciate it, and here goes." He took a deep breath, let it out, then said, "I want you to marry me."

It was the very last comment she'd expected, and it was so bizarre that she was surprised she didn't fall to the floor in shock. "You want me to what?"

"You heard me: I want you to marry me."

If she'd been greedy and selfish—more like Peggy, for instance—she might have immediately accepted. But she wasn't avaricious or proud, and he'd recently returned from his journey after suffering years of torment. He was in no condition to attach himself. He was definitely in no condition to propose to *her*. She was a commoner, and they were barely acquainted. It was ludicrous.

Before she could reply, he said, "I realize I sound rash and unhinged, but why shouldn't I have proceeded? We've only just met, but I feel as if I've always known you. Don't you feel that way too?"

"Yes, I feel as if I've known you forever, and I can't imagine traveling home in September."

"Exactly. Why should we separate?"

She sighed with dismay. "Oh, James, you're pressuring me horribly, and I wish you wouldn't. Your health and mood are precarious, and at the moment, you shouldn't wed anyone. Most especially me. You've just arrived in England, and you're still recovering your equilibrium. With how disordered you've been, it's ridiculous for you to think of matrimony."

"We've already established that I'm not right in the head, and I doubt I will ever be. I'm not the man I was when I left. I don't remember who I was, and I'm someone else now."

"Yes, you're an earl, from one of the best families in the land. If you suppose you're capable of picking a suitable wife, then you should rush to London and start courting debutantes. You can't consider me."

"No, you're wrong. You'd be perfect. You've spent several weeks in my company, and you've observed how I'm faring without running away in terror. You've figured out how to deal with me. Could you picture me fettered to a debutante? How could a young girl cope with my quirks and odd disposition?"

She chuckled. "No, I couldn't picture it. The very idea is hilarious."

"When my father shackled himself to Bernice, it was a typical aristocratic union, and from practically the first day, he recognized how incompatible they were. He was miserable for the rest of his life. I won't put myself through that sort of quagmire."

"You presume *I* could deliver a better conclusion than what your father found for himself?"

"I'm sure of it. We're so fond. Why shouldn't we stay together? Why not?"

His optimism was dangerous, and it appeared to be catching. She was asking *why not* too. Why not wed him? Why not live happily ever after?

What was her other option? Would she stagger to Hexham at the end of the summer and never see him again? For years ever after, would she regret her cowardice? Why shouldn't she latch onto him? *He* had obligations to his name and title. *He* had peers who would snicker over how he'd married down. She could bind herself to any man she liked. Why not choose him?

He would be risking all—reputation, esteem, status—while she would be lifted up very high. The situation at Hexham was dicey and in such a state of flux, so it might be very wise to consent. He'd have to support her, so she'd be secure and protected. Why decline such a precious gift?

"Your stepmother and brother wouldn't like me to be your bride," she said. "Aren't you concerned over how it might upset them?"

"I don't care about their opinion. Have you heard the rumors about their conduct when I was away?"

She shook her head. "No. What did they do?"

"After my brother, Edward, died, they tried to have me declared deceased so they could glom onto the estate bank accounts. They even held a funeral for me. I'm a tad bitter about it."

She smirked. "You're a tad bitter about many issues."

"It means they don't get to judge my behavior. They're lucky we're still speaking. Most times, we aren't."

They quarreled regularly, and their vitriol was so depressing. Should she attach herself to the gloomy group? What would it be like to have them as her kin? Yet if he didn't interact with them very often, how could it matter?

"What about your friends?" she asked. "What would they think?"

"Nearly all of my friends have abandoned me. There is such hideous gossip swirling that I'm viewed as a very noxious fellow. They claim they never knew me, so why would I agonize about any of them?"

She gazed down at the rug, assessing the benefits and detriments. The benefits seemed personal and wonderful: She'd have him as her husband. The detriments accrued to strangers or to the Covington family members she didn't particularly like. Why allow them to ruin this golden opportunity?

"Here's my biggest fear," she said. "We're content at Wave Crest. It feels as if we've met while traveling, and we're engaged in a holiday amour. What if that's all it is? What if we ultimately discover there's no foundation beneath us? It's not as if we have the underpinnings of ancestry or station to carry us forward."

"I'm trying to be an optimist, and I won't let you be a pessimist. What if we discover instead that it was the best notion ever?"

"Then how about this: In the future, I assume your health will continue to mend. What if you start to wish you had your old life back? What if you start to ask yourself how you could have been stupid enough to pick me? Where would I be then?"

"First off, I would never wed a debutante, so please stop worrying that I might. And second, I would never deem myself stupid to have picked you. In fact, I predict I'll constantly be smug because I shrewdly grabbed onto you when I had the chance."

She exhaled a heavy breath. "You make this sound so easy."

"It will be so don't fret and stew over it."

"How and where could it transpire?" Upon voicing her question, she blanched. Gad, was she considering it?

"I thought we'd elope to Scotland."

"Elope! That would be terribly scandalous."

"Or I could send for a Special License. We should forge ahead immediately, so we can't come to our senses."

"You've just stated the exact reason we should hesitate. This isn't a decision we should arrive at in a slapdash way. At least *you* shouldn't. I'm a spinster, with no prospects or responsibilities to weigh me down, so I can rush into any ridiculous situation. You, on the other hand, have burdens that ought to check any wild impulses."

He grinned. "These days, I only have wild impulses. After my ordeal in the Arctic North, I learned that life is too short, so it's silly to delay or ponder. Why deny myself the things I desire the most? Why not take the merry course, the joyous course? What if I dropped dead tomorrow? I'd never know what it would have been like to be your husband. You wouldn't force me to have that as my ending, would you?"

She chuckled, but miserably. "Heaven forbid that I keep you from having whatever you want before you drop dead."

He slid off his chair and onto one knee. "My dearest, Emily, will you marry me? Say *yes*. Say you will."

"Ooh, it's so hard to refuse you."

"Then don't refuse. Why would you?"

Her heart was pounding so furiously that she was surprised she could hear him speaking. He seemed so sure that it would all work out. Why not believe him? If it fell apart later on, she could always point out that she'd tried to dissuade him, but he wouldn't listen.

She braced, as if she was about to suffer a fierce blow. "Yes, James, I will marry you, but don't you dare be sorry in the future. Promise you won't be. Not for a single minute."

"How could I ever be sorry?" he asked. "With you by my side, I shall be happy forever."

"You better swear I'll be happy too."

"You absolutely will be." He kissed her, and he was quite desperate about it too. "Let's elope to Scotland. What do you think? We can sneak away and return as man and wife. The deed will be accomplished before anyone realizes they should have prevented us."

It was precisely why they shouldn't hurry: that others might have a negative view of their conduct. But she grinned too and said, "I've never participated in a genuine adventure, and an elopement to Scotland would definitely qualify."

"An elopement it is."

"ARCHIE! WAIT!"

Peggy raced down the hall and grabbed his arm, pulling him to a halt.

"You look distraught, Miss Shaw. What's wrong?"

They were next to a deserted parlor, and she dragged him in and shut the door. Since she'd staggered back from her walk into Baywick, she hadn't been able to corner him and confront him about Temperance Moore. There had been no chance at supper, and after the meal was over, he'd slyly absented himself from company.

He was staring at her as if they were strangers, as if he didn't know who she was. They were married! They'd been celebrating their union in her bedchamber every night. He'd sworn he'd tell his mother about them very soon, but his mother had finally waltzed in, and he hadn't uttered a word.

"Would you like to explain Miss Moore to me?" she demanded.

He glared with confusion, as if she'd babbled in a foreign language he didn't understand. "Miss Moore? Why would you inquire about her?"

"She's bragging that she's your fiancée! You were eager to keep our marriage a secret, but you have to set her straight. I don't care what sort of arrangement you had with her, but it's over now, and she needs to depart."

"What are you talking about, Miss Shaw? To what secret are you referring?"

"Don't call me *Miss Shaw*. Call me Mrs. Covington, which is my rightful name."

"Are you deranged? In what bizarre world would you be allowed to call yourself Mrs. Covington?"

She started to shake. "I'm your wife, Archie!"

He whacked a palm on his ear, as if his hearing had been affected. "Did you just say you're my wife?"

She gaped at him as if he were the Devil, risen up from Hell to torment her. "Don't act like this," she fumed. "We had a wedding, and Gordo officiated at the ceremony."

"You're claiming Gordo is a vicar?" He laughed in a very cruel way. "Gordo is many things, but if he boasted of possessing a religious title, the Earth would spin off its axis."

"He officiated! You can't deny it!"

He clucked his tongue like a fussy nanny. "I have no idea what game you're playing, Miss Shaw. You and your cousin were in dire straits, so my brother welcomed you into our home, and I can only suppose you're a confidence artist. You assessed our affluent circumstances and figured you could obtain a benefit. Is that it?"

"You're my husband!"

"No offense, Miss Shaw, but I'm an earl's brother, and—should he pass away—I'd become earl. I would never shackle myself to a girl of your low status."

She was practically sputtering with alarm. "We recited the vows and signed a marriage license! Your friends were there. Gordo was there!"

"You would pretend there were witnesses? There was a license?"

"Yes, a Special License! You applied to a bishop so we could proceed immediately."

"I have *never* applied for a Special License in my life. You can check with every bishop in the kingdom. As to my purported *friends* attending our wedding, I can safely state that they will never admit to such a farce—for it never occurred. Inform me as to the date of the ceremony, and they will recollect that they were in London."

If he'd taken out a knife and stabbed her, she couldn't have been any more devastated. "We're married," she repeated, as if she was explaining a difficult concept to a child.

"What is your ploy, Miss Shaw? Will you spread an allegation that you've been ruined by me? Will you assert that I am the culprit? If you are a slattern, and you've gotten yourself into a jam, I fail to see how that could be my fault or my problem. I suggest you consider the consequences before you level any spurious charges."

"They're not spurious, and our wedding was a real event! I won't let you slither out of it."

"How will you stop me? You should remember who I am and who you are, and you should also clearly recognize that there can be extreme legal penalties for slandering a man of my class and reputation."

"Archie! Why are you treating me like this?"

"First of all, Miss Shaw, I don't give you permission to use my Christian name. Second of all, you're mad as a hatter and this conversation is over."

He walked to the door and reached for the knob. She rushed after him and seized his wrist so he couldn't slink out like the cur he apparently was.

"I'll talk to your mother in the morning," she said. "I'll tell her I'm your wife."

"Then I shall tell her that you are a trollop and a liar. Which one of us do you imagine she'll believe? I'm sure it's not you."

"We're in love." The comment—when voiced aloud—sounded pathetic and absurd. "I'm going to make you happy forever."

He tsked disdainfully. "How would you have? You're a plain, ordinary girl, from a family of rural nobodies. What could you bring to the table that would interest me in the slightest?"

"You said I was lively and fun. You said we shared the same tastes and relished the same entertainments. You said I would be the perfect bride for you."

"You're deluded, Miss Shaw. Miss Moore will be the perfect bride. She's very rich, and our betrothal is in place so I can have her fortune."

"Bigamy is a crime so you can't marry her."

"With every word you speak, I'm more convinced that you're out of your mind. I'm not certain it's wise to have a female on the premises when she's suffering from such blatant hysteria, so you and your cousin will need to depart at once."

"Archie! Please!"

"Your scheme has been foiled, and you ought to be ashamed of yourself."

"I'll destroy you," she pointlessly threatened. "I'll announce to the world that you begged me to have you."

"If you wish to prove yourself an unhinged doxy, you're free to behave that foolishly, but you should ponder the ramifications. I can guarantee you won't like what they will turn out to be."

He yanked her hand from his wrist and sauntered away. Her knees gave out, and she stumbled over to a chair and eased down.

Her heart was beating so hard that she thought it might burst out of her chest. She frantically contemplated the past few days. There had been a wedding—with witnesses. She'd signed a license, but it suddenly dawned on her that she hadn't seen it again. He'd tucked it into his coat and had kept it. Where had he put it? Why was she fearing it had been burned to ash in a hearth?

Had he tricked her? Had the ceremony been carefully orchestrated so she'd assume it was genuine? Is that what had happened? How else could he so blithely deny her?

There were occasional stories about wealthy dandies pulling this sort of stunt, but she'd always figured they were masculine fantasies that couldn't possibly be true. After all, how could a female be so stupid?

Yet he was insisting no wedding had been held, so he must have engaged in subterfuge, and she'd gleefully fallen for it. She'd deemed herself cleverly wed to a rich, important man, but his plan had simply been implemented to leave her ruined and disgraced.

Bile roiled in her belly, and she leapt up and raced to a potted plant over in the corner. She vomited over and over, as panic assailed her. She had to find Emily and tell her about Archie.

Emily would know what to do. Emily would fix everything.

Chapter Nineteen

EMILY WAS LYING ON her bed, wrapped in James's arms, as he slumbered deeply. It was late and quiet, although Peggy had knocked furtively and agitatedly on numerous occasions, as if she was suffering an emergency and desperate for Emily to be apprised. Emily couldn't care less.

Luckily, the door had been locked, so she'd ignored her cousin, and finally, Peggy had muttered furiously and had slunk off, so Emily had been able to revel in the moment. She was so happy, glad she'd agreed to marry him, but terrified too and figuring she shouldn't have.

She was very British, and she understood that a person should recognize his or her place and stay in it, so she was jumping up to a position she wasn't qualified to occupy. She loved him though, so she would forge ahead and become his bride. But she wondered how much time would have to pass before she would feel more confident about the spot she'd wrangled for herself.

They'd talked about their elopement, and about the future they hoped to have, until they'd run out of words. His excitement had left him totally drained, and he was napping. She should have scolded herself for letting him doze off, but she wasn't certain it mattered. They'd be wed shortly, and while there were sticklers who would claim it was sinful to cuddle so intimately prior to the vows being spoken, she, apparently, wasn't one of them.

It seemed as if the universe had furnished her with a special duty to watch over him, and she had an obligation to keep him safe and steady. If he wanted to fall asleep on her bed a few days before the ceremony, she wouldn't argue about it.

When the sun rose, it would be Wednesday, and they'd decided to sneak away to Scotland on Thursday. They would pretend to be taking a drive along the coast, and they'd pack light and stow their bags in advance, so as not to arouse any curiosity. They would send a note on the road that they were actually bound for London and would return soon. People at Wave Crest would speculate as to their plans, but when they came back, they'd be husband and wife.

Suddenly, James mumbled and violently shook himself. He gave a vehement exhalation of *No!* and swatted at an invisible foe. Then he lurched up as if someone had poked him with a pin. He glanced around quite frantically, as if he couldn't remember where he was, then his gaze rested on her, and he relaxed down on the pillow.

"Were you having another nightmare?" she asked, as she snuggled nearer to hold him tight.

"I always have nightmares," he admitted.

"Was it the same one you had that afternoon at our picnic?"

"Yes, but it's not all that dramatic. I'm lost in a blizzard. I can't see anything, and I'm searching for my men. I can't ever find them, so it's exhausting."

"Did that happen to you? Were you lost in a blizzard and searching for them?"

"It happened on dozens—perhaps hundreds—of occasions, so I guess it's not a dream. It would be more precise to say it's my mind replaying a genuine event."

He shivered, and she tucked in the blanket, attempting to capture more of their bodily heat.

"You're not about to rush out and fetch a winter coat and hat, are you?" she asked.

He chuckled. "No. Since I met you, my chills have been considerably reduced. You're having a palliative effect on my condition." He dipped down and kissed her, then peered out the window. "What time do you suppose it is?"

"Three? Four?"

"Dawn must be about to arrive. I should tiptoe out," he said, but he didn't move.

"There's no hurry. Let your dream fade a bit before you stagger off."

"Are you glad about our elopement?"

"I'm glad, but I'm nervous too."

"Have you been loafing here in the dark, fretting and stewing?"

"Yes. I'm a worrier. I constantly focus on the things that could go wrong. I've suffered several tragedies over the years, so I'm always braced for catastrophe."

"What tragedies have you suffered?"

The question underscored how reckless they were being. Couples generally wed after a lengthy acquaintance, and they marched to the altar, surrounded by relatives and friends who'd known them since birth. They didn't ride off to Scotland, while keeping the whole endeavor a grand secret.

As far as she could recall, she'd never even told him she was from Hexham. If she'd traveled home that very second, he'd have no idea where it was located.

"My mother died when I was a baby," she said, "so I was raised by my father."

"He was a gentleman?"

"Yes, and he was wonderful, but he was bankrupted in a financial scheme. He invested in a swindle, lost all he owned, and perished from a broken heart. I was sent to live with my uncle. After he passed on, my aunt found out he'd been a spendthrift and gambler."

"But she held onto the property? Right?"

"Yes. She's managed to stave off the creditors, but she's been ill, and I can't imagine what will transpire after she's gone." Emily wrinkled up her nose, hating to mention negative topics in his presence. "Our situation has been dicey."

"Maybe I could pay off the debts and buy the place for you. We don't need to permit the creditors to seize it. You'll be my wife, so it could be my wedding gift to you. Would you like that?"

He tossed out the possibility as if they were discussing pocket coins, and it emphasized the differences in their circumstances. It would be marvelous to save Hexham, but she never wanted to sound greedy or have him assume she was coveting his fortune. She was marrying him because she loved him, and she would never take his wealth for granted.

"We can talk about it after we return from Scotland," she said, recognizing it would be difficult to get used to having money. For most of her life, she'd been balanced on the edge of fiscal ruin, and it would be a relief not to have to count every penny.

He eased her onto her back, and he shifted so he was stretched out atop her. He kissed her, and the embrace began sweetly, but it quickly intensified. His tongue was in her mouth, his hands in her hair. Their torsos were crushed together, and she reveled in the weight of him. It set off feminine instincts she hadn't realized she possessed, and she was swiftly thinking she'd likely commit whatever sins he suggested.

He was touching her all over, caressing her breasts, her tummy. Each stroke of his palms was like a bolt of lightning to her anatomy.

She was attired in her nightgown, and with her covered just by the thin fabric, she might have been naked. The sensation he produced was naughty and shocking, and she was treading on very dangerous ground. There was a wicked ambiance to the event, so she was eager to cast caution to the wind and act in every debauched way—even though she couldn't have explained what any of them were.

His ministrations had her so distracted that she scarcely noticed when he tugged down the straps of her nightgown, when he bared her bosom. He abandoned her lips and nuzzled a trail down her neck and across her chest. Without warning, he sucked on a nipple, and it was so decadent and so delicious that she was stunned. She didn't try to stop him, but lay like a statue and allowed his torment.

He kept on and on, nibbling on one nipple, then switching to the other. He went back and forth, back and forth, until she was quite overcome and feeling as if she might simply explode.

At the same time, he was drawing the hem of her nightgown up her legs, past her calves, then her thighs. Eventually, he'd worked it high enough that he'd reached her private parts. She was riveted by what was occurring, but alarm bells were ringing too. Matters were escalating so fast, and she thought they should step off the ledge where they were perched and debate where they were headed.

"What are you doing?" she asked.

He was still nursing at her breasts, and at her question, he glanced up at her and grinned. "I'm making love to you. Do you like it?"

"Yes, I like it, but I'm worried we're walking down a road we shouldn't travel."

"We'll be married soon. Why can't we misbehave?"

"It would be wrong to continue."

"Some people would claim that it is."

She smirked. "Not you, I take it."

"You're aware of my opinion about life. It's short and we should grab for all the pleasure we can. Let's have this be our wedding night."

She scowled. "You mean right now?"

"Why shouldn't we? Would you rather wait until we're in Scotland? Will we consummate our vows in a foreign coaching inn? You can't want that."

"I hadn't really stared that far into the future. This is happening too rapidly for my liking."

"And it's happening too slowly for mine," he said. "We shouldn't delay the best aspect of matrimony."

"What is that? Snuggling like this?"

"Yes. We can carry on like this for the rest of our lives. We don't have to ever leave our bedchamber if we don't feel like it."

His expression was warm and fond, and when he looked at her as he was, she couldn't refuse him. She supposed this was how they'd always interact. He'd smile and ask sweetly, and she'd agree to his every request.

Shouldn't they treat it as their wedding night? Why not? She hadn't had much of a chance to ponder the details of their stealth trip to Scotland. It was bad enough that they were eloping. Did she wish to proceed with the consummation in a noisy, decrepit coaching inn?

They were sneaking off like escaping bandits, telling no one and inviting no witnesses. Shouldn't they celebrate now, in her comfortable bed at Wave Crest?

"Should we stop?" he asked. "Would you like me to return to my room?"

She blanched. "Don't you dare."

His grin widened. "That's my girl."

With no further comment, he began enticing her again, and with her acquiescence, he'd been pitched into a fevered state. His kisses were more desperate, his caresses more fierce. He couldn't seem to hold her closely enough, couldn't kiss her deeply enough. He was so certain of the correct direction that she simply let him lead the way.

He dipped to her breasts and was fixated on her nipples. He pinched and bit them, sucked and twirled them, and she was writhing with a misery she couldn't control. His fingers slithered under the hem of her nightgown, and he slid them into her womanly sheath.

She wanted to ask what he was planning, but he knew exactly what had to transpire. He pushed his fingers in and out of her body, the feeling so exciting that her hips flexed against his hand. It was as if her anatomy was aware of what path to take, and she allowed instinct to spirit her away.

He flicked his thumb at the tender spot located at the vee of her thighs, as he captured a nipple with his eager lips. Suddenly, she was flying to the heavens in ecstasy. She seemed to shatter, and she spiraled up and up until she reached an apex, then she tumbled down and landed safely in his arms.

He was laughing, preening, proud of the devastating response he'd wrought.

"Was that marital desire?" she asked when she could speak again.

"Yes, and it was a very fine example of it too. You've just proved that you and I will be a lusty, happy couple."

"I hope so. Is that kind of pleasure common?"

"Yes—if the man is skilled on a mattress."

She snickered merrily. "Why am I positive you're about to brag that you're an expert at amour?"

"I won't brag, but I will admit that I've never been a saint."

"You don't keep mistresses and dally with trollops, do you?"

"No, I'm much too reserved for that, and I'm too tight-fisted with my money to waste it on doxies."

"I'm delighted by that statement, and you better be telling me the truth."

"It is the truth, and when I can have you as my bride, how could any other female ever tickle my fancy?"

It was a dear remark that thrilled her. It stirred her affection for him, and it bolstered her confidence that she was right to bind herself. He would be her devoted husband.

She noticed that he was on edge, while she was relaxed from his ministrations, and she asked, "You're awfully tense. What's wrong?"

"There's more to this than we've attempted so far."

"What else has to happen?"

"Has no one explained it to you?"

"I've only been told that it's very physical."

"A man can experience the same type of pleasure that just swept over you."

"He can? That sounds so peculiar. I'd like to do it for you, but I don't know how."

"I'll show you what needs to occur," he said.

"Can you describe it first?"

"It's easier if we simply start in again."

"Can you at least give me a hint?"

He scowled, dithered, picked his words. "Men and women are built differently in their private areas. I have a sort of rod between my legs. It's usually flaccid, but it grows very hard when I'm aroused."

"How fascinating. What's it called? Does it have a name?"

"A phallus or a cock."

"Oh, I've heard of those." Always uttered as derogatory slurs. "I had no idea what they meant though."

"It fits in your woman's sheath, so I will join our bodies together and move it in and out. It will bring me enormous satisfaction, and it's how I could eventually plant a babe in your womb."

Her innards clenched at the thought, and evidently, there was much more taking place than a hasty romp that probably shouldn't have been initiated.

"A babe!" she said. "I hadn't even considered it."

"It's referred to as fornication, and it's how you wind up with child."

She was practically breathless with shock and excitement. "And you accomplish it by putting your phallus into me?"

He nodded. "Yes."

It was a strange process, and she struggled to envision how it was achieved, but she couldn't fathom it. She flung out her arms as if she was being crucified. "Have your wicked way with me, but you better promise I'll like it."

"You'll like it, Mrs. Covington. I promise."

At being called Mrs. Covington, she rippled with pride and pulled him close and delivered a kiss of her own, then he shifted onto his knees and tugged off his shirt to bare his chest. His shoulders were broad, his waist slender, and there was a smattering of hair across the top. It narrowed down his tummy and disappeared into his trousers.

She tried to recollect if she'd ever viewed a man's chest before. She didn't think she had, and the sight exhilarated her in a manner she didn't comprehend. It fueled her worst impulses, making her yearn for both of them to be naked. It was a savage, inexplicable urge, but it felt exactly right.

He snuggled down, their skin connecting and generating such heat that it seemed as if sparks were shooting around the room. The moment was that electrifying.

He was past the point where he could continue chatting. They'd become physical beings, with the pursuit of the conclusion their only goal. He started driving her up the spiral of desire yet again. He touched her everywhere, massaged her everywhere, each stroke of his busy hands sending her higher and higher.

Gradually, she realized his actions were intended to distract her, to keep her from focusing on what was actually occurring. He'd widened her thighs, his torso dropping between them, and he was unbuttoning his trousers, yanking them down to his flanks. All of it transpired so casually, and was such a natural progression, that she scarcely paid attention to any of it.

He was prodding at her private parts, his fingers working inside her, then something else was there, something bigger, and she recognized it to be his phallus. They were swiftly marching toward the end, and she was terribly glad that he'd clarified what he would be attempting. If he hadn't, she would have been frightened out of her wits.

As it was, she was ecstatic and eager, cataloguing every detail for later reflection. She wasn't anxious or afraid. She was curious and ready.

His ardor was burning at such a hot temperature that he couldn't delay, couldn't slow down to allow any acclimation. He could only rush ahead to the bliss that awaited. He was pushing into her most sensitive area, the pressure increasing, her body protesting the invasion and trying to prevent it, when suddenly, he gave a fierce thrust with his hips and burst into her.

He froze, the significance sinking in. The deed was done, she was ruined, and they were totally bound. There could be no going back.

He smiled down at her, appearing a tad strained, as he asked, "Are you all right?"

"I'm fine. Are we finished?"

"No, there's a bit more."

"What should I do?"

"Move with me. Like this."

That was the extent of the conversation he could manage. She hugged him tight, as he shoved his hips against her own. For a minute or two, it was awkward, but she figured out the rhythm and participated with a reckless abandon.

The tempo escalated. He would pull out all the way, then push himself in, until she thought they might just ignite from the friction they were creating. It was wild and debauched, and much before she was prepared, he groaned and collapsed onto her, his weight pinning her down. He didn't feel heavy though. He felt wonderful and welcome.

How could she have lived to be twenty-five, but not have known a woman could engage in such a boisterous act with a man?

Eventually, he drew away and slid onto his side. She rolled too, so they were nose to nose. They were grinning, delighted with what they'd accomplished.

"I've got you now," he said. "You'll never be able to escape my dastardly clutches."

"I've snagged you too. If you have regrets in the future, I'll remind you that it's too late to complain."

He scoffed. "As if I would ever regret picking you."

Mentally, she whispered a prayer that his current opinion would always remain true. "Might you have planted a babe? You said this is how it happens. Could it the very first time?"

"It's a possibility whenever we're together like this."

"What if we discover you're about to be a father? I'm not sure you've fully contemplated the ramifications of being a husband, so I'm positive you haven't considered being a father."

"If you're with child, I will hope every second that we will have a little girl who looks just like you." It was the dearest comment he could have uttered, and tears flooded into her eyes. He was stricken and asked, "What's this? Tears? You can't be sad. Not when we're at the beginning of everything."

"I'm not sad. I'm happy, but I'm overwhelmed too."

"I am an overwhelming fellow, so I completely understand, but I can't have you crying on me. This is our wedding night, and my poor ego would never survive it."

She sighed with joy, as he shifted onto his back and draped her over his chest. It was her favorite spot in the world. Her ear was directly over his heart, so she could hear it beating. If she'd died that very instant, she'd think her entire life had been worth it merely to have had the chance to be with him like this.

"What time do you suppose it is now?" he asked after a bit.

"If it was four o'clock when you inquired previously, it's probably five." She rose up on her elbow and glanced out the window. The sky was starting to lighten. "Dawn is breaking."

"I better sneak out while I still can. Until we're wed, I can't have the servants find me with you. Not before I have a ring on your finger."

"Thank you. I appreciate it. Once I'm your wife, your servants will be *my* servants, and I can't have them assuming I'm a tart."

"Well, *I* have learned you have a few loose tendencies, but I'll keep that news to myself."

He eased away and sat on the edge of the bed, then he peered at her over his shoulder. "I don't want to leave. I wish I could loaf in here all day."

"That would give the staff plenty to talk about."

"Let's meet for breakfast," he said. "How about around eleven?"

"I would like that, but is it wise for us to dine? I'll gape at you like a besotted ninny, and people will notice. I won't be able to hide my infatuation."

"I won't be able to hide mine either, so I guess we'll have to risk it."

He slid to his feet and straightened his clothes, then he chuckled as if he was embarrassed. "I just realized I deflowered you, and I was in such a hurry that I didn't even take off my boots."

"You're a terrible scoundrel."

"Am I forgiven?"

"Yes. I've already figured out that my life will be a long slog of you committing mischief and my pardoning you for any lapse. Where you're concerned, I have no spine whatsoever."

"Aren't I lucky?"

He leaned over and kissed her goodbye. The embrace was sweet and luscious, and she shoved him away.

"Go," she said. "If you don't, you'll be caught with me and that would be a disaster."

"I'll see you at eleven."

"Yes, in the dining room."

He didn't pull away though, but remained hovered over her, his beautiful blue eyes searching hers. "I'm glad we did this," he said. "You're not suffering any regrets, are you?"

"No. No regrets."

He stood and went to the door. He peeked into the hall, then crept out and departed. She sat very still, trying to hear his strides as he tiptoed away, but he was being too furtive, so it seemed as if he'd vanished into thin air.

She plopped onto the pillow, wincing as her feminine parts protested their new condition. She was truly a woman now, having lain with the man she loved, the man of her dreams, the man who would be her husband very soon.

The night of amour had exhausted her, and she snuggled under the blankets and fell into a deep slumber. As she drifted off, she was smiling, focused on James and nothing else.

Chapter Twenty

EMILY WAS DRESSED, A maid about to pin up her hair, so she could head downstairs to locate James. She was running late and kicking herself for having overslept. It was noon already, and she hoped he hadn't waited for her to stagger down to join him for breakfast.

Typically, she rose early and liked to be busy first thing in the morning. She would hate to have him think she was a slacker.

Suddenly, Peggy barged in, and she was fuming, as if Emily had missed an important appointment. "There you are! I've been searching for you. Where have you been hiding?"

"I wasn't hiding. I was exhausted after supper, so I snuck off to bed. Now, I'm having a lazy start to my day."

"I needed you last night, and I knocked and knocked."

"Yes, so?"

"You should have answered." Peggy scowled at the maid and told her, "Would you excuse us? I have to speak privately with my cousin. I'll finish her hair."

The maid was taken aback at Peggy's abrupt manner, and Emily smoothed over the awkward moment with a smile and said to the maid, "You can abandon me. If my cousin can't arrange my hair, I'll call for you to return and fix what she couldn't."

The woman smirked and left, then Peggy shut and locked the door. She dragged two chairs over to the far side of the room, placing them very close together. She gestured to one of them and said, "We have to talk. Sit down."

"What's wrong?"

"Sit! And keep your voice down. I can't have anyone loiter in the hall and eavesdrop."

"For pity's sake. Why all the drama?"

"Don't argue, Emily!"

Emily sighed with exasperation, but she stomped over and plopped down. Peggy sat too, and she didn't look well. Her color was high, her eyes red, as if she'd been crying for hours. She appeared feverish, as if she was catching an influenza.

"I have to tell you an awful story," she said. "It will shock and upset you, and you'll be angry, but please don't scold me. We're beyond lectures or reprimands."

"Oh, no. What did you do?"

To Emily's great astonishment, Peggy burst into tears, and her anguish was alarming. Emily braced, frightened over what was about to be revealed.

She had kerchiefs in the dresser, and she walked over and grabbed one. She had wine on a tray too, and she poured a glass. Peggy had to calm down or they'd never get to the bottom of what had transpired. She'd be too distraught to explain.

Emily handed over the kerchief and the wine, saying, "Drink down the contents, then let's see if you can spit it out."

Peggy was unusually obedient. She glugged down the wine, then swiped at her tears and mustered her aplomb sufficiently to choke out, "I doubt you've noticed it, but Archie Covington and I have been flirting, and it's grown into an amour."

Emily groaned with dismay. "Don't confess this to me. I can't bear to hear it."

"He's the reason we were kicked out of Mrs. Darlington's hotel. I was gambling with him. It's why I came in so late."

From Peggy's morose condition, Emily figured she could guess what had occurred, and she asked, "Are you ruined? Is that what you're about to confide?"

"Yes, but it's worse than that."

"What could be worse? The only more damning admission would be an announcement that you're increasing with his child, but isn't it too soon to know?"

"No, it's not that. Not yet anyway."

"What is it then?"

For once, Peggy was ashamed. "He's been so fond of me, and he constantly pressured me to climb into his bed, but I wouldn't, not unless he married me. I was very adamant about it, so we wed a few days ago."

"Did you just say you're wed to him?" Peggy nodded vigorously, and Emily said, "But Peggy, he's engaged to Miss Moore. She and his mother were very clear about it. It's not possible for him to have proceeded with you. He's previously contracted."

"We had a secret ceremony. There's a small church down the road, and we snuck there and recited our vows. There were witnesses, and we signed a marriage license and everything. Then we celebrated our wedding night."

"What's the problem then?"

"Archie is insisting there was no ceremony."

Emily gasped. "What? How could that be?"

"I'm devastated, afraid, and very, very angry. You have to tell me what to do."

"Is he claiming you imagined it? You're lying? You're deranged? I take it you've talked to him. What is his position?"

"He's claiming I'm lying, but his friend, Gordo, officiated. Archie told me he's a curate in his father's church, so he's allowed to perform weddings, but apparently, he has no ministerial authority."

"Of course he has no authority! He's a wastrel and a drunkard. Why would you have believed such an outrageous falsehood?"

"I'm in love with Archie! He seemed so besotted, and he was going to change my life! Why wouldn't I have believed him?"

At Peggy's gullibility, Emily couldn't tamp down a wince. "What about the witnesses? Who attended? Have you spoken to any of them?"

"They were Archie's friends, the fellows you've met at supper. They'll claim they weren't in Baywick on that date."

"What about the license? What happened to it?"

"Archie stuck it in his coat, and I never saw it again."

"Why am I suspecting it was his idea to keep the event a secret? What was his excuse?"

"He needed time to persuade his mother and his brother that I would be a suitable bride. He assumed, if he sought their blessing, they wouldn't give it. He couldn't risk that they'd refuse."

"That was terribly convenient for him." Emily was being very sarcastic, but Peggy didn't notice.

"How can I fix this?" Peggy asked. "I'm Archie's wife, so we have to apprise the Earl and his mother. Then Miss Moore has to depart immediately. On that point, I will remain firm. It's nonnegotiable."

Emily gaped at Peggy, wondering if she wasn't touched in the head. Or perhaps she'd been counting on Archie Covington so desperately that she couldn't face reality.

There were always stories about the rich, spoiled sons of the aristocracy and their penchant for fake weddings. The rumors regularly circulated, but Emily hadn't thought they were true. She simply couldn't picture a young man being so vicious. It was such a cruel subterfuge and all of it implemented merely so a wealthy cad could convince a naïve girl to lift her skirt.

She supposed part of the *fun* was the chase and the surrender. They were deceiving their prey, and in their sick minds, that amounted to high entertainment.

"Peggy, listen to me," Emily said. "You're not married to him. He tricked you."

"No, no, it was a real wedding. I swear it was!"

"You're in a frantic mood, but you have to stop being so silly."

Despite Peggy's comments, her pathetic expression indicated she understood that she'd been duped. She was struggling to hold onto the dream of being Mrs. Archie Covington, and the blasted oaf was precisely the sort of cretin Peggy would have adored. Once he'd paid her the slightest bit of attention, she wouldn't have been able to resist.

She broke down and wept as if the world was ending, and Emily sat quietly, waiting for the deluge to pass. A clock ticked over on the mantel, and a bird chirped outside, but other than those two sounds, there was only Peggy's sobbing.

The tears gradually slowed, and Emily said, "Please tell me you recognize your folly. I can't continue discussing this if you're determined to act like a lunatic."

"I've been debating," Peggy said, "and I've decided I might have been fooled, so we have to have a second ceremony. And don't forget: I might be increasing. Even if the first one was a sham, he has to step up and behave appropriately. The Earl and his mother have to force him into it. Otherwise, what will become of me?"

Emily doubted Bernice Covington would be willing to intervene in the debacle. As to James, Emily might have some sway, but who could guess for sure? She barely knew him, and aristocratic families were a strange species. They supported each other in every situation. They closed ranks. Who could predict what he might do?

Suddenly, she was as weary as Peggy. She'd presumed she was engaged herself, and she suffered a momentary surge of fear that *she* had been tricked too. Might James have slyly seduced her, as Archie had seduced Peggy?

After all, James was an earl, and from the beginning of his infatuation, Emily had been dubious. She was as lonely and gullible as Peggy, so she'd have been easy prey too. Had James realized that about her? What if he was as corrupt as his brother?

No, no, James wasn't Archie! He wouldn't deceive her. He wouldn't hurt her.

She tried to remember that fact, but she was shaking with alarm. She couldn't imagine where this would lead. She'd been expecting to elope with James. Would that still occur? What if it didn't? Where would it leave her?

"I will meet with Lord Roxbury," Emily said, "and I'll ask his advice. He's kind and I trust him."

"Archie has to marry me, Em. If he won't, I'll just die!"

Emily clucked her tongue. "No one is dying, and you have to quit being so hysterical."

"I can't help it. I've been so afraid."

"I understand that you have been." Emily rose and went to the bed. She pulled back the blankets and pointed to the mattress. "You've had a terrible shock. Why don't you rest for awhile? You could take a nap."

"I should accompany you," Peggy said. "If we confront the Earl together, he'll have to believe us."

Emily could think of no more wretched circumstance than to have Peggy howling and hurling demands. "You stay up here, and I'll see what I can accomplish, but you have to brace yourself for bad news. You're aware of what these noble families are like. I have no idea what their opinion will be about this."

She didn't give Peggy a chance to argue. She clasped her arm, lifted her to her feet, and guided her onto the bed. She tucked her in as if she were a child.

"Go to sleep," Emily said.

"Come up the minute it's been resolved."

"I will, and you must promise you won't strut in after me and start any quarrels. Let me handle this."

"You're the best, Em. I've always thought so."

"I agree. I am the absolute best."

Peggy was quickly drifting off, and Emily tiptoed away and headed downstairs, her spirits heavy, her confidence destroyed.

"May I talk to you?"

"Yes, of course."

After a bit of searching, a footman had informed Emily that James was in his library. He was on the other side of the ostentatious room, seated at the desk. There were huge windows behind him that looked out at the garden and the ocean beyond. The sun was shining brightly, so he seemed to glow with a golden halo.

Attired like the aristocrat he was, he was wearing a dark blue coat, a white shirt with an extravagant cravat. His fingers were covered with expensive rings. In contrast, she'd risen late and had dressed hastily. Her maid hadn't finished styling her hair, so it was simply tied with a ribbon. She felt plain and even a tad unkempt.

The differences between them had never appeared more stark, and she was very nervous, as if she'd transgressed and had been caught in the act.

She didn't want to discuss Peggy with him. Previously, he'd been apprised of the debacle with Mary Darlington, so he grasped that Peggy was capable of great mischief. She couldn't bear to confess that Peggy had stirred more trouble.

He'd been eager to marry her, but a couple never wed as quickly and recklessly as they were planning, and this was a perfect reason as to why not. They hadn't even packed their bags yet, and a calamity had already developed.

She was curious as to how James would assess his brother's role in the fiasco. From the few comments he'd shared about Archie Covington, she'd learned that he and Archie weren't that close, but she couldn't suppose he would like to have her make horrid allegations about his sibling. What if he deemed them to be specious? What if he called Peggy a liar?

What then? What then?

The questions flew by, and she inhaled a deep breath to calm herself. He'd only ever been courteous to her, and she wouldn't ascribe bad motives to him. Still though, as she entered the room, she was trembling slightly. She approached the desk, and there was an empty chair across from him, as if they were about to conduct a difficult employment interview.

She smiled and said, "I'm sorry I missed breakfast. I overslept, and I—"

She'd intended to open the conversation by mentioning their scheduled meal, but he cut her off. "I've asked my stepmother to join us." He waved to a corner, to where Emily hadn't noticed Bernice Covington staring out a window. He added, "I hope you don't mind."

How was she to reply to such a request? She minded very much! She needed to confer with him in private, and she couldn't abide Bernice Covington.

Her pulse began to race. Why would the Countess be present? Had Mr. Covington revealed the situation to them?

When Emily had told Peggy she'd meet with James, it hadn't occurred to her that Mr. Covington might have gotten to him first, and whatever he'd imparted, it was obvious they'd accepted his version of events. Emily was stumbling into the debate ten steps behind him. How would she ever catch up?

James gestured to the empty chair, and Emily eased down. The Countess pushed away from the window and came over to stand beside James. The positioning couldn't be an accident. They were sending a signal that they were allies and their interests were aligned against hers.

James's expression was unreadable, but the Countess's was filled with loathing and spite, and Emily recognized that any examination of Archie Covington's actions would be pointless. They wouldn't listen.

"I expect I know what topic you're about to address," James said.

"If it's about your brother and my cousin, then yes, you've guessed the topic."

"We deliberated this morning, and this is how we will proceed."

Emily blanched. "You decided without talking to me? Without hearing Peggy's side of the story?"

"We didn't need to hear it." James's tone was cold and infuriating.

"May I speak on behalf of my cousin who has been the victim of a hideous charade?"

The Countess scoffed with disgust. "No, Miss Shaw, you may not state an opinion, and you most especially may not blather on about your cousin."

Emily wasn't in awe of Bernice Covington, so she might have hurled a caustic retort, but James held up a hand, urging them both to silence.

"I won't tolerate any bickering," he said.

Emily ignored him. "Your brother was anxious to seduce Peggy, and when she refused to oblige him with carnal conduct, he swore he'd wed her in order for it to be allowed. There was a ceremony with witnesses. She signed a marriage license."

The Countess hissed, "There was no wedding! Don't you dare spread such a false claim."

"Bernice!" James was very curt with her. "I warned you that I won't have any quarreling, and I meant it." The Countess bit her tongue, then James focused his attention on Emily. "Archie came to us the minute Peggy raised her accusations. I'm not sure what to think."

"It's not hard to figure out," Emily said. "He arranged for Peggy to recite vows in front of a minister, but it appears now that it was a ruse he implemented merely to lure her into his bed. If the ceremony was genuine, then they're good and truly shackled. If he faked it, then he's ruined her with wicked intent, and she might be carrying his child. We should immediately have another wedding and make the union official."

The Countess muttered under her breath, and James tsked with exasperation. "I'm sorry, Miss Shaw, but Archie informs us that Peggy has been inappropriately flirting with him from the moment she arrived in Baywick. Several of the servants have verified Archie's account. She's been flaunting herself outrageously, and on numerous occasions, he asked her to stop, but she wouldn't leave him alone."

"It was all his doing," Emily fumed. "She was innocent prey, and he chased her down like a determined huntsman. He was playing on her insecurities, babbling that he loved her, that he'd marry her."

"Why would he have told her that?" James gently inquired. "Think, Miss Shaw. Please. He's been engaged to Miss Moore for the prior year, and no offense, but your cousin is far beneath him in status and station. Even if he fancied her, he wasn't free to propose. Why would he have encouraged her?"

"How about because he's a scoundrel?" Emily was angry and embarrassed, and tears flooded her eyes. "I demand he fix this mess."

James's expression became pitying. "He's saying he never touched Peggy and she's a liar."

Emily bristled with temper. "Bring him in here at once. Let him tell me—to my face—that the wedding never occurred."

"He left for London," James said. "We felt we should get him out of the house, so we can deal with this issue without his presence exacerbating matters."

"He left?" Emily's jaw dropped. "Like a cur? Like a swine? Like the dog he is?"

The Countess seethed over Emily's insults, but James didn't react. He remained very calm. "Yes, he's gone, so you and I have to pick up the pieces. How would you suggest we accomplish it?"

"I've already announced the only resolution we'll accept: He has to return to Wave Crest and wed Peggy without delay."

"That's not an option." James shook his head as if Emily was a dunce. "We can't have them under the same roof another minute. It's best if he's away."

"Best for whom?" Emily asked, but he didn't answer.

Instead, he said, "I'm at a loss as to how we should handle this situation. Your cousin is raising many claims, but Archie has vehemently denied them. You and I have to meet somewhere in the middle and figure out a suitable ending."

"An ending for Peggy, you mean. It sounds to me as if your brother's conclusion has been arranged. He behaved egregiously, then skipped away unscathed."

"He insists she's deranged and hoping to trap him into a marriage he never pursued. If that's the case, how can I allow it to happen? How can I deduce what is true and what isn't?"

"You could believe *me*," she said. "We're friends, aren't we? We're close?" She yearned to mention their own secret engagement, but with the Countess glaring down her snooty nose, she didn't dare. "Your brother tricked Peggy by staging a false wedding."

"What if she's lying to you, Miss Shaw? Have you considered that possibility?"

He gazed at her so sweetly, his blue eyes searching hers. They both knew that Peggy wasn't trustworthy, that she regularly stirred mischief, and briefly, Emily's tenacity failed her. What if Peggy had invented the incident? Mr. Covington was precisely the sort of cad Peggy expected to have as her husband.

Once in her life, her father might have chosen a lofty spouse for her, but his fiscal misfortunes had pushed them down the social ladder to where Peggy couldn't receive the swain she deserved. What if she'd seen a solution in Mr. Covington?

Was Peggy capable of that type of duplicity? Was she so corrupt in her morals, so jaded in her attitudes, that she might employ any ruse in order to obtain what she sought?

Suddenly, Emily was questioning every facet of the disaster. Peggy might participate in any dubious antic to acquire what she craved. Ever since they were young girls, Emily had understood this about her cousin. Peggy's lack of scruples, coupled with her vanity and narcissism, had constantly wreaked havoc.

Was this one more hideous jam, perpetrated by Peggy who could never seem to behave any better? If Emily hesitated, it was only because Peggy had been absolutely bereft when she'd shared her tale about Mr. Covington. Peggy was many things, but she wasn't an actress. She couldn't have feigned such an intense level of woe.

"She's not lying, Lord Roxbury," she quietly stated. "I'm certain she's not."

"I need you to contemplate this rationally," he said just as quietly. "I beg you to picture it from my perspective so you'll grasp why I'm dithering."

Their strong affection was still in place, and Emily caught herself leaning toward him. He was leaning too, and the Countess noticed their overt fondness. She snapped, "James! Stop being so polite to her! Stop pretending there is a viable *side* to her cousin's ridiculous story."

Her sharp words cut into the air like a knife, and James and Emily lurched back in their chairs. James said, "I don't want any fighting, Bernice. Can't we get through this without you barking and condemning?"

"I won't stand here and let Archie's good name be destroyed. That hussy will not glom onto him! Not while I draw breath in my body!"

At hearing Peggy called a hussy, Emily quaked with fury. "Don't insult her. She's always been like a sister to me, and I wish you wouldn't resort to character slurs."

"I would suppose you don't wish it," the Countess sneered. "You're much too cozy with the Earl. Are you imagining, if you simply bat your lashes, he'll ignore your cousin's misdeeds? Why am I positive *you*—like your cousin—glanced around Wave Crest and decided you could accrue many benefits from your acquaintance with us? Are you thinking you'll plead her case and, if she wins it, you'll enjoy some of the spoils?"

"Bernice!" James scolded, as Emily said, "It's not like that. Peggy was viciously ruined by your son, and he should have to marry her."

"The Earl might be willing to put up with your nonsense, but I'm not. Archie advises me that your cousin is an experienced trollop."

Emily gasped. "After his depravities have been exposed, you're accusing *her* of immorality?"

"I'll do more than accuse her," the Countess said. "I'll flat-out declare that she had carnal relations with several of his friends. Right in this very house! When you went up to bed at night, she would sneak back down to revel with them. She drank excessively, until she was stumbling about in a near stupor, then she'd carouse in foul ways. The servants witnessed it."

"That's not true!" Emily hotly claimed. "She was an innocent maiden before she crossed paths with Mr. Covington."

"No, she wasn't, and his friends can testify to it. They returned to London, but Archie was still in residence. Is that why she picked him to be the culprit in her scheme? It's obvious she was intending to land a highborn husband, but with the rest of them gone, Archie was the only one she could blame."

"What an outrageous allegation!" Emily huffed.

"Your cousin is a whore," the Countess said, "and if she winds up with a babe in her belly, it could be any man's child. I won't permit her to foist a bastard on us and insist we've incurred an obligation."

Emily was so stunned she couldn't respond. She gaped at the malicious shrew and wondered how to deflect her venom. Finally, she yanked her gaze to James and said, "You can't believe any of that. Please tell me you don't."

He killed her by shrugging. "I'm bewildered by the whole debacle. Archie swears his friends would line up to confirm that she's fornicated with all of them."

"Of course he'd say that. Of course they'd lie for him. They're obnoxious peas in a scandalous pod, and they can't waltz away with no penalty. If they pulled this stunt on Peggy, it can't have been the first time they've tricked an unsuspecting girl. It was too coordinated, and it seemed too real. They must be called to account—starting with your brother."

"I'm debating the best resolution," he maddeningly said. "I'll interrogate his friends, but what if they verify Archie's story? What then?"

"You could listen to me." Emily was almost begging. "You could trust me."

The Countess replied with, "Why would he listen to you, Miss Shaw? You are kin to a skilled harlot. Why would your assurances matter to us? Every word that comes out of your mouth is tainted by your unwavering support of her."

Emily asked James, "Is that your opinion? Do you think my words are tainted?"

"I don't think that," he said. "I think you're loyal to your cousin, and you assume she's been honest with you."

The Countess butted in again. "We're finished dickering over this issue. While we were talking, your bags were packed."

Emily scowled. "Wait, what? Am I departing?"

The Countess snickered with disdain. "You can't have imagined you could tarry at Wave Crest. After your cousin spewed her spurious falsehoods, why would you be welcome?"

"I did imagine we could tarry." Emily looked at James. "Is this your decision? Are you asking me to go?"

She stared him down. This was the moment he could announce their engagement to his stepmother, that Emily was his fiancée, but he was infuriatingly silent.

"Peggy can't remain here," he said. "I promise I'll investigate the situation, but for now, she has to leave. You can stay though. I would be happy with that."

The Countess jumped in with, "No, James. Absolutely not! She is not staying with us. Not after her cousin caused all this trouble. I refuse to allow it."

Emily had felt tears threatening, and a few of them dripped down her cheeks. She was embarrassed to have them appear, but she needn't have worried. Neither Roxbury nor his stepmother noticed her emotional display.

As his stepmother had been venting and insulting Emily, why didn't he order her to shut up? Why didn't he defend Emily?

To her great horror, she was certain that his proposal had also been a sham, that he'd proceeded so he could persuade her to lift her skirt. Was it a ruse regularly practiced by the Covington brothers? What else could it be? It had to be a sort of twisted entertainment for them.

He'd slyly offered matrimony, and she'd merrily given him what he'd sought, but she couldn't justify her acquiescence. During the weeks of their burgeoning amour, he'd been charming and marvelous, and she hadn't been able to resist him. Wasn't that exactly how Archie Covington had behaved toward Peggy?

She and Peggy were a pair of foolish ninnies. They'd traveled away from home, with no older, wiser chaperone to supervise them. They'd been enticed by rich cads, and they'd immediately been ensnared in inappropriate relationships with them. There had been no one to counsel caution, other than Mary, and Emily had ignored her.

Hadn't she recognized from the beginning that Roxbury's affection was very odd? Hadn't she understood that it was peculiar and misplaced?

She couldn't blame Roxbury for her idiocy. Yes, he was wealthy and sophisticated, but he hadn't lured her in against her will. She'd leapt in with both feet, but she was a mature adult who knew right from wrong. She never should have involved herself, and she simply yearned to slither away and lick her wounds in private.

"If you'll excuse me," she said, "I should see to my cousin."

"There is a carriage out front," the Countess interrupted before Roxbury could comment. "Our driver will transport you to the coaching inn in Baywick. I expect the two of you to flee the area on the mail coach tomorrow morning."

Emily didn't bother to glance at her, but said to Roxbury, "Is there anything you'd like to tell the Countess about me?"

She was providing him with a chance to redeem himself, to reveal their betrothal, but he didn't take it. Again, before he could remark, the Countess said, "Go away, Miss Shaw. We are weary of your company."

Emily hesitated a second, then a second more, furnishing Roxbury with an opportunity to speak up, to claim her, to apologize. But apparently, he'd been struck dumb.

She whipped away and left.

Chapter Twenty-One

EMILY WALKED INTO HER bedroom, worried over what she'd find. When she'd gone downstairs, Peggy had dozed off in her bed, but her cousin was up and pacing. Emily had traveled to Baywick with two trunks and a portmanteau. They were stacked by the door. The staff at Wave Crest was very efficient, and as she stood, gaping, two footmen arrived and carried them out.

"What's happening?" Peggy demanded, and she ran over and clasped Emily's arm, looking frantic and perplexed.

"It's not good news."

"I figured that out on my own. Several housemaids came to pack your belongings, and when I asked them what they were doing, they only knew you were leaving immediately."

"Unfortunately, *you* are leaving with me," Emily said. "You should head to your own room and check to be certain they didn't miss anything. Then I'll meet you out in the driveway. A carriage has been harnessed to take us into Baywick, and we'll stay the night at the coaching inn."

"And then what?"

"We'll return to Hexham in the morning."

Peggy was flabbergasted. "How could you have wrecked this? I sent you down to fix the dilemma. You were supposed to talk to the Earl and the Countess for me. Were you fighting with them?"

"There was no opportunity to quarrel. Mr. Covington had conferred with them before me, so they'd made up their minds. They believed him rather than us."

"What did he tell them?"

"He's claiming you invented the whole story to trap him. He's claiming *you* were the pursuer, that you've been flirting shamelessly with him, and when he didn't share your interest, you initiated this nuptial scheme."

Peggy's jaw dropped. "How could he say that? Is Miss Moore departing? Please assure me you arranged that part at least."

Her cousin seemed to be wallowing in an unhinged reality, and if she was, Emily couldn't deal with it. Roxbury had refused to declare himself engaged, so she had too many of her own issues to consider.

"Could we not argue?" Emily's shoulders slumped with defeat. "The entire conversation was hideous and I'm exhausted."

"Should I confront the Countess? Would that work?"

Emily blanched. "No. You definitely shouldn't confront her."

"She's my mother-in-law. I can't help it if she doesn't like that fact."

Tears flooded Emily's eyes. She could not cope with this situation. It was simply beyond her. She glanced over her shoulder to be positive no servants were lurking, then she murmured, "I will mention this once, then we will never discuss it again."

"What is it? What's wrong?"

"Mr. Covington told his mother that you have lain with all of his London chums."

Peggy quailed with alarm. "He what?"

"He said you would sneak down to revel with them late at night, after I was in bed. He said that you would drink to excess, then disport with them in a wicked manner. He said—if you are in the family way—it's not his problem because he has never touched you, and anyway, there could be no method for determining who the father might be, for it could be one of a dozen men."

At the accusation, Peggy trembled violently. "How could he deny me?"

Emily couldn't abide another repugnant scene, not after the one she'd just endured, and she grabbed Peggy and shook her. "That's what Mr. Covington's mother and brother think of you. We are not welcome to remain and we will not remain. Now *go* to your room and check that you've left nothing behind. We won't ever be back, and if the maids forgot anything, it will be lost to you."

She shoved Peggy toward the door. Her cousin staggered, then hesitated as if to refute the terrible words that had been hurled, but Emily couldn't bear any debate. She couldn't defend Peggy. She wouldn't take a side.

A dreadful incident had transpired between Peggy and Mr. Covington, and she'd been thrown into the middle of it against her will. She couldn't repair it or alter the conclusion. She could only flee and whisk Peggy away to safety.

She didn't know what she believed. Peggy would pull any stunt in order to glom onto Archie Covington. But Mr. Covington was a swine and a cur, so it was highly likely too that he'd have tricked her. In their unscrupulous tendencies, they were exactly alike, so how was she to guess what was true?

She didn't suppose Peggy would have been debauched enough to consort with his friends, but she wouldn't bet on it. There had been constant rumors around Hexham that Peggy was no better than she had to be. The main reason her fiancé, the loathsome Teddy, had tossed her over was because he'd discovered she was free with her favors. Would she have displayed them for Mr. Covington's horrid companions?

She might have—if she thought it would make them like her. She was that intent on being accepted by those she viewed as the *right* kind of people.

Emily was convinced Mr. Covington had behaved badly with Peggy, but Peggy was capable of any shocking deceit, and Emily had been sufficiently humiliated during her first trip downstairs. She wouldn't repeat the experience.

Peggy hadn't moved, and Emily said, "I'm heading down to the carriage. You can come or not; it's your choice. If you don't ride with me, you'll have to walk into Baywick. We've been kicked out. You have no standing to tarry and you won't be permitted to plead your case."

"I have to locate Archie. I'll drag him to his mother and force him to confess."

Emily scoffed with derision. "Archie Covington has scurried away like the fiend he is."

Peggy's knees buckled. "He can't have abandoned me."

"He crept away like a thief who'd stolen the silver, deserting you to face the debacle without him. He's on his way to London, and Lord Roxbury will travel there too, so he can question his brother's friends about your licentious conduct with them." Emily glared, her expression so cutting she was amazed she didn't draw blood. "May I hope you haven't exhibited any?"

Peggy's cheeks heated to such a hot temperature that Emily could only assume her cousin was guilty of committing many risqué acts. Who could predict what the men would confide about her to the Earl? The prospect was so mortifying that Emily was nauseous and seriously wondering if she might vomit on the floor.

"Do what you will, Peggy," she said, "but I am leaving. I have to check my own dressers, then I'll be down in the driveway."

"If I depart with you, I'll probably never see Archie again."

Emily spat out a morbid chuckle. "If you stay or if you don't, I can guarantee that you will never see him again. He has renounced you, and you are a fool to dawdle and pine over him."

Peggy burst into tears and raced out.

"Will you join me in the carriage?" Emily said to her retreating back. "Don't be an idiot about this."

Peggy mumbled a comment Emily couldn't decipher, but it didn't matter what it was. She was simply desperate to escape herself. A maid had placed her bonnet and shawl on the bed, and she went over and was tying the bonnet's ribbons when footsteps sounded behind her.

She'd expected it would be a footman, looking for more luggage, but to her great annoyance, it was Lord Roxbury. How dare he barge in! Did he imagine they'd chat? About what topic? He'd been plenty blunt down in his library. What could he possibly wish to address?

"I'm sorry," he said to start the conversation. "This has been a terrible morning, and I didn't handle our discussion very well."

"I beg to differ," she snottily retorted. "I thought you were extremely clear."

"I was taken by surprise, and I wasn't sure what to think."

He approached her warily, as if she was a wild animal that might bolt. That's precisely how she felt: wild and out of control. He reached for her, and she lurched away, refusing to let him touch her. She was so angry that she could barely force out any words.

"You weren't sure what to *think*?" she repeated to him. "You allowed your stepmother to call Peggy a harlot and a liar. I sat there, while she insulted me over and over, and you blithely concurred with her assessment that her son is a saint and my cousin a sinner. Was there any portion of it that I didn't comprehend?"

She grabbed her shawl and stomped to the door. He appeared totally bewildered, as if he couldn't deduce what he was observing.

"You're not leaving," he said. "You can remain here. It's just your cousin who has to go."

"You actually presume I would tarry without her?" She was sputtering with affront. "You figure I'll ignore what occurred, ignore the Countess, and loaf under your exalted roof as if we're all bosom buddies? What is wrong with you?"

"Bernice is an expert at theatrics. She revels in her antics. Don't pay any attention to her."

"Fine. She was being overly dramatic. I'll agree that she was. What about you? What is your excuse?"

"I told you that I'm perplexed over how to view the debacle. For a temporary solution, I requested that both Archie and Peggy depart the premises. They shouldn't be in such close proximity as we evaluate the conundrum."

"Yes, because Peggy is such a temptress! She lured your poor, innocent brother to folly, and he is such a weak, gullible character that he couldn't resist her feminine wiles. Oh, wait! I forgot. He engaged in no misconduct."

"I never said that."

"No, you merely had the Countess say it for you. She accused Peggy of trapping him into marriage on a lie. You took the coward's route and let her do your dirty work."

"I won't declare that Archie is a saint. Nor is he innocent or gullible. I'm puzzled over what to believe."

"How about *my* version of events?" she demanded. "Would that have been so hard?"

"I'm willing to admit that something dastardly happened, but are you certain Peggy is being entirely truthful? You've confided in the past that she's selfish and self-centered, and she got you in that trouble with Mary Darlington. Are you completely positive that you know what transpired? Should you be so adamantly incensed?"

Emily wasn't at all certain. She suspected there had been a fake wedding, but what about the rest of it? What about Mr. Covington's chums and his assertion that Peggy had disgraced herself with them? What about Mr. Covington's insistence that—if she was with child—they couldn't identify the father?

It was such a foul story that Emily would never mention it to anyone. She most especially couldn't share it with Florence once they were home. Nor would she debate it with Lord Roxbury who was staring down his pompous nose as if he were a king and she a serf.

"I'm sick of talking about this," she said, her fury rising.

"I'm not too keen about it either, but I wish you'd stop being so angry. Why are you? I feel as if you're blaming me for what went on between them."

"I'm not blaming you for their mischief. I'm blaming you and your stepmother for how you treated me."

"I've admitted to being overwhelmed and that Bernice revels in her hysteria. I'm caught in the middle of a dreadful quagmire."

"How are you caught?" she sneered. "Your brother spewed his false tale, and you swallowed it hook, line, and sinker. You didn't bother to wonder what *I* might have told you."

"I realize I acted too quickly in judging the situation. I should have delayed and considered more fully, and I regret that I didn't."

"It's convenient for you to claim that now."

Her temper was on a sharp edge, but his was rising too. She'd never seen him when he was irate, and it was another strike against the ludicrous amour they'd pursued. She'd hoped to be his wife, yet she knew so little about him that she'd never observed him when he was enraged.

What sort of people wed when they were strangers?

"I'm sorry," he said again, a muscle ticking in his jaw.

"Great. You're sorry, but would you like to clarify this pesky detail for me? The Countess hurled her venom at me quite vehemently, and you never butted in and ordered her to be silent. Why didn't you tell her I am your fiancée? Why didn't you apprise her that she was speaking to the next countess? Explain that to me—if you can."

"It wasn't the appropriate moment to announce our engagement."

"Why wasn't it? And in your grand estimation, when would be the appropriate moment?"

"When . . . ah . . . things calm down."

"It sounds as if we won't be traveling to Scotland tomorrow." For an instant, he gaped blankly, as if he was confused as to what trip she referred, and she said, "We were eloping, remember?"

"Yes, I remember, but we should delay for a bit. Just until I can resolve matters here. We'll proceed then."

She smirked with derision. "At what point, precisely, would that date arrive? Why am I predicting you'd never think it's the right time?"

"I intend to wed you."

"Really? Then go downstairs and inform the Countess that it's your plan with regard to me."

He frowned. "I don't even like her. Why would I discuss my marriage with her?"

"How about because she's been your mother since you were a boy? How about because she's the reigning matriarch in your family? What problem could there be in informing her?"

His cheeks heated. "I am none of her business, and I'm not about to debate Bernice with you. Could we stick to Archie and Peggy?"

She scoffed. "It's silly—and a little late—for me to mention this, Roxbury, but it's recently dawned on me that I don't know you very well."

"You know me well enough, and don't call me Roxbury. Call me James and don't be such a brat about this."

"A brat!" At the slur, she was so incensed she was surprised the top of her head didn't blow off. "Your brother is a deplorable scoundrel. He staged a fake wedding merely so he could convince Peggy to lift her skirt."

"That's her version of what transpired. According to *you,* she has a dubious reputation, and until I investigate a tad more, I won't blindly accept her story. Her conduct in my home might not have been very proper."

"Let's leave Peggy out of it and focus on this: Why am I worried that you possess many of your brother's same base qualities?"

"What are you talking about?"

"You've flirted with me for weeks. You brought me to live with you, and you wore down my defenses. Then, when I was isolated and adrift, you coaxed me to ruin myself—with the promise of marriage. Imagine my astonishment when I discover that we're not sneaking off to Scotland."

"We'll proceed very soon! Why won't you listen to me?"

"I won't listen because I don't believe you. It seems to me that duplicity runs in your family."

He bristled with offense. "You're comparing me to Archie?"

He appeared so shocked that she would have laughed if the situation hadn't been so serious. "Yes, I'm absolutely comparing you. Now then, I'm finished bickering. Why don't you stroll down to your library and enjoy a celebratory drink with your stepmother? The two of you vanquished my cousin without breaking a sweat."

"We didn't vanquish her," he ridiculously claimed. "We are simply trying to figure out how to handle the dilemma."

"Yes, by kicking her out."

He snorted with disgust. "You can't assume she would be allowed to tarry. Not after the charges she leveled."

"No, I don't think that. Of course you'd support your brother over her, even though he's a cad with despicable habits and friends."

"Could we not argue over his character?"

"There is no other issue on the table, Roxbury. In any other house in the land, Archie and Peggy would be marching to the altar. We'd be having a very quick ceremony to repair the damage he's done, but because you're rich and important, that ending hasn't even occurred to you. Goodbye."

She started for the door, and apparently, she'd exhausted his patience.

"Where are you going?" he snapped.

"I'm meeting Peggy down in the driveway, and we're heading into Baywick. As the Countess has demanded, we will depart for home tomorrow morning. It is my specific intent that we never cross paths with any of you ever again."

"*You* don't have to depart. How many times must I repeat myself?"

"How many times must *I* repeat myself? I would never stay with you when I have been so hideously disrespected. Your brother is the culprit here, and I am struggling to fathom how *I* have become the guilty party."

"I'm not blaming you for any of this," he insisted.

"No, you just haven't stood up for me once. And you've decided we're not marrying, but then, I doubt you ever expected to."

"Don't accuse me of bad motives."

She smirked. "I'm quite sure, Lord Roxbury, that bad motives are the only sort you possess."

She stormed out, and he barked, "Emily! Hold it right there! You don't have my permission to flounce off."

She halted and whirled around. "You suppose you can command me? Me? You have the gall? You are not my father or my husband. You have no authority over me, and I deem it typical that you would speak to me as if I'm your servant. I'm certain now that it's how you've always viewed me."

"You're being totally absurd," he muttered, as if she was an alien creature beyond his understanding.

"Yes, and you are being a complete ass, and since we've arrived at the point of trading insults, this appalling conversation needs to conclude."

She kept on again, and he followed her into the hall. He called to her, "You've obviously forgotten one vital detail."

She glared back at him. "What, in your infinite wisdom, would that be?"

"What if you're increasing? What then?"

She gasped with outrage. They were out in the open, so their remarks could easily carry to others who shouldn't hear them. What if a servant was approaching? What if Peggy was around the corner? If gossip spread about her, she'd die of shame.

"If I should ever have the misfortune to discover I am increasing," she said, her tone furious, her volume a quiet hiss, "I will buy a gun, return to Wave Crest, and shoot you in the middle of your cold, black heart!"

She raced to the stairs and pounded down them. He shouted to her twice more, but he didn't chase after her, which was a miracle. He was the kind of arrogant fiend who would.

To her enormous relief, the carriage was parked out front, the driver in the box and waiting for her to appear. Peggy was inside, which was another miracle. She was white as a ghost, on the verge of fainting, while Emily was teeming with ire and eager to lash out at the whole world.

"Are you ready?" Emily asked.

"Yes. Please get me out of this terrible place."

Emily clambered in and banged on the roof, and the driver whisked them away. She tried to seem stoic and resigned, but in the end, she couldn't help but peek out at the manor vanishing behind them. It was located in such a pretty spot, centered in the most beautiful meadow, the ocean a sapphire strip in the distance.

From the moment she'd first visited, she'd wished it could have been her own. When Roxbury had begun to flirt with her, she'd foolishly assumed it could wind up as hers someday. But that had been a fantasy.

She studied the windows, stupidly thinking Roxbury might glance out to watch her leaving, but she didn't see him anywhere. Why would she have expected to see him? Why would he want a last glimpse? She was deranged; there was no doubt about it.

She shifted on the seat, and she gazed in the other direction, toward Baywick and the road that would take them home in the morning.

Chapter Twenty-Two

TEMPERANCE WAS APPROACHING THE door to the Earl's library, when she heard Bernice say, "I'm glad they're gone. We're shed of them quicker than I imagined we'd be."

The Earl responded with, "We're not discussing it, Bernice. I'm sick at heart over the entire affair, and I won't listen to any of your sarcastic comments."

Bernice continued speaking anyway. "I'm not surprised that Margaret Shaw slithered away with her tail between her legs. She was too much of a coward to put up a fight, but I am surprised by Emily Shaw. I thought she would stand her ground, but she's just as spineless as her cousin."

"Bernice!" the Earl snapped. "Have mercy on me. I won't chew over it like a tough piece of meat."

"The little harlot's ruse is ended with their departure, and there's no reason to point any fingers at Archie."

Temperance took that as her cue to brazenly enter the room.

There was some sort of drama unfolding in the house, although she couldn't guess what it was. She'd asked various servants what had happened, but they'd claimed to have no information. She couldn't forget the prior evening and how Margaret Shaw had been following

Archie, and with Archie's name being bandied, she was incredibly suspicious.

The Earl was seated behind the desk, and Bernice was perched in a chair across from him. They weren't exactly startled by her arrival, but they weren't delighted by it either.

"Was there some trouble this morning?" Temperance asked as she tromped over and sat next to Bernice. "I inquired of the servants about the shouting and slamming of doors, but they wouldn't tell me what had transpired."

Bernice smiled in her typical sneering way, as if Temperance was a child. "It doesn't concern you. We simply demanded the Shaw cousins leave the property. Previously, they'd had some problems finding lodging in the village, so the Earl had tried to help them by inviting them to stay at Wave Crest, but they're the kind of girls who can't be helped."

"Meaning what?" Temperance asked. "Were they caught stealing the silver? Were they hiding candlesticks in their traveling trunks? They seemed rather harmless to me."

Roxbury hesitated forever, debating, then he said, "It's not important."

"I must beg to differ. I was eavesdropping out in the hall, and Archie's name was mentioned in conjunction with Margaret Shaw's. What did he do to her?"

Roxbury snorted with disgust, but didn't reply, so Bernice said, "What a silly question. Archie barely knows the ridiculous ninny, so how could he possibly have *done* anything to her?"

"You're the worst liar," she told Bernice, causing Bernice to sniff with offense.

Roxbury said to Bernice, "You might as well spit it out. Miss Moore ought to learn the truth about the cad who'll be her husband."

Bernice bristled. "Archie is the innocent party in this situation, and Miss Shaw is deranged. You agreed that she is, so don't pretend her nonsense has merit."

"I didn't agree with you," Roxbury said. "I felt I needed more time to evaluate their divergent stories. That's as far as I'm willing to go on Archie's behalf."

"A high defense, I'm sure," Temperance snidely muttered.

She stood as if she'd march out, and Roxbury waved her down, saying caustically, "You might have noticed that your betrothed has vanished."

"Yes, I noticed."

"This is what has been revealed: Margaret Shaw has leveled some shocking accusations about Archie. She claims he wed her in a secret ceremony, attended only by his friends."

"James!" Bernice said. "You will not give credence to that trollop's fantasies."

Temperance ignored Bernice and asked Roxbury, "Is Miss Shaw married to him? She's Mrs. Covington?"

Roxbury shrugged. "Miss Shaw believes she's his wife, but Archie vehemently denies it. Her cousin, Emily, insists Archie faked the event so he could seduce her."

"He tricked her with a fake wedding?" Temperance's tone was bland and detached, even though she was raging on the inside. "Is that your opinion of what occurred?"

"I don't have an opinion yet," Roxbury said, but Bernice huffed at him, "You're being absurd. The annoying tart is a fortune-hunter. Nothing more. Nothing less. I don't care what tale she spreads or what amount of damages she seeks. She will not get a farthing from us!"

"You are out of line, Bernice, so be silent." Roxbury's expression was thunderous, and he turned to Temperance and said, "I sent Archie to town, so we could deal with Miss Shaw while he was out of the house. Then I sent Miss Shaw away too. In light of her allegations, it wasn't appropriate for her to remain on the premises. I will investigate further by riding to London and interrogating Archie's friends."

"You will not interrogate them!" Bernice fumed.

Roxbury didn't so much as glance at Bernice, but he said to Temperance, "I apologize for disclosing this dilemma to you, but you are planning to marry Archie, so I don't suppose we should keep this from you."

"Is there a chance he's wed to Miss Shaw?" Temperance asked him.

"Yes, there's a chance, but if it was a bogus ceremony, then he's *about* to wed her in a genuine one."

At the comment, Bernice appeared as if she might faint. "Wed him to that doxy? Are you mad?"

"I'm not mad," Roxbury said. "I'm very, very angry, and if he deceived that poor girl, then he's a fiend who must be brought to heel."

Bernice scoffed. "That slattern will *never* glom onto him. Besides, he's not free to attach himself. He's been engaged to Temperance for the past year, and we should squelch any rumors by moving up the wedding date. I was hoping to hold it by Christmas, but perhaps we should obtain a Special License and proceed immediately. What would you think, Temperance?"

Was Bernice unhinged? Did she assume Temperance was deaf? Or that she was an idiot? She'd heard every word Roxbury had uttered, and she'd comprehended all of them.

She said to Bernice, "I won't shackle myself to your son. The engagement is severed."

Temperance might have punched Bernice, and Bernice said, "The nuptial contract is between your father and me. It's not up to you to decide if it will continue or not."

"By all means, contact my father. He never liked Archie, so he'll be glad I'm crying off."

"We'll sue you for breach of promise," Bernice stupidly threatened.

"With what money will you hire an attorney?" Temperance calmly asked. "As far as I'm aware, you and Archie don't have any."

"How dare you!" Bernice whipped her furious gaze to Roxbury. "Will you let her speak to me like that?"

He frowned. "I have no authority over her. If she wants to insult you, how can I stop her? Now then, if you'll excuse me?" He pushed back his chair and stood.

"You're not leaving!" Bernice pointed rudely at Temperance. "Not with this impertinent child sassing me. Put her in her place! She can't cry off. Tell her we won't permit it."

Roxbury smirked. "You just advised her, Bernice, that the matter is between you and her father. It has naught to do with me. I suggest you take it up with him."

He started around the desk, and Temperance had no idea if she'd ever see him again, so she said, "My offer still stands. I intend to use my dowry to purchase a title. I'd be happy to give it to you and become your countess."

Roxbury gaped at her as if she'd grown a second head, and Bernice squealed, "No, no, no! Absolutely not! James, don't encourage her! That money is Archie's. She can't give it to you!"

Roxbury ignored Bernice. He exhaled a deep breath, then politely stated, "Thank you for your interest in me, Miss Moore, but if I accepted, I would be the third Covington brother you've considered as a spouse. It's a little too peculiar for me."

"Temperance!" Bernice was practically shouting. "You can't contemplate this betrayal of Archie. What is wrong with you?"

"Don't listen to Bernice," Temperance told Roxbury. "If you'd like, I can have my father meet with you to discuss the terms."

"It will never be necessary," Roxbury said, "for I'm already betrothed. We just haven't announced it."

Temperance and Bernice both gasped, and Bernice asked, "Have you tipped off your rocker? Why would you make such a preposterous claim? You're not betrothed."

"Yes, I am," he said. "To Emily Shaw."

Bernice snorted with derision. "I refuse to believe it. Don't jest."

"I'm not jesting. She and I are engaged, and she's quite vexed with me—because of you and Archie. I allowed her to depart Wave Crest, merely so I could get her cousin out of the house, but I'd best track her down so I can apologize."

Bernice's mouth was opening and closing like a fish tossed on a riverbank. "You're not serious. You're not marrying that . . . that . . . nobody."

"She's not a *nobody*," he retorted. "She's very special to me, and I am in love with her. Your opinion is irrelevant."

He marched by them, and Bernice shrieked, "James! You will not go to her."

He tsked with exasperation. "You have completely overstepped yourself. Let's review, Bernice: When have I ever heeded you on any topic?"

"Well, you will heed me in this! Emily Shaw is as much of a gold-digger as her cousin, and you will not chase her down."

Roxbury rolled his eyes and said to Temperance, "Goodbye, Miss Moore, and good luck in your future marital search."

He bowed curtly and left, and Temperance sat with Bernice, the silence settling around them.

"Will he actually wed Emily Shaw?" Temperance was stunned that the pretty, pleasant woman had enticed him. How had she managed it? The prospect was too ludicrous to fathom.

"No, he will not," Bernice seethed, "and I will not debate the situation with you." She jumped up so abruptly that her chair tipped over. "You'll have to excuse me too. I've had all of your company I can abide for one day. If you need me, I shall be in my room."

"I won't need you," Temperance replied, as Bernice stormed out.

She dawdled, waiting for Roxbury to leave, waiting for Bernice to lock herself in her bedchamber. Temperance wasn't eager to run into either of them again.

Once she was sure the coast was clear, she tiptoed out and proceeded to her own room. She'd brought maids with her, and she had them furtively pack her traveling trunks. Then she summoned a carriage to convey her into Baywick, where she would hire a coach to transport her to London.

Archie's scheme toward Margaret Shaw had been revealed, so Temperance had dodged a bullet. She wondered if he'd ever notice that she'd cried off, and she supposed it would occur to him when her dowry funds never flowed into his depleted bank account.

It was such a fascinating pile of money. She'd pictured it as a living thing that could change a man's life. Archie had been too reckless to glom onto it, and Roxbury had been too foolish, so she'd have to offer it to someone else. There had to be one blasted male in the kingdom who would like to grow rich with scant effort. She'd have to have her father search for a new candidate.

Her trunks were carried down to the driveway, her luggage quickly loaded, and she climbed into the vehicle. She relaxed on the seat, and as they lumbered away, she didn't glance back.

MARY DARLINGTON WAS SITTING at the desk in her office when a maid peeked in to apprise her that Lord Roxbury had arrived.

"Will you see him?" she inquired. "He says it's urgent."

Mary concealed any reaction. Her sole connection to Roxbury had been through Emily, and her friend was staying with him. She was immediately certain that she wouldn't like what he was about to impart.

"Yes, I'll see him," she said. "Please show him in."

Her office was small and tucked away at the rear of the hotel. It was filled with file cabinets, paperwork, and the general disorder of a hectic business. It was an awful place in which to host a visitor, but she didn't want him to linger, and the cramped space would hasten the conversation.

She rose as he entered and gestured to the only other chair. "Lord Roxbury, this is a surprise. Would you like a refreshment?"

"No, thank you."

He sat down, and he was so tall that his knees were wedged against the desk. He had to be incredibly uncomfortable, which was a benefit. She intended a short meeting.

"What brings you by?" she asked. "How may I help you?"

"I have a curious request, and I hope you can oblige me."

"I will if I can."

"Emily Shaw has left Baywick, and I need to speak with her." Mary didn't respond, and he added, "It's very important."

His sudden appearance made her suspect he'd behaved badly toward Emily, and her hackles were up. Calmly, she inquired, "Wasn't she residing with you?"

"Yes, but she departed. She should have been at the coaching inn until tomorrow morning, and I tried to catch her there, but I guess an afternoon mail coach was available. She booked a spot on it and was gone before I could stop her."

His cheeks heated with chagrin, and Mary frowned, feigning nonchalance. "Why was she at the coaching inn?"

He hemmed and hawed, struggling to pick a comment that would paint him in a good light. Finally, he said, "Look, I'll just put my cards on the table. We had an unfortunate incident."

Mary gasped. "She was injured?"

"No, no, it was nothing like that," he hastily explained. "Her cousin, Peggy, was involved in some mischief with my brother, Archie."

"What sort of mischief?"

"I'd rather not discuss it, but I had her exit Wave Crest without delay. I had Archie scurry off to London too."

His firm tone provided no opening to seek details, but she didn't need any. Archie Covington was a regular source of gossip in the town, and he might have engaged in any antic with Peggy Shaw. She would have gleefully joined him in it.

They were a matched pair of degenerates, and in Mary's view, they deserved each other. Apparently though, Peggy's immoral conduct had impacted Emily yet again, and Mary felt very sorry for her.

"Why would you include me in this morass?" Mary asked.

"I'm very fond of Emily, and we quarreled about the situation. I begged her to remain at Wave Crest, but she accompanied her cousin. We were both angry, and we spewed remarks we shouldn't have voiced."

So it was *Emily*, was it? Not *Miss Shaw*? Clearly, he'd grown much too attached, and Mary could barely keep from leaning over and whacking him alongside the head. Why were noblemen such idiots?

"I understand why she went," Mary said. "Peggy Shaw can be a nuisance, but Emily is very close to her. Why are you hunting for her?"

"I have to apologize, and I'd like her to return to Wave Crest."

As your what . . . ?

Mary bit down the question. She'd never liked knowing that Emily was residing with him, and she recognized, from her own horrid experience, that a rogue like Roxbury was impossible to resist.

If he hadn't seduced Emily, it was only a matter of time before he succeeded. Was that why he was hoping she'd return? Was he still wearing her down? Had she fled before he'd reached his goal?

She hadn't seen Emily since the day she'd learned that she'd moved to Wave Crest. Emily was smart and savvy, but amour could make even the most pragmatic female behave in outrageous ways.

Mary was suffering from the strongest urge to protect her friend from Roxbury, but she couldn't decide on the best route. What had happened between them? How hideous had it been? Might Emily have told him to never contact her again?

"Why are you here?" she asked, stalling. "I haven't spoken to Emily recently. What were you expecting I could do?"

His cheeks heated to an even deeper shade of red. "I will be very blunt with you and admit that I am a vain ass."

She chuckled. "I'm scarcely acquainted with you, so I will offer no opinion on that assessment."

"I've been cordial with Emily for several weeks, but I'm so self-centered that I never asked her where she lived. I realize it's a rural estate, but I never inquired as to its name. I seem to remember that she corresponded with you prior to her coming to Baywick, and I will throw myself on your mercy and beg you to furnish me with the information I require to track her down."

The words, *track her down,* rang ominously, and she was torn over what her role should be. She never supplied personal details about her guests to anyone, and there was no reason to start with Roxbury.

Why would he chase after Emily? Mary was terribly afraid that it was for salacious purposes. Emily was an adult, and if she wished to stay in touch with him, she could write to him on her own. Why should Mary get involved?

She fibbed to him with a carefully blank expression. "I had her address in the past, but I don't usually retain a customer's mail once she leaves. I may have already tossed out any letter, but let me check my records."

She spun to a cabinet behind the desk, and she opened a drawer and pretended to search through it. He stared at her back, his sharp focus cutting into her like the blade of a knife.

After a bit of riffling, she turned around and said, "No, sorry. She sent me a letter months ago, but I don't have it any longer."

His shoulders slumped. "I figured that would be your answer, but didn't you befriend her while she was here? Did she ever mention the name of her estate or maybe a nearby village?"

"We didn't have many intimate conversations," she lied. "I try to keep my customers at arm's length. It's never wise to delve into their issues at home, and they generally wouldn't like me to be too nosy."

He glared at her, obviously assuming she wasn't being truthful, but he was too polite to accuse her of it. She couldn't bring herself to divulge Emily's location. Who could guess if Emily would like him to show up there?

She'd think about writing to Emily herself, so she could ask how to handle the dilemma. If Emily gave her permission to provide her direction, then Mary probably would, but she was nervous about facilitating the relationship. She didn't view herself as being callous, but she wouldn't participate in whatever scheme he was pursuing.

"If you hear from her," he said, "will you reply and tell her I stopped by? Will you tell her I'm looking for her?"

"If I ever hear from her, I will apprise her, but I had a quarrel with her too over her cousin's conduct. I evicted Miss Shaw because of it, so we didn't part on the best of terms." It was a huge falsehood, but she told it with a straight face. "I don't suppose she'll be a guest in my hotel ever again."

"Thank you for seeing me. I apologize for bothering you."

"It was no bother. May I escort you out?"

"I can find my own way."

He stood, bowed, and departed. She listened as his footsteps faded down the hall, then she pulled out a file that contained the half-dozen letters Emily had posted before she'd journeyed to Baywick. They were filled with a typical traveler's questions about lodging and activities, about rooms and costs. Mary retrieved a piece of paper and started to write.

Would she ever mail it? Should Emily be notified of the Earl's visit? Mary couldn't decide.

She finished the missive, then put it back in the drawer. The quandary, one that included moral obligation and ethical duty, would entail significant reflection, and she had no idea when she'd have it resolved.

"You should have sent a message. We'd have come home right away."

"I didn't want to ruin your holiday."

Emily eased a hip onto the mattress of her Aunt Florence's bed. The older woman was tucked under thick blankets, but she couldn't warm up, no matter how completely she was covered.

In the weeks Emily had been gone, Florence had wasted away to skin and bones, so she could have been a skeleton that was barely alive. Her hair had fallen out, and there were purple circles under her eyes, purple bruises visible around her joints as if her veins were leaking blood inside her body. Her lungs sounded as if they were full of water, and she wheezed when she tried to talk, but she didn't try very often.

The effort of speaking was too painful, and she could hardly converse.

Emily was shocked and ashamed. While she'd been reveling at the seashore, while she'd been merrily disgracing herself with Roxbury, her dear Florence had been quietly dying. Florence was the mother she'd never had, an optimistic, caring person who'd thrived in difficult circumstances.

Her husband, Emily's uncle, had been a reckless, detached spouse, and her stepdaughter, Peggy, was a rude snot and troublemaker. Florence had remained sunny and unbendable, never complaining over her lot, never shirking a task, or railing over the unfairness of her condition.

Emily endeavored to emulate her in all aspects of her life.

"You're back early," Florence said. "How was Baywick? Didn't you like it?"

"It was lovely, but we missed you too much," Emily fibbed. "We couldn't bear to be away from you for the whole summer."

Florence smiled wearily. "You were always such a good girl."

"I'm honored that you've thought so. I hope I've been worthy of your many kindnesses over the years."

"You definitely have been. Tell me about your trip. Tell me every detail you remember, so I can pretend I was there too. I've pictured you strolling on The Promenade, with the sailboats drifting by. Was it exactly as you envisioned?"

Emily described Baywick, painting it as a sort of fairyland, where everything was beautiful and perfect. Florence's eyes would flutter shut, and she'd appear to have dozed off, but then, she'd ask a question that proved she was hanging on Emily's every word.

"I'm glad you went," Florence said. "I'm glad you had the chance."

A coughing fit ensued, where Florence hacked up blood. She required constant nursing, and a housemaid rushed over with a bowl and a towel. She shoved Emily away, tending to Florence until the spasm had passed. The maid dosed her with laudanum, then she fell asleep. Emily waited a few minutes, to ensure she wouldn't reawaken, then she tiptoed out.

Their housekeeper was hovering in the hall, and Emily whispered, "How long has she been like this?"

"She collapsed right after you and Miss Peggy departed. I think she sensed what was approaching, but she hid it from you. She was determined that you have your adventure."

"You should have written to me," Emily said. "I would have raced to her side immediately."

"She didn't want you to come home. She felt the future was too uncertain and after . . . well . . . after her ordeal is over, you might never have another opportunity to get away."

"That's precisely the attitude I would have expected from her."

"She pondered you every second, wondering if you were enjoying yourself. It made her happy during this terrible period."

"What is the doctor's opinion?" Emily asked.

The woman shook her head. "I won't sugarcoat it. She won't last long, and I'm relieved that you arrived when you did. If you'd delayed at all, you might have been too late. It will be a great comfort to her to have you here at the end."

She gave Emily's hand a supportive squeeze, then Emily continued on to the stairs and down to the front parlor where she supposed Peggy would be loafing.

In an odd way, it seemed as if Roxbury had done her a huge favor by kicking them out. If he hadn't chased her away, she'd still be in Baywick, without having any hint of Florence's mortal peril. Florence had been suffering from consumption for years, but her health had never worsened overly much. There had been brief intervals where she'd been incapacitated, but she'd always rebounded.

When Emily had first read about Mary Darlington's hotel for young ladies, Florence had been the most excited about it. She'd urged Emily to contact Mary for information, and Emily agreed with the housekeeper that Florence had probably concealed the rate of her decline, so Emily had been free to traipse off on her holiday. It was entirely typical of her aunt to be that selfless.

They were suddenly wading into uncharted territory, and Florence's demise and funeral would be hurdles that would have to be jumped over. After the debacle Emily had endured with Roxbury though, she couldn't muster the fortitude necessary to cope with Florence's passing too.

She'd intended to confess her amour to Florence. She'd needed the advice of a wiser, shrewder female, one who'd seen enough of life and men to furnish solid counsel. It wouldn't happen now. Now, there would only be a death watch as they counted down Florence's final hours. From this point on, whatever occurred, however Emily chose to proceed, she was on her own.

She entered the parlor, and Peggy was there, pacing and drinking an alcoholic beverage. Before they'd journeyed to the coast, had Peggy been a drinker? Emily couldn't recollect, but evidently, her cousin had adopted many bad habits while they were away. Her quick descent into depraved conduct underscored the general consensus that women shouldn't travel alone and unsupervised.

The trip back to Hexham had been difficult. Luckily, they'd been able to flee Baywick immediately. When they'd reached the coaching inn, after slithering away from Wave Crest, the mail coach had been there, with open seats, so they'd boarded and escaped without much reflection.

Their swift exit meant that Peggy had had no chance to storm back to Wave Crest and quarrel with Bernice Covington. In that regard, their fast egress was a blessing for which Emily would always be grateful.

On the coach, they'd argued occasionally, but there had usually been other passengers with them, so the presence of strangers had prevented Peggy from raising embarrassing topics. They'd bickered when they'd debarked the vehicle to eat or stretch their legs.

In those short breaks, Peggy had been brimming with plans as to how she'd locate Archie, how she'd obtain a genuine marriage to him. She'd assumed she'd drag Florence into the disaster, that Florence would intervene with the Covington family, but that prospect would never transpire.

"Where is Florence?" Peggy asked, not yet having bothered to track down her stepmother. "Why hasn't she come down? Isn't she delighted to have us back? I thought she'd be jumping for joy."

"While we were gone, her health failed significantly."

Peggy snorted with disgust. "Isn't that just like her? I need her to help me with Archie. She can't be under the weather."

Emily nearly marched over and slapped her cousin. Peggy was such a selfish person, and Emily's custom was to ignore her faults, to look the other way, to tiptoe behind her and sweep up her messes. Well, Emily's horrid summer had brought many issues into sharp relief.

Her days of excusing Peggy, of justifying her excesses, of bracing against her petty cruelties, were over.

"Florence is dying," Emily said, "and I would appreciate it if you would mind your manners as we stagger to the end."

Peggy scoffed. "She's not dying. I refuse to believe it's that grave."

"I'll be surprised if she's still alive tomorrow morning."

"But I *need* her. If she's sick, who will write to Bernice Covington for me? Who will sue that old witch for breach of promise?"

"You're about to be left to your own devices, as I will be left to mine. We'll be tossed out into the world without Florence as a foundation to keep us afloat."

"Don't be ridiculous. Florence has been ill forever, but she mends rapidly."

"Not this time," Emily grimly said. "Best prepare yourself."

Nausea roiled in her belly, and suddenly, she felt as if she might vomit.

Ever since she'd stood in Roxbury's library and had listened to him denigrating Peggy, she'd been dizzy and queasy. She was simply an ordinary female, from a small village in the country. She had no idea how to maneuver through the quagmire Peggy had stirred with Archie Covington. All of it was beyond her ability to manage. Who wouldn't be devastated? Who wouldn't be anxious and distressed?

She whipped away and raced up to her bedchamber. She dropped to her knees and grabbed the chamber pot under the bed. She vomited over and over, until there was only bile in her stomach. Then she dragged herself up onto the mattress and began to weep.

She realized that her trauma would eventually wane. Her morose condition would get better. The stress and tension would fade. It would happen gradually, and she would recover from her summer of trials.

But just that moment, when her heart was broken and she was at her lowest ebb, she couldn't imagine when or how it could possibly occur.

Chapter Twenty-Three

JAMES WAS SITTING AT a table in a corner at a packed gambling club. He was trying to remain invisible, observing the activities, but not participating.

Archie's friend, Gordo, was across the room. The lazy oaf was frantically tossing dice, as a crowd avidly waited to learn what numbers would land. From the amount of chips scattered on the green baize, there had to be a fortune hanging in the balance.

James had never seen the point of gambling. Nor did he understand the thrill that players received. They lost too often, so where was the fun in that?

He was back in London, feeling morose and adrift. Emily had fled Wave Crest, so it had been too dreary to tarry there. Bernice had tarried with him, and he'd been so irritated by her that he'd left too. He'd assumed his escape would lighten his mood, but so far, it hadn't helped.

He was staying at his town house, but unfortunately, Archie was there too, and James was more aggravated with him than he was with Bernice. He ought to head to his main manor of Roxbury. He'd inherited it while he was away in the Arctic North, and since he'd returned to England, he hadn't spent any time there. He had to take charge at the estate, but he couldn't make himself travel to the property.

After he arrived, he'd only have himself for a companion, and the silence would have driven him mad. He was so glum that he'd considered inviting his old shipmate, Pettigrew, to visit, but he wouldn't inflict himself on anyone.

He still couldn't decide what he believed about Archie and Peggy Shaw. He supposed Archie had treated her abominably, but he also suspected she was an experienced tart. Did James have an obligation to save her?

He didn't think so, but Emily had been very clear in voicing her views on the matter. She'd snuck away before he could apologize, and she hadn't contacted him again. She knew how to get hold of him, and the fact that she hadn't was blatant proof that he hadn't been forgiven and probably wouldn't be.

He yearned to convince himself that her severing of ties absolved him of any duty toward her cousin, but if Archie was so corrupt that he would trick a young lady into a fake marriage simply to lift her skirt, what other monstrous antics might he attempt?

James was suffering from the most compelling perception that he should obtain an answer to that question so Archie couldn't commit any other sins.

Gordo lost his wager. There was a collective groan from the men who'd been watching him. Another player scooped up the chips, and Gordo staggered away, drink in hand, looking as if he might have squandered his last penny.

He wandered by, and James gestured for him to stop and pull up a chair.

"Roxbury!" he said as he plopped down. "What brings you to town? I thought you were hiding from the newspapers."

"I was bored in the country, but I'm bored here too. I was wishing I could find some entertainment that is more risqué."

"There are whores upstairs."

"I don't want a trollop. Will it shock you if I admit I'd like someone more innocent? Archie tells me they're very amusing. He never shuts up about it. He claims you and your friends lure gullible girls into debauchery. He suggested I might like to join you. Would that be possible?"

James must have appeared genuinely curious because Gordo launched into a lengthy narrative about how they'd invented a game where they made bets over who could most ruthlessly ruin a naïve maiden. They trolled places like Vauxhall Gardens, searching for easy prey. Archie was a master at it, usually winning the biggest purses for seducing the most trusting females.

With scant coaching, Gordo waxed on about the bogus wedding Archie had arranged for Peggy Shaw. He bragged about pretending to be a preacher.

James scowled, as if he was confused. "What was your opinion of Miss Shaw? Was she loose with her favors? Archie said she'd lain with all of you."

Gordo snickered. "No, none of us had her but Archie. From the moment they met, she was wild for him."

James's expression grew thunderous, and Gordo frowned and asked, "What's wrong? Have I mucked up my description of how the game is played? You can talk to Archie about the rules. He can explain them better than I."

"I understood you, so I will give you this word of warning: I plan to call on your father first thing in the morning."

"Why would you?"

"I will inform him of how you deceive and harm women in this city. I will demand that you enlist in the army immediately so you can learn a bit about responsibility and sacrifice."

Gordo huffed with offense. "You have a lot of gall. You're not tat-tling about me to my father, and I'm not joining the army."

"It's up to you whether you remain in England or not." James's tone was very casual, but his eyes were shooting daggers of outrage. "But if in the next two weeks, I discover that you haven't bought your commission and left the country, I will kill you."

Gordo scoffed as if they were sharing jokes. "You'd kill me? You're being absurd, and you're proving the rumors about your mental state to be true. You're quite mad."

"Yes, I am mad. I never deny it, so you should escape my wrath by enlisting at once."

"Why are you so upset about this? Peggy Shaw was a flirt and a tart. Who cares if Archie tricked her? I certainly don't."

James hadn't meant to cause a scene, but he didn't like Gordo. The cruel lout was a brutal villain with no conscience.

He rose too fast, his chair tipping over behind him. Before Gordo realized what James intended, he stepped around the table and punched him just as hard as he could. He flew out of his seat and crashed to the floor in a bloody heap.

There were shouts of *Hey, Hey!* and *Whoa! What goes there?* and several burly footmen ran over to intervene.

James waved them off, then he took a final glance at Gordo and said, "Two weeks, you little prick, or I'll hunt you down. Don't make me. I'd like it too much."

Then he walked out into the cold night and headed home to have a chat with his brother.

"MAY I ASK YOU a question about Peggy Shaw?"

Archie frowned at James and said, "Her name is Margaret, and no, you may not ask me. I shudder with dread just from hearing you mention her. I'd like to enjoy my breakfast without suffering indigestion."

They were in the dining room at their London house. A buffet was arranged on the sideboard, and a pair of footmen were lurking, waiting to be useful. James had already eaten, and Archie was trying to eat, but James kept interrupting.

"I was wondering if she ever told you where she was from," James said.

"Why would you wonder that?"

"I'm merely curious. She was so determined to trap you that I picture her tucked away at her rural residence and busily drafting lawsuits for breach of promise."

"She's too stupid to prosecute a lawsuit against me."

"So she never talked about her home?"

"I think it was Hexham maybe? Something like that. I seem to recollect it was on the road to Guilford, but I wouldn't stake my life on it. When Miss Shaw was babbling, I barely listened to her." Archie shrugged off the topic and sipped is tea. "Don't let her ruin your morning."

"You never ponder her?" James inquired.

"Why would I?" Archie's frown deepened.

James was in a surly mood, and he could be relentless at beating a problem to death. "You came awfully close to being leg-shackled."

"Mother would never allow Miss Shaw to ensnare me. She's helped me previously when a crisis like this arose, so she's aware of how to nip it in the bud."

The words slipped out before he could bite them down. His mother had interceded in many of his carnal escapades, but it was a secret he shouldn't have revealed. He had a terrible hangover and had momentarily forgotten to be circumspect.

"How has Bernice assisted you in the past?"

James focused in like a hawk swooping down on its prey, and a shiver slithered down Archie's spine.

"Oh, you know how it is." Archie was blithe and dismissive. "Girls occasionally misconstrue a fellow's purpose. They complain when they shouldn't."

"You've had complaints leveled about you to Bernice?"

Archie snorted as if the notion was preposterous. "Don't mind me. My head is pounding, so my reasoning is muddled. I'm spewing nonsense."

"Well, I'm absolutely fascinated by this situation, and I beg you to tell me more. Be particularly precise about how Bernice helps you to weasel out of sexual jams."

Archie froze, his perception of danger increasing dramatically. "I didn't say that."

"Yes, you did, and I should probably confess that I bumped into your old chum, Gordo, last night."

James had never been interested in Archie's friends, and his bowels clenched. "How is Gordo? I haven't seen him in weeks."

"Why is that? He's in London. You're in London. Is he avoiding you? Are you avoiding him?"

"No, why would I be?"

James sipped his own tea, his gaze cutting and direct, as if he was expecting Archie to utter a comment he shouldn't. After a fraught silence, his brother said, "Guess where I'm off to?"

"With your odd schedule and habits, I wouldn't dare to speculate."

"I will be conferring with Gordo's father."

It was the strangest remark ever, and Archie asked, "Why would you speak to him?"

"Gordo will be joining the army shortly."

Archie snickered. "Gordo? A soldier? I doubt that very much."

"He will be enlisting, and *you* will be getting married."

"Yes, to Temperance Moore."

"She's cried off."

Archie grinned. "I'll win her back. Women can't resist me, and in the end, she won't be able to either."

"You won't ever wed her," James said. "Even if you could convince her—and in your deluded state, you seem to assume you could—I won't permit it. You're marrying someone else."

"You're being so ridiculous. Mother picked her for me, so who, in your exalted opinion, would you select instead?"

"You know who."

"I don't; I swear."

"Then let me be very clear."

James stood and loomed over Archie. He was much taller than Archie, and he was much brawnier too. He looked positively murderous, and Archie cringed in his seat.

"Gordo explained the rules of your game to me," James said.

Archie couldn't completely swallow down a gasp, but he managed to ask, "Game? What game?"

"Your game where you trick gullible young ladies like Margaret Shaw. Your game where you seduce them and take bets over it."

Archie shook his head. "I have no idea what you're blathering on about. I haven't played a game with Gordo since we were on teams in boarding school."

"Liar."

Suddenly, and with no warning at all, James punched Archie in the face. The blow was brutal and vicious, and it lifted him off his chair so he crashed to the floor. He curled into a ball, wheezing, struggling to breathe, as James grabbed him by his shirt and hit him again.

Archie had never been hit before. Not by anyone, and he couldn't believe how much it hurt. Blood dripped from his nose and mouth, and for a moment, he suspected he blacked out. Once he could focus again, he was still on the floor and staring at James's boots.

"What is wrong with you?" he mumbled.

"That was for every girl you've ever harmed." James kicked him in the ribs, making it even harder to breathe. "And *that* was for Peggy Shaw."

"Peggy Shaw, bah!" Archie spat. "Why would you care about her? She's nothing to us."

"She's nothing to *me*," James said, "but she's about to be your bride."

"I'd throw myself off a cliff rather than wed her."

"Fine, be my guest, but when you die, you'll be her husband, so she'll be widowed and instantly shed of you. I'm arranging an immediate wedding."

"Mother won't allow it. She's always insisted I have a greater destiny."

"Your mother will have no say."

James whipped away and marched out, and Archie was huddled on the rug like a ragdoll, unable to move, unable to jump up and chase after him.

"James!" he forced out. "You can't abandon me. Where are you going?"

"I told you: I have an appointment with Gordo's father to ensure he's punished for his mischief with you, then I'll begin the steps required for you to become a married man."

"I won't shackle myself to Margaret Shaw. Despite how furiously you nag, you'll never persuade me."

"Won't I? If that's what you suppose, then you don't understand the power I can wield against you. Make ready."

James stomped out, and Archie was left alone to assess his dazed condition. After a bit, a footman skirted around him and started clearing the plates from the table. Archie lay at his feet, like a ghost that no one could see.

⸻ ⸙ ⸻

"What are you doing?"

"I'm leaving."

Peggy and Emily were in the front foyer at Hexham. Peggy had just finished breakfast and had been walking toward the stairs to climb to her bedchamber when she'd stumbled on Emily. Her cousin was wrapped in her cloak and tying the ribbons on her bonnet. Her traveling trunks were stacked by the door, and as Peggy watched, a footman carried them outside.

"It looks as if you're planning an extended trip," Peggy said. "What brought this on?"

"I'm returning to Baywick."

Peggy scoffed. "Why would you? It was a pathetic little town, and nothing good happened to us there."

"Mrs. Darlington offered me a job, and I've decided to accept it."

"You'll work for wages?"

"Yes, but then, I'm not a grand personage like you. I'm not a lady of leisure, and I've overstayed my welcome at Hexham. I have to build a life somewhere else. I won't sit here as the creditors arrive to toss me out. I previously lived through that dire experience, and I'm not inclined to live through it again."

"But what about me?" Peggy asked. "How will I manage without you to advise me?"

"I guess you'll have to figure it out on your own. You're so smart and so shrewd, and I'm simply a fool who constantly steers you in the wrong direction. What advice could you possibly need from me? You have matters under control, so you'll have yourself squared away in no time."

Emily was being very curt, very snotty, which was bewildering, but also a tad frightening. She was always pleasant and happy. She never complained or chastised. She never found fault or quarreled. In that, she was a lot like poor, deceased Florence had been, but they were weak traits Peggy couldn't abide.

She liked females who were more like herself: confident, tough, eager to fight, eager to win. She was destined for a bigger future, and Emily realized that fact. Or at least, Peggy had assumed Emily realized it.

For once, Emily wasn't being kind or sympathetic. She was gaping at Peggy as if Peggy was a stranger she'd met on the street. Peggy would be the first to admit that she wasn't easy to like, but Emily had tolerated her with an unusual forbearance. What could have transpired to alter her into this miserable woman Peggy didn't recognize?

"Is this about the funeral?" Peggy asked. "Are you still angry about it? I've apologized repeatedly. Why can't you move on? I certainly have."

To everyone's amazement, Florence had lingered for several weeks after they'd returned from their holiday. It had been a grueling interval that had devastated the entire household, and Emily had valiantly nursed her until the bitter end.

As they'd ridden home from the funeral, Peggy had mentioned that she was glad Florence was dead. She'd meant that she was relieved Florence's suffering was over, but the sentiment had been clumsily voiced. She'd sounded heartless, as if she was coldblooded, as if she was delighted by Florence's death.

Emily had been so aghast that, for a few days after the service, she'd locked herself in her room and had refused to come out. When she'd finally emerged, she'd been glum and quiet. She'd claimed she comprehended Peggy's intent, that Peggy had been forgiven for her bad choice of words, but it didn't seem as if she'd been forgiven.

"It's not about the funeral," Emily said. "With Florence having passed away, this period of my life is over. I won't loiter here as the walls crumble around me. I have to settle in a new location where I'll be safe."

"You can't desert me like this."

"You'll be fine. Isn't that what you always tell me? I'll depart, and you can implement perfect solutions, without me urging caution. You won't have to listen to me anymore."

The comment was polite enough, but underneath it, there was a hint of sarcasm, as if Emily thought Peggy was an incompetent dunce.

They might have bickered, but the footman poked his nose in the door and said, "Your bags are loaded, Miss Emily, and might I suggest you hurry? You're running late, and you don't want to miss the mail coach as it travels through the village. The driver won't wait for you."

"You're correct; he won't." Emily spun and followed him out.

Peggy was so stunned that she was frozen in place, like a bump on a log. Then she shook herself out of her stupor and raced after her cousin.

"You're really going?" she said. "Just like that?"

"Yes, just like that."

"What if I have to contact you?"

"Mrs. Darlington will know where I am."

"What if the creditors show up? What shall I do?"

Emily shrugged. "I have no idea what's best, but I'm sure—with your stellar intellect—you'll devise a glorious plan."

Peggy was weary of Emily's derision, but she ignored it. She reached out and squeezed Emily's hand. "Don't leave me. I can't imagine how I'll get by without you."

"You've never needed anybody, Peggy. You've especially never needed me. You'll muddle through."

"Maybe I should come with you. Maybe I could find a situation for myself in Baywick. Why not? It might be fun."

She was merrily thinking of how she might cross paths with Archie if she was there, but Emily swiftly tamped down that notion. "Mrs. Darlington wouldn't welcome you back."

The footman cleared his throat, a subtle reminder for Emily that she was dawdling too long, and she climbed into the vehicle.

Peggy was flabbergasted and even a tad alarmed. "Won't you say goodbye to me?"

"Goodbye."

The footman latched the door, then motioned to the driver. Peggy could see Emily in the window, but Emily wasn't looking at Peggy or the home where she'd been so happy. She was staring in the other direction, as if she couldn't be bothered to catch a final glimpse of the spot.

It almost seemed as if she'd never lived at Hexham, as if she'd already forgotten Peggy. Her skin was a ghostly white, and there was no expression on her face. She might have been an ice statue that would never thaw out. What could have thrust her into such a deplorable state? And why was she so miserable?

Peggy was the one who was in jeopardy. The banks were demanding money she didn't have, so she was about to lose Hexham. She'd be trapped in a morass, while Emily would fly free, like a prisoner breaking her chains.

"I'll miss you," Peggy said, which was true.

Emily tsked with exasperation. "You'll miss me? I doubt that very much."

The horses began to pull, and in the blink of an eye, the carriage vanished down the lane. Peggy tarried until the dust settled, and she figured Emily might realize how ridiculous she was being, that she'd turn around. But she wasn't coming back.

Peggy whipped away and went inside. Most of the servants had quit after the funeral. They'd been owed wages, but with Florence being so ill, they hadn't pestered her over it. After she was deceased, they'd greedily insisted Peggy cough up the amount, and when she couldn't, they'd stomped out as a group.

It meant the house was too empty, too quiet, and she was all alone.

"Miss Shaw is here."

On hearing the maid's announcement, Bernice gasped with outrage. "Margaret Shaw is here? She would dare to loiter on our stoop?"

"It's her cousin, Emily Shaw. She asked after the Earl, but he's in London, so I thought perhaps you could speak with her instead. Are you available?"

Bernice was loafing in a rear parlor at Wave Crest, having an afternoon glass of wine and peering out at the ocean. She was in no mood to converse with Emily Shaw—or anyone else for that matter.

She'd just received a curt summons from James, ordering her to town. There had been another letter too, from Archie, and he claimed that James had beaten him to a pulp and was forcing him to marry Margaret Shaw. He was begging her to stop James, but how could she? He'd grown to be a dangerous, erratic fiend, and there was no reasoning with him.

She couldn't abide the prospect of sparring with him over Margaret Shaw, and the very idea of him presuming the wicked tart would be an appropriate bride for Archie was too preposterous to be believed.

Bernice had to focus her energy on Temperance Moore's father. He'd written that they were crying off, but Bernice wouldn't let them. She and Archie desperately needed Temperance's dowry, and if she didn't deliver it to them, they'd have to survive on James's charity. That predicament qualified as a genuine catastrophe.

Why would Emily Shaw have traipsed in? Earlier in the summer, James had insanely boasted that he was engaged to her, but after she'd scurried away, he'd forgotten about her. Out of sight, out of mind.

Once she'd left Baywick, he hadn't uttered her name again. Bernice couldn't imagine what she might want, but she would never allow the trollop to inflict herself on James.

"She's not staying," Bernice said, "so I'll confer with her in the foyer. I won't permit her to stroll through the manor. She might steal some of the silver on her way out."

At the horrid slur, the maid's eyes widened with shock, but she knew better than to comment. She led Bernice out to the front of the house, and as they approached Miss Shaw, Bernice said to her, "The Earl is away, Miss Shaw, so I've agreed to speak with you."

She waved the maid away, then marched over to where Miss Shaw was hovered by the door like a frightened rabbit.

Bernice seized the initiative. "You are the very last person I ever hoped to darken my day. In light of the trouble you and your cousin caused, you have some gall to slither in. Why are you inquiring about the Earl?"

"I have to talk to him. It's private."

"Is it really? Well, James hides nothing from me. State your business and be quick about it."

Miss Shaw was trembling, and she was very pale, as if she'd been ill. Bernice studied her caustically, thinking that there was only one *private* topic she would need to address with James. How far had their affair progressed? Was she increasing? Was she anxious to apprise him, so he'd wind up supporting her forever?

Or might she be lying as her cousin had lied? Had she arrived—another Shaw girl—about to spew falsehoods and snag Bernice's stepson into a quagmire?

The Shaw cousins had more audacity than any two females she'd ever met. They'd spent a few weeks at Wave Crest, then they'd decided to glom onto some of the family's wealth. On many previous occasions, Bernice had dealt with their ilk. Archie repeatedly landed himself in jams with slatterns who yearned to ensnare him. Bernice was an expert at crushing grasping doxies like Emily Shaw.

"The Earl is in London," she said, "preparing for his engagement ball."

Miss Shaw blanched, then sagged slightly. "He's engaged? To who?"

"To Temperance Moore." Bernice smirked. "I'm sure you remember her. She was a guest when you were here too. She's an heiress?"

"Wasn't she betrothed to Mr. Covington?"

"She *was* betrothed to him, until you spread your fictions and ruined his chance, so Miss Moore is marrying the Earl instead. James was tantalized by the amount of money she was offering, and he snatched her up—right under his brother's nose."

It was a terrific fabrication, and she was proud of herself for having so cleverly devised it.

"He's proceeding with her already? So fast?" Miss Shaw asked. She appeared so wounded that Bernice might have punched her.

"Yes, he's proceeding that fast, Miss Shaw. You wrecked my son's life, and I will never forgive you. Archie's loss is all your fault, so whatever *private* discussion you hoped to have with the Earl, he wouldn't be interested in your petty problem. He's about to be a husband, so why don't you get out of my house?"

Bernice stared her down, and Miss Shaw was a tough character. She pulled herself up to her full height, and she looked as if she might hurl a pithy retort, but in the end, she didn't. She realized it would be pointless to quarrel, and she skulked out.

Bernice followed her, watching as she trudged down the steps and out into the driveway. There was no carriage in the yard, so she must have walked from Baywick. She started down the lane that would take her back to the village.

Bernice couldn't resist calling after her, "Will you give your cousin a message from me?"

Miss Shaw glanced over her shoulder. "Why would you send her a message?"

"The Earl has a bee in his bonnet where he's insisting Archie will wed her."

Miss Shaw stiffened with surprise, then she cackled in an eerie way, sounding like a witch. It made the hair stand up on Bernice's neck.

"They're perfect for one another," Miss Shaw said. "I'm certain they'll be very happy."

"They won't be happy, Miss Shaw, and she will marry him over my dead body. Tell her that for me. A marriage between them will never happen!"

"Tell her yourself. I really don't expect to speak to her ever again."

She continued on, and Bernice would have shouted a few insults, but the idiotic ninny wasn't worth the bother. Besides, Bernice had tricked her by informing her that James was engaged. She'd never come sniffing around in the future, so Bernice had gotten the last laugh. Piling on a heap of invectives would have been like kicking a puppy.

"EMILY! I CAN'T BELIEVE you're here."

Mary Darlington rushed across the front parlor of her hotel to hug her friend. She looked lost and scared, beaten down by life. The vibrant young lady who'd been a guest earlier in the summer had vanished, and this unhappy shell of a woman had taken her place. What could have happened?

"Could I talk to you alone?" Emily asked.

"Yes, certainly. Follow me."

She led her down the hall to her apartment at the rear of the building.

"What is it?" Mary inquired, as they stepped inside, and she shut the door.

"I'm in a desperate spot and I need help. I didn't know where to turn, so please forgive me, but I came to you."

"Oh, no . . ." Mary murmured.

She held out her arms, and Emily fell into them and began to weep as if her heart was broken. Mary maneuvered her over to the sofa and eased her down. They sat together, with Mary clutching her hands until the tempest had waned.

"I traveled to Baywick to speak with Lord Roxbury," Emily said, once she'd caught her breath. "I stopped at Wave Crest, and his stepmother told me he's in London, preparing for his engagement ball."

"He's engaged?"

"Yes."

Roxbury had pursued Emily with the determination of a military general on a war campaign, but while he'd been seducing her, had he been betrothed to someone else? Could he possibly be that much of an unscrupulous knave?

Well, yes, where a nobleman was concerned, any duplicitous conduct could occur.

"I have to confess a terrible secret," Emily said. "When you hear it, I hope you won't hate me."

"I could never hate you, but what is it?"

Mary could guess what was about to be revealed, and Emily instantly confirmed her worst suspicions.

"I think I'm increasing."

Mary sighed with resignation. "From the minute I learned you were staying with him, I was worried this might be the conclusion."

"He proposed to me," Emily said on a sob. "Before I ruined myself? We were going to elope to Scotland."

"Of course you were."

It was always the same galling story: An aristocrat promised he would furtively ride off to matrimony, without apprising his family, without any of his friends or kin deducing his intent. The gullible maiden never paused to wonder *why* he'd behave that way.

"Are you sure about your condition?" Mary asked.

"No, but I've missed my monthlies, and I'm nauseous constantly."

"I have an acquaintance who's a midwife. We'll have her check you."

"What would you advise me to do?"

Mary sighed again, embarrassed that she was such an expert on this topic, but personal experience was a hard teacher.

"If you're having a baby, you can't prevent it. The only choice you have is whether to keep it or have it adopted. I can't imagine you carrying on unwed and with a bastard to raise. You'd have to proclaim yourself a widow, then move to a different town and start over as a stranger in a strange place. It would be so difficult."

"I'm such an idiot, and I'm so ashamed."

"Don't be ashamed," Mary said. "Just be sensible now. You weren't in the past, but you'll have to be shrewd in the future. There's a good home for unwed mothers outside York. You can give birth there, then they'll handle the adoption arrangements."

"Could I keep the baby, then come to work for you? I could pretend to be a widow in your hotel. I wouldn't have to hide myself and reside among strangers."

Emily was so eager that Mary couldn't bear to hurt her, but she could be very ruthless when circumstances required it.

"You couldn't bring a baby here," Mary gently told her. "People in Baywick have met you, and my servants would remember how recently you were a spinster. You'd have to relinquish the child first. Then you could work for me."

"I don't know what's best." Emily practically wailed the comment, and she began to cry again.

"You don't have to figure it out this afternoon," Mary said. "You've had a rough summer, and you need to rest and regain your strength. Let's put you to bed, and you can take a nap. We have a month or two before you have to decide how to proceed, and we'll avidly debate—so you're positive."

"Thank you," Emily said. "You're being so kind. If you'd slammed the door in my face, I have no idea what would have happened to me."

"You're in a very lonely spot, so I won't abandon you. You'll always be safe with me."

"You can't make me."

Archie watched James through a slitted eye that was painful and swollen from when his brother had pummeled him. They were in James's biggest, fanciest coach and parked in the driveway of the paltry rural house called Hexham. Margaret Shaw was inside and expecting she was about to become Archie's bride.

For the prior week, he'd been James's prisoner. Despite how Archie had protested his innocence, he'd been fettered from head to toe and locked in his bedchamber. When James had declared it time to depart for the country, the footmen had hauled Archie out to the vehicle, as if he were a sack of potatoes, and tossed him in bodily. His wrists and ankles were bound with ropes, the restraints attached to the bench on which he was sitting, so he couldn't jump out and escape.

"If you'd rather be prosecuted for fraud and rape," James blithely stated, "I'm fine with that ending. Shall we return to town? I can drop you at Newgate Prison, and your incarceration can commence tonight."

"You wouldn't dare," Bernice fumed. James had forced her to accompany them, with her objecting and cursing his name every second.

"You should stay out of this," James said to her, then he continued to harangue at Archie. "If you'd like to risk a trial in the law courts, I should probably explain that I will find some of the other girls you've tricked, and I'll have them testify against you. Once you're convicted, I'll argue for the harshest sentence to be imposed. It will be a quick hanging or transportation to the penal colonies in Australia. I'll request a hanging."

"I'm your brother," Archie spat, as if James had forgotten.

"You're just barely my brother, and I no longer wish to claim a connection."

"You can't mean it," Archie moaned. "If you cut your ties with me, you won't have any family at all."

James snorted with amusement. "I will view that as an enormous benefit, so please tell me the punishment you prefer. Hanging or transportation?"

"Mother!" Archie said to Bernice. "Can't you stop him?"

"He's being completely unreasonable," she replied. "As usual. The minute he staggered in from the Arctic North, and we realized how deranged he'd grown to be, I should have had him committed to an insane asylum. If he was shut away for a lengthy interval, he wouldn't be quite so cocky."

James focused his deadly gaze on her and said, "If you open your mouth one more time, I'll gag you."

"I am your mother, and I shouldn't have to—"

"Be silent!" James shouted it so loudly that the wood of the carriage vibrated. Then he leaned toward her, looking so lethal that she lurched away.

"Do you think I never hear from my servants?" he demanded. "The butler at Wave Crest wrote to me. Apparently, Emily Shaw visited and asked to speak with me."

Bernice glanced away, appearing guilty as sin. "How is that my problem?"

"You told her I was engaged to Temperance Moore. You sent her away believing I had betrothed myself to that ridiculous ninny."

"What if I did?" Bernice retorted. "Emily Shaw is a strumpet, just like her cousin. I hope she's devastated forever."

"Quit baiting him!" Archie seethed.

"He's being a beast," she responded. "He deserves to be baited."

"Temperance's dowry is mine," Archie said to James. "You can't steal her fortune right out from under my nose."

James whacked Archie alongside the head. "Are you deaf? Or are you just very stupid? Temperance Moore has reneged, and you're marrying Margaret Shaw immediately. It's either that or I'll convey you to London to be jailed."

James glowered at Bernice. "I should clarify a few points for you, Bernice. From this moment on, you will not be welcome in any of my homes. I will also be running notices in the newspapers that I will not pay any of your debts."

James's dire financial edict got her attention, and she reined in some of her snide attitude. "I'm your father's widow. You're obligated to take care of me."

"No, I'm not. He bequeathed funds to you, so you could support yourself, but you've frittered them away. If you hadn't been so cruel to Emily, I might not have treated you like this, but I've never liked you, and I'm sick of you. I'm severing our affiliation."

"You can't be serious." Her tone was beseeching and sycophantic. "Not when we've been so close to each other over the years."

James scoffed with disgust. "Archie's friend, Gordo, admitted that you intervene for Archie when his carnal games go awry."

"Of course I intervene. We couldn't allow those tarts to besmirch our good name."

James rippled with malice. "If you don't stop aggravating me, I'll have you prosecuted too—as an accomplice."

The threat rattled her. "If I can't live with you, where am I to live?"

"You can remain here at Hexham with your daughter-in-law or you can wallow in a ditch. It doesn't matter to me, but I suggest you be kind to her. If you irk her overly much, she'll kick you out, and then, I can't imagine what your fate would be."

Bernice bristled. "That slattern will never be my daughter-in-law."

"It's up to Archie. Not you." James reached for the door and climbed out. He stared into the vehicle and said, "What's it to be,

Archie? Are you marrying Margaret Shaw this morning? Or will I transport you to jail?"

Archie gaped at James, wondering when he'd become such a tyrant. Archie wanted to reason with him, wanted to throw himself on James's mercy, but his brother had been turned to stone in the Arctic North, and he had no mercy to share.

Why not wed Margaret? She was a gullible fool, and she was madly in love with him. After the vows were spoken, any money she had stashed away would be his. He'd steal it, then flee. Evidently, she'd recently inherited Hexham too, so he'd force her to sign it over to him, then he'd sell it and pocket that money as well.

He'd hurry back to town and resume his debauched life. If she protested or demanded to join him there, he'd lock her in a convent.

"Yes, I'll marry the bloody girl," Archie snapped.

"A wise idea," James said.

Bernice wailed, "Archie! You can't shackle yourself to that doxy."

"It will be fine, Mother. You needn't worry about me."

James yanked the door wider, and two footmen lifted Archie to the ground. They helped his mother out too.

"Your devious mind is whirring," James said to Archie. "You're plotting how you'll bleed Miss Shaw dry of any assets, then vanish and leave her destitute."

"I wasn't thinking any such thing," Archie huffed, trying to appear offended.

"Hexham isn't hers," James said. "It was seized by creditors and sold at auction for pennies on the dollar. The new owner has agreed to let her tarry as a tenant, but she'll have no income from the farm. Her dowry is spent too, so she has no wealth to deliver to you."

Archie's jaw dropped. "How will we get by?"

James shrugged. "I won't attempt to guess. This arrangement will be a sort of prison for you. I want you trapped in the country, so you can't show your sorry face in London for at least five years."

His decree was the limit for Archie. He pulled himself up to his full height, but with his limbs fettered, it was hard to intimidate. "Now see here! I've had enough of your coercion and posturing. You can't forbid me to visit London."

"I can and I have. If I stumble on you there, or if I hear gossip that you slithered in, I'll have you arrested, despite any promises to the contrary."

"Bastard!" Archie muttered.

"Aren't I though?" James grinned evilly and gestured to the front door. "Shall we go in? The vicar—and your fiancée—are waiting."

Archie hemmed and hawed, fretted and fumed. James seemed to hold every card, as if he were omnipotent. How could Archie fight him? How could he win? What was Archie's other option? Arrest? Prosecution? A swift execution? How had he been reduced to this pathetic point?

"Yes, we can go in," he ultimately said, "but I will never forgive you for this."

"I don't care."

James spun and led the way into the house, and Archie hopped along behind.

PEGGY WAS SEATED AT the dressing table in her bedchamber when a maid knocked to announce that Lord Roxbury had arrived with Archie. It was her wedding day, and Archie Covington was the man of her dreams. She would be happy forever. She just knew it!

Lord Roxbury had fixed everything. He'd written to inquire if she'd still like Archie to be her husband. With her affirmative reply, he'd scheduled a second, true ceremony.

After weeks of drama and uncertainty, she'd assumed her problems were perfectly repaired. Florence had died, and Peggy had inherited Hexham, but her relief had been temporary. Creditors had seized it, but then, a buyer had magically swooped in to purchase it. She'd received a letter from a lawyer, advising her she could stay on as a tenant. Rent free! Fancy that.

She simply had to keep the property from deteriorating further, and she'd been delighted to accept his terms. Who wouldn't have been?

Her sole regret was that Emily had left in a snit. She would have loved to have her cousin in attendance at the wedding, and it was sad that the only guests would be a handful of servants. Peggy had no kin to witness the event, and no neighbors had been interested. Her reputation was that bad. She was a pariah.

She didn't have any money, but she was about to have Archie for her very own! What more could a girl want? And Archie was rich, so *he* would have money. She'd provide Hexham as their main residence, and his fortune would allow them to live in a grand style. They'd occasionally be invited to the Earl's homes too.

She was so excited!

"How do I look?" she asked the maid.

"You look fine, Miss Peggy."

"It's not Peggy; it's Margaret. Don't forget to remind the staff."

She swept out, and as she reached the stairs, she descended slowly, anxious to make an impressive entrance, but as she strolled into the parlor, she was stunned to discover that Archie's ankles and wrists were bound. His eye was blackened and swollen shut, giving every appearance that he'd shown up very much against his will.

Well, he'd definitely been eager when they'd snuck off to that dark church with his friends. What was wrong with him? Would he rather have a boring heiress like Temperance Moore?

The realization raised her hackles. He could be a vain idiot, and she'd even the score by tormenting him in small ways until he stopped being so mean.

"Greetings, Lord Roxbury," she said to the Earl, then she saw Bernice Covington was in the room too. It was to be expected that the harpy would be present. After all, she was Archie's mother, but Peggy hadn't pondered her for a single minute. She rudely pointed and asked, "Why is she here?"

"Bernice will be living with you," Roxbury explained. "She's not happy about it, and if she grows too irksome, you can kick her out. It's entirely up to you."

"She has to do as I bid her?" Peggy relished the notion.

"She doesn't have to obey you," Roxbury said, "but if she's ever too obnoxious, you can demand she leave. She doesn't have anywhere to go though, so I presume she'll be less of a shrew with that cudgel hanging over her."

"I want her to depart immediately," Peggy said.

"You can discuss it with her after we're finished," Roxbury said, "but all of you should know that *I* am now the owner of Hexham." There was a collective gasp of dismay, then he continued. "I will install a team of servants to spy on you, and they'll report to me, so I can evict any of you whenever I feel like it. Hopefully, that will keep you on your best behavior."

Peggy was frantically trying to deduce the benefits and detriments of having Roxbury as her landlord, of having Bernice Covington on the premises. On the spur of the moment, she couldn't delve into the advantages and perils.

She turned to Archie and said, "Hello, Archie. It's nice to see you again."

"Bugger off, Margaret," he seethed, and he told the vicar, "Let's get this charade started, so we can get it ended."

The vicar nodded, his expression bland, as if he didn't notice Archie had been dragged to his wedding fettered, beaten, and vehemently opposed. She figured Roxbury had bribed him to officiate, but she didn't care why he'd forge ahead. She was about to be Archie's wife!

"If you'll take your bride's hand?" the vicar said, then he remembered Archie was shackled. "Oh, sorry. How about if we proceed straight to the vows."

"Hurry, would you?" Roxbury said. "I've had about all of these miserable creatures I can stand, and I'm keen to escape their wretched company."

Peggy should have protested the comment. She should have insisted that matters would work out, but she glanced at Bernice Covington, then at Archie. They were livid, and some of her certainty vanished.

"I'm ready," Peggy said. She stepped next to Archie. Her skirt brushed his leg, and he blanched and hobbled away, putting more space between them.

"Don't worry about him," Roxbury said to the vicar. "He's a bit gun-shy, but he'll speak the vows." Roxbury leaned in and murmured, "Won't you, Archie?"

Roxbury moved between Archie and the door, blocking his path so he couldn't flee, although how he could have attempted it with his ankles bound was a mystery.

Bernice tsked with affront and went over to hover in a corner, as if she couldn't bear to watch. But Peggy grinned, ecstatic over the future that was about to arrive, and delighted to finally be Archie's wife in truth.

"Lord Roxbury! We meet again."

"Hello, Mrs. Darlington"

"How can I help you?"

Mary's tone was polite, but cool. She wouldn't ever be insolent to him, but she was swallowing down a thousand scathing remarks, and she simply wanted to be shed of him as rapidly as she could manage it.

They were in her office, with her seated at the desk, and Roxbury wedged into the chair across from her. He'd stopped by a few months earlier, searching for Emily, but Mary had never told Emily about it.

Emily was increasing with his child, but he was marrying another. Perhaps he was already married. Why apprise Emily of his visit? It would have been needlessly cruel.

"My butler at Wave Crest has notified me that Emily Shaw is in Baywick. I've been in contact with her cousin, Peggy Shaw, too, and she claims that you would know her whereabouts." He paused, furnishing her with a chance to supply the information he sought, and when she didn't, he said, "I'd like to talk to her."

"She's not here."

His gaze narrowed, and he grew visibly aggravated. "For reasons I can't fathom, it's obvious you don't like me. I would inquire as to why, but I don't have the patience to bother with you. I have to see Emily immediately. Will you hide her from me?"

"She left, my lord. Seriously."

His shoulders slumped. "Where did she go?"

Mary studied him, thinking he was such a handsome man, and it always amazed her that handsome men seemed to be the most debauched. He was determined though; she'd give him that.

"Could I ask you a question?" she said.

"You can ask, but from how you're glaring, I probably won't answer."

"How was your engagement ball?"

He sighed with frustration. "I am not engaged to Temperance Moore, so no ball was ever held."

"Why would your stepmother spread that story?"

"How about because she's a witch and a harpy? She was anxious to hurt Emily."

His harsh choice of words shocked her. She wasn't an intimate of the Covington family, and it was outrageous for him to hurl such a derogatory comment.

"You're not betrothed to Miss Moore?" she asked.

"I never considered it for a minute."

"You're still a bachelor?"

"Yes, but I hope I won't be for much longer."

Mary's pulse raced. "You've picked someone?"

"Yes, Mrs. Darlington, and while I don't believe it's any of your business, I will declare that it's to be Emily."

Mary could have fallen off her chair; she was that stunned. "You want to marry Emily Shaw?"

"Yes, and I'd like to proceed as quickly as possible. Is she here or not?"

"Swear to me that you mean it," Mary said. "Swear that you intend to propose."

He scowled. "Do I look like the sort of person who jests? Would I tease you about such an important matter?"

"No, definitely not."

She smirked with astonishment, being completely floored by how wrong she'd been about him. She'd convinced herself he was a cad and a liar, just as her prior beloved had been. Who could have predicted he was a different kind of man entirely?

"She's several days away," Mary said, "and if you truly wish to speak with her, you'll have to travel quite a distance to accomplish it."

"Why has she departed? I thought you'd offered her a job. What happened?"

Emily was safely ensconced at the unwed mother's home where Mary had birthed her own child so many years earlier. It was on the other side of the country, and after her ordeal had ended, she'd moved far away from that spot. She'd had to ensure she never bumped into anyone who might have been present during that terrible interval.

"I have a surprise for you, Roxbury," she said, as she pulled out a piece of paper and jotted down the directions to the facility. "I can't imagine what your reaction will be, but you've claimed you're anxious to marry her. If this news changes your mind, I will throttle you, so don't you dare disappoint me."

She shoved the paper over to him, and he scrutinized it, then said, "What's this?"

"This is where you'll find her. It's a home for unwed mothers."

He frowned, the clueless dolt not understanding. "Why would she be there?"

"Why do you suppose, you thick oaf? Congratulations! You're about to be a father."

He sucked in a sharp breath, then he grinned from ear to ear. "I am? Well, then, I guess I'd better hurry to fetch her away so she can become my bride."

Chapter Twenty-Four

EMILY SAT ON A bench, staring out at a decrepit garden. It was a chilly autumn afternoon, a brisk wind blowing, angry clouds whipping by. She fought off a shiver and tugged her cloak more tightly around her body.

The unwed mother's home rose in front of her. It was an old monastery, three stories high and constructed of a grey brick, so it exuded a sinister air, as if it was a prison. In light of the morose mood of the inhabitants, it might have been one. It definitely wasn't a spa, and no effort had been exerted so it would be more comfortable.

Some of the women were under a version of house arrest, locked in their rooms on orders from their parents who'd shut them away. They were mostly young girls who'd fallen in love with the wrong boy and were positive—if they could just escape and be with him again—their lives would be perfect.

Emily, as an adult, was free to come and go, and in fact, she could change her mind about giving birth at the facility, or about the adoption, but she wouldn't do that. She would face the music and was marching toward the future as best she could.

There was a general perception in the place that they were all sinners who deserved what had happened to them. Emily certainly pictured it that way, although she was trying to move beyond her sense of guilt and shame. Mary had insisted she would eventually forgive herself for being such a fool, that the ordeal would make her stronger, but at the moment, she simply felt invisible and adrift.

How had she arrived at such a desolate, solitary spot?

She'd always viewed herself as a smart, shrewd person. She'd risked all—for a nobleman! How could she have been so stupid?

An aristocrat like Lord Roxbury never wed *down*, but she'd been so fond of him that she'd started to believe she was special, that the restrictions limiting other females didn't apply to her. She'd truly assumed he'd marry her, and she hadn't been able to deflect his wily seduction. She hadn't wanted to deflect it, and look where her idiocy had left her!

Alone. Friendless. Penniless. If she hadn't met Mary Darlington over the summer, what would have become of her? Who could she have turned to for help? The rest of her life, she would work hard to show Mary her undying gratitude.

Did Lord Roxbury ever think of her? Did he ever wonder how she was faring? Had his wedding been held? Was he delighted with his bride?

She doubted he would be. Temperance Moore had been such a vain snob, and Roxbury was a funny, lost soul. They were such a mismatch, and as she caught herself obsessing, she shook her morbid musings away. It was pointless to ponder him or remain fixated on the past. She couldn't alter what had occurred, and she had to stagger forward and gird herself for the pending tribulations of childbirth.

It was a dangerous, often fatal endeavor, and she needed to focus on that and naught else. She had to let memories of James Covington fade into the distance.

A servant exited the building and called to her, "You have a visitor, Miss Shaw."

Emily blanched. "*I* have a visitor?"

In the entire kingdom, she couldn't imagine who it might be. She was lodged on the other side of the country from Mary, who was busy running her hotel, so it wouldn't be her. The only other possibility was Peggy, but Peggy would never have bestirred herself to check on Emily. Her cousin wasn't exactly the type who would sympathize or offer assistance.

"Who is it?" she asked as she stood and walked over.

"I wasn't apprised. The matron simply sent me to fetch you. You're to use the private room next to her office."

Emily knew the room to which she referred. Visitors weren't encouraged at the facility. They fueled division and unhappiness, and while few people stopped by, there were occasional discussions with relatives that could grow very contentious. Parents liked to blame their daughters for their immorality, and it wasn't unusual for muffled shouting to waft up the stairs.

Whenever those noises were detected, Emily hurried off to another part of the property. It was too depressing to be reminded of how disgraced they were. What about the men who'd put them in their shameful situations? Why was there no penalty for their sins? Why wasn't there a decrepit prison for them?

She followed the servant inside, and her anxiety soared. She was so miserably gloomy, and if she was about to endure a horrid encounter with a rude or cruel dolt, she wouldn't stumble through it with much grace.

As she approached the correct door, the matron was standing in the hall. Her firm glower had Emily lurching to a halt.

"This is highly irregular, Miss Shaw," she said. "You're residing with us due to your prior bad decisions, so please reflect carefully about this. Don't behave more foolishly than you already have."

Emily had no idea what the woman meant, and there was no opportunity to inquire. The matron practically pushed her into the room, and the door was shut after her.

There was a man over by the fire. His back was to her, so she couldn't see his face, but she'd have wagered a hundred pounds that it was Lord Roxbury. Yet he was in London, planning his engagement ball. Or maybe he was on his way to Italy for a romantic honeymoon. There was no chance at all that he would be at an unwed mother's home near York.

He heard her enter and spun to her, and yes, it was James Covington. It really and truly was, and the sight of him was so bizarre that she was dizzy. How had he found her? Why would he have searched? Mary must have tattled over where she was. Why would she have betrayed a confidence?

"Hello, Emily." He grinned like the cad he was. "Fancy meeting you here."

"Lord Roxbury? What are you doing?"

"I've come to whisk you away. I've brought a carriage, and the matron informs me you're not locked in, so we can leave immediately. Let's get your things."

He took a step toward her, as if he'd escort her out. His expression was warm and fond, as if they'd never quarreled. Could he actually assume she'd flit off with him? To what destination? To what conclusion?

For some odd reason, she was afraid of him, and she sprinted behind a sofa, using it as a barrier, as if he was a violent beast about to strike her. Her obvious alarm irked him, and he frowned, as if she was being a nuisance.

"What's wrong?" he asked. "You can't be eager to tarry in this dreary spot. I'll never believe it."

"I'm incredibly confused by your arrival. What is your purpose?"

"I told you: to whisk you away."

"Why are you so sure I'd want that?"

"The better question is: Why wouldn't you want it?"

There were a thousand issues vexing her, but she voiced the most pertinent one. "How did you find me?"

"How would you suppose? I forced Mary Darlington to tell me where you'd gone."

Rage swept over her, and she felt aggrieved and abused. How dare he bluster in! Was there no justice in the world? Could a modest, humble woman ever receive recompense for the depravities inflicted on her by a handsome rogue?

"How was your engagement party?" she snidely asked.

He growled with annoyance. "There was no party."

"A likely story," she fumed. "Your stepmother boasted of it to me. Why was it cancelled? Were you so excited about Miss Moore's fortune that you rushed to the altar without delay? Are you a husband now? If you are, I must categorically state that it's contemptable for you to have visited me."

A muscle ticked in his cheek, a clear sign that she'd aggravated him. As if she cared! She was so far beyond consideration of his tender male ego that she couldn't even see him. He might have been invisible to her.

"Would you sit down?" he said, struggling to remain calm.

"No. I can't fathom why you've sauntered in, but the days where I would hang on your every word have ended. You've had a lengthy journey for nothing, and I'm busy. Would you excuse me?"

She moved as if she'd stomp out, and she was determined to escape before she burst into tears. Ever since she'd discovered her condition, she'd been an emotional wreck. The smallest little incident had her weeping. She couldn't bear to have him stroll in, looking dashing and wonderful. It had her recalling how happy she'd been, how stupid she'd been, how reckless she'd been.

She yearned to fall into his arms and confess how much she'd missed him. She yearned to beg him to save her, to carry her off to a place where she would be content, but he was a fiend and a liar who'd seduced her with wicked intent. Then he'd trotted off to London and betrothed himself to an heiress. He was that despicable.

"Sit, Emily!" he commanded. "I insist."

There was a table in the middle of the room, with chairs around it, and he pulled one out and gestured to it. What was he hoping to achieve? Was he about to explain why he'd tricked her? How he was surprised that his antics had hurt her? How he was sorry for being so awful? Well, he could choke on his apology. She shouldn't have to listen to it.

But despite her roiling fury, she was too much of a coward to march out. She trudged over and plopped down, but she didn't speak. If he had comments to share, he could share them, then depart. She wasn't about to make the conversation any easier for him.

"Would you like to know why it took me so long to get here?" he asked.

"No, because I haven't been waiting for you. After how Peggy and I were treated by you and your brother, you can't have presumed I'd be pining away."

He tsked with offense. "You're so angry with me. Why is that exactly?"

"You have no idea? Maybe that's the problem for us. You are a clueless male idiot, and I am a witless female ninny. How could two such ridiculous people ever have assumed they were friends?"

"At least you admit we were friends in the past. I suppose that's progress."

He pulled out a second chair and set it directly in front of her, then he sat down too. He'd kept some space between them, for which she was grateful. She didn't want their legs entangled. When he touched her, she couldn't think straight.

"After we quarreled," he said, "you retired to the coaching inn."

"I remember it well." Her tone was snotty, her patience exhausted.

"Were you aware that I showed up there, so I could persuade you to return to Wave Crest?"

"No, I wasn't aware."

"You jumped on the mail coach and fled, so I couldn't catch you."

"I didn't flee," she caustically seethed. "I went home where I belonged."

"Yes, and I was eager to chase after you, but I'm such a self-centered ass that I never inquired as to the name of your family's property or where it was located, so I didn't have any notion of where you were."

"Why would you have worried about it? I'm so puzzled by this."

He ignored her taunting remarks and said, "I visited Mary Darlington and pleaded with her to jot down your address, but she claimed she didn't have it."

The news was a tad distressing. Why would Mary have pretended not to know her whereabouts? Was Mary being loyal? Disloyal? Emily couldn't decide.

"I told her," Roxbury continued, "that if you ever contacted her, she should reply and inform you that I was searching for you. Didn't she apprise you?"

"No, but I didn't contact her. I arrived at Hexham, and my Aunt Florence was dying. I was pitched into a very painful death watch, and I never pondered you for a single minute."

"I tried not to ponder you either, and I still don't understand why you were so enraged with me that day at Wave Crest." She would have launched into a tirade, but he held up a hand to stop her. "We'll have to disagree about it. I thought I was cautiously assessing the facts with regard to your cousin, but obviously, you don't view it that way. It split us apart."

"We were never together," she said. "At this late date, don't rewrite our history."

"We weren't together? If my memory is correct, we were about to elope to Scotland, so who is rewriting our history? It certainly isn't me."

The comment rattled her. He seemed to believe they were still fondly attached, that an elopement was still a possibility. Was that the message he'd come to convey? It was such a peculiar prospect that she couldn't accept it to be the case.

"Yes, we were about to elope," she said, and she waggled her fingers at him. "As you can see, I'm wearing no wedding ring, and I am tucked away, out of sight and in disgrace." She smirked derisively. "I guess we never proceeded."

"Because you left in a snit."

"Because you kicked me out of your house!"

He rolled his eyes. "Will we go around in circles all afternoon?"

"We will if you constantly utter ludicrous falsehoods that I can't abide. Are you finished?" She pushed back her chair as if she'd leap up and storm out.

"No, I'm not finished. I'll tell you when I am, and it will be after I've explained several important matters."

She could have marched out anyway, but she figured he wouldn't leave her alone until he'd spewed his justifications. "Fine. Get on with it. You keep blathering, but you never offer any statements worth hearing."

He exhaled slowly, as if she was a great trial. Then he said, "After you abandoned me in Baywick, I was very angry. I felt badly used by you and Peggy, and I convinced myself I'd been a fool to become involved with you."

"Join the club, Roxbury. I wasn't too delighted either."

"I returned to London, and one evening when I was out and about, I ran into Archie's chum, Gordo. Remember him?"

"Oh, yes, I remember him. He is the obnoxious dandy who officiated at Peggy's fake wedding."

"Yes, that's him. He was very drunk, and with a bit of prodding, he revealed the entire charade."

Emily had been braced to learn that Gordo had denied the sham, but with his admitting the ruse, some of the wind went out of her sails.

"He confessed it?" she asked.

"Yes. Archie and his friends played a game with young maidens. They frequented popular venues where they'd flirt with unsuspecting girls whom they could deceive and seduce. They wagered over their antics, and according to Gordo, Archie was the best at trickery, so he was usually the winner."

"My goodness," Emily murmured. "Please assure me Gordo was punished in some fashion. I hate to suppose he walked away with no penalty."

"I pummeled him, which was personally satisfying, then I spoke to his father and demanded he enlist in the army and depart England. At first, his father was reluctant to oblige me, but I threatened to expose the whole, sorry affair, and the pompous boy was gone the next morning. I've insisted he stay out of the country for at least five years. I hope he'll acquire some humility while he's away."

"I wouldn't count on it," Emily said quite bitterly. "What about your brother? I pray you've inflicted a hefty penalty on him too."

"For starters, I pummeled him even more thoroughly than Gordo."

"Thank you. I'm grateful." She meant it too.

"And I forced him to marry your cousin."

"You what?" Emily banged a palm on her ear. "Did I hear you correctly? You made him marry Peggy?"

"Yes." He grinned as if they were conspirators. "He was vehemently opposed, and I dragged him to the ceremony with his wrists and ankles bound."

"You didn't!"

"I gave him two choices: He could wed Peggy or I'd have him prosecuted for fraud and rape. I'd have testified against him, so he'd have been hanged. That prospect definitely got his attention."

"They're wed? You're not joking?"

"He complained every second, but I'd scared him to death, so he's shackled to her."

"What is Peggy's opinion? She must be ecstatic, but I can't imagine why any woman would want your brother as a husband."

"She was thrilled, but I doubt her merry attitude will last. It's only a matter of time before Archie disappears on her."

"He's a very dodgy character," Emily said, "so if he flees, it won't surprise me."

"I agree, and Peggy has some issues with her new mother-in-law. Bernice is difficult to tolerate, but then, so is Peggy. Bernice will reside with Archie and Peggy, rather than me, and I can't fathom how they'll carry on. They just might kill each other."

Emily couldn't envision how Peggy would weather the grim task of being Archie's wife or the Countess's daughter-in-law. "Where are they living? Do you know? She'll expect me to write and congratulate her. If I don't, she'll nag at me forever."

"Actually, they're at Hexham."

"That's not possible. The creditors were about to swoop in, and I left so I wouldn't have to witness it."

"Yes, the creditors arrived, and the property was put up for sale. Guess what?" He was preening and smug, and his cocky expression was unnerving.

"What? What is it?"

"I bought it—for pennies on the pound too. It was a real bargain."

"You own it?"

"Yes. It's your family's home, and you shouldn't have to lose it merely because your uncle was a spendthrift."

"You bought it for me," she mumbled, trying to understand the kind gesture. "I'm too stunned to comment."

"Is there another *thank you* in there somewhere?" he asked. "Although I must admit that I can't predict how this will resolve. Peggy and Archie are at Hexham—with Bernice—and when I snuck away, they were fighting like cats and dogs. Among the three of them, they don't have a farthing to their names, so their situation is dire. I've supplied them with a roof over their heads, but that's it, and I've printed notices that I won't pay any of their bills."

"Some of my rage is fading," she said. "I'm delighted by this story, but aren't you worried about them? They'll be awful custodians."

"I've installed some competent employees to watch over Hexham for me. They won't allow Archie to wreck anything, and Peggy is too flighty to cause much trouble. It will survive long after they've moved on to greener pastures."

"And your stepmother?"

"I can't guarantee her conclusion. I'm betting Peggy will give her an apoplexy."

"You are horrid," she said, finally smiling, "and *yes,* there's another *thank you* in there. I'm absolutely bowled over by this."

"I was hoping you would be."

Suddenly, he slid off his chair and dropped to a knee. She frowned and tried to scoot away, but he gripped her thighs so she couldn't escape. There was only one reason for a man to be in that position, and it was to propose.

Her pulse started to thud with dread. He'd proposed previously, and she'd consented. In the intervening months though, she'd realized that he hadn't been sincere. She couldn't immediately turn in the other direction and claim he wasn't a scoundrel. She'd been too successful at convincing herself he was a rogue.

Yet, here he was, about to attempt it again. How could she refuse him? Where he was concerned, she'd never been able to erect any barriers and keep them in place. How could she on this occasion?

She needed some time to ponder the consequences. Had she changed? Had he? Did she trust him? Would he follow through? It was happening too fast, and he'd broken her heart once before. She couldn't allow him to break it again.

"What are you thinking?" she said, stalling.

"You know what, now be silent and listen to me."

"You're scaring me."

He scowled. "How am I scaring you?"

"I'm so afraid you're about to utter comments you don't mean."

He blew out an exasperated breath. "You are the most obstinate woman in the kingdom."

"And you are the most deranged man. It appears you're about to propose, and we've already walked down this road. I'm not certain we should walk down it again."

"Emily, let's review where you are. You're locked away in an unwed mother's home. You're having a baby." He rested a hand on her tummy.

"*We* are having a baby. We don't have the luxury of pretending we won't be husband and wife."

"You don't want to marry me. Not really."

"Who told you that?"

"No one," she said, "but you're Lord Roxbury, and I'm Emily Shaw from Hexham. It's a bizarre notion."

"At the moment, I may be Roxbury, but I wasn't always an earl. For much of my life, I was just James Covington from London."

"You were always quite a bit more than that." She'd never permit him to denigrate himself. "You deserve to wed very high. You could have a duke's daughter or even a princess. You should be in town, chasing debutantes."

He clucked his tongue with irritation. "Could you imagine me shackled to a debutante? I'm touched in the head, remember? Everyone agrees that I'm not sane."

"You're fine," she insisted. "You've developed a few odd quirks, but they're easily managed."

"It's precisely because you deem my quirks to be irrelevant that you are the perfect bride for me."

His declaration that she would be the *perfect* bride was riveting and terrifying. It made her anxious to cast caution to the wind, to furnish whatever he sought, but a more rational part of her brain took hold.

"You barely know me," she said.

"That's true—if we measure our relationship in the number of weeks we've been acquainted. But if we measure them according to how close we are, it feels as if I've known you forever. Don't you sense it too?"

She couldn't lie. "Yes, I sense it too."

"From the instant we met, we were drawn to each another. It's almost as if Fate decided we should cross paths."

"Maybe," she grumbled.

"After you left Wave Crest, I told myself it was for the best. I told myself I didn't need you and I ought to move on, but guess what?"

"What?"

"I can't bear to live a life that doesn't include you. If you won't be mine, what will become of me?"

He looked positively bewildered, as if he'd been wandering in the wilderness, and she was a beacon that had brought him to safety. It rattled her; it ignited a fire under her optimism so she assumed any marvelous ending might be possible.

He was the one with the exalted name and position, so he had very much to lose by picking her. If he didn't care about the differences in their class and station, why should she? She was suffering from a powerful urge to dissuade him, but she couldn't forget that she was increasing with his child. What if it was a boy? What if he was destined to be the next Earl of Roxbury?

She couldn't remain unwed and have him be a bastard.

She'd heeded Mary's advice, had hidden herself, having resolved to birth her baby, then put it out for adoption. In the period she'd spent at the facility, she'd wiled away the dreary hours, coming to grips with her situation. She'd persuaded herself that her choices had been correct, but she hadn't had the heart for it.

In the past, she hadn't believed she'd ever have a child. Having no dowry or prospects, no beau had ever been interested in her, but James was offering her a chance to be a mother, to keep it, to raise it. It was a special blessing, a special gift. Could she toss it away?

She clasped his hand and brazenly said, "Ask me to marry you— fast—before my courage flags."

He smiled. "My dearest, Emily, will you do me the very great honor of being my wife? Will you be my bride so I can be a father to this son or daughter we've created? Will you have me—flaws and all?"

"Yes, James, I will marry you, but on one condition."

"Without even hearing what boon you seek, I can adamantly say *yes,* I will meet any condition you impose. What is it?"

"I don't mean to insult you, but I don't exactly trust you to walk to the altar."

"You don't trust me? After I traveled all this way to fetch you?"

"I was thinking you should have to work a bit harder to prove you're sincere."

He smirked, but with amusement. "I'm down on bended knee and begging you to have me. How much more sincerity will you demand?"

"We're in the north of England, so Scotland is a short distance. I'd like to get a ring on my finger as quickly as I can. Might we still elope? If you agree that we can proceed directly to Gretna Green, then we can have an immediate wedding."

"How could I refuse? Haven't you figured out why I'm doing this?"

"I have no idea what's driving you, but you should be good and truly bound so you can't change your mind."

"I'll never change my mind. For you see, I love you, Emily Shaw, and I will love you until my dying day."

"I love you too," she admitted, the rightness of it sinking in.

He dipped in and kissed her, and they both sighed with pleasure.

"You're so stubborn," he said as he drew away. "I'm stunned to have convinced you."

"Is this an indication that you're not marrying me because you have to? You're marrying me because you want to?"

"Yes, I want to marry you more than I've ever wanted anything. I plan to live happily ever after. How about you?"

"I plan to live happily ever after too. Starting this very minute."

She stood and tugged him to his feet, and he pulled her into his arms and kissed her for an eternity. As their lips parted, they were brimming with contentment, and she had tears of joy in her eyes.

"Will you pack your bags?" he asked. "Have I worn you down sufficiently that you're ready to leave with me?"

"Yes, you've worn me down, and I'll hurry too. I'm not about to give you an extra second to ponder your decision."

"With me it's forever," he said.

"With me too. Aren't I lucky?"

~ THE END ~

Did you enjoy your holiday in Baywick?
Would you like to visit again?

LOVE EVER AFTER

the story of
Mrs. Mary Darlington
and
Captain Jackson Pettigrew

Coming Soon!

About the Author

CHERYL HOLT IS A *New York Times, USA Today,* and Amazon "Top 100" bestselling author who has published over sixty novels.

She's also a lawyer and mom, and at age forty, with two babies at home, she started a new career as a commercial fiction writer. She'd hoped to be a suspense novelist, but couldn't sell any of her manuscripts, so she ended up taking a detour into romance where she was stunned to discover that she has a knack for writing some of the world's greatest love stories.

Her books have been released to wide acclaim, and she has won or been nominated for many national awards. She is considered to be one of the masters of the romance genre. For many years, she was hailed as "The Queen of Erotic Romance", and she's also revered as "The International Queen of Villains." She is particularly proud to have been named "Best Storyteller of the Year" by the trade magazine Romantic Times BOOK Reviews.

She lives and writes in Hollywood, California, and she loves to hear from fans. Visit her website at www.cherylholt.com.

Made in United States
North Haven, CT
08 April 2022

18010335R00225